SPAWN OF THE CONDOR

The arrow-pierced, dying condor landed in front of Navron, the servant of the evil wizard Alyubol. Then the huge creature seemed to burst apart. The body crumbled away, and blood flowed everywhere, dissolving into stinking fumes. The brown feathers squirted blood as they fell from the wings like leaves in an autumn gale. And over all rang the insane laughter of Navron.

Then a strange metamorphosis began. Each feather which had fallen grew, changed, and became a grim warrior, brandishing a deadly sword. Two of them sprang to Navron's side to guard him. But the others moved with dark determination to where Princess Berengeria stood, staring in shock at the impossible scene.

In moments, they had surrounded her. Her belated scream rang out once and then was cut off...

By Dennis McCarty
Published by Ballantine Books:

FLIGHT TO THLASSA MEY

WARRIORS OF THLASSA MEY

WARRIORS OF THLASSA MEY

Dennis McCarty

A Del Rey Book

BALLANTINE BOOKS • NEW YORK

A Del Rey Book
Published by Ballantine Books

Copyright © 1986 by Dennis McCarty

All rights reserved under International and Pan-American Copyright Conventions. Published in the United States of America by Ballantine Books, a division of Random House, Inc., New York, and simultaneously in Canada by Random House of Canada Limited, Toronto.

Library of Congress Catalog Card Number: 86-91377

ISBN 0-345-33911-8

Manufactured in the United States of America

First Edition: January 1987

Cover Art by Darrell K. Sweet

THE AUTHOR WOULD LIKE TO DEDICATE THIS VOLUME TO HIS LONG-SUFFERING MOTHER, PAULINE GERTRUDE WINTERS MCCARTY. HI, MA!

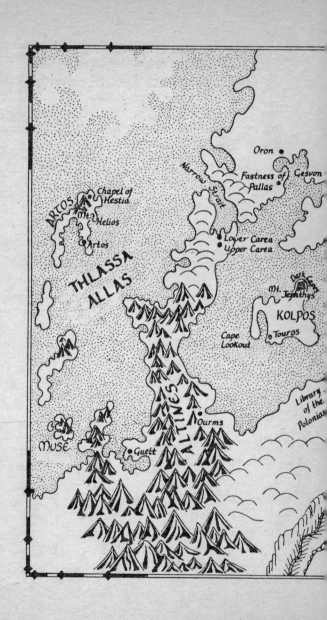

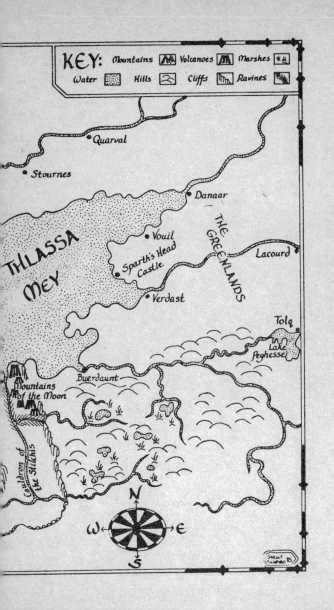

KEY: Mountains Volcanoes Marshes
Water Hills Cliffs Ravines

Quarval

Stournes

Danaar

THLASSA
MEY

Vouil

Sparth's Head
Castle

THE
GREENLANDS

Lacourd

Verdast

Tolq

Lake
Feghessel

Buerdaunt

Mountains
of the Moon

Cauldron of
the Stilchis

N
W   E
S

Chapter One:
The Forest of Tolq

IN ALL THE lands across the Thlassa Mey there was no place like the forest east of Tolq. Towers of oak, beech, and hazel smothered everything. Traveling there was dangerous; the forest teemed with wolves and wild boar, not to mention deer and countless small animals. Respectable men seldom ventured there except in groups, and—despite all the game which lurked beneath the heavy branches—the forest was seldom hunted. But the endless hiding places could shelter anyone who wished to avoid prying eyes, though there was also plenty of cover for those who desired to spy on anyone who did go there.

On a glorious autumn day in the forest, two stout men sprawled across a lichen-covered boulder at the edge of a ravine and watched the drama taking place below them. Their names were Diomedes and Leander; they were housecarls in the service of Count Clauvis of Galliardy. They kept as silent as knives hanging in a cutlery; but if silence had not been necessary, they would have snickered at what they were viewing.

Two people were talking as they strolled through the

shadows. They were both striking in appearance. The young woman was tall and of great loveliness, with hair that was a dark, deep red, eyes that were large and lustrous, and a face that was as perfectly formed as a ripe fruit. The man was nearly as handsome as the maiden was beautiful. He was taller than she, his hair was glossy black, and his body tapered from noble shoulders down to muscular hips and thighs. He sported a thin, black mustache, neatly trimmed, and was exceptionally tidy in all ways.

They sauntered along arm in arm, pressing their bodies together as they passed through the shadows. The man laughed as they paused at the base of one great tree, then he faced the young woman and laid a finger across her lips. He smiled; then they embraced.

Their lips clung together, and they sank to their knees in the soft foliage. The youth's arm circled the maiden's shoulders, and he lowered her until she lay before him on the lush grass, then he kissed her once more.

The maiden's bosom surged like a tempest. She tilted her head nervously and watched as the youth's hand moved to her shoulder, then slid the soft material down, down, to reveal skin white as rose petals. Her eyes closed and she trembled as her lover's mouth flitted across her body. "Take care, take care." She barely whispered the words; her lips hardly even moved.

The young man's eyes flashed with ardor. He lifted himself with a sudden motion, stripped off his leather jerkin and the linen tunic beneath it, and embraced the maiden once more, the flesh of their torsos meeting, the warmth of the contact carrying away all other sensation. The maiden's eyes fluttered and there was an inner light behind them, but she stirred in the fervent embrace. "Kind sir, you grow too hot."

He laughed again. His teeth were firm and even. "The heat we feel's nothing yet. Wait a moment and it'll melt us together like copper and zinc." He lifted himself until he was kneeling over her and his hands played a rhapsody over the sensitive curves of her body.

And still he had no idea he was in danger; he smiled

as joyously as ever. "You own every ounce of love that's in my heart, Bessina, but my body loves you as well. And if you're not playing me false, I swear your body loves mine."

Bessina spoke breathlessly. "It does."

The young gallant threw himself forward and their lips met again, but even as he moved he felt a blow to his back; sickening pain forced him to roll onto the meadow grass. Then the lovers both saw the brightly colored shaft of the crossbow bolt sticking up from the ground beside them. The young man's sudden motion had caused the shot to miss by the breadth of a man's hand—the difference between life and death—but the bolt's head had still raked across the flesh of his bare back. His blood stained the grass beneath him.

Haste deadened pain. He leaped to his feet and pulled Bessina up with him as a second bolt whacked into the oak tree beside them, to quiver before his staring eyes. They darted behind the great trunk. Bessina was still breathing heavily; her belly and bosom heaved and her carelessly held blouse only half concealed her beauty. But her lover's attention had turned elsewhere, along with hers.

He peeked out at the slope that stretched above him, but there was no movement. His breath came in gasps, and he wiped his hand across the small of his back. When he drew it forth to look at it, it was covered with blood. "Who would try to kill me?"

Bessina tore a strip of cloth from her bodice to bind him. "Methinks there is no lack of men to hunt you down, my Flin, you brigand. Many know of you. You've luck; that razor head just sliced a shallow gash; the wound's a clean and harmless one."

"Maybe, but there'll be more wounds behind that if we don't hurry. And who can know what will happen to you when they've done with me." Flin leaped upward, caught hold of a stout branch a cubit above his head, and pulled himself onto it. Then he reached for her. "Leap up and I'll catch your hand."

She obeyed, grasping at him as she did so. She clawed

at his suntanned forearm, and his hand enclosed her wrist in a vicelike grip, until her arms felt as if they were being pulled from their sockets. But he easily hauled her into the crotch of the tree with him, and they climbed together until they were sure they were concealed by the foliage.

Once they had reached a secure place, he gazed at her for an instant, then cradled her face between his hands, kissed her lips, and smiled. "Farwell, my love."

Her eyes widened. "You cannot leave me."

"I go where I have to go. Can you climb down from here without my help?"

"I can, but still I want you here with me. Where will you go without me?"

He hardly seemed to notice the question. "Have you a weapon?"

"No."

He handed her a dagger. "I always carry extras. And don't be afraid to use it, though I doubt you'll need to." He looked about as he spoke. "As to your question, I'm going to repay someone for the gift he almost gave me. It'll be grand sport."

"Will I see you again?" Her expression was a mixture of anger, surprise, and amusement as he prepared to move away.

His arms circled her shoulders and their kiss lasted a long time. "Send a message whenever you want. I'll not fail you." Then he released her and made his way out along a branch, reached an intersecting limb from another tree, and was gone. His passing was indicated only by rustling which quickly faded from her hearing.

"Flin," she called after him, panic creeping into her voice. "Flin." She sat for a moment, her eyes wildly sifted the golden branches, then she calmed herself. At last she broke into an incredulous smile. "My Flin, you are the very prince of rogues."

She was by herself. She sat in the tree and listened for a sign, a sound from either Flin or the unknown assassins who had tried to kill him. But there was no sound, no shout. The sky grew cloudy, gloom crawled over the forest like a spider, and the squeaks and chitterings of squirrels and small birds hid the silence.

She waited a long time. The excitement that had buoyed her up while the young brigand had been at her side drained out of her. She found herself alone. She was a young woman with no one to help her face the shadowy depths of the forest; that fact rasped at her nerves as time crept by, which was odd. She had not felt that way before.

Then she heard a scream, a human scream that echoed along the forest aisles, full of agony and fear. Caught by surprise, Bessina nearly leaped from her branch; her fingers flew to her lips as the sound faded in the gloom. Who had screamed; had it been Flin or his antagonist? Was she now more alone than ever?

Her passion for him was a curse and she knew it. He was bursting with the mixed qualities of joy and danger; he made her laugh and feel afraid at the same time, but she knew to the depths of her soul that great troubles would be her portion as long as he was in her life. And now he was in danger; the scream could have come from his lips. She felt smaller and more afraid than ever.

She had to leave the forest. The rain would soon fall; the gathering gloom and the wandering breeze which sifted through the leaves told her that much. Worse, the afternoon was growing old and weary and would lapse into evening; then the wolves would come to turn the forest byways into a deathtrap. So she stiffened and slid from her branch, carefully dropping onto another, lower one. She peered between the leafy boughs to assure herself nothing and no one was waiting for her, then slipped to the ground, making the drop with great caution. A fractured ankle would be death at this time and in this place.

She flitted between the trees like a nymph, noting all sights and sounds, keeping track of climbable trees in case of emergencies. She would be in danger until she could pass from the gloomy forest to the fields that surrounded the city of Tolq; even there she would have to keep out of sight.

She was Bessina, daughter of Count Clauvis of Galliardy, a fact which made her smile. Even though he knew

her by her real name, Flin the Brigand did not dream of
her noble parentage.

She had gone to a bazaar unescorted, and they had
met there, these unmatched ones. She knew Flin well;
she had heard of him and he had told her all about himself.
But for all he knew of her, she was a crumb sweeper at
the lowliest peasant hearth about Tolq. That was her one
advantage. Flin had captured her, she could not deny it;
her hidden nobility was the single lonely advantage she
retained over him.

Darkness covered the land by the time she reached the
plowed fields that surrounded Tolq. Her margin of safety
had been slight and she knew it; in fact, she was still not
secure among the peasant dwellings that dotted the dark
landscape. She cautiously kept to the shelter of orchards,
fences, and hedges. A pair of guinea hens signaled her
presence loud and long at one of the larger peasant holdings, but she managed to pass without being challenged.
It became dark as basalt; a thick blanket of clouds hid
every star and planet and forced her to make her way in
a world of sounds and deep shadows.

At last she saw the light of the gate watch where the
road passed into Tolq. The other lights of the town were
few, but that one gleaming lantern was enough to guide
her to safety. She hurried; she had to be in her chambers
in time to clean herself and put in an appearance in her
father's great hall to avoid suspicion.

The wall that surrounded Tolq was poorly kept up. It
was low and easy to climb and she knew it as well as she
knew the callouses of her own feet. She turned her steps
toward a good place near the gate and crept toward it,
using the darkness as cover. Fallen stone provided both
shelter and a ladder to the top of the wall; but just as she
reached it, she heard travelers approaching along the road
she had left. Curious, she paused in the darkness to see
what she could see, to hear what she could hear. She saw
a pair of horses. The lead horse was ridden by Diomedes,
one of her father's housecarls, a hulking bully who was
easy to dislike; the second horse bore only an unrecog-

nizable burden. But her skin grew cold and started to crawl as she glimpsed Diomedes' crossbow slung over his shoulder. Did the second horse bear a body?

Diomedes' arrival caused a commotion at the gate, and another guardsman joined the watch while Diomedes climbed off his horse. Then the three of them went to the second horse and—horror of horrors—removed the body of a man. But it was not Flin. She could see that much as she watched anxiously; she went limp with relief as the sagging form they carried off in the lantern light turned out to be one of the other housecarls.

The guards' words were low and hard to understand, but Diomedes' voice echoed off the walls. He told of the villain he had been sent to kill, a slippery, well-known brigand whose presence in the region had come to the Count's attention. And then a smile curled his heavy features as he added, "The Count ordered the rascal's death for a good reason. Why, if I told you all I knew, your ears would blaze for a fortnight. We thought he was dead meat, but he got clean away and paid poor Leander off with a dagger thrust. He's a foxy one."

One guard gazed dryly at Diomedes. "If you let him get away, it won't sit well with the Count or his chamberlain."

Diomedes made a sound that was midway between a grunt and a growl. "He'll be back. And then he'll die."

Bessina stifled a gasp. Her father knew; he had found out about her budding affair with Flin the Brigand and he was going to end it by killing the would-be lover. She had to get back to her chambers. Her breath made little squeaky sounds as she scurried over the wall and rushed along the dark streets of Tolq toward her home, Castle Gnoffe, which loomed as a hard, dark mass ahead of her. She would have to slip past a second pair of watchmen, but that would be no trouble.

What was she going to do? Her father knew, but how much did he know? She was tempted to confront him, to rage and argue, but they argued often, and he did not always let her have her way. What would she do? Should she plead, should she hurl things, or sing or beg or bawl? She had no idea, but she had to do something; she had to do whatever was necessary to save Flin's life.

Chapter Two:
The Prisoner

VISIONS OF FLIN'S murder haunted Bessina, even though she tried to set a reasoned pace. She planned her approach. She would wash herself, change out of her soiled clothing, and make herself presentable. But she was desperate to be on her way and, for all her resolve, she hurried breathlessly. Haste warred with method, but one thought stood above all—she had to preserve Flin's life.

At last she was ready. She had bathed, her clothes were fresh, and she was delicately scented with rose water, a gift from her father which she knew he would notice. Her mind raced ahead of her footsteps as she hurried to Count Clauvis' chamber, followed by a servant bearing a torch.

When she arrived, she saw a weak glow still peeking from beneath the heavy wooden door to her father's chamber and she heard low voices within. But she could not wait; she was too agitated to do that. The pearls of her teeth pressed her lower lip as she rapped smartly against the door. The voices within stopped. Then the door swung open and she found herself gazing into the squinting face of Crecche, the Count's chamberlain. She grimaced. She did not like that face. It was dry and tightly drawn about the mouth, like an old money pouch. But even though she disliked Crecche, her rôle and her mission forced her to take care in her actions; she took pains to execute a polite curtsy before she spoke. "I came to see my father. Is he here?"

Crecche looked her up and down, fondling her with his eyes before he replied. "He is. Come speak with him." He stood aside; beyond him, she saw Count Clauvis standing before a leaping fire, looking soft and approachable in his evening robes—at least compared to the wizened chamberlain. He was staring into a goblet of wine, but he looked up from it at her approach and his face hardened; the flickering firelight made the shadows of his short-cropped beard leap across his features. "Good evening, daughter. What attracts you up into our midst?"

Bessina hesitated; she did not like the situation. It was plain that the wind lay badly. What approach would be best to take with her father? Could she make Crecche leave? "My Father, I wish to speak with you but I will wait until what business you may have with our good chamberlain is done."

Crecche eyed her and his scraggly white whiskers moved with his smile. He motioned for her servant to enter and then closed the door and shuffled toward Count Clauvis and Bessina, his laugh creaking like an old squeezebox. "I'll tell you what she wants, my gracious Lord," he said, wiping the laugh from his lips. "She's come to beg you for the life of that young knave whose plans to take her virtue ran afoul of your two housecarls late this afternoon." He gazed up at her. "Am I correct? Your silence tells me that my words strike close."

Bessina's mouth slipped open and her mind clouded at Crecche's words. She was undone; there was no way she would be able to wheedle her father on the matter now; Crecche's words showed that she was outflanked on every side. Her mouth twisted bitterly and she turned on the chamberlain as her hatred of him seized control of her tongue. "Since when has this low commoner the right to speak so easily of the affairs of us, his betters, Father? Tell me that."

Count Clauvis looked at her but did not reply; Crecche replied for him. "I am his true adviser, child. My words concerning his finances and estates have made him wealthier than many lords. Why, then, should I not give my counsel when his daughter drags his name into the muck?"

"You have no right to speak so brazenly of things which don't concern you. What am I? Am I a prisoner, that all my deeds and travels, meetings, and acquaintances must now be overseen by snoops and spies?"

Crecche smiled at her, then turned away and bent to a small table which held a pitcher of wine and a goblet. He picked up the goblet and poured musically from the pitcher, still smiling, still smug. "There is no need for a charade. We all know the particulars involved. Young Flin the Brigand he is called by some, the son of Leuval, proud lieutenant in a company of knights who loot and burn in sorties from their Greenlands castle keep. This Flin's a valiant knave in his own right, a daring and resourceful enemy, as he has shown in killing our good man." His eyes narrowed. "It's also said that he has mastery o'er women's hearts without a rival all across the lands that ring the Thlassa Mey. From seeing the effect he's had on you, I say such rumors stand on solid feet."

Bessina's glare speared Crecche one last time, then she turned toward Count Clauvis. "My Father, have you not a thing to say?"

Count Clauvis cleared his throat and replied. "The words he says are true; our facts are quite as solid as the keep in which we stand. I fear you have our mother's lusty heart, and we cannot allow that to erode the name and reputation of this house."

Bessina's eyes shifted between the two men who confronted her. Her father's face was firm, hard, and resolved, and Crecche's smile had become a smirk. Was her love to be shut off so easily, like milk from a cow's teat? Her temper flared and she turned on the other man, the counselor. "And so you take your joy from my disgrace and hope to turn some profit by my grief. I have a lusty heart, my father says. Perhaps that's true. Yet I say Flin is just as nobly made, as capable of earning my regard, as nimble-witted and courageous, as any mate your council might select."

"Perhaps, my Lady. Still, the proper steps must be observed in seeking out a man to fill your nuptial bed. Some stranger whom your father's never seen, whom you yourself have only met by chance, perusing in some unbecoming, lower-class bazaar, can hardly fill requirements of estate. The Count is right; it shows you lack gentility when you must seek companionship all unescorted in so low a place. It shows base qualities that must be crushed from one who is this province's sole heir."

"Ah. My ignoble traits besmirch the place that I was born to occupy." Tears of rage and shame moistened Bessina's cheeks and several strands of her hair were swept free, which gave her a disheveled look. "You worm. What is ignoble? Mine's an honest love, and were you honest in your counseling, we'd never need a hiding place to meet. But you spew loathsome venom from your lips and turn my father for your own advance. Thus, I must have the husband you select and any other love must be erased."

The chamberlain looked up at Count Clauvis. "I must protest such disrespectful speech."

But rage and despair controlled Bessina; words flowed form her lips like a volcano's belchings, and she could no more stop their fall than control the lightning. "It's I who should protest. How many years have your hearth-taxes made the peasants groan? How great a share of all their crops and goods has gone for your advancement, and how many peasant girls have yielded up their maidenheads to you to gain remittance from your levied curse? You make my father wealthy, but these lands all groan beneath the weight of your misdeeds. Our vassals are the wretchedest of all who scratch a livelihood around the Thlassa Mey."

"Enough," Count Clauvis said.

"You say I am immoral. Yet I never once have harmed a living soul with such an avarice as you have shown."

"Enough." Count Clauvis' roar bounded off the chamber's stone walls. He glared at both of them, then took a draught of wine as he composed himself. "This argument is meaningless. The final word is mine. Young Flin must die!"

Bessina felt her insides crumble. Such a thing could not be; the smile on Flin's face could never be allowed to fade, the broad arms could not be allowed to go slack and be eaten by maggots. How far would Galliardy's housecarls go to seek him out? If he returned to the lands of his origin, would that gain him a remittance against the sentence?

Even though she was fighting to hold them back, Bessina felt tears burst from the corners of her eyes. Her father and the chamberlain were committing an unspeakable crime against her, against Flin, and against the love they bore one another. How could they do such a thing? She gazed up at her father. If it were not for Crecche's presence, she could still bargain for Flin's life. How she hated the grasping wretch!

A rapping at the chamber door interrupted the argument. When Count Clauvis told the caller to enter, one of the sergeant-at-arms' men appeared. "What's your business, sirrah?" Count Clauvis asked.

"My Lord, I stand the duty watch in the donjon tonight and I was sent to tell you the prisoner's dying. We've called the physician, and he says the man will be in Hades before the sun rises tomorrow."

Bessina stared at the messenger in puzzlement. What prisoner? Who was dying? What was he talking about?

But Count Clauvis seemed to understand well enough; he received the news with a simple nod. "I see." An interesting expression passed across his features and he glanced at Bessina. He did not smile as he spoke. "Now, madam, this is most propitious, most appropriate, this villain's death. He wronged me foully many years ago, and since has rotted in my donjon's depths. No torture could repay his shocking crime, but I have paid him back in spite of that. So come with us and you shall see the fate of any man who dares to wrong me in so foul a way."

"What crime did he commit?"

Count Clauvis shook his head. "It does not matter." Then he turned to the gaoler. "Lead on, sirrah. Take us to the place." He gestured for a torch-bearing attendant to accompany them and strode to the chamber door, followed by the others. Bessina noted that even the chamberlain was following silently, apparently put off his stride by the turn of events. That was odd. Crecche practically ruled Count Clauvis on most things, but he seemed to have nothing to say on this matter.

They left the Count's chambers and descended the tower steps, passing through the great hall and down into the castle's donjon. They entered a region Bessina had never before seen. She could tell they had passed below ground level by the wicked looking moisture which coated the red stones of the passage and the foetor which oppressed the air. They had to be approaching the oubliette, the castle's great refuse pit.

Castle Gnoffe was an ancient place; it had been old when Count Clauvis' father had been a child. Bessina had spent many a night in her girlhood daydreaming about the treasures that could lie hidden beneath the massive foundations. But she had never pictured such a worm's lair as the one they entered.

After a long walk, the corridor opened into a large cavern; they had reached a torture chamber. It was a room she had never even dreamed of: grisly instruments cluttered the broad floor, from great, wooden monstrosities to simple tools—tongs, branding irons, gougers, flailing knives. All bore the dust and cobwebs of long disuse; in fact, there were dust and debris everywhere.

Cells opened off the large chamber. The door to one of them stood ajar and the flickering of a torch within showed it was occupied. Count Clauvis pushed past his own attendant and entered, while Bessina hesitated, horrified by the place. How could civilized men have constructed such a home for nightmares? What horrible deed could the prisoner have done to be cast into such a pit?

A grumbling of low voices issued from the cell for a time, then Count Clauvis reappeared, his face lit by a strange, terrible expression. Although she had often argued with her father, Bessina had never considered him a violent or cruel man by nature—but the cruel atmosphere within this lair seemed to have laid hold of him. He walked from the cell, strode straight to Bessina, and grasped her by the shoulder. There was no tenderness in the touch; she had never seen him so charged with anger, violence, and hatred. He snarled and shoved her toward the cell, causing her to reel through the cramped doorway. "See there, young harlot. Feast your eyes upon the wages brought by sin and earthly lust. For more than your own lifetime has this wretch decayed in this foul chamber for his crime. For ten and seven years has he been caged within this place. Look well upon him, daughter, for his fate will duplicate the end of your own Flin, and that's *my* counsel, my *own* policy."

Bessina staggered forward; then her eyes fastened upon the prisoner, the victim of her father's hatred. He lay on a filthy cot, his body resting on the vermin-riddled remains of what once must have been straw. There were two other men in the tiny cell but she hardly even noticed them; she could not remove her horrified eyes from the poor man.

He was a living, rotting skeleton. The odor which rose from him assailed her nostrils and sickened her more than the sight of him. He had once been a man of considerable height and breadth of shoulder, but he had become a wasted, sore-caked ruin, already more dead than alive. Pus oozed from the great, open sores; infected blue bruises dotted the emaciated body, writhing with maggots that had begun their work even though the soul had not yet freed itself. He was completely bare; the hair had long since rotted or fallen from his skull and none was to be seen anywhere else on his naked form.

She tried to keep her gaze from traveling the length of his putrifying body, but she could not. She looked at the area below his waist with a kind of morbid fascination and what she saw brought a gasp, almost a scream, from her lips. The pitiful creature lay in a stinking, drying pool of his own excrement; even as she watched, the tortured

bowels added another blood-traced blot of watery substance. And that was not all. She could not remove her
gaze from him; she could not keep from comparing the
most private area of his body to the glory of Flin's form,
which she had never seen, but which she had pictured in
secret moments.

What was her father doing to her? Why had he brought
her to see the pitiful wretch? She was seventeen years
old and had never had a suitor until she had met Flin.
Her father had become a different man since that time;
he had always been firm, but the way he was showing
her such a sight still seemed cruel and perverse.

She had never beheld a naked man and now she was
forced to look upon this human ruin in all its exposed
shame and horror; her face grew cold and she could feel
many eyes upon her. She had sometimes wondered what
the unclothed male form would look like, had found herself dreaming of Flin's concealed parts. But this sight
would only give her nightmares; she was already on the
verge of gagging or screaming—or both.

Between the prisoner's legs was nothing; he bore only
the livid, unmistakable scars of brutal castration.

She tried to shrink away, but Count Clauvis had come
up behind her; his hands gripped her shoulders and held
her in place. "Look well upon him. See his manly form—
a younger man than I am, in his prime. And this shall be
the fate, I swear to you, of Flin, your brigand lover." He
raised his voice and addressed the prisoner. "Listen, you.
Awaken, meet this tender, virgin maid, a creature of such
beauty you've not seen for countless lifetimes spent within
this cell. She is my daughter. My daughter." He screamed
the last two words without thought for diction or rhythm.
His terrible passion choked off words; he released Bessina
and she could hear the sound of his footsteps as he staggered away. Then she heard a crashing sound. He had
snatched up some instrument of torture and was flailing
away with it in his rage, knocking over stools, shattering
chairs, and pounding the floor.

But she could not look away from the prisoner. His
eyes had retreated into two cavernous holes; they had

remained closed all the time she had watched him. Either he was asleep, or the effort of his feeble breathing had weakened him so much he could not open them. But they did open. They opened and an expression of the most pitiful horror grasped his sunken face. He blinked his eyes rapidly, the sticklike arms moved to cover his midsection, and a strange noise came from the hollow mouth, a noise Bessina could not easily identify. She did understand after a moment. The poor, pitiful fellow was weeping. And more than that, he was trying to make words; she could not understand them at first. "Sa sha. Sa sha. Sa sha."

He was an animal. He had lost the power to speak, perhaps even to think. "Sa sha. Sa sha," he mumbled and stared up at her with pitiful eyes.

She tried to turn away but she was transfixed by the vision. "Sa sha," he said one last time, then tried to turn over. More words came and then she understood. None of the words meant anything; they were no longer words at all, yet he had communicated with her by his unknown, unspoken tongue. For an instant there had been a bond of understanding between them and she had *sensed* his meaning; she had understood everything he had been trying to say. Her eyes welled over, tears raced down her cheeks, and she collapsed into sobbing, such was the pity she felt for the miserable wretch. He was not an animal. His body was decaying; it was dead and it rotted away from him even while he still clung to life. What a man he must once have been to have survived his terrible punishment for even seventeen years! He had been a man of breeding and dignity, and she understood what he had been trying to say, even in his last moments of life. His speech and thoughts were those of a nobleman, a man who had not been looked upon by a woman for seventeen years, certainly not by a young maiden. "Such shame, such shame. This is the worst of all."

The scene overcame her; was this to be her Flin's fate? She sagged into an attendant's arms and had to be half-dragged from the chamber while the physicians hovered over the dying prisoner. Crying out, casting away the iron he had been wielding, Count Clauvis went with her, panting out a last word of instruction to the chamberlain. "Attend to this; I'll look on him no more. I leave disposal to your judgment."

Then they went away, accompanied by the servant with his torch, back through the ancient torture chamber, along corridors and up stone ramps and staircases. Bessina began to recover as they went, but she was terribly shaken by the experience—she felt as if she had taken a beating herself. Seventeen years had that pitiful creature been caged in that tiny cell—that was the span of her entire life, all the sunrises and sunsets she had ever known in the world. Flin had to be spared such a fate.

It took time, but she finally felt able to walk without support. And her father also seemed recovered, as if he had spent his passion for the moment. She glanced at him from time to time, trying to study his features. He was pale; his face, the face which had been so animated all the time he had glared down at the prisoner, now bore a kind of washed-out look. His fury had passed, leaving only weakness behind. And she also noted that Crecche no longer accompanied them.

She did not hesitate. Flin had to be saved and there would never be a better moment to make one last plea for his sake than the present. "My Lord," she said. "I see your vengeance is a thing both terrible and awful to behold. Pray tell, what things are contemplated in pursuit of him I hold next to my heart?"

He shot her a withering glance. "If brigand Flin is next to your young heart, then best you tear it out and cast it down onto the dusty soil. Speak not of him."

Bessina was dismayed by her father's sensitivity to even the mention of her love's name. She would have to be more careful, even without the chamberlain about. "Then I apologize. But still, what is his fate?"

The working of Count Clauvis' mouth betrayed the turmoil which seethed behind his face; she could see his passion building once more, as visible as an angry cobra's spreading hood. "Tell me the truth," he said. "In his pursuit, has he pushed you beyond the bounds set by the rules of chastity?"

She was amazed at such a question. "No, no. I swear it."

"Do not play me false. Remember, my physician has the means to find the truth about your innocence."

"I know. I speak the truth." She felt tears rising once more at the prospect of such an examination. Why was he so ready to humiliate her?

He nodded at her reply and seemed to relax a bit. "It's well. I see your attitude has changed; respectfulness becomes you more than wrath." He looked down at her and the least trace of fondness softened his brow. "Your mother has been dead for many years and I have had you reared the best I could. You mean a deal to me, although my many tasks have held me from your long upbringing's full delight."

Bessina said nothing. Fear of uttering the wrong word paralyzed her tongue.

"And had this brigand's lust achieved its aim and used your maidenhead as payment for his foul desires, my vengeance would have been far harsher than the measures you have seen adopted with the prisoner you saw."

Bessina still said nothing. What could have been more horrible than that wretch's fate? But Count Clauvis quickly satisfied her curiosity. "The torture chamber would have been rebuilt," he said, "and utilized in many awful ways. His family would have never dared to set a foot upon my farthest lands because I would have seized them, treating them the same." He was again becoming excited; it was an ugly spectacle and it frightened her all over again. "They'd suffer as I seized them, just the same as I have suffered at the foetid hands of that foul prisoner you just beheld, as I would suffer if this raw young man should now preempt my fatherly control. And I would do such things..." He choked, gagged on his own anger. "The man you looked at crossed me by no greater space than is the length of two extended fingers. Flin would suffer as no villain ever has. I'd stop him..." His rage throttled him again; he halted for a moment, one outstretched palm braced against the stone wall. Slowly, he regained control of himself. "But such has not been done, if you speak true. Be that the case, the measures I discussed with Crecche, my lord chamberlain, were only these—young Flin's to be destroyed where he's found and decent burial provided for, yourself to be betrothed unto the man to whom I owe good fortune, Crecche, himself."

Now it was Bessina who nearly fell. The corridor wheeled about her and she was barely able to keep her balance. She could not bring herself to touch her father for support and he offered none; her fingers rose to her temples and she stood like one who had been struck a mighty blow. "No, no, it cannot be."

"My word will measure out the boundaries of what may be for you. You are a wanton, willful maiden, much the way your mother was, without her sense of obligation and propriety. In Crecche's care, you'll learn your duties."

"Please." She tried to calm herself. "And he suggested this solution?"

"Indeed. I know your meaning; yes, I will admit you are attractive and he finds you so. Your auburn hair reflects your humor and your eyes are green as liquid velvet. Still, his counsel's good, whatever be his thoughts."

There was no one with them except one servant who bore a torch which he replaced from time to time from the set of extras he carried at his belt, and who watched, bemused, as she pleaded. "Oh, Father, do not do this awful thing. I cannot marry Crecche, nor see my Flin snuffed out in all the richness of his youth. My waywardness I will admit, but show us kindness, please, and spare us both."

Her panic and full-flowing tears were real. An hour or two gone by, she might have tried wheedling her father and playing on his affections—but the capacity for that had been wrung from her. And Count Clauvis seemed to sense that fact; one hand strayed forth to caress her disheveled hair.

Her words had to contest with her sobbing. "I claim all fault as mine; Flin only showed the feelings he had honestly discovered by my hand. He doesn't even understand my title. Please believe me, for I kept from telling him the truth about my own identity; he doesn't dream what maiden he pursues. You cannot have him killed, the crime's not his. Had he suspected that I was your line, he'd not have even looked upon me. I will swear that much upon the gods." Her speech was broken once more by sobbing. "Do not destroy our lives with your revenge, by killing this young man and forcing me to bear a living death within the arms of that old, wrinkled toad, the chamberlain."

She raved on without any idea whether her pleas were doing any good; through tear-misted eyes, she could not tell whether there had been any softening in his expression. "I have my beauty and have not been touched. I have good value as prospective bride to any nobleman across this land. I'll never protest more; my wantonness and willful attitude have been destroyed. But match me not with Crecche and stay the hand that hovers over Flin. I'll do what deeds you ask; I'll wed whomever you may choose. My loyalty and daughterly respect will all be noted in the farthest courts, if you will stay your hand. These things I swear." Her speech dissolved into endless weeping and protestations of her willingness to do anything, to wed anyone other than the chamberlain, if only the two acts of her father's revenge might be prevented.

For his part, Count Clauvis seemed genuinely moved by her outburst. His features became tense with the workings of his mind, then he spoke. "There is one way, if you remain as mild and abject as you seem to be tonight."

"Just name conditions; they will be fulfilled." The words came with difficulty as she wiped her eyes upon the kerchief he handed her.

"First, you shall be as meek and mild a maid as ever lived or curtsied to a guest. And if I bid you marry some old crow with rotten teeth and rheumy, glazing eye, you'll do so and there'll be no argument. And if I bid you lick up after dogs that tear the scraps before my great hall's guests, you'll do it. If you one time play me false, I'll seek for your young Flin and have his heart."

She nodded quietly, choking back her emotion. She was not sure she had any more tears to shed.

"And since my heart is set against this man called

Flin; he shall not live the life he lived before, despoiling maids and riding with his band. My last condition's this— send him a note, arrange a rendezvous at some set time. A band of men will apprehend him there and transport him, all bound up, to some seaport where he shall be placed aboard a ship to serve as crewman till his dying day. Impressment, then, shall be the fate for him."

Her fingers clenched as a look of exquisite wretchedness gripped her features. "And his betrayal shall be at my hands."

"It's not betrayal, for he shall not die; by your own hands he lives. But make your choice."

She did not know whether to feel relief or not, but she did know there was only one reply she dared give him. "Yes. I agree."

His expression changed. He smiled warmly down at her and drew her to her feet, embracing her tenderly, pressing his bearded face against her moist cheek. Was that all that had been needed? Had mere submission made him a happy father? "Now you're my daughter," he said. "All the rancor which has separated us through all these years is turned to soothing mist. You now are my own blood and shall remain so while your heart is true." He held her face between his hands and looked into her eyes. "My sweet Bessina, all this day's travail is purchased with these tears and your consent. My heart is glad. Now take you to your rooms and heal yourself with sleep's refreshing balms."

He gave her one last embrace, then he went with her most of the way to her chamber, one hand about her shoulder. At last, he kissed her warmly on the forehead and watched as she opened her door.

For her part, Bessina was overwhelmed by the shock of the evening's events. It had all been like a dream, the chain of actions that had swept her up since the sun had set. But she was no fool; she still had the presence of mind to hold onto one awful reality—her nightmare had been real. When morning came she would have to betray her love; she would have to send him to a life as an impressed deckhand on some nameless vessel.

She went wearily to her bed; but all the long night, sleep eluded her like flies hazing an outstretched hand. She had never seen her father act the way he had acted. What had come over him? They had argued before. She had disobeyed him and had committed a peccadillo or two over the years. But she had never let a man near her before, had never felt love before. Was that it? Was that what had caused the change?

She had fallen in love. Why did that fact so enrage her father? Who had the dying man in the donjon been? What had been his crime? Was her father going mad? She lay in her bed, her head thrust between two goosedown pillows. She could not erase the two images of her father's rage and the prisoner's disfigurement.

Reality was reduced to one fact—she did not dare do a thing that would lead to Flin's death. She had to send the message which would lure him into a trap. She was forced to appoint a rendezvous which would cause her love to be taken by her father's housecarls.

Chapter Three:
The Assassin

WEST OF TOLQ and south of Buerdaunt lay a land of rolling hills and forests. As a refuge for game it was not equal to the great forest which lay east of Tolq but it was more favored by nobles; it was less mysterious and less deadly, yet a day of riding with dogs and lances seldom failed to produce meat.

Lothar the Pale, King of Buerdaunt, rarely took time for such diversions; still, he was like his rival, Berevald of Carea, in that he had nobles to entertain. War between the two lands was coming. It might come before winter, it might wait a year or even two years—but it would come. That made it a time for cementing relations with the powerful nobles of his land.

So it was that Lothar had spent the day with a large cadre of his own counts and barons, riding after his hounds and mastiffs. It had been a good day, too; he enjoyed such diversions when he took the time for them. Now, behind the returning train of nobility, attendants were bearing many stags as well as a boar or two, all to be rendered into the next evening's feast. So the King sat comfortably astride his palfrey and followed the road to Buerdaunt's great eastern gate.

The city's towering walls rose beyond the groves of oak and beech which lined the roadway. The fortifications which defended Buerdaunt were mighty because the King was a careful man. The walls stood twenty cubits high and bore a massive hoarding, a gallery of the hardest oak, from which defenders could drop hot pitch, oil, or other forms of death onto any besieging enemy.

The eastern gate stood open before the returning party; the portcullis had been raised and the massive wooden doors swung wide. But were they to swing shut and the great bar to slam into place, any attacking army would need help from the gods themselves to break through. And even if that happened, the invaders would face a still greater obstacle—Lothar's own stronghold, Pomfract Castle, with its crenelated towers, massive gatehouse and barbicans, and its great, tall keep.

No, Carea would not be able to attack Buerdaunt directly. But Carea held sway over the Narrow Strait, gateway to the world's trade, and could strangle Buerdaunt's commerce without a single Carean knight setting foot in Lothar the Pale's dominions. But that would be taken care of. Lothar had pulled many necessary puppet strings; that problem was being sorted out even as he rode toward Buerdaunt at the head of his nobles.

With great pomp and a drumming of hooves, the hunting party passed through the gate, beneath the raised portcullis, and into Buerdaunt. Guardsmen raised their weapons in an enthusiastic salute as the cream of the land's chivalry passed by.

Then bedlam erupted. As Lothar the Pale passed into the city, a single figure bolted from the throng and leaped onto the back of the King's horse, throwing his arm about the royal neck. The assailant's right hand rose and the blade of a dagger glinted in the sunlight, then flashed downward. Lothar the Pale struggled furiously against his assailant in spite of his own small size; he twisted in the saddle, caused the dagger's blade barely to graze his chest, and struck a return blow with his elbow.

The King's bailiff, red-haired Gymon, had been riding beside the monarch but the assassin landed two blows before he could respond. He finally did act as the knife descended again; he clutched the assassin's arm, hauled him off the King's horse, and all three fell together. They landed on the paving stones in a heap. The King was knocked senseless, but the attacker scrambled to his feet, only to disappear beneath a wave of humanity as nobles, soldiers, and townspeople surged forward to the defense of their monarch.

Attendants rushed to the King, lifted him, and tore open his doublet. He was still breathing, but two gashes bathed the paving with his blood. They quickly bound his wounds, and someone offered him a goatskin of wine. In the absence of other authority, Gymon tended to the prisoner and had him dragged to his feet by the guards. The man struggled for his life, kicking, trying to free his arms, even biting one of those who restrained him, but he exhausted himself after a moment, and his movements became sluggish as fatigue crushed his limbs. Gymon brushed the dust off as he confronted the fellow. His face was grave. "You putrid scum, what causes this attempt?"

The would-be assassin glared at the bailiff. "If my first blow had been true, I'd have disappeared into the crowd and you never would have taken me."

"That may be so. Still, taken have you been, and it will go more easily with you if you reveal your reasons for this deed."

"Be damned, by all the gods." The prisoner tried to struggle once more, but could not break free or even keep up his efforts for long; there were too many arms and bodies restraining him. "I know I'm a dead man no matter what I say. You'll not get a word from me." He managed to jerk his head forward and spit into the bailiff's face.

Gymon's features twisted furiously as he wiped away the spittle, restraining himself with obvious difficulty and glaring at the unrepentant captive. "Perhaps we might surprise you," he said. He eyed the soldiers, then turned toward the city gate. "Follow me."

The soldiers hustled the prisoner after Gymon as the

bailiff strode through the gate. Once they were all outside the high wall, he gave a strange order. "Release this man. If then he can escape, he'll have his life to squander as he may."

There was an uproar and the soldiers stared at the bailiff. Gymon's face reddened; he repeated his order, and they reluctantly complied. The prisoner stared about for only an instant before he dashed for the nearest grove of trees, about fifty cubits away. But he had only started when Gymon shouted another order, this time to the keepers of the hunting kennels. "Release the dogs. Make haste or heads will roll."

It took only a motion of the wrist for one of the big dogs' keepers to set the creatures free. In less than a heartbeat, half a dozen of the fierce canines stormed after the fugitive, followed by several more. Their baying made fierce thunder as they pursued him.

The man reached the edge of the grove, plainly terrified by the dogs; he ran no farther, but attempted to scale the first tree he came to. He leaped up, grasped a low branch, and tried to lift himself high enough to hook one leg over the limb, to heft himself out of the reach of the sharp-toothed pursuit. But he missed and slipped back. One lean hound reached the tree before the rest and leaped; vicelike jaws closed on a dangling leg and there was a scream as the dog dragged the man from his refuge and pulled him down among the baying beasts.

The end came quickly. Blood-curdling screams were cut short as vicious teeth clamped into arms, legs, throat, and belly. The animals made horrid, gargling snarls as they tore at their prey, crushing muscle and tearing flesh away from limbs, ripping skin open, and flinging this way and that the bits and pieces of what once had been a human being. The brutal execution was quickly over and the corpse was no longer even recognizable. The dogs finally grew bored and lost interest in their unfamiliar food. They dropped what pieces were left and trotted back to their keepers, broad tongues again dangling from ragged mouths. Gymon seemed satisfied with his work as he sent a brace of servants to bury the remains. What was left of the assassin would not even hang in chains to remind the townsfolk that the attempt on the King's life had ever taken place.

As for Lothar the Pale, he was carried to his chambers and physicians came to undress him and examine his hairless body. They determined that none of the wounds was serious, although they did apply bandages. Lothar himself revived during the examination, called for wine, and then asked what had happened to the assailant.

Gymon quickly answered. "The rascal did not long regret his act. His blood now soaks the sand outside the city's gates."

Lothar the Pale frowned as Gymon gave him the details of the fellow's violent end. "Perhaps, if he'd been spared, he might have told the names of those who hired him for the deed."

"I have to doubt that," Gymon said. "For he swore he'd die before he said a word, when I interrogated him."

"One question quickly put is nothing. Men who boast of their resolve will often speak once torture has begun to tear their frames."

Gymon bowed his head. "Then I regret my haste. I simply thought that rapid retribution for his act would make a good example of the man, discouraging all those with like intent."

Lothar the Pale hardly seemed to notice the apology; he was already deep in thought. "We know, of course, that someone sent him here," he said at last. "He didn't strike the blow from any personal dislike; I never saw the fellow in my life. Some noble knave has sponsored him, for no man would have struck me, not unless he had been promised escape by someone with the power to make good."

"That does seem likely and that very thought was in my mind as well. That's why I had him executed hastily, before his freedom could be gained by stealth."

"Who put him to the deed?" Lothar the Pale mused. Then he sipped his wine, sat up, and dismissed the physicians from the dark chamber. He rose and called his attendants to dress him, standing only as high as their shoulders as they carried out his orders. He lifted his arms and allowed them to slip his clothing onto him with the air of a fine stallion used to being groomed and tended. The workings of his colorless face showed he was deep in thought. Once the attendants had finished, he put down his goblet and scratched his head, his fingertips rubbing the cornsilk tassels of his hair. "Perhaps my distant rival, Berevald, believes my death would multiply Carea's sea advantage during war."

"Perhaps." Gymon pursed his lips. "I must misdoubt it, all the same. Old Berevald so dotes on chivalry that knighthood's tenets form the strategy by which he makes his wars."

Lothar the Pale nodded. "And I agree. Some other man has set this fellow to his deadly task." He looked up at Gymon. "Come, sit. We must discuss this for awhile."

Gymon did as he had been ordered. He chose a campaign chair in one corner of the little room Lothar the Pale used for sleeping quarters, seated himself in it, and carefully eyed his monarch.

Lothar the Pale became stern and hard. He had plainly reached a decision. "It's my desire you make me up a list of every lord across my broad domains who owes me debts or underpays his tax, or stands in gain in any other way from my untimely death."

"Already it is done." Gymon smiled with pride as he answered. "I keep just such a list; it's well maintained to serve you in a moment such as this."

Lothar the Pale nodded. "Ah, that's my loyal Gymon. I did well to make you bailiff for your services. You always run a step before your foes and use whatever measures can be found and ready to your hand as you maintain the order of my realm." His face betrayed no emotion as he spoke; there was no telling what his humor was. "I wonder, do you always use your gifts to work for such advancement of the Crown? Or are you ever tempted to intrigue for purposes which do not match my own?"

Gymon gazed at his master. The applelike knob which protruded from his throat bobbed as he swallowed. "Why no, my Liege."

Lothar the Pale's mouth formed the least shadow of a smile. "Of course not. Fetch your list."

While Gymon went to fetch his list of nobles, Lothar the Pale sent all his attendants from the narrow chamber; the servants left torches on the walls, then departed one by one. The King mused while awaiting the bailiff's return. "The loyalty of vassals is a thing which must be reinforced from time to time by gifts and loving strokes. And Gymon can be kept within my circle by such means. He is as grasping and as devious as any man can be, but now our roads run parallel. He keeps his list for reasons all his own, but it shall be of use to me as well. And as for his ambitions, I am sure he shall bear watching, for the time may come when those ambitions can no longer be quite satisfied by piddling honors which I might bestow. When such times come, advisers are dismissed."

He sipped his wine and waited for his counselor to return. "But still, his shot comes very near the mark when he describes old Berevald; it's not that ruler's way to send one man to kill his enemy with dagger thrusts. The man who seeks my life lies near to home. Who might he be? The mighty gods may know, but they do not inform me. Even so, reprisal must fall on the head of someone, for examples must be set. A head must roll in payment for this perfidy. Whatever name my bailiff may provide, as long as it is not some bosom friend or relative, his days shall soon be troubled. By my faith, I care not what the fellow's name may be, for one's as good as any other, just as long as we convey across this realm the message that the King is not a babe. To flail my enemies and preen my friends is how I make my person sacrosanct."

The bailiff did not take long; he returned, opened the chamber door without knocking, and slipped in as quietly as a mongoose. His chest still heaved with the exertion of his errand. "My King, I hurried to my rooms and back."

"I see that by your rasping, gasping breaths," Lothar the Pale replied. "What names have you to show me?"

Gymon opened his red silk robe and produced a folded piece of parchment, which he presented to the King. "As you can see, there are a dozen names of lords to watch.

Some have been holding taxes back. A few have uttered words or phrases that give cause for deep concern about their loyalty."

Lothar the Pale casually eyed the document. As the bailiff had pointed out, there was a considerable list of names, each neatly printed beside the reason its owner lay under suspicion. There was no doubt the bailiff took great pride in the list; it plainly represented much labor and a considerable network of spies. "Much effort went into this information," Lothar the Pale said carelessly. "But we cannot execute some dozen lords."

"There is no need. My pen has listed many who run cool to having you upon the throne, or who are lax in yielding funds which have been designated for the Crown's own use. But none, I feel, has treason in his bones, save him." He extended a knobby finger toward one entry. "This Count. He has not fully paid his tithe unto your treasury for years. He has not sent ship money; his support for you has been lukewarm at best."

The King gazed at the name. "The Count of Galliardy." He looked doubtful. "Are you quite sure of him? I've heard he spends his every waking hour a'counting coin deep in his treasure room. He has not worn his armor but for show in many years, and frankly I don't see how he can pose a threat to me. I grant his greed's to be condemned, but if I act to seize each miser's lands, I shall be fighting civil wars for years and have no other time for policies."

"No, there is more. He has a counselor whose avarice is famous through the land. Informants have told me this grasping pair would greet your death with joy, for it would free them from some claims the Crown has held upon that fief. And last to say, when invitations were extended to the nobles of the realm to come and join the hunt we held today, Count Clauvis sent regrets and stated that he had some business to attend to, which would keep him from your presence. So he did not come. But what could be more crucial than a call to ride to court and pay the homage due his monarch? He has nothing else to do. The only reason he would stay away was that he knew some violence would come unto your royal person. By my troth, it's certain that he fears reprisals for his crimes. He sent that man who tried to kill you for that very cause."

Lothar the Pale pondered for a moment. Count Clauvis held one of the more powerful provinces of the realm. No other lord of his importance had missed the hunting holiday; what was he doing all alone in his castle far up the River Priscus? Although he was disposed to accept any name given him by Gymon, the King preferred not to attack that powerful a noble. But what was the fellow up to? "In many of the castles of my realm, men loyal to the Crown are sent to serve among the knights and guards. Have we such men in service of this Count?"

"Indeed we have. A dozen men are in his pay, but loyal to yourself. That many men can open up his gates, allowing entry to the host you bring to put him in his place."

Lothar the Pale nodded but he did not speak. After a moment, the bailiff put a question. "My Liege, I ask a boon."

"What might that be?"

"The Count of Galliardy has a daughter, clear of eye with lovely auburn hair as rich as aged wine. The moneys of his treasury are past sufficient to repay this campaign's costs but still, if we should seize this traitor's fief, his daughter would be worthless baggage. I will take her from you and defray all costs, for I am told her beauty beggars words."

Lothar the Pale did not change his expression; he only studied the nervous courtier. But another man watching the conversation might have been tempted to laugh. So this was the game Gymon was playing; he was urging the King against Clauvis, Count of Galliardy, for the sake of his daughter's beauty. That was not important; as long as the proper message was sent to any traitors in the realm, one burned castle was as good as another. But the entire affair tended to raise another question: since the attempted assassination had proven so useful to the bailiff, would it have been beyond possibility for him to have ordered it himself?

The King spoke at last. "You cannot have the maiden.

She will go unto the destination I appoint and you must rest assured that it shall be a long way from Buerdaunt. Now, does that change your view that I supress this Count?"

Gymon made half a shrug. "Why, no, your Grace. If it is not to be, it's but some nights of recreation lost."

The answer seemed casual enough. Still, Lothar the Pale would have liked to probe more deeply into the matter. But that could be done later; time was crucial to his present course. The operation had to be finished quickly, before war with Carea could break out. "Then we shall gather knights and other troops and march upon this Clauvis. I want word conveyed to all the men we have within the walls of Castle Gnoffe. Then, on the night that we appoint, the gates shall open wide. My aim's to take the castle in a way that shall strike terror into all my foes— no siege, no battle; Castle Gnoffe must fall as rapidly as lambs fall to the wolf. I do not want the fact that we have marched to be conveyed to any excess ears; one day we will reside within our court, the next day in the castle we have seized. It must be brilliant, instantaneous."

The bailiff nodded.

"And when we have this Clauvis, it's my wish he not be harmed until I have him here. I'll have him under torture and I'll know the facts which lie behind this brace of wounds." The King indicated the two dagger marks left by the dead assassin. "Now get you gone. You have enough to do."

Gymon rose from his seat, bowed deeply, and left. He would carry out the royal command. He was an energetic and devious minion; a task such as the mysterious, instant seizure of a powerful castle was a challenge at which he would excel. Within a few days, Lothar the Pale would have his example and Count Clauvis and all his goods and chattels would be in royal hands.

Chapter Four:
The Oracle

CASTLE CONFORTH WAS a massive citadel which surged up from the rocky mountainside above Upper Carea, a fortress known both for its fine strategic location and its regal luxury. Just off the grass-covered grounds of the inner ward, King Berevald's great hall served as a setting for fantastic fetes and banquets in the evenings, as well as audience in the daytime.

On this fine, fall day, the old King and his courtiers eagerly awaited the return of the heir, Palamon. The Prince had sailed off a fortnight earlier to consult the mysterious Oracle at Euelpis.

King Berevald had fathered five children. Of these, all that remained were Palamon and his sister, Berengeria. All five had been struck by the mad wizard, Alyubol; two had been slain by him while a third, named Berethar, had vanished, never to return. Decades had passed without a breath of the Prince's fate. At last Palamon had been sent to consult the Oracle.

So the King waited. And outside the great hall, Princess Berengeria also waited. She stood with a few attendants and her eyes studied the castle's towering gatehouse. From that place would come the first news of the tall Prince's arrival.

The clarion call of trumpets pierced the air; there was a commotion at the gatehouse and a young page scrambled toward the great hall. A clatter of hooves announced the arrival of many horsemen.

Then Berengeria clenched her hands and beamed; her eyes glistened like a dolphin's scales. Palamon rode into the castle's inner ward at the head of a column of knights. She rushed toward him and hugged him as he swung from his saddle. He was a tall man, broad-shouldered, and with powerful limbs. He wore a suit of gleaming chain mail, a hauberk which was rumored to be magical. But his face, though it was lean, handsome, and adorned by a full mustache, bore the lines of nearly forty years of sorrows and troubles. Still, he smiled down at the young woman who hugged him; his affection for her was great.

"What word have you for us?" Her eyes danced as she put the question.

He shook his head. "Our father must be first to hear my tidings, though I will tell you they bring no encouragement."

Her face fell. "Then I must take it that the news is bad."

"What news, indeed." The harsh voice cut the air between the two siblings. Turning, they saw Ursid, the young noble from Buerdaunt. "What has your Oracle to say of me, who aided both of you to flee my own far land and reach this court? What word for me, who bled from many wounds for love of Berengeria?"

Ursid was a man without a country, a lonesome, star-crossed lover. He had been feted and honored in the strange land to which he had come; he owned fine clothes, costly weapons, and a place of honor near the palace of the King. That was his wage for his part in Berengeria's rescue. But he was still a stranger, still out-of-place and alone. Despite the love he bore for the Princess, she did not love him. It was at last becoming plain to him that he would never win her hand.

So now he stood before the object of his passion, bitter and insistent. "The time for talk has passed, Princess. If I now ask the King for your fair hand, then what will he reply to my request? Will he say 'yes' and clasp me to his breast or will I hear postponing words again?"

Berengeria's face was suddenly drawn and strained; it showed sympathy for the young knight, but it showed the stress of the sudden interruption even more. Resentment made her eyes gleam as she spoke. "Ursid, no one denies your worthiness to seek my hand, but might I rest awhile? While you have seldom spoken to my face, I hear of all your applications to my father and to Palamon, as well as other persons. You have spoken much, and much of what you said was loud and not well pondered." She turned her glance from him. "I do not see myself as being some possession, your prize ewe."

As for Palamon, he was torn by sympathy for both of them. Ursid had labored long and hard for Berengeria's hand, yet she had often told Palamon that she did not and could not return his love. Which one should be pleased? Where was the answer that would not bring tears to one or to the other, and what was Palamon's own place in their dispute?

Ursid continued, raising his voice so all could hear. "I am a stranger here. I have few friends. But still the deeds I've done in her behalf support my suit for Berengeria." Once more he addressed his plea to the Princess herself. "My countenance is not what it once was, Princess, but still the scars that I exhibit all were gained in your defense."

"I am aware." The agitation in Berengeria's voice grew like a tumor; though she did not look at the young knight, Palamon could see her eyes flash. Her jaw was working violently. She bore the look of a woman who has been insulted in her own home and she snarled through clenched teeth. "By all the gods, cannot this subject be allowed to rest? Must you speak marriage now?" She gestured toward the onlookers. "Must my affections be displayed before the ears and probing eyes of all the world? You have not given me a moment's peace when I could rest, free of the question: what man shall possess my virgin body, out of all of those who slaver for it? Peace, I beg of you."

Ursid's eyes also flashed. "You say that you want peace, but for how long? A month? A year? Your hand is owed to me—I simply want what, by all rights, should be my own." He gestured angrily. "And yet I will not have it said that I have been unreasonable. Just pledge to me your word your hand shall come to me in eighteen months. Then I shall leave these shores and travel 'cross the sea, far from your view. And thus you'll have the peace you've spoken of."

Berengeria threw up her hands. "Oh, Hestia," she cried. "Will you give unto this knight the wit to understand the words I speak? He does not listen to my plea for peace and time alone; the only words he hears are those his mind has reconstructed from the things I say. His ears are deaf, except to what he wants to hear." Her face writhed with her anger and frustration; she looked as if she were about to tear her hair out.

Palamon had listened to the argument before. The dispute had to be stopped, but what was he to do about it? Although Berengeria was his sister, she was also the maiden whose spirit and determination to reach her homeland during the flight from Buerdaunt had captured his heart. And most of all, it hurt him to watch her writhe in the flames of Ursid's persistence. "Methinks I have some say in this affair."

Every face turned toward him, and a grim expression curled across his features as he spoke. "Before I learned my own relationship with Berengeria, I won her hand in combat, in a tournament of knights. Although you fought with prowess, young Ursid, 'twas I who gained the laurel wreath about my brows; the victory was mine. 'Twas I who stood with arms borne high aloft while you were carried from the cluttered field. Thus, while your claim is honorable, it still is I who vanquished you. So it's my right to treat disposal of her hand as I see fit."

Ursid smiled a horrible smile. "And how shall you receive my suit, new Prince?"

Palamon's own expression never wavered; it had

become fixed on his face like a scar. "It's not a subject to be lightly taken, for brave suitors soon shall come from many lands about the Thlassa Mey. All suits must be considered, for the hand of our Princess is no small prize. Alliances and dowries proposed must all be cataloged ere we decide; her hand's a public property, and public weal is of most high account. This is my word: Carea's future must be satisfied before some gallant can receive her hand."

Ursid looked as if he could spew acid. Palamon remembered a time when those features had been rounded, unformed, and pleasant; it had not been long ago. It tweaked him to see Ursid looking the way he did. "Is that your *kind* reply?" Ursid sneered. "A dowry? Alliances will show who wins her hand? And such a knight as I, who have no land, who have forsaken all my properties to spring her from her place of hostageship shall have small place in such a competition.

"I see what treatment I can now expect at all your hands. Your dear Princess is safe; the service that I gave now slips your thoughts as quickly as the water from a weir. I shall be kept and fed and gawked upon, an orphaned knight of small utility. I must apologize, for I can see that I grow burdensome when not of use."

Lady Aelia, tall, slender, and astute, was chief among Berengeria's attendants. She had listened to Ursid's remarks; now she spoke. "There's merit to this statement and the claim our friend Ursid has brought. He should not be so easily dismissed."

But Ursid turned on her, his brown eyes full of rage. "I understand your meaning. Now you say my pride should not be injured; hold awhile, considering my plea. When time has passed to make refusal seem a trifle less obtuse, then issue your denial. I must go. I fear I am an inconvenience here." He wheeled and stalked away, pushing past anyone who happened to be in his path as he left the castle.

Silence reigned, for there was some truth in the young knight's words. For his own part, Palamon felt wretched; he had been a traitor to a brother-in-arms. Ursid's service for Berengeria's sake had been gallant and crucial; no one could know that more than those who had made the trek from Buerdaunt to Carea. He had received little enough reward for all he had done.

But Berengeria did not love him; her heart rebelled at any mention of Ursid as a husband, all the more because of the young knight's persistence. And who could blame her? She had not chosen Ursid; he had chosen her. The entire matter was distasteful to Palamon.

And there were other matters to attend to; Palamon had to bear the Oracle's message to the King. He looked one last time at Berengeria, touched her shoulder, then strode into the King's presence chamber. All eyes rested on him, heralds shouted at his entry, and pages scrambled before him. But the confrontation with Ursid had tangled his thoughts. He had no words as he approached the dais and the white-haired monarch who was waiting for him. He reached the throne, knelt, and placed a slip of parchment into the old man's hand.

Berevald looked at the tall Prince with questioning eyes. "The Oracle addresses this to me?"

"Indeed, your grace."

Berevald frowned as he looked the paper over. It contained a single verse, the Oracle's only answer to all the questions Palamon had put to her.

O Palamon, your overspreading fame
Has long preceded you to this retreat.
All Berevald's five children suck'd the teat
Of fortune, drinking honor, downfall, shame;
Of all those five, it's you who hold the claim
Of quaffing most the bitter and the sweet—
A heady brew—but ere your life's complete,
You'll drink more of a vintage much the same.
To Berethar, your brother, fortune's draught
Was poisonous; while still he was a youth,
He did succumb. He had no child to feed
And call his own. Two more words end this sooth:
Of vulture's wings, beware when feathers bleed,
And by the Axe's Blade is found the truth.

The King's lips moved silently as he read the prophesy over and again; then he read it aloud for the entire chamber to hear. When he was done, silence reigned in the great hall. At last the Queen uttered a sigh. "Alas, it says my Berethar is slain.'While still a youth he did succumb,' it says. How many years have passed since his red blood surged through his veins?"

Palamon went to his mother's side and tugged at her shoulders to lift her because she had doubled over with grief. "My mother, it was not for you to know. The gods allowed events to pass in such a way that you could never learn his fate. Had you suspected he was still alive, you still could not have done the slightest thing. Fair Berengeria has been restored to you, as well as I myself. The plotters who removed three other children from your arms performed their evil work in spite of all your efforts to resist. You cannot suffer guilt for anything."

She sighed once more as she gazed up at him and at Princess Berengeria. "The words you say are wise. I shall oppose the heartbreak and the grief which wait to drag me to despair. I have you two restored to me; therefore my blessings will I count. But still it is my fate, a mother's fate, that even were my children all returned but one, for that one child I still should grieve far more than I'd rejoice for all the other four."

Berevald had left his great wooden chair and also approached his Queen, making his way through the press of attendants. Palamon stepped aside as the old King took her hands into his own and gazed into her eyes. "But still there may be answers to be found. Now read with us the Oracle's last line you shall see a clue to learning more about our second son. It says 'Of vulture's wings, beware when feathers bleed.' This is a passage we cannot make out but we believe the next is plain as day. 'And by the Axe's Blade is found the truth.'" He drew himself up to his full height. "We know the meaning of that simple line."

Lady Aelia had also joined the group. "Perhaps," she said."But you must take the greatest care if you would read the Oracle's veiled passages."

Berevald shook his head. "We say it's plain as day.

For we now hold within our donjon's cells that foul Navron who is the confidant of Alyubol, the evil wizard and my greatest foe. For Alyubol was he who stole each child of ours in its own time, and this Navron must know the secrets of them all."

He turned away and commanded a brace of attendants. "You men! Go out at once and fetch the guards. Remove Navron from prison; bring him up. We'll bind him to the stake which stands alone within the inner wall. 'Tis many weeks since he has seen the sun—this time will be the last unless he speaks. 'And by the Axe's Blade is found the truth.' An execution, plain and simply put. Unless he speaks and tells us of the death of Berethar, an axe's blade shall cleave his scraggled skull."

The two soldiers hurried from the vast chamber, their armored feet scuffing across the tiled floor. The King walked after them as they went, descending the dais with his purple robe spreading behind him, his family walking along, attendants and courtiers following him into the bright daylight. There was a dreadful sense of purpose about him; plainly no doubt lay in his mind that he saw through the veiled phrasing of the prophesy. Already there was shouting across the inner ward as guardsmen bestirred themselves. A fraction of an hour would bring one of two events: either evil Navron would reveal the hidden fate of Palamon's brother, or the villian's brains would be spilled onto the courtyard's paving by the executioner's axe.

Chapter Five:
Vulture's Wings

ROYALTY AND ATTENDANTS poured out of the great hall and into the castle's inner ward, a broad courtyard surrounded by kennels, barracks, mews for hunting birds, and stables. In the center of the great, cobbled square stood a high post, higher than a man's head, cut square, its breadth twice the span of a grown man's fingers. A soldier was summoned from the barracks; his arms were as big around as mutton hams, and he wore no hauberk or jerkin. Dark hair sprouted everywhere—from his broad chest, from the massive arms, and even from the great, square back. He had a heavy beard and he walked with a brutal sense of purpose.

"He comes," the Queen observed quietly. "For months together he must wait; you have not summoned him this year nor last. But now he comes."

Palamon did not know the man but he could guess his office. "So," he said. "You've asked the executioner to come?"

"I have." The King's voice was rough as a grindstone.

The executioner arrived and bowed before the royal

family. "The notice has been short, your Grace. I have not dressed. Should I prepare myself?"

"Not yet. Let's see your blade."

The fellow rose and presented his weapon, a great battle-axe. Palamon had seen such a weapon wielded in more than one fray, although not one as heavy as this. But judging from the rippling muscles of the great shoulders, the man doubtless could use it well. His name was Adrastus.

The great stake was prepared. Scurrying attendants brought leather thongs, carried up faggots, and arranged them about the stake, leaving a space open so the prisoner could pass through. Then there was a commotion at one end of the courtyard; a knot of men appeared, escorting a white-robed figure. The King glanced in that direction, placed his hands on his hips, and glared at the approaching prisoner. "So, knave. Our lodgings, are they well within the boundaries of your taste, or do you find they lack the luxury of those afforded by your master?" The irony dripped from his words like fluid from an old wound.

Navron grinned back at the King. He was a sinister looking fellow of average height, clean-shaven except for a thin, black mustache, and he wore the white woolen robe which marked him as one of Alyubol's ministers. His face bore a look of evil that was ground into it the way dirt was ground into a peasant's hands. He looked about himself at the crowd of nobles who had come to watch the interrogation and he laughed at them all.

He did not struggle against his escort; he allowed them to bring him before the King and he stood smirking up into the older man's face. "Your quarters have met all my physical needs. But fear not, for they cannot contain me for long."

Berevald controlled his anger; his tone became strained, but he did not raise his voice. "What is your name, you knave?"

"My name is Navron, as you know well enough."

"Indeed. You are the minion of foul Alyubol, who stole from me my children and my joy and caused cruel tears to stain my poor wife's cheeks."

Navron's expression never faded as he surveyed his surroundings and answered the King almost as if it were a second thought. "My master is yours. Your defeats have the numbers of sand."

"Indeed, that might well be. But even so, you ne'er shall witness either more defeats or victories." Berevald turned to the guards. "Now bind him up, my men."

A half dozen warriors leaped to obey the command. They hustled the pale-robed Navron to the stake, bound him to it, and stacked the faggots about him. He continued to smile but his expression became forced as the preparations continued. "Am I to be burned alive?"

"No. Weakling that I am, I have no heart to burn a dog alive, much less a man, though whether you be man or animal is hard to tell. But I shall put a question to you, sirrah; if you answer truthfully, your life shall then be spared and you will spend your days in moderate captivity. But if you should refuse to answer, then an axe shall split your skull and roaring flames shall rid the earth of your foul corpse forevermore. Adrastus," Berevald summoned the executioner. "Show this man your axe's blade, for by the axe's blade is found the truth."

The burly executioner's arms bulged as he lifted his great weapon. The blade glinted in the late afternoon sun.

Navron swallowed. "Then say what your question might be."

Berevald began to reply but was interrupted by a buzz of conversation. Some of the people who had crowded into the inner ward were looking up into the sky, for a great bird of prey had appeared and was circling above the castle's battlements, its broad wings guiding it gracefully through the ether. "What thing has now appeared?" the King demanded.

"A mountain condor," one courtier said. "Several times this month has it appeared far from its mountain lair high in the Altines, south of Carea. It wheels about for some short space of time, then disappears, returning to its home."

The King watched the great bird for a moment, then turned back to the prisoner. "You'd have the question put? Then very well; what was the final fate of Berethar, our son, whom Alyubol, your master, swept away from us long years ago?"

Navrón laughed. "The secret shall die on my lips."

"You must speak out, for there can be no doubt your brains shall soon be spilled if you do not." But before the King could say more, the buzz of voices grew louder across the courtyard. He looked up again. The condor had spiraled even closer to the ground; its vast wings were holding it only a few fathoms above the onlookers' heads. Each feather could be seen working at the wingtips to stabilize the brown body.

Berevald glared up at it, then he called every archer within earshot. "We'll not be interrupted as we seek to learn the fate of our poor missing child. All bowmen who can hear us, nock your shafts and put an end to interferences by downing this o'erflying fowl. And when that's done, we shall begin again."

Palamon had only recently returned from Euelpis and his visit to the Oracle; his mind was still full of the holy presence. He stepped forward and placed a hand on the King's shoulder. "My Lord, none can be sure that would be wise."

But it was too late for discussion; the deed was instantly performed. A volley of brightly fletched arrows sang into the air; many missed, but others pierced their target. With a scream which chilled the bone, the condor spun toward the ground, landed beak forward, and crashed into the piled faggots at Navron's feet. As for the minion of Alyubol himself, he seemed delighted and amused; he laughed as if his sides would split, throwing his head back, shaking his shoulders with mirth so great it caused his fetters to quake.

King Berevald pointed toward the fallen condor and roared orders. "Remove that creature, then we shall begin once more to pry the truth from this man's lips."

A pair of soldiers tried to obey. But as they grasped the condor by its huge wings, wings as broad as the height of two men, the creature seemed to come all apart. The body crumbled away from them and blood flowed everywhere, dissolving into stinking fumes which overcame everyone nearby. The great, brown feathers squirted blood as they fell from the wings like leaves in an autumn gale, turning over and over again as they fluttered to the paving about the stake. And over all rang the insane laughter of Navron. Something even stranger followed. Each feather which had fallen from the stinking carcass grew, changed, and became a grim, hulking warrior dressed in dark leather armor, brandishing a deadly longsword.

Two of the mystical soldiers sprang to Navron's side as his bonds fell away, loosed by some spell he uttered. Then onlookers' screams pierced the air, followed by the shouts of Berevald's own guard drawing their weapons. Adrastus the executioner was the first Carean to fall. His axe cleaved one opponent from shoulder to the navel, but he was unable to strike again before he was run through.

Several guardsmen grasped the stunned King and Queen and hauled them away, dragging them unceremoniously toward the safety of the keep itself. Another pair hauled at Palamon, but he shrugged away from them, stood his ground, and stared at the struggle before him. Where the great condor had fallen, a fearsome battle developed as the defenders of the castle withstood a great number of brown-clad invaders.

Carean guardsmen dashed toward Berengeria to remove her from danger, but they were too late. The invaders cut them down like cattle, surrounded her, and began forcing her away, out of Palamon's reach. Led by Navron, they made for the castle's gatehouse.

A few of them turned toward Palamon, fought their way past Carean soldiers, and fell upon the tall Prince with snarling fury. But Palamon did not move. He stood motionless before them, staring, concentrating. To him there were no brown-clad attackers. They were imaginary; their blows fell, but did not harm. He breathed a single word, for he knew what kind of army they were. "Alyubol." The mad wizard who was his father's great enemy had sent a deadly illusion to free Navron.

Palamon's discipline had defeated the illusory warriors, but only when they had attacked him; the ones which had seized Berengeria were still forcing her away.

He ran after them, shouting at the top of his lungs, "Disbelieve them—you shall then fall free." But she could not hear him. The illusions around her had set up a shout to drown out his words and they bore her away too quickly for him to catch up.

Though the illusory army could not strike Palamon, it did grisly work upon the Carean warriors. The high gatehouse had never been designed to be attacked from within; the men who kept the portcullis and drawbridge were hacked down, and the magical force erupted from the castle, led by Navron, and bore the screaming Princess away as they carved a bloody swath toward the city of Upper Carea.

Once they had departed, the debris of the carnage assaulted the eye all across the castle's inner ward. Men lay everywhere, dogs sniffed at corpses, and survivors groaned, nursed wounds, or bound one another. From outside the walls rose the cries and clanking of armor as the knights and city provost's guards donned weapons and mounted steeds to set off in pursuit. Palamon smiled grimly. The pursuit would come to nothing, for it was a response Alyubol would surely have planned for. And the mystical soldiers who had fallen were already beginning to fade from view. Palamon's neck bent, his eyes surveyed the damage at his feet, and he murmured something. "Of vulture's wings, beware when feathers bleed." The thirteenth line of the Oracle's prophesy had already come to pass, fulfilled by the great race of condors which inhabited the mountains to the south; condors were huge, dignified, carrion-eating birds—vultures.

He pressed his lips together as he walked toward the stake to which Navron had been tied. Alyubol must have known, from the moment he had sent his clever minion to be captured in Carea, that he had the means to bring him forth again. And he had recaptured Berengeria in the bargain.

All at once, the Prince cried out and sagged against the stake. He had been able to defend himself against the mad wizard's illusion, but what good had that done? He had not been able to protect Berengeria. His voice had

not been loud enough, and his feet had been too slow.
Now Berengeria was gone, and no man could even know
where to search for her. Would she be taken to Alyubol's
island stronghold? To Buerdaunt? Elsewhere? Nothing
mattered anymore. He had loved her more than a sister
and now she was gone.

A hand pressed against his shoulder and he turned to
see Aelia standing behind him. "Now peace, Sir Knight.
We have no time for grief; we must forget all nonessential
things, prepare ourselves, and pledge a solemn quest to
seek her out." Aelia's face was drawn by her own emotion
but her coolness conquered all.

Palamon sighed and turned, gathered himself together,
then pulled himself upright and gazed into the slender
woman's eyes. "Indeed we must. Your counsel's always
wise." What did she think of him? Berengeria had been
in her care for twenty years and Palamon had not been
able to halt the Princess' capture. What must Aelia think
of him? Palamon knew a secret that made the question
of more than academic interest.

Then a new thought shouldered all else out of Palamon's mind. Ursid! The young knight was still furious
over losing Berengeria and had just left the castle—what
rôle would he play in the matter? Had he been a part of
the plot? The Crown had presented the young knight with
a luxurious townhouse nearby; was he there now or had
he joined the mystic legions bearing the Princess toward
her unknown destiny?

Palamon grasped Aelia by the wrist. "We must bestir
ourselves and hurry to the dwelling of Ursid."

She caught his meaning instantly. "Indeed we must, to
see what part he plays in this affair."

Together they dashed toward the gatehouse. They did
not bother to obtain horses; the townhouse was only a
short jaunt. They ran like lunatics through the gatehouse,
past bodies, and into the streets of Upper Carea. Palamon
stopped once to allow Aelia to catch up, but left her far
behind again when the building they sought came into
view.

The mystical army had left a river of destruction which

led directly to Ursid's dwelling. Palamon did not know what to make of it; the townhouse's door stood open and the interior was a shambles. He had misjudged Ursid entirely; the place had been the scene of a bitter struggle. Inside the furniture had been overturned and broken, and servants were dead; there could be no doubt that Ursid had been attacked and had defended himself nobly.

So the young knight had not been in league with Navron. The trail of his struggle was undeniable; it led from his sleeping chambers downstairs, through the rooms which led toward the door. One terrified attendant who had survived confirmed it: "The young master was hauled off like a bag of grain, once they got ahold of him."

Once Palamon and Aelia had learned all they could learn, they returned to Castle Conforth, neither one speaking. Both knew it would be futile to pursue Navron and his minions; mounted men were already doing that, though it was not likely they would run the abductors to the ground; Alyubol would have made allowances for such pursuit.

The royal chambers were desolate. Palamon and Aelia found the King and Queen surrounded by attendants in the Queen's chambers, pale but composed. The King stood and the Queen greeted them with glances from recently wiped eyes; then all except for Berevald seated themselves about the room.

Palamon spoke first. "There's only one course fit for us to take. I'll go alone unto the Isle of Kolpos, where I can begin to seek for news or rumors of our Berengeria."

"Why Kolpos?" the Queen asked.

"On Kolpos lies the lair of her abductor, fearful Alyubol," Aelia said. "But hold; how may we know her destination is his foul abode?"

"Because his lust for her will make it so," Palamon said. "When she was in his clutches once before, his passion was aroused. His fatal flaw is that he lacks control; if he still wants her, she'll be taken there." He paused to shake his head. "It is a fearful thought: our Princess held and at the mercy of a madman known to be as merciless as any demon."

"We shall not think of that," the Queen replied quietly. "But I have thoughts. Why will she not be taken to Buerdaunt? The Buerdic King, our enemy, Pale Lothar, held her once as hostage. Why will Alyubol not sell her back to him? It's known that they have been allied before."

"Two reasons light my mind," Palamon said. "The first is that she has, as I have said, excited lust within the madman's soul. He therefore will desire she stay with him. She cannot fetch the ransom she once did from Lothar, for no longer does she stand alone as heir to proud Carea's throne."

"And she escaped from Lothar once before," Aelia added. "Old Alyubol's mad memory shan't forget."

"But she escaped from Alyubol as well," the King said.

Aelia shook her head. "Indeed, but that will not count in his mind. Where there is risk, he'll want her near at hand, to slay or keep as whim directs his addled brain."

Berevald struck the chamber wall with his clenched fist. "Buerdaunt provided funds for the support of Alyubol before. They shall again; they do not have a scruple and they know the way foul Alyubol opposes me." His jaw worked. "Pale Lothar blackmailed me for three long years; it's sure he stands to profit by my grief once more by purchasing my daughter. I will not be blackmailed. I shall have the fleet prepared; Buerdaunt and Kolpos both shall be blockaded. We shall see if Alyubol and Lothar are well pleased by the result their intrigues bring about."

Palamon was silent for a moment. When he did speak, it was with obvious reluctance. "My Liege, if I'm not to seek my sister's rescue, I'd prefer the Thlassa Mey not be at war. To seek her will be difficult at best, but if all ports are locked by conflict, it will be impossible. I beg you to postpone your warlike actions."

"Our legions can be landed on the shores of Kolpos and we'll bolt him from his lair."

"He'll kill her for his vengeance ere he flees," Aelia said with a pleading glance at the royal couple. "If she is to be saved, then the attempt must be a tiny operation of no more than two or three. The risks are great, but not as great as if a company of men began to seek her."

The King turned away and slapped his fist into his palm. "How certain can we be she even lives?" There was a note of despair in his voice.

"It is an honest question." Palamon looked graver than ever; it seemed that he was actually in physical pain. "Still, we must act upon the supposition that she lives. If she is dead, all meaning then is lost." He paused, then continued. "I want to seek her out on Kolpos' shores. A passage on some vessel can be bought and I will search that land unrecognized."

"Nay, nay," Aelia said, shaking her head. "You ne'er shall go unrecognized. His spies will lurk on every street of Touros and all other seaport towns of Kolpos. I must go along with you; my features are more common than your own and I know how to trap elusive tales and glean what information there might be. It is agreed we must not send a force of men to Kolpos; Alyubol might flee to places where he never could be found. But we, together, will accomplish more than you can by yourself, O Palamon."

"Perhaps. But there is danger in this quest."

Aelia laughed. "Have I not met with danger eye to eye and faced it down? Sweet Berengeria and I knew danger's tingling breath upon our necks before we ever met with you." Aelia's gaze pierced Palamon as she spoke.

He smiled back at her and nodded reluctantly. "Indeed. Your words are true. I must admit I underestimate your skill and your resolve. And who can know? My heart may fail, and you may need to bolster up my spirits ere this deadly mission sees an end." He turned to the King once more. "Father, will you give the two of us a chance to travel incognito and seek out poor Berengeria on Kolpos' shores?"

Berevald looked from one of them to the other, then back again, his features softening. "Ah, Palamon, that is a hard request. Our daughter has been snatched away from us and now our son is also asking for the right to leave, to follow her into the deep, uncharted realm in which she's held." He heaved a sigh. "When I interpreted the Oracle, I'd no idea it would come to this. If you are lost upon some unknown shore, the long years left to us shall be like torture."

He clapped his hand on Palamon's shoulder. "You two are both experienced; you know the risks involved and how to counter them. Therefore we would be wrong if we forbade to you the chance to save our Berengeria. The full resources of the kingdom shall be placed at your disposal to produce the best disguises for your safety's sake."

Palamon did not smile but he nodded. "I thank you."

The King raised his palm. "Wait a bit; I am not done. A fortnight shall you have to search for her, but on the twentieth day from your departure, Carea's fleet shall sail. We shall not risk you for a longer time and cannot let Pale Lothar do his blackmail once again. Therefore, if you should not gain your success before that span of days has passed, you must be on your way back to our shores."

Palamon looked into Berevald's face. The King had acted with the greatest restraint all the years Berengeria had been a hostage of Lothar the Pale; his limit had plainly been reached. Palamon could not condemn his actions. They would have a fortnight, then they would have to return and the war would begin. It was a daunting prospect.

Chapter Six:
Lothar the Pale

LOTHAR THE PALE, King of Buerdaunt, rode through damp darkness, his armor resting heavily upon his shoulders. He was leading the cream of Buerdaunt's heavy horse, five hundred handpicked knights. Many were directly loyal to him; the others owed fealty to Count Guntram of Jolier, who rode at the King's right side. Gymon the bailiff rode on the other side, looking less than comfortable in his burnished armor.

They were marching toward Tolq and did not yet need secrecy. The royal treasure and Gymon's intrigues had seen that the sentries who guarded Castle Gnoffe would not be zealous in their duties. Besides, Count Clauvis' castle was still half the night away. The King had carefully planned his attack; it would fall just before the first light of dawn, when the castle and its defenders would be least ready for it.

Unlike many nobles, Lothar the Pale had no great lust for battle; it was a state duty, like sharing the bed of a Queen who did not appeal to him. As far as the conduct of the battle itself was concerned, he doubted his presence was even necessary; affairs would be in capable hands. Guntram of Jolier was a masterful leader and so was Gymon, as out-of-place as he might look astride a war-horse. But a King had to lead his army into the fray, if only for appearances' sake.

The road to Tolq was a major highway. The trees had been cut back from it for thirty cubits to deny shelter to would-be robbers and highwaymen. Even at that, the great body of knights which Lothar the Pale led filled the space between the trees, and their horses filled the night air with a steady, low thunder, as from a combat between clouds far away. The night was full of the creaking of leather, the click and chime of armor plate against plate, and the breathing and snorting of the great animals. But that was as close to silence as so large a force could come.

Ahead of the horsemen and along each flank, torch-bearers held their brands high, flames dancing in the breeze. Their role was to cast enough light to prevent some knight from being swept off his mount by an over-hanging branch or injuring his horse on a snag or boulder. The light was faint, but it was enough to keep the front rank from accident, and those who followed more or less stayed in the tracks of those before them.

The Count of Jolier's armor glinted in the darkness as he spoke to the King. "My Liege, what manner of crime has been performed by Clauvis, Count of Galliardy, that he deserves to be attacked within his castle keep? My stout knights and myself will march to battle under your command; still, I would learn the reason for the fray."

Lothar the Pale's long, near-white hair swept across a metallic shoulder as he looked at the Count. "Disloyalty—or treason, if you wish."

The Count of Jolier stared at him. "A grievous charge."

"It's proven well enough," Gymon said.

The King's pink eyes were steady. "Ostensibly, good Count, his crime is that he is suspected as to honesty of tithes; above all that, however, there is more. As shown by correspondence, his support for me is less than hot, and there's no knowing how he will respond if foreign armies trespass on our land. And Galliardy lies in the path

of any force which would oppose us. Thus, his crime is
that he has conspired to occupy the wrong location at a
time that's also wrong."

"I see."

"I think you do. I must be sure that Galliardy is held
by loyal hands, if war should come. So Clauvis' lands
and titles, chattels, goods, and holdings shall be distrib-
uted between such men as I deem fit. That's if the battle
goes as well as I am sure it will, when we at last reach
Tolq."

"It shall, your Grace," the bailiff said. "All things have
been prepared."

While the army marched, Lothar the Pale and his bailiff
reviewed their plan for the benefit of the Count of Jolier.
Castle Gnoffe stood on a point which jutted out into Lake
Peghese itself. It was in poor repair; Count Clauvis had
long been too interested in his riches and his pleasures to
give consideration to his defenses. It was said the walls
were so crumbled that in some places an agile man could
climb them without a ladder. Still, the castle had originally
been well-built and, if stoutly defended, could be costly
to take.

But intrigues would prevent that. There was a passage
by which refuse was carried to the lake and water brought
into the castle. If properly manned, it would have been
as inaccessible as a gatehouse; a few brave soldiers there
could have withstood an army. But some of Count Clauvis' housecarls were in the royal pay. It had been arranged
for a company of men to be allowed entry to the castle
by the passage, to approach the gatehouse by secret corridors, and to signal the subversion of the castle by casting
a torch over the gate itself. The force would have to kill
the men in the gatehouse, jam the twin portcullises so
they could not be dropped, and prevent the other internal
defenses from being used.

"This fact must be remembered," the King said. "This
attack must gain success so rapidly no lord will dare oppose
the dictates of the Crown. Our victory must be so quickly
won that all who hear the news will be amazed by what
transpired."

"So it shall be," the Count of Jolier said. "No strategy was ever as complete as this which both of you have laid before me."

As they approached Tolq, they were met by a force of light cavalry which had been observing the castle. The officer-in-charge conferred with Gymon for a moment, then Gymon spoke to the King. "Your Grace, they say the town is all asleep. Although they did not dare approach the keep too closely, it appeared quite unprepared."

Lothar the Pale nodded. "Then let us hurry on; the night grows old."

First light was casting a faint glow above the trees behind them as they rode down on the outer walls of the city. They rode quietly for fear of raising an alarm. But there were no watchmen at the main gate when they arrived; Gymon's subversion had succeeded in eliminating the first line of opposition.

The army of knights rode through the town, filling the streets the way water would fill a sluice. Each knight kept to his station. Careful instructions had listed the dire fate which would befall any straggler who caused an alarm to be sounded. But there were no alarms. They rode through the darkened city like clopping ghosts, poured into the square before the castle, and challenged the dumbfounded sentry, demanding entry for the King.

The hapless watch officer stood aghast, too amazed to answer. When he finally did manage a reply, he stammered and made little sense. Even that did not matter. His response was interrupted by a blood-curdling scream, followed by the sight of a torch being flung out over the castle's gate. Then the gate itself swung ponderously open; the sappers had performed their task perfectly and Castle Gnoffe lay open to assault.

"My hearty men, ride forward," the Count of Jolier cried. "Take this keep by all the gods of battle. Victory or death." Couching his lance, he spurred his own steed and charged, pebbles flying from the animal's hooves and five hundred handpicked knights galloping after him.

Even from the ground, the dismay on the faces of the men atop the wall was clearly evident. In an instant, they had drawn longswords to repel the charge and had thrown themselves down ladders and stone steps to meet the invaders. But they were defeated before they could even begin; many were ridden down by the first charge. All they could do was die gallantly in a hopeless fight against mounted knights who drew weapons and beat down upon their heads in a deadly manner. Led by the captain of the watch, many of the guardsmen were hacked and battered to pieces, and their blood was splattered across the inside stones of the gatehouse and the curtain wall.

Others fled; they escaped over the crumbling walls or out the gate and ran screaming into the night. Some knights rode after them, while others carried on the battle inside the castle walls, pursuing their vanquished foemen across the inner ward, into towers, up staircases, and along halls and galleries. Serving women, attendants, and servants were rounded up and herded into a corner of the wall, where they looked about and begged for mercy. Blood and the cries of stricken men were everywhere.

Lothar the Pale forced his head into his helmet and joined Gymon in riding through the vacant gatehouse to observe the carnage. Men and women were scampering all about the castle, closely harried by armor-clad pursuers. Then flames erupted from within the castle's hall; the dancing orange light provided grisly illumination for the spectacle.

Screams erupted from many a tower window. As the two fathers of the massacre proceeded across the bailey and into the inner ward, they saw a number of their knights once more mounting their steeds. "To Tolq," one of them cried. "The city next must fall to us."

With savage cries, they thundered out of the castle toward the entrails of the defenseless city. They were a great number, and Tolq was no better defended than the castle which had been built to protect it. Still, the King made no move to stop the pillagers; he did not even turn in his saddle to watch them go. "The city has no hope of fending off so great a horde of greed-crazed plunderers," he observed calmly. "How many maidens shall be raped or slain, how many children shall the sunrise find all moth-

erless or dead or lying by the corners of the streets,
bewailing fate which could so callously destroy their world?
Lives shall be ended, hopes shall come to naught, and
honest expectations shall be snuffed at lance's point.
Before this new day ends, the wealth of this fine city shall
be gone, and refugees shall hobble down the highways,
stripped of hope.

"But these things touch me not. They have no weight
beside the nation's needs in these hard times. The wealth
of Tolq and Clauvis shall pay off this horde of knights and
whet their appetites for more. When war with far Carea
comes, they shall be fairly drooling for the fray in hopes
of reaping more such benefits. And all this crumpled,
crushed humanity shall issue from the slaughter, bearing
word Buerdaunt's own King will not be compromised or
mocked by serf of haughty nobleman. Those monarchs
who maintain that progress comes from seeking out men's
higher instincts all are fools, for human greed, corruption,
lust, and simple selfishness are all the tools a knowl-
edgeable king requires. There is no number low enough
to be denominator for mankind."

Gymon nodded at Lothar the Pale's statement. "Indeed,
your Grace, my mind is much like yours."

Unmoved by the carnage taking place about them, the
two men waited for word of Count Clauvis himself. Gradually the courtyard became quiet; the shouts and metallic
clash of battle gave way to the flaming crackle of pillage
and the whimpering of fragmented beings dragging themselves to safety. An anguished wail rose up from the city,
along with the glow of spreading fires.

Then a knot of moving bodies emerged from a tower
and approached the King. Four of Lothar the Pale's warriors, two knights and two cavalrymen, were dragging the
disheveled form of Count Clauvis of Galliardy, still in his
nightshirt. "Your Highness, we have found him. He was
hid down in the deepest levels of the keep."

Count Clauvis was a picture of bewilderment and defeat.
He staggered toward the King and went to his knees, his
arms raised in supplication. "My Liege and Lord, what
brings you to this place? Why bring you arms of massacre

into the land of one whose loyalty's complete? About me I see screaming, dying men who were my housecarls only hours ago, and flames dance in the windows of the rooms where once I slept and supped. Why was it done? Why persecute a loyal vassal, Sire? No crime have I committed to deserve such punishment from you."

One of the cavalrymen placed a boot between Count Clauvis' shoulder blades and shoved; the tall, balding man pitched onto his face, and the carefully trimmed beard collided with the paving stones. "Respect your betters, sirrah," the horse officer said in a sneering voice. "And we all are now your betters, whosoever we may be, for no man is a traitor as you are."

"A traitor?" The captive's eyes stared from his round face; his expression showed the beginnings of real terror. "No, it never has been so. In no way has my loyalty been stained by traitorous thoughts or deeds in all my life."

The bailiff climbed down from his courser and stood over the fallen noble. He still wore his basinet, which made his voice sound tinny and sinister. He had a fearful look as the light from the unborn dawn crept over the parapets and glinted off the helmet. "Is it not true your coffers are o'erfulled with gold and jewels and ill-gotten gains?"

"Oh, no, my Lord. I am a wealthy man, a happy state which I attribute to my lucky birth and fortunate descent from landed nobles and well-dowried maids. My lands are rich, my fields are green and lush, and Crecche, my treasurer, has husbanded my widespread finances and broad accounts. I would be better praised than chastised for thus marshalling my wealth to serve the crown."

The bailiff stooped, removed his helmet, and placed his face only a finger's length from Count Clauvis' face. "Your wealth was never used to serve the crown; that much is known. 'Twas used for luxury, debauchery, and ends more sinister."

"No, no. It is not so. It is not so." Count Clauvis paused. "And if it were, 'twere hardly treasonous."

"From all the taxes passed upon your lands, you never have sent on the rightful share which should be due the

King. To what ends have you held the balance out? What enemies shall benefit from funds scraped up by your embezzlement?"

Count Clauvis' bafflement was real; there could be no doubt he did not know why he was being questioned. "Such things have not been done within my fief; my chamberlain will swear that much to you, for quarterly he adds the tallies up and forwards them to all their several goals."

The King had remained silent throughout the interrogation; now he spoke in a soft voice. "Who is this chamberlain?"

Gymon turned to look up at him. "A man named Crecche, your Grace."

"Then seek him out and question him as well."

"It has been done, your Grace; men search for him who know him by his face. He shall be brought to us to speak his piece, to tell us of his part in these intrigues. And also, I might say, this fellow's daughter shall be brought to us."

Lothar the Pale became silent and the bailiff returned to his questions. "Why sent you that assassin to strike down your Lord and Liege, your one annointed King?"

There was an interruption before Count Clauvis could reply. Guntram, Count of Jolier, returned from the last of the fighting. His sword was still unsheathed and its blade was nicked and stained by the work it had been doing— it fairly dripped as he approached the King. "My Lord, all resistance is overcome. This castle is securely in your hands and its defenders all are prisoners or dead."

Lothar the Pale merely nodded, and the interrogation went on as before.

But the interruption had allowed Count Clauvis to gather his wits and compose himself; he drew himself up and replied with dignity. "Your Highness, I am truly horrified to hear attempts were made upon your life. But still you must believe me when I say that such an act was not inspired by me.

"I see things happening I cannot change. My castle has been captured by your knights and in the distance I still see the glow of fires which burn my city to the ground.

This afternoon gone by, I was a Count, a noble high in honor and in goods; I now have nothing. I am not a fool; I understand that my wealth and lands shall soon be parceled out unto the favorites my King shall choose. And I myself? Perhaps my execution shall take place today or on the morrow; maybe I shall live in poverty, a broken, homeless man, or maybe, as the mean between those two, my days shall pass with me your prisoner. But still I say you judge me falsely and whatever punishment is meted out, it lands upon a man who's innocent. My sins are sins, but treason they are not."

There was another interruption before the bailiff could reply. More knights arrived, some escorted old Crecche, the chamberlain, while others led Bessina, who writhed against their grip. Even as they reached the impromptu hearing, she shook free of her escort and stood glaring, her eyes blazing at those who had captured her father's castle. But when her gaze finally fell on Count Clauvis himself, her expression changed and became something harder to describe. Her face softened and fell, and her glare became a look of woeful recognition and pity. She plainly understood that her father was a prisoner of the King and her home was no longer her home.

"So you have found them," the bailiff said, "and I know them both. This man, this wizened, pinched-up bag of bile, I met some years ago." He gazed into Crecche's face. "We'll deal with you, good sir, in just a wink. But first we all must look upon Bessina, who is known for many leagues about. I know her by the reputation that such beauty brings. Stand tall, young lady; look upon your King, and let all eyes devour your fair form. All gold and earthly goods are easily lost, but beauty such as yours will live in songs and minstrels' tales long after you are gone."

Bessina shrank beneath the bailiff's approving eyes; and for his part, Lothar the Pale looked her over without emotion. She was indeed beautiful. Her dark vermilion hair and the endless green of her eyes were striking, even in the doubtful light. Many a man would deem himself lucky to have her for a bride, even though no dowry could now accompany her hand. For his own part, however, Lothar the Pale was not impressed. He could see through her in an instant; she was like all her sex. There was a coarse and slatternly air about her; she was shallow, simple-minded, and selfish. She was not for him.

It was plain that Gymon had difficulty even taking his eyes from Bessina long enough to turn toward Crecche. But he was finally able to do it, and his face darkened as he glared at the councillor. "Now, sirrah," he said. "Tell us all. Tell how your master came to send a man to kill the King. Are others in the plot?"

The chamberlain looked genuinely confused. He answered like a man who did not even understand the question. "A plot? Oh, Sire, I know not."

Lothar the Pale caught Gymon's attention with an impatient cough. "The taxes," he said when the bailiff glanced up at him.

"Ah, yes." Gymon peered at the chamberlain again. "Indeed, you old, corrupted toad. The swords are drawn which soon shall end your life, should you refuse to tell us how there came so little funds into the coffers of the King when yours is such a wealthy land."

This was a different question, one Crecche plainly did understand. He stammered but his roughly bearded face filled with hate and fear. He glanced at Count Clauvis. "I only did the things that I was told to by my master, Galliardy's own Count."

An expression of stunned betrayal clutched the face of the man Crecche had spoken of, but Bessina leaped at the old chamberlain, her eyes again ablaze. "You ancient, baneful scoundrel, how you lie! For years you've stolen half my father's funds and now, when caught, you try to place the blame on him for your own foul embezzlement. Oh, how I hate you. Go someplace and die."

"You are a wanton wildcat, red-haired girl. Were you the daughter any man deserved, he'd not been driven to illegal means."

"What say you, Crecche? You lie; I am undone." Count Clauvis rose from his knees and stared at his chamberlain.

"For years I trusted you to guard my wealth, but now I see your ways have ruined me."

Bessina turned to him. "My father, I forewarned you many times. Your trust was placed onto a thieving rogue, a villain whose intent was the enrichment of himself. How many times were you required to speak to him for wearing clothing which was far too gaudy for his blood or his estate? It never worried you, although it showed his grasping humor and his covetousness. If he had served another nobleman he'd have been fined a score of times. Now you can see the deepness of his loyalty, his thanks for all the kindness you have shown."

The chamberlain plainly saw the battle going against him. His eyes shifted between his former master and that man's daughter; then he turned to the King and threw himself onto the ground before the monarch's warhorse. "Your Highness, it's my oath that they both lie and all things that I did were at commands which he—my master, Clauvis—issued me. What use have I for gold or earthly wealth? I am a simple man of ledgers, lists, accounts, and records, not a farthing more."

"He lies, he lies," Bessina cried. "No accusations are too base for him. He'd cheat the gods." One of the knights grasped her about the waist and clamped a hand over her mouth; she struggled but could not break free. As for Count Clauvis, he stood silently, his head bowed, his world shattered.

Lothar the Pale watched the byplay without expression. Once Bessina was silenced, he turned to his bailiff. "What use have we for either of these men?"

"But little, Sire. The chamberlain is old and much too crafty to receive a trust. This fallen Count himself is but a man of paper. By my faith, the only one of promise is this red-haired wench herself, who might be pleasing bride material for sale to any wealthy merchant who would like to buy her father's title for a price. And such a sale would help replace the taxes lost."

The Count of Jolier spoke. "To my own mind, the guilt lies with that man, the chamberlain. The Count himself just erred in placing trust in someone who is proven all corrupt."

Crecche's eyes widened with desperation; no one was restraining him at the moment, and he suddenly dashed toward the castle's gatehouse. It was a hopeless move; the King did not bother to watch as several knights leaped after the fugitive. They had no trouble apprehending him; his foot caught between two paving stones, twisted, and he went down with a scream. Two knights grasped him roughly beneath the arms and hauled him to his feet; it was plain that the ankle was broken. His cries and whimpers filled the courtyard.

Lothar the Pale spoke to Gymon quietly. "We'll not transport him wounded to Buerdaunt. Your judgment's sound; do with him what you will."

Crecche's cries died down as he watched the bailiff speak with one of Count Clauvis' housecarls, a man called Diomedes. Crecche appeared puzzled that the fellow was on such familiar terms with the King's adviser.

Diomedes nodded and looked at the chamberlain. Then his eye came to rest on one of the loose paving stones which lay about the courtyard. "Place him there," he said of Crecche, gesturing toward the paving beside the loose stone.

"No, no," Crecche cried, his screams redoubled from what they had been before. "You cannot do this thing to me."

Diomedes walked a little way toward the broken butt of a lance which lay untouched, a remnant of the storming of the castle. He picked it up and walked back toward Crecche, whistling. "Hold him, now," he said. While many hands pinioned the struggling Crecche, Diomedes pulled up the loose paving stone. It was a large, flat stone about the size of a man's boot, and he placed it beneath the Chamberlain's neck. Then he stood and faced the bailiff. "Your Lordship, I will give him an execution which fits well the kind of man he is." But the bailiff was not even listening. Diomedes shrugged and went on with his task.

Crecche's eyes bulged in terror as he looked up at his self-proclaimed executioner. Holding the shattered lance butt in both hands, Diomedes raised it over his head and brought it down the way a woodsman would bring a great hammer onto a splitting wedge. The butt struck the chamberlain's throat with a sickening sound; his body heaved in the grip of the men holding him. Diomedes swung again. Three more times he swung; then the body of what had been Count Clauvis' corrupt adviser lay quietly, except for a quivering of the fingertips.

"It's done, then," Diomedes said. "Take him out and bury him wherever the common dead are put away."

Bessina watched in fascinated horror; then a hand touched her shoulder and she looked up. It was her father; his face was drawn and it looked gray, even in the ruddy glow of the torchlight and the approaching dawn. "Dear maiden," he said. "What shall now become of you?"

Before Bessina could reply, Lothar the Pale gestured toward her father. "I want some men to bind this fellow up. I want him taken with us to Buerdaunt, where we can question him in more detail concerning charges laid against his door."

Men leaped at the King's command. Count Clauvis was seized once more, a length of rope was produced, and he was bound securely. Gymon looked up at his monarch. "Your Majesty, we're now left with the girl. I still advise we take her back with us as well and find for her some suitable position in the kitchens. At some time, we may find that she proves useful in some way."

Lothar the Pale shook his head. "I do not think I can agree with that. She has two witch's eyes; I think it best that they be placed behind some convent's walls. Count Guntram of fair Jolier, have I not heard that somewhere in your realm there stands a chapel dedicated to the rehabilitation of such maids as this?"

"Indeed, your Highness," the Count of Jolier said. "On a grassy hill above the Tanguine River stands a chapel dedicated to the twelve divinities. It's peopled by religious women from all walks of life. Their days are spent in prayers and songs and fasts. It is a convent of quite high repute, and pilgrims journey there each spring to listen to a mystic who resides not far outside the boundaries of the place."

"Then take her there," Lothar the Pale ordered. "I place her in your charge. Instruct the prioress of my intent, that she be kept there, dedicated to the rites prescribed within that holy place, and taught for the salvation of her soul." He then stood in his stirrups and addressed all the knights and other warriors who were within earshot. "Our business here is finished. All the aims which we had hoped to gain have been achieved. We shall remain here for another day to see to redistributing the lands and goods of this low-fallen count."

Count Clauvis began to weep upon hearing the words. Scribed onto his face was the knowledge that his journey into torture and nothingness was about to begin.

But the King ignored him and continued. "These prisoners depart at once unto the separate destinations we have set. Let all who view this long night's hard events be warned of what awaits all men who dare to plot against anointed kings."

A horse was brought for Bessina; her hands were tied and she was lifted up and forced to sit astride it as best she could while the reins were controlled by the knight who led the animal. The Count of Jolier accompanied her, along with a score of other mounted knights, as she was led toward the gatehouse.

But what of her Flin? How was he ever going to find her, even if by some chance he did return from the imprisonment he had been sent to? And what of her father? What lay waiting for him in the donjons beneath Lothar the Pale's castle? As she was led away, she gazed over her shoulder; her last look at her father came as he was clapped into irons and roughly rolled into a litter which had been brought. He was going to be transported to Buerdaunt lying helplessly in a litter.

Would she ever see him again? It seemed unlikely. She felt tiny and orphaned; then their eyes met for only an instant before he was hauled from view. In his face was a painful mixture of fear, regret, and terrible loss.

Chapter Seven:
The Lash

CAREFUL PLANS HAD been laid, transportation had been secured, and Palamon and Aelia had become a noble couple journeying to Kolpos to see their daughter married. Their daughter in this case was a handmaiden named Chroma, who would accompany them as far as the Kolpian port of Touros. Then she would remain with relatives while Palamon and Aelia sought Berengeria at Alyubol's secret stronghold.

They had been given only a fortnight to find Berengeria—and then Carea's fleet would sail. Therefore, they had made their arrangements quickly; they had gathered up Chroma, traveled to Lower Carea, and purchased passage on the first Kolpos-bound ship they had found, an old cog which was moored at the great mole in the harbor, off-loading lumber and furs. They boarded her in the afternoon and saw to the stowage of their luggage, which included Palamon's wondrous armor, his mighty sword called the *Spada Korrigaine*, and two chests full of treasure for the purchase of information and favors.

Then Palamon turned in early; he had hardly slept since

Berengeria had disappeared—and even when he had, it had been a light doze; he had awakened at the slightest disturbance. So it was that, after he and the two women boarded the roundship in the afternoon, he hoped to nap at least a little while before the ship sailed in the morning. Once they were under way, sleep would be more impossible than ever. Palamon did not sleep well at sea.

He, Aelia, and Chroma each occupied one of the roundship's three passenger compartments. Cabins would have been too expansive a word; the tiny chambers were more closets than anything, with barely enough room for a cot, a hammock, and some parcels of luggage. But that was good, in a way. Palamon and Aelia were playing the role of Chroma's parents on their way to a wedding in Kolpos; the cramped quarters provided an excuse for them to sleep in separate compartments. Thus, Palamon was not yet faced by the dilemma of proper conduct at too-close quarters with Aelia. He knew a secret which he had not dared reveal to her for many weeks; when he had gazed on the goddess, Pallas, the deity had promised Aelia to him as a bride.

That vision was still as fresh in his mind as the scent of apple blossoms. And it had left him in a soul-tangling dilemma. It was not that he did not know Aelia well enough; after all, they had been constant companions all summer while fleeing the clutches of Lothar the Pale. The problem was that he still had no idea how to act toward her, given that he would someday have to ask for her hand. She was not Berengeria; she was withdrawn, dignified, and aloof, and he could never escape the feeling that she was looking more deeply into him than he would like.

She was the bride selected for him by the Divine Maiden; she was the woman of his vision. But he was a knight whose childhood and youth had been spent in the celibate surroundings of the Fastness of Pallas; no number of visions could make him love her or help him court her. He could only wait. Perhaps the time would come when he would be able to speak to her of more than missions and responsibilities.

But when would he come to love Aelia? Or was that

even important? If she was the bride fate had chosen for him, did love matter? It might not matter to the gods; still, he did not see how he could wed Aelia without feeling it.

With such thoughts swirling through his brain, Palamon did at last doze off far, far into the night. But it seemed as if he had not slept a moment when he awoke to the sound of voices approaching the ship along the mole. His eyes fluttered open, and he stared into the darkness as he listened; the sounds were soft and faraway, though they were coming closer. Were he not so easily awakened, he never would have noticed them. He heard several pairs of footsteps mounting the brow that led up to the vessel's deck; there was much milling and talking, and it sounded as if the number of voices was becoming ever greater.

What was happening up there? Was it a danger, something he should investigate? After a moment Palamon decided to do that very thing; he rose and donned clothing in the darkness. He did not take the time to put on his armor but he did strap on a sword, a simple longsword, not his two-handed blade. He did not dare carry that until the ship had sailed; the whole population of Upper and Lower Carea had heard of the *Spada Korrigaine*. Dressed and his feet hastily inserted into sandals, he stepped from his tiny cabin and onto the deck.

The sun had not yet risen, but the sky was a pale blue in the east. A whispering breeze put lines onto the waters of the bay and the main deck of the vessel was alive with sailors; it looked as if every man of the vessel's crew was present, along with men from other ships. But they were not getting under way. The sailors milled about the deck like sheep, some watching, some acting as if they were trying to keep their eyes averted from what was going on at the base of the mast.

A wooden grating had been lashed to the mast itself, and a man was being bound to it hand and foot, his back stripped bare. It was a young seaman Palamon had noticed the day before, a tall, attractive, dark-haired fellow. The ship's officers all stood in a row to watch, led by Hrusk, the master. Palamon did not like Hrusk. He was tall, lean, and light-complected. From a loop at his waist, below the middle of his back, dangled a great ring of keys. Palamon knew Hrusk to possess a sort of charm, but he also had the impression that the thin, blond shipmaster would have sold his whole crew into slavery, if it could have advanced him a cubit.

As the officers faced the mast, a swarthy fellow appeared from the forecastle with a sack. Another crewman piped a shrill note on a whistle, and Palamon watched, fascinated, as the sailors shifted their eyes to Hrusk. The master made a short speech. "You all know the new man who was taken on board while we lay in the Tanguine, off Verdast. I took him into the crew because I was told he was under death sentence for horrible crimes..."

The prisoner strained against his bonds. "Love's no crime, you biscuit eater."

There was a ripple of laughter among some of the crewmen. Slight smiles played across the faces of others, but such amusement was snuffed out by Hrusk's glare. His face became red; his back stiffened as if he had been struck a blow. "Go ahead, fellow. Mock me, show your ingratitude for the way we took you in, offered you shelter and food." He turned to one of the officers. "Gag him."

The gag was applied in spite of the dark youth's struggle and the way he swung his head back and forth. While that was done, Hrusk went on. "He's deserted us twice, once off Gevson and again last night. The second time he even corrupted another man, a good hand. I won't tolerate this sort of thing." He emphasized the last sentence with a stamp of one foot, his face growing red once more. "Show him the lash."

The rangy seaman unlaced the top of his sack and hauled out a short-handled whip. Several rawhide strips the length of a small man's arm dangled from it, each one tipped with an iron barb. Murmurs of recognition rose from several throats as the whipper shook the instrument before the eyes of its victim, allowing the iron barbs to drag across the youthful face.

The shipmaster went on. "This hellion, this useless bundle of disrespect, could have avoided the death sentence if he'd been a good sailor. Instead he was disloyal at every turn, he wheedled a shipmate into deserting with him, and he placed this vessel in jeopardy. There's only one punishment for him. He'll be lashed until he hangs from the straps, until his blood soaks the deck—until he's dead. When we cast his body into the sea, it will be a lesson to everyone like him."

The shipmaster approached the young man, placed a hand on his shoulder, and spoke to him in a voice loud enough for all the men on deck to hear. "This is a painful death and only the worst breach of duty would deserve it. But to show that I don't want to be unfair, I'll have the gag removed and you'll be allowed to scream."

At his order the gag was removed, but the young man responded with more defiance. "I'll not cry out for you."

"We'll see." Hrusk moved away and watched while the first officer signaled the whipper. With an experienced air, the man swung the nine lashes slowly behind him, then struck, grunting with the effort. The metal tips of the lashes made a surprisingly innocent slapping sound as they struck. There was a hissing inrush of breath through clenched teeth as the young man reacted, bowing his back with the pain. The lashes had made nine read weals, perfectly spaced tracks which began to rise on the tanned skin.

The second blow fell; again the victim received it in silence, though his fingers clenched the grating to which he was bound and blood trickled where the weals crossed on his back. There was a third blow and he did cry out. He made the cry of an animal in pain, or of a man who was being reduced to the state of an animal. With each succeeding blow, his back became redder with his own blood and his cries became more intense than before.

The whole affair was uncivilized; Palamon crossed the deck and touched the shipmaster on the shoulder. "I want this stopped. It's neither time nor place for torturing a man to death."

Hrusk smiled back at him. "It's simple discipline."

"Though it may be, it's still not to my taste. You know my office, sir, that I might buy or sell this vessel at a whim or have it seized. The sun is rising; when the tide begins to turn, I want us under way in greatest haste." Palamon raised his voice enough to allow the other ship's officers to hear him.

Hrusk's mouth curled angrily and he gave an order for the lashing to stop. About a dozen blows had fallen but already the man wielding the lash dripped sweat. He paused to watch the exchange, wiped his brow, and ran the lashes between his fingers to clean the blood from them. The shipmaster turned back to Palamon, his anger showing in his features. "The discipline of any man is my charge, sir. You overstep your bounds when you don't allow me to take steps that are proper and necessary."

Palamon smiled a mirthless smile. "Ah, yes. All necessary acts should be performed. But come and let me speak to your young miscreant." He walked toward the young man and looked into his eyes, which were half-glazed from the ordeal. The skin of the fellow's back had been turned into a bloody, hashlike mass by the iron-tipped lashes. He was soaked with blood and sweat, and his eyes hardly seemed to comprehend as they met Palamon's.

Palamon frowned and his heart went out to the lad; whatever crime he had committed, how could a man not pity anyone who had to suffer so? He glanced at the shipmaster with a frown. "It was a clever punishment; it seems to me that we should show such cleverness in treating men as humans. There might be a deal less hardship in the world. Perhaps the ground might suffer from the lack of blood to fertilize it; still I think it worth consideration, by my faith."

Hrusk said nothing. He only glared at the tall Prince, who had turned back to the victim. "Now what's your name?" Palamon asked. "If you are able, speak."

The young man's mouth worked, then he managed to produce a word. "Flin."

"Now tell me, Flin, explain to me the crime which led to your impressment in this ship."

"There was no crime."

Palamon shook his head. "No man receives a punishment without first claiming to all ears there was no crime. Speak truthfully and tell me what you did, for I can help you if you do not lie."

There was another pause as Flin gathered himself. Finally, he managed to utter a complete sentence. "I loved a nobleman's daughter in Galliardy."

Palamon's eyebrows raised. "Were you impressed because you loved a maid?"

"She was the Count's daughter. Rather than have her love a commoner like me, he had me captured by his housecarls and taken to Lacourd, where I was put into a gang and taken to sea."

"And your imprisonment was meted out for love?" Palamon lifted his head and gazed at the shipmaster, half laughing. "Was that his crime—to love a noble maid?"

Hrusk looked uncomfortable. "What he did isn't important. You know how sailors get put on ships. But he deserted twice since then and we had to send parties ashore to haul him back this last time."

Palamon disliked the shipmaster but he forced himself to don a pleasant expression. "Unbind him. It's my order that you do."

Hrusk hesitated. It was plain that Flin's release was the last order he wanted to obey. "My Lord, you're a noble in your own land, doubtless with power over life and death, but on this vessel I'm the master."

Of course he did not know that Palamon was the Prince of Carea; he could not know. Unfortunately, such was the nature of Palamon's mission that the tall Prince also did not dare reveal the secret—still, there was another way to appeal to a man like Hrusk. "Tush, fellow, it's with ease such problems are erased. I've funds enough to cover hurts you may receive by setting this man free. He interests me and I desire he live." He turned and spoke to Flin once more. "Young man, I've means to purchase your release, but ere I do, you'll make an oath to me that you shall never flee this vessel's deck again until we all have come to reach our destination, namely Touros on the Isle of Kolpos. By what gods do you swear?"

The first comprehension flickered in Flin's eyes that

his ordeal was over. "My Lord, I'll swear to whatever god you choose. They're all the same to me."

Palamon laughed at the young man, with part of the laughter turned inward. After all, every man could not be expected to live with one eye on the heavens the way the tall Prince did. "It's easy, then, to see how you've arrived in straits as desperate as these. Ah, well, I'll hear you swear your oath upon the name of her you say you love, for if you break your word, she'll be the one who grieves for her dead lover, lad. But swear and cheat the lash."

"My Lord, the gods sent you to save me."

Palamon laughed again. "Perhaps; at least it is a pleasing thought." Having made that jest, he became serious once more. "Now swear that you shall serve this vessel well, at least once you've recovered from your wounds. Swear that you ne'er shall flee again, that you'll obey your betters with respect, and in all manner ways you shall become a proper seaman till I set you free."

Flin nodded weakly. He seemed quite excited, but the blood which had streamed from his back had weakened him and made him pale by its departure. "I swear."

Palamon turned to the shipmaster. "And in my turn, I shall defray whatever costs arise from treating all this fellow's hurts, as well as any damages he might cause in the future, if he breaks the oath we heard him make."

Hrusk gestured impatiently to a pair of his officers. "Set him free."

"Have you a surgeon?" Palamon asked.

"No."

"Then take him down and place him on my cot. My wife can then administer to him." It brought a strange feeling to refer to Aelia as his wife, even though it was the ruse they had agreed upon.

And so it was done. Two seamen cut Flin from the grating and took him to Palamon's tiny cabin, where he was laid out on Palamon's cot—a hammock was too rough for a man with his back cut to ribbons. Then the sailors left and Aelia treated the young man's torn flesh as ably as she could.

She had brought along many parcels and they contained all manner of items; among them was balm and a large quantity of linen for making bandages. By the time she had finished, Flin had fallen asleep with fatigue and the injuries of the flogging; he lay on the thin cot, snoring, as motionless as a stump.

When Aelia had finished she wiped her hands and rose to face Palamon. "And now, good Prince, will you explain to me this kindness to a man you do not know."

Palamon smiled grimly. "I have my reasons."

"By my chosen faith," Chroma said. "It made my heart go out in sympathy to see them whipping him with such cruel verve. That whip brought shudders to the spine. Sharp bits of iron were used in place of knots as lashes and to cause the blood to flow. The master of this vessel is a fiend."

Aelia nodded. "Indeed, I cannot say he is a saint. But still, O Palamon, you cannot save the life of every seaman we might find."

Palamon smiled back at her and nodded, but his mind was elsewhere; he was considering the features of the tall, dark youth, as well as the crime for which he had been cast into servitude. These things flooded his mind with a host of other images. It was unjust for any man to suffer as the lad had suffered, simply because of the gossip that he had loved the wrong maiden. "I cannot argue, Aelia, for I know your wisdom makes your eye more clear than mine. For all of that, I could not let him die."

A shadow of a smile curled Aelia's lip and she looked up at Palamon once more. Her expression pleased him as she spoke. "If there are saints of flesh, I know of one. But we must not pursue philanthropy unto the point we place ourselves at risk."

The vessel's motion informed them that lines had been cast off and they were floating freely on the waters of the bay. Still, they did not go up on deck to watch their progress out into the Narrow Strait; they had been abroad before. "What's your intent when we reach land?" Aelia asked. "If you can purchase freedom for this lad, then do you mean to have him go with us in seeking out the lair of Alyubol?"

"I do not know," Palamon said. "We know him not at all."

"Indeed. We cannot judge his loyalty, or whether he has belly for our quest."

"His loyalty remains unknown," Palamon replied. "But as to belly, we all watched him take the lash courageously and speak his mind when punishment was done. To me it seems he has a stalwart spine, although the covering's been mussed a bit."

Aelia spoke again. "But even so, our plan would best be this—he should remain with Chroma, with her mother's family, until we have the information we seek. If we can find a way to reach the salt-encrusted keep of Alyubol, and if this fellow shows a willingness to carry arms, then we could ask him to accompany us. If any doubt remains before the time that we prepare to bring this matter to strong blows, then we should leave him there."

"Remember," Palamon said. "He is searching for the maiden that he left behind. His wish may be to make his way to her without consideration for our quest."

"In that case, he's a waste of time," Aelia said.

The conversation ended in that vein and the three Careans went onto the deck so Flin could sleep. When Palamon returned a little later, Flin had awakened and he had climbed into a hammock, where he was still lying on his side. He looked up as Palamon entered. "Who are you?" he asked. "Why do you save the life of a man you don't know?"

"I am a nobleman who journeys to the Isle of Kolpos in the Thlassa Mey, to see my daughter wed in Touros. Who are you? What is your story, lad?"

Flin laughed softly and laid his head on one arm. "By the gods, there was a moment when I really did think my goose was cooked. But you came and saved me. You know, the gods must truly exist; they sent you to scuttle old Hrusk."

"Oh, yes," Palamon said. "The gods exist, you may be sure of that. But speak now of yourself, my lad; you seem in cheerful spirits for the hurts which lately have been laid upon your back."

"I'm a cheerful man. Do you have any wine?"

Palamon reached into a cupboard, produced a wine skin, and handed it to the young man who raised it stiffly. When he had finished tipping the skin to his lips, Flin pointed beneath the cot, toward the long leather wrapping which housed the *Spada Korrigaine*. "That looks like a sword," he said.

Palamon blinked. "Indeed? It's just a burnished leather case."

"You're a smooth one, aren't you?" Flin replied. "But a package like that holds either a very large sword or a walking staff—and you don't look to me like a man who needs help getting about." He put down the wineskin. "Look at yourself. You've got a heavy tan, a lot of crow's-feet around your eyes, so you've lived outside most of your life. You're also lean and well-muscled and you've got some nasty scars on your arm there." Flin gestured toward Palamon's left forearm with a grin. "So you're a warrior and that's a sword. Can I see it?"

Palamon sighed, then shrugged and pulled the package into the open. When he untied the leather and unwrapped it, the great *Spada Korrigaine* lay gleaming in the dim light and Flin's eyes grew large. The young man reached for the jewel-encrusted handle, but Palamon caught his wrist. There was powerful magic in the sword, and even Palamon did not know all its secrets. But he did know the blade had intelligence that was nearly human; he had seen it burn men's hands when they had tried to grasp it against its will. He did not know how it would respond to Flin's touch and he had no desire to find out.

Flin looked offended. "Can't I pick it up?"

"You do not want to pick it up."

Flin looked at the mighty weapon longingly. "That's funny. I thought I did."

Palamon rewrapped the sword and slid it back under the cot. "But we digress," he said. "Inform me of your past, of who you are and from what land you come."

Flin hesitated, a little gleam in his eyes as he looked at the leather case once more; then he began to tell his story to Palamon—how he had ridden for a half dozen years with the Red Company across the lands north of the Tanguine River, how he had come to meet Bessina at a bazaar while relaxing in Galliardy, how they had fallen in love, how the soldiers had captured him, and how he had discovered only then that his love had been the daughter of the lord of the province, Count Clauvis, himself. Then he asked Palamon a question. "But tell the truth. Why do you want to know?"

"I have my reasons. In a little time, perhaps, you may be told a fact or two you might find interesting. Until that time, or for this day, at least, I shall allow you to recover here within this chamber. Then, when you can work, you must return to your appointed place, at least until our destination's reached."

"What's your real destination?"

Palamon looked at him. How much had Flin guessed, or had he guessed anything more than the fact Palamon was a warrior? "Touros, as I have already said."

Flin studied Palamon, smiled, then stretched like an overgrown cat. "Then I have the rest of the day to lie and dream before I go back to my sailor work. The masters of this ship never had a reason to complain about my work, I can tell you that. I'd have been the best hand ever, if they'd agreed to let me go at the end of the voyage." He looked at Palamon eagerly. "Will you do that? Even if I have to stay aboard when you reach Touros, I can stand it, if I know I'll be free when we reach Lacourd. I have to return to Bessina, you see."

"And if your freedom means so much to you, what might you do to gain it?"

"Anything." Flin's face showed absolute sincerity.

"Ah, anything. Would you agree to die?"

"Of course not." The way Flin wrinkled his brow told Palamon that he knew the question was a joke. "But I'll do anything within reason."

"She's worth that much to you?"

"With ease. I'll conquer her father's army and take her for my own—there's risking my life for you—and then we'll live together in happiness the gods will envy."

Palamon could not keep from breaking into a smile—

not his usual wry smile, but a smile of real enjoyment; Flin had great charm and the Prince could not help liking him. Lying in Palamon's hammock with his arms folded behind his head and his torso swathed in bandages, he was a refreshing oasis of candor in a world of lies and appearances. Palamon placed a hand upon his shoulder. "Then rest assured. Your freedom shall you have, and may it do you all the good for which you hope. We all seek maidens in this world; you have your reasons and I have my own. I'd be a cruel man to keep you from your quest while I pursue my own odd destiny."

Flin grasped Palamon by the wrist. "Thank you. Thank you. I'll never forget it."

Palamon left the younger man to his rest and journeyed back onto the deck to stand with Aelia and the maiden Chroma. The two women were leaning against the rail, watching the steep Carean cliffs march past the vessel, pointing the way out to the Narrow Strait and the Thlassa Mey. At that stage of their voyage, there was little to do but watch the vessel's progress, so he joined them.

They all stood watching the shoreline. Palamon glanced at Aelia more than once, for she was beautiful in her own way. He furtively observed her slender shape, her straight, aquiline nose, and her arched eyebrows. She was much of an age with him, but there was not a trace of gray in her dark hair, even though his was sprinkled liberally with that color. What did that mean, he wondered? Was it simply a sign of the way her body worked or did it mean she was tougher than he was? He would not have argued that matter, if someone had asserted it; she had been through many hard times over the years, she and her Princess.

His eyes strayed to her lips, her bosom, the rest of her slender figure. She was a priestess of Hestia; had she ever kissed a man? Her lips had been faded and chapped by worry and weather; they were not as red and full as Chroma's lips, for instance—or Berengeria's. It seemed impossible that Aelia's lips could ever meet his for any reason. Palamon could not help laughing at himself. What a trick of fate it was. He was a former Knight of Pallas, and she was still a priestess of Hestia; both orders demanded the chastity of their members foremost among all vows. Yet the holy Maiden, Pallas, had told him Aelia was the woman he would marry. All his years of celibacy were to end in the nuptial bed of the woman he was now watching, this chaste Hestian priestess. The gods certainly possessed a well developed and ironic sense of humor.

But he was ashamed of himself. He was mooning over Aelia, eyeing her body, thinking thoughts of love—both physical and spiritual love—without ever having decided how he would earn that love or how he would return it. His years as a Knight of Pallas had not prepared him for the courtship of a spirited and aloof woman; it was all very distressing. Pallas had to be laughing to herself, the bell-like tones of her mirth ringing out over paradise the way they had rung out during his vision.

When evening came, Palamon returned to his cabin. He was suspicious he might find young Flin slyly examining the *Spada Korrigaine*—curiosity was a universal plague, after all—but he was pleased to find the young man still lying in his hammock. The lad's youthful vigor was overcoming the effects of the flogging; he showed less stiffness than Palamon would have expected as he rose and left the cabin.

And Flin did become a splendid, willing seaman, at least as far as Palamon was able to observe. He shrugged off the pain which must have spread from his scars, performed each task willingly and with considerable strength and stamina. Surely the shipmaster could no longer find fault with him, at least until the ship reached land.

For several weary days the vessel reached endlessly along the coast of the Montaigne Peninsula, Carea's southernmost province. At last they turned east to pick up a favorable breeze toward the island of Kolpos and its only large city, the fishing and trading seaport called Touros. There the quest to find Berengeria would begin in earnest.

But as the sun started toward the horizon behind them and they looked to the east for the low, blue mound that was Kolpos, Palamon saw something unpleasant approaching from their starboard quarter. The sea behind them was a rolling lake of sparkles and over the top of it a black sail rose in the distance, steadily overtaking them. The new vessel was hull-down for a long time, but the narrow bow grew visible as it drew closer. On and on it came, until Palamon could see the froth where the cutwater slashed the waves and the many oars which rose and fell, rose and fell, like the legs of some demon centipede. There were many men lining the vessel's bows, exhorting their comrades at the oars, and they all carried weapons; already some of them were nocking arrows to their bows.

Aelia joined Palamon on the deck; her face was grave and she reached toward him, the slender fingers of one hand grasping his wrist. "Pirates," she said. And she was surely right; there was no other possibility. Their vessel was being overtaken by pirates. Already the ship's officers were screaming orders and sailors scampered about.

"Pirates." What an awful world of frustration and catastrophe lurked in that single word.

Chapter Eight:
Raiders

THE CORSAIR WAS constant in its pursuit of the round-ship. The men aboard her howled and shouted, for they would board their quarry within the hour. Throughout the pursued vessel, work stopped as sailors and passengers alike stared back at the dark-hulled craft. Palamon looked about. Hrusk and his officers were standing as though frozen. No orders had been given, no preparations were being made. He approached the shipmaster. "We must move quickly; weapons must be raised and preparations made to fend attack."

"'Twill make no difference," Hrusk replied, his face an ashen color. "We only have a score of men; they have dozens. We can't defeat them, and it will be death for all of us if we try."

Aelia was close enough to enter the conversation. "The King's own gold lies in this vessel's hold, the King's own servants stand before you here."

Palamon spoke again. "Indeed, and you should know the fates of those poor women who fall into corsairs' hands. Foul treatment, rape, and ransom are the best they might expect from this pursuing crew. I go to fetch my weapon. If I must fight you as well as them, so be it, sirrah."

He strode to his tiny cabin to don his armor and fetch his great, two-handed sword; as he did so, Aelia transfixed the shipmaster with a withering glare. "Perhaps you have no stomach for a fray, but not all men are cowardly as you." She turned toward the crewmen. "If you are men, you must take up your arms; you must withstand this grim assault which looms above us. This ship bears the King's own goods, which must not be surrendered. My tall knight has gone to fetch his weapons and shall stand beside you through the fray which now approaches."

Seamen looked at one another in dismay. "To stand up to them is death," one said. "If we don't fight them, they'll only take the cargo; no one will be killed."

But Flin leaped from the rigging to argue with his shipmates. "Coward's talk," he cried. "This woman is a better man than any of you when she looks forward to a fray and you all try to hide between decks while your ship falls without a battle." He faced Hrusk, whose thin face became livid beneath the younger man's stare. "I call you a swine to your face to preach surrender while your passengers have to fight. I stand with them."

"It's an easy thing for you to say," the shipmaster replied. "The knight saved you from the lash."

"I'd say it anyway." He turned to Aelia. "Lady, find me a weapon and I'll fight to the death. I'm Flin, after all. Find me a sword and no boatload of fish-chewers and ale-pissers can make me yield. I'm a fighting man, a leader of companies and a waster of castles and I won't hide like these sheep. Together we'll make a meal those raiders will find too hot by far."

"Well spoken, lad," Palamon said as he returned to the deck, bearing his own sword and wearing a suit of lustrous, greenish-gold chain mail. The hauberk had been hastily donned and Palamon had not brought his helmet in his hurry. His rich crop of brown, gray-streaked hair was open to the sun as he turned back to the shipmaster.

"Now you must surely see we mean to fight, whatever be your choice."

Then he spoke to the crewmen. "Who stands with us?" A few men half-heartedly raised their hands; none of the ship's officers stood among them. "The number does not matter," Palamon said quietly. Then he spoke to Hrusk once more. "Bring up some swords, so that we may oppose those brigands, while I give my extra blade to Flin, who has the courage to support our stand." Palamon would use the *Spada Korrigaine*; he pulled out his extra longsword and handed it to Flin, who was delighted.

"It's an easy thing for you to say, my Lord," Hrusk retorted, "since you're practiced in the arts of war and assured a ransomed life if you're taken. What about us? If we're taken after a fight, we'll die as surely as the rain falls." He had raised his high-pitched voice so the entire crew could hear him.

"Then do whate'er you wish," Palamon said. "Do not oppose them, yield your vessel's goods. But bring the weapons pleaded for by those of us who want to fight against all odds—then you can stand and watch and wager on who'll fall and who will not. We'll make a thrilling entertainment for your pleasure."

Hrusk's mouth twisted as if he wanted to say something more, but he turned and spoke to an officer. The man vanished into the sterncastle to bring forth a half dozen rusty longswords. He threw them on the deck and went back for more.

While the few crewmen who were willing to fight chose from among them, Flin admired the sword Palamon had loaned him. The way he slashed the air with it demonstrated that he had used such weapons before. "It's a fine blade," he said. "I swear I'll make a few of them hop with it."

Palamon's reply was grim and subdued. "Our numbers are so few we have small chance. Fight closely at my side; our only hope is that together we might form a stone upon which their assault will break apart."

Flin wore a smile of real anticipation as he looked up at the tall knight. "You're a great warrior—I can tell that—

and I'm Flin. It's that boatload of fish-biters who should be afraid."

The officer dumped another armload of swords onto the deck. The weapons were poor in quality and pitifully few in number; for all that, there were more than enough to fill the hands of the few seamen who chose to take them up. Aelia bent over the blades which lay unused and picked one. "A clumsy thing it is," she said. "My dagger's handle fits my grasp more comfortably, withal. But still, 'twill cleave a jerkin, one or two."

Palamon shook his head. "Nay, nay. You must not join us here on deck."

"I'll hold my own."

"I grant that much. But still, if you or Chroma perish in the fray, I never will forgive myself your deaths. I could not bear to lift my weapon more for watching your pure blood bewash these planks. Please go beneath the decks, the two of you—for my sake, even if it's not your wish."

"I'll take them," Flin said. He grasped the two protesting women by the arms and escorted them to the stern-castle. That done, he returned to Palamon's side, to join the tall prince and the four other sailors who would fight the corsairs. Even then, the corsairs' gleaming vessel surged alongside the roundship. The din from the opposing deck was terrible; drums pounded, trumpets and hautboys screeched rough notes, and men shouted and screamed as grapnels hurtled toward the target. The hooks clutched the roundships' railings bow and stern. Oars were shipped in the corsair vessel and sweating, shouting men hauled upon the lines that drew the two ships together the way a trapdoor spider draws its prey into a hole.

A stout, barechested man at the rail of the attacking vessel cupped his hands about his mouth as he shouted. "Surrender your ship. You have no chance against us."

Hrusk attempted to shout a reply but his voice was drowned out by Flin. "Do your worst, you piece of bilge waste. You'll be sorry you ever laid eyes on this ship."

There was an instant's shocked silence aboard the attacking vessel. Palamon could not help smiling as he watched the surprised expressions Flin's reply had brought to the rough, bearded faces. But the reaction passed in a heartbeat. There was a cry of rage, a shower of hand axes hurtled across the space separating the two vessels, and one defender fell with a scream.

Then the battle began. Attackers worked their way out along the corsair's spar and dropped among the defenders. Shouts rose from both decks as the two vessels drew together. The direct assault from the roundship's own deck made Palamon's strategy of keeping his pitiful number of defenders in a tight group a hopeless dream. He turned to face one pirate and struck a lightning blow with his *Spada Korrigaine*. The weapon cleaved the top of the man's torso from the rest of his body while the arms waved spastically. But as the tall knight turned to face the next foe, he saw the bulk of the roundship's company retreating into the safety of the forecastle.

Flin joined the melee with fierce joy, wielding his bright longsword with all the ferver of a knight using a well-made weapon. Whatever the outcome would be, and he seemed to know in his heart that the gods would have to reward his struggles with victory, Flin showed that the fighting was a welcome change from the drudgery of ship-board life. A pair of men from the corsair leaped toward him, waving wickedly curved blades. He slew one in a duel which raged across the deck, then forced the other back to the rail, disarmed him, and finally forced him over the side. The fellow landed in the water between the two ships with a scream and a splash.

But the odds were overwhelming. Where Flin had faced two opponents, three replaced them, and more were streaming onto the roundship's decks. Another of the sailors defending the vessel fell. The corsairs had not won the battle yet. Flin was holding his own with his adversaries and a heap of bodies marked the place where Palamon stood against the onslaught, his mighty weapon drinking deeply of brigand blood. But another defender staggered away from the fray, blinded by blood which streamed into his eyes from a vicious slash across the forehead. He screamed, clutched his face, and danced in a ghastly circle; Flin could hear him but did not dare look. Fighting required all his attention.

Then he felt a blow from behind. In his wilderness of pain and fear, the stricken man had run headlong into Flin's back; the young warrior threw up his hands as he lost his balance and hung perilously over the ship's rail. He was helpless. He watched as one opponent aimed a thrust at his exposed belly.

There was nothing to be done about it. He yielded himself to gravity, rolled across the rail and into the emptiness of air. Even as he fell, he heard the *chunk*! as the curved blade bit into the rail he had so recently vacated. He fell for what seemed to be an eternity; then the wind was crushed from him as he struck the vicelike space where the hulls of the two ships rubbed together. For an instant, he felt himself being squashed as if he were being masticated by giant jaws. Then a swell of the sea parted the two vessels for an instant, and he dropped into the salty water, groaning.

He had dropped Palamon's longsword, but he was not dead; that was important. He bobbed to the surface, coughed the water from his lungs, and saw that he was safe for the moment. The fighting still raged above him; he could hear the clash of arms and the cursing of the pirates. When he looked up, he could see that some of them still remained aboard their own ship; an extended arm and a pointed finger told him that much. He saw another man climb up and straddle the corsair vessel's rail, then drop back onto the deck. Evidently some of the attackers were reluctant to throw themselves into the fray; perhaps, if the defenders could hold out long enough, the raiders would withdraw and seek easier game.

Swimming carefully, Flin rounded the stern of his own vessel so he could climb back up the side and rejoin the fight. As he reached the ship's open side, he viewed a line trailing from the mast into the water. That would make it easy to climb up, so he stroked boldly toward the dangling line, grasped it, and hauled himself toward the deck.

As his eyes cleared the scuppers and he could view the bloody expanse of the vessel's main deck, he saw that the situation had grown serious, but was still not hopeless. Palamon and two other men had been forced back toward the forecastle; they were all that was left of the defenders. The corsairs had become wary attackers; they feinted in and out but were careful not to get within reach of Palamon's deadly sword. They pressed the two men who flanked the tall knight, but only at intervals; if Flin could put his hands on another sword and counterattack, victory could be won.

But even as he tensed to clamber onto the deck, Flin watched foul treachery. Hrusk must have been pondering the fate of officers who refused to defend their own vessels; he must have decided Palamon could not reach port with the roundship. Before Flin could gain the deck, the crafty shipmaster appeared from the forecastle companionway and rose up behind Palamon like a specter, clutching a stout piece of hardwood. Flin heard the grunt as Hrusk struck Palamon a terrible blow on the back of his exposed head. The tall knight crumpled and the attackers leaped on the two other sailors, slaughtering them like a couple of pigs. The battle was suddenly over; the decks became quiet. Without a sound or motion which would reveal his presence, Flin allowed himself to slip back into the water.

He looked about. Afternoon was growing into evening, the sun was setting, and darkness would soon spread her veil across the placid waters of the Thlassa Mey. Above him, Flin could hear the sounds of pillage as the victorious corsairs ransacked the ship. Did the knight Palamon still live? It did not matter; the two ladies were alive. Flin had to take their part; certainly none of the corsairs or the shipmaster would. And even if he could remain out of sight until the galley sailed away, he knew Hrusk would order his death as soon as he climbed back onto the ship. There was too much between them for him to harbor hopes on that matter.

So there was no way for Flin but to continue the battle, alone if need be. And if the tall knight still lived, that would be all for the better, but he would have to wait for the time being. The skies grew dark, the salt water softened Flin's skin and aggravated the scars on his back. He heard voices from above and hoped for his own sake and the sake of the two female passengers that one belonged to Palamon.

Chapter Nine:
The Douzainium

ONE OF THE largest of the stone structures of the Douzainium lifted its gray-tiled roof near the refuge's wall, beneath several towering beech trees. It was the Dormitory of the Three Virgins; it housed those maidens who had been brought to the refuge within the last year. The declining moon sent soft, oblong patches of luminescence through the tall windows and into the building's single large chamber; the paleness lay across the cots lined along the walls, splashing over the sleeping feminine shapes and onto the tiled floor.

But even though it was past midnight, one of the occupants of the room did not sleep. Bessina's cot stood beside the handcarved shrine at the rear of the chamber, at the end of an entire row of cots. It was a position which marked her place as the most recent addition to the order. She had been in the refuge, the Douzainium, for two days; already she wore the white linen robes of a new postulant and the Abbess had received a large grant from the King of Buerdaunt, along with clear instructions concerning her education and indoctrination.

But Bessina was not about to stay. She knew her father lay in Lothar the Pale's donjon and she knew Flin, her brigand lover, was by now serving on one of the many ships which plied the Thlassa Mey. Besides, she knew her presence in the place suited the King's purpose and perhaps that of his loathsome bailiff, which alone was reason enough for her to seek escape.

So she would not stay. She would leave the Douzainium as soon as she found the opportunity; she now sat in her cot, sensing the approach of that opportunity. The acolyte who slept with the new members had passed into the land of dreams, albeit fitfully. She lay in a cot in the middle of the hall, stirring occasionally.

Just as each stone, building or tree within the Douzainium was a religious symbol, so the position of each cot bore its own meaning; Bessina's cot stood on the left side of the hall, closest to the shrine on that side. That marked her as the most recent arrival at the refuge. The maiden who slept in the cot next to hers had arrived a few days earlier and so on and on around the chamber until the last cot, the maiden who slept nearest the shrine on the right side of the room. She had been a postulant over a year and would soon take holy orders.

All the young women were sound asleep except Bessina. The air sometimes stirred with a sigh or a soft snore, but the only steady sound was the breeze which vibrated the hall's six great, arched windows. Bessina sat up and looked about like a bird guarding nestlings. When she had watched and listened long enough to feel safe, she rose and tiptoed the length of the chamber, toward the great oak doors at the far end.

She had nothing. Everything she had ever owned had been left at Castle Gnoffe. All she would take with her from this place would be her wits and her desire to reach the two people who meant everything to her—Flin the Brigand and her father. She was not even certain where she was, other than northward from Tolq; but once she had escaped, she would find her way.

She would make her way to Buerdaunt; it would not be hard to find the capital. And once she was there, she would find a way to remove her father from the donjons of Lothar the Pale. Flin was beyond her grasp for the time being; she did not even know where he was. But she would see her father out of Buerdaunt and she would see him safe. Then she would seek Flin until she found him.

She had not made a plan—planning would have led to despair—but she knew her father would still have friends among the nobles of the land, although she had seen that the Count of Jolier was no longer among them. She and her father would go to someone and ask for help; if none was given, the two of them would find refuge elsewhere. She would do whatever needed to be done. Even though he had wronged her, she could not allow her father, her own flesh and blood, to perish.

She held her sandals as she tiptoed to the great doors, but when she tested the two towering panels, she found both locked. She glanced back toward the acolyte's bed. The maid's slender form was aglow with the moonlight that washed over her and she was certain to have the key.

But where would she keep it? Bessina turned toward the sleeping maiden and crept the length of the hall, watching the softly curved form in the moonlight. Was the key on a chain around the sleeper's neck? Was it in some inner pocket in her robe? Bessina's heart crashed against the walls of her bosom as she bent over the sleeping form. Then the sleeper stirred, coughed, and rolled over. Bessina scampered around the corner of the shrine to watch the maiden sigh and mutter in half-sleep, then fall silent once more. But it had been an awful moment; Bessina heaved with great draughts that threatened to burst her. She did not dare fail; she had seen the cells which awaited unruly postulants in the convent, and the Abbess had told her in the plainest words that attempts to leave would not be tolerated. She was there under the King's orders.

There was a statue of the goddess Actaea within the shrine; Bessina had seen it in the daytime. It was a marble figure of great beauty which showed the divine patron of the forest in flowing robes, riding a mare and holding a drawn bow. Even the enclosure about the shrine was a work of considerable craftsmanship; the hardwood lattice was actually a bas-relief which featured hunting scenes, religious scenes, and scenes of life within the heights of Paradise.

In a while, the acolyte would awake, rise, and replace the candles which had burned out about the shrine. In fact, the young woman stirred even as Bessina watched. Would she awake soon? Bessina glanced about. She did not want the acolyte to see her dashing across the open floor to her cot; she had to remain hidden. Her eyes fell upon the shrine once more. If she could climb the carved wood of the enclosure, perhaps she could reach the top and hide up there. Then she would be in less danger of being discovered.

She made her way up the carvings, holding her sandals in her teeth while her hands and feet searched for purchase. It was the work of a moment for her to haul herself into the hidden safety of her goal. And wonder of wonders, there was a carefully shuttered vent in the wall over the shrine; it was right in front of her. She could hear the breeze whispering softly through the louvers and, by searching carefully with her hands, she found a latch.

Then she heard the acolyte stir, yawn, and stand up. Her heart nearly stopped. What if the maiden should lay eyes upon Bessina's empty cot? Bessina quickly undid the latch and opened the louvered door, listening all the while to the movements below. She heard a cupboard being shut; the acolyte was getting out new candles and preparing to light them, which meant she had not yet noticed the cot.

Bessina thrust her head into the chilly evening air. The drop to the ground was a fair distance, easily twice her height, but behind her she could hear the acolyte softly chanting the prayer which accompanied the lighting of the new candles. There was no turning back now. With a quick glance across the leaf-strewn lawn before her, Bessina climbed out, hung down as far as she could by gripping the sill with both hands, then let go.

She had to choke back a scream as she hit the ground and felt one ankle give beneath her. She nearly sobbed with pain. But she could not remain on the cold ground beside the Hall of the Three Virgins; she had to find a place to hide and some way to scale the convent's wall.

She clenched her teeth and rose shakily, hobbling toward a spreading tree which extended its branches near the stone wall itself. Her left leg felt as if she were holding it in a flame, so great was the pain each time she put weight on it; but she made it to the tree and managed to haul herself into the branches the way Flin had taught her. Gasping, she climbed onto the crotch of a stout limb, safe for the moment.

She gazed between the half-stripped branches and studied the grounds. The wind was brisk and cold and it searched through the folds of her robe and chilled her as if she were naked. It picked up armies of fallen leaves and sent them dancing and frolicking, scurrying in circles which played across the lawns like tiny, rustling skeletons.

The moon was setting; soon it would leave her in total darkness, alone with the chill, her thoughts and fears, and the thousands of whirring leaf-voices to serenade her. She had to hurry; she knew that much, even before she heard a cry and the sounds of people rushing about. A torch-bearing figure issued from the far end of the building Bessina had fled and hurried across the grounds toward the Abbess' retreat; Bessina watched as the torch moved away, flickering in the wind. She had no time to wait; she had to do something. She felt her way in the darkness and crept along the heavy branch toward the night-shrouded stone wall. The thought of jumping from that height onto her injured limb was enough to bring tears to her eyes, but it was the only course she could conceive. She had to get outside the wall as quickly as possible.

So she hurried along the creaking branch. Then the wall was beneath her, its broad stones a looming mass, and she could see a light a little way beyond. Where was she going? Was she moving from the relative safety of the tree to a place where there was even greater danger of discovery? It did not matter; she had to take a chance. She could already hear voices approaching the Hall of the Three Virgins and that meant they were also approaching her hiding place. She hoped for the best, held her breath, and jumped.

There was crunching and crackling; the air was driven from her body, and she felt her flesh brutally scratched as she landed in some kind of bush which had lain hidden beneath her in the darkness. She tried to collect herself, then clambered to her feet and fled.

She could hardly see a thing except that she had closed the distance between herself and the light she had noticed before. Then her breath rushed from her in disappointment; she had reached another walled yard, this one tiny compared to the compound she had escaped. She was in a garden, no doubt at the rear of a house occupied by one of the convent's administrators.

Sighing, crawling both from pain and for the sake of concealment, she made her way toward the light. She could tell it issued from a casement window in the basement level of the tumbledown stone cottage before her. There was not enough light to show her a gate or break in the wall which surrounded the garden; and if the garden was searched, she would quickly be discovered. She was trapped. Her only path of escape lay over the wall again or through the old dwelling itself, a pleasant thought.

She was both curious and desperate. The casement window attracted her. The light flickered, ebbed, and grew strong again, then repeated the process. She looked about and saw that no one had yet come into the garden, so she gathered her nerve and crawled across the damp ground and into the window well, which was large enough to allow her to peek through the thick pane without being seen.

She found herself peering into a small chamber, a little room below the rest of the building. The glass was thick and filled with bubbles from the crude blowing process, but she was able to wipe away enough of the dust and dirt on it to make out the solitary figure of an old man. He stood at a workbench, pumping a leather bellows into some kind of small forge; each time he leaned on the goatskin air bladder the flames before him leaped up. That was what produced the light which had attracted her in the first place.

She could not judge the man's age, because his face was turned away; still, she knew he had left his youth far behind him because of the close-cropped white hair which covered his head. He wore a priest's cassock, but what a male priest's role was in this refuge for women and maidens she could not begin to guess.

Made bolder by the fact that his back was turned, she pressed her face against the glass of the windowpane in order to observe the chamber more carefully. It was small and looked more like a storeroom than anything else. There were wooden boxes lying about, a small bookcase, and two or three chairs which had capes and other clothing thrown over them. The light thrown by the little forge was so dim it was impossible to make each article out clearly.

Then she saw something moving beside one of the chairs on the far side of the old man, who was apparently watching the fire burn in the forge. The thing moved again. Whatever it was, it was small, about dog-sized, and hairy. Then the creature stepped out into the light and she gasped as she looked upon it. It was a demon of some sort, some kind of familiar spirit—a mocking travesty on human form, covered with coarse dark hair, with a leathery face and a mouth which sported massive canine teeth. The thing moved across the room, walking upon all fours, working its blubbery lips as it went. It exuded evil. What place had she stumbled across, hidden within the embrace of the holy Douzainium? Or was the refuge itself evil in spite of all its supposed holiness?

In her dismay, Bessina's hand had floated to her lips, a movement which must have been visible from within. The demon familiar saw her. It stopped stock-still and stared up at her with an indescribable expression; then the floppy lips pulled back from the gleaming teeth with rage, accompanied by a shrill, chittering scream. The old man's head jerked about. The thing bounded toward the window with incredible quickness, leaping up and grasping the sill, screeching and baring its fangs in the most horrible of grimaces.

Bessina uttered a scream herself as she scrambled up and out of the window well toward whatever escape she could find. Even if she had to lift herself into the spreading beech tree once more, had to risk recapture and a beating, that would be a refuge compared with another confrontation with the horrible creature.

She tried to run with a hobbling gait around the corner of the house, only to land in the hairy arms of a man who had emerged from the rear of the structure. She struggled frantically, beat the man's chest with her fists, and cried out, "Let me go. Please let me go."

Chapter Ten:
The Soothsayer

BESSINA'S CAPTOR DID not respond to her cries and he was too strong for her to escape him. He forced her against the building's wall, spun her body about, and pinioned her arms behind her, before hustling her back through the open door. She tried kicking at him, but was hampered by her injured ankle as he hauled her along an unlit corridor and into a book-lined chamber. He forced her into a corner, pinned her there, and pulled twice on a cloth bell rope.

Bessina's struggles weakened; the man was simply too strong for her. She had no choice but to bide her time, which turned out to be a wise decision. As soon as she ceased fighting, he released her and stepped back, though his body still blocked any exit.

She brushed an auburn hair from her face and glanced about the room. It was a marvelous-looking chamber, a library. There had never been a library in her father's quarters at Castle Gnoffe; he had never had any use for such a place. So she looked about the room, marveled at the shelves of polished hardwood, and inhaled the musty smell of old paper, not to mention the sweeter aromas of leather and vellum. She could almost smell the learning that filled the place.

She had been forced into a corner between two high wooden racks which held scrolls, bound books, and other articles she could not identify. Perhaps they were religious relics; she could not be sure, but there were all kinds of odds and ends reposing in clear glass vials. There were bits of wood, of bone, and of metal. They made strange, living shadows in the light of the fire that cracked and grumbled in the chamber's great stone fireplace.

As to the man who guarded her, he was less exceptional. His features were plain, blunt, and ordinary; he was bald and of middle age and he wore the tunic of a house servant. He never spoke a word as he stood before her, using his body as a gate to block her escape.

Then Bessina heard a sound and turned to see the elderly man himself enter the chamber. His face was intriguing, though not as interesting as his library. The mouth was thin and apparently toothless, the face clean-shaven, and the nose stubbed and mediocre. But the dark eyes had fire in them, a brilliant twinkle which drew her attention away from all his other features. He stopped before the two of them and stared at her, nonplussed. "Is this the reason why you called me up from all my study and my meditation? Why's this maiden outside her own walls?"

The servant—for that was apparently his office—did not answer with words. Instead, he made a rapid series of gestures, accompanied by incongrous little squeeks and grunts. Bessina understood immediately; he was a deaf-mute, or at least a mute. As for the elderly gentleman, he nodded and his bushy eyebrows moved together. "You say you caught her prowling in the garden?" He looked Bessina up and down.

She stared back at him, partly in fear of the strange things she had spied him doing, partly in desperation to be away from the place. "I beg you, sir, to let me go."

"Indeed. Does my old friend the Abbess now instruct her postulants to spy and burglarize?"

"I have no time. I beg you, let me go."

"Unless you stop your fidgeting and hold your tongue except to answer questions, maid, the first thing I shall do is see you flogged. Your clothing marks you as a newcomer into the abbey. How, then, did you come into my garden?"

Bessina was surprised by the question. She had supposed everyone in the refuge knew why she had been brought to the Douzainium. After all, she had been accompanied by the noble Count of Jolier. "Do you not know of me?"

"I am the mystic Peristeras, maid. I am not part of your Douzainium. They give me bread and quarters and they tend to all my other needs because I have a gift giv'n by the gods. Do you know of me? I sometimes speak the sooth."

She shook her head. "I came into this place two days ago."

He nodded and turned toward a large chair before the fireplace. "I thought as much."

With that movement, and seeing the servant had relaxed a bit, Bessina made a desperate dash toward one of the corridors entering the chamber. But she did not get far: her leg buckled beneath her and she fell before she had gone two steps, crying out as she sprawled across the floor.

The servant and the elderly gentleman stared at her. "You're hurt. You should have said so. You must wait while Omo brings you bandages and gauze. You'll not escape, and if you try again I swear you shall be sent back to the walls of that same refuge you so eagerly escaped."

Bessina looked up at him. His concern over her damaged ankle reassured her for all his threats. Besides, the member did need to be wrapped; the pain was nearly enough to make her weep. "I'll not attempt it more, but help me, please."

Peristeras' expression softened; he really did seem moved by her injury and her plight. He stepped toward her and examined the affected member, then looked up as the servant reentered the chamber. "Good Omo, will you wrap this maiden's leg?" The mute fell to the task and the old man resumed his seat with an apologetic air. "I have no skills of medicine or craft; I have my gift, no more. But tell me who you are."

Sitting up while Omo administered to her, Bessina studied the old gentleman's face. Could she trust him? Did she have a choice? At last she began to speak, to tell him the story of Lothar the Pale's sack of Castle Gnoffe, of the capture of herself and Count Clauvis, and of her journey to the refuge.

He listened patiently and his eyes poured over her in a manner which made her uneasy. There was nothing improper in her movements, and his expression really had little in common with the way filthy old Crecche had looked at her. There was nothing at all sensual about his observation of her, but it still made her uncomfortable, as if she were being subjected to a medical examination without being asked her consent.

She finished her tale at last, as much of it as she dared tell, and he nodded slowly. "You interest me. The color of your eyes, your hair, the contours of your face, they all are features which may indicate there's more to you than even you may know. You say you do not know me?"

Bessina shook her head. "No."

"I think I shall believe you." He turned his own head toward his servant. "Omo, you may now depart from us. I feel assured this maid will not refuse our hospitality, especially when she learns I am inclined to aid her in her quest for freedom."

Bessina's heart leaped to hear the old man's words. Was he telling the truth? It was too good to believe. But Omo nodded and moved from the room, his broad shoulders swaying. Bessina watched him go, unable to decide whether she felt more or less comfortable, now that she was alone with the singular old man.

As for the soothsayer himself, he sat and studied her with his chin resting on the back of one hand. At last he spoke once more. "They say I am a mystic, for I bear the gift of seeing things beyond the veil of time and space. Do you believe my words?"

She hesitated. "I do not know."

"Your answer's natural and wise. You know me not." He rose and extended his hand. "If you'll accompany me into my vault, I think you will be wiser for the deed. Do you believe your leg will let you walk?"

"Perhaps it will." She clambered to her feet and took a couple of steps to test her bandaged ankle. Though she limped badly, she could walk.

"If you'll grasp my hand, I'll balance you." The tone was firm, although it was polite enough. Still, she was hardly certain whether she should fear the old gentleman or not, even though he seemed polite and frail and was a finger's width shorter than she. Reluctantly, she laid her hand in his and found it cool and dry to the touch.

He led her from the chamber, bending his arm so he could lend her more support. She appreciated the gesture; she offered him a quick smile by way of thanks, and he smiled back at her, although his smile seemed to be mostly from politeness. "You claim to be the daughter of the Count of Galliardy," he said. "Then tell me, can you write?"

"I can."

He nodded. "Ah, that is well." They walked through a darkened chamber and paused at the head of a narrow stone stairway; an irregular light could be seen at the bottom of the rough-cut stone steps. Bessina hesitated as she looked down. She knew this chamber was the one in which she had first spied him.

Did he perform some sort of evil rite in there, some sort of blasphemy against the gods themselves? Was the demon familiar still there? Or was there anything at all to fear? After all, she did not know the length or depth of the rites required for the select worship of any god. With her hand held lightly in his, Peristeras noticed Bessina's hesitation. "Come," he said. "There is nothing here to do you harm."

Thus encouraged, she followed him into the embrace of the cellar room. There was a heaviness in the air, a bit like the odor of her father's kennels at Castle Gnoffe or of a forest cave where a bear had been hiding. She shivered slightly; she knew it was the odor of the demon. And the demon was indeed there; Peristeras pushed a squat oaken door the rest of the way open, and she saw the creature standing before them in the dim light of the forge, silently watching her. As she entered the chamber, it opened its mouth and bared its great fangs again, though it did not make a sound.

She hesitated once more. "Will *that* hurt me?"

Peristeras glanced toward the creature, then back at her, and smiled. "She shall not harm you; she is but an op, a creature brought to me some years ago from lands which lie far north, upon the far side of the ocean." He stepped forward to shoo the creature away. "Go, disturb us not."

It gazed uncertainly at the two of them, then retreated toward a corner of the room where there was a wrought-iron ladder, a bowl of fruit, and a pitcher of water. It stopped, eyed them once more, grasped the pitcher in a manner disconcertingly human, and took a draught of the water, spilling some. Then, with startling quickness, it leaped up the ladder to a platform and lay down to watch them with enigmatic eyes.

The elderly man pulled a chair out of another corner of the room, removed some items from it, and gestured toward Bessina. "Sit, I beg you."

She did so, looking about as she settled into the luxurious leather upholstery. He drew up another smaller chair, but did not use it. He watched her while she glanced about uneasily; then all at once he fetched a quill and a piece of parchment. He brought the items to her and thrust them into her hands. "Now write for me your name, your father's name, the name of this young man you love, and be as certain as you can you spell them right. You must write down each name as it appears in records kept by scribes in your own land."

She was full of questions, but she took the implements and began to write, holding the parchment across the broad arm of the chair. The quill ran out of ink and he had to dip it for her; still, she was quickly finished. Once she had completed the last letter, she blew across the ink to dry it, blotted it, then offered the parchment to him.

To her surprise, he refused it. "No, I'll not read it. Place it with your hands into this crucible I show you now." He produced a large stone crucible, or pot really, and made her tuck the parchment into it so that not a corner stuck out. Then he took it from her, placed a cover on it, and thrust it into the forge. He added faggots to the flame and pressed on the bellows until the little fire danced and roared.

What was he doing? Bessina sat in her chair and watched him. Was he mad? What was the sense of writing something on a piece of paper only to consign it to the flames? Still, he seemed intent on what he was doing; he said nothing and the only sounds in the chamber were the working of the bellows, the complaints of the flame itself, and the sound of the familiar as it watched the odd rite. Bessina had seen soothsayers, or at least men who had called themselves soothsayers, but never had she laid eyes upon such a proceeding as this.

At last he released the bellows and removed the crucible from the flames with a pair of tongs. It had become exceedingly hot; it glowed red as he removed it from the furnace, and a last wisp of smoke escaped the cover. He examined it for a moment, then cautiously removed the cover and peeked in. The beast on the platform behind him watched with an intensity that was more than animal as the old man peered at the contents of the container. Then his face grew dark. His eyes raised to look at Bessina and he frowned. "You lied to me about your father's name."

She became frightened; she could see his anger reflected in the face of his familiar. "No, no," she protested. "I wrote it down as carefully as you instructed me."

"Yet something's wrong." He studied her face, then hurried to fetch another piece of parchment. "You must write down your mother's maiden name. Move quickly now, before the vessel cools."

Some of his urgency communicated itself to Bessina; she scribbled the name and handed the paper back to him, and he instantly folded it and dropped it into the crucible.

It puffed into flame from the heat retained by the stone. Once the smoke had cleared, he gazed in at the ashes once more, and a worried expression crossed his face. He wrote something on yet another piece of paper and dropped that in. While it burned in its turn, he looked up at Bessina, his face showing great concern. "Move not a muscle. When the paper's burned, I'll read the truth contained within the ash. But I must read it ere it settles down into a meaningless small pile of naught."

The parchment burned itself out and the smoke ceased to rise from the crucible. Beneath his familiar's watchful eye, Peristeras the soothsayer rubbed his chin, made a holy sign, wiped his hands upon his cassock, and bent low to examine what was left. His face filled in turn with concentration, comprehension, and then dismay. He fell back from the workbench and landed painfully on the stone floor while the familiar chittered and screeched from its perch above him. "I'd no idea," he said. "This is terrible." He looked up at Bessina, his face as gray as glass, then rose. "The gods instructed you to come to me. The Moirae are upon you; only you are given power to protect the world from conflagration at a demon's hands." He had become pale. The only color left in his face was the red of the fire's glow.

For her part, Bessina was frightened. What was he talking about? Was he really mad? As he approached her, she rose from her chair, stammering. "What is it that you mean to do with me?"

"Be not afraid of me. It's you I fear. You are caught up in great events, events which you can hardly comprehend. Your past is filled with far more than you know; your present, too. Nor could I read it all before the ash decayed and decomposed." He was suddenly interrupted by the tinkling of a bell in one corner of the chamber, near the railing. He ignored the sound and tried to reconstruct his train of thought, but the bell sounded again. Clenching a fist, he strode toward the doorway with a forcefulness she had not expected of him. "Wait here. I shall return."

He stalked from the chamber, leaving Bessina alone

with the familiar. She glanced toward the creature's platform, then started to see that it was no longer there. Was
it back at the far end of the shelf where she could not see
it or was it stalking her? She was afraid to seem frightened,
so she sat stock-still, wondering what was to become of
her.

.Her thoughts were diverted by the sounds of Peristeras' footsteps echoing from above, growing softer as
they moved toward the far end of the dwelling. Then she
heard a confusion of voices, some of them female voices.
Her hand fluttered to her lips; the Abbess was there. The
hunt for her had carried the officers of the Douzainium
to the cottages. Would the old gentleman yield her up?
How could she know and what would she do about it,
even if he did?

The sounds continued for a moment, then she heard
the old man's voice rise above the others. "I know of her
and what becomes of her lies in the hands of the immortal
gods. You do not serve them by pursuing her." The voices
went on a bit longer, then there was silence.

In a moment, he reentered the chamber more agitated
than he had been when he had left. "Your friends have
called," he said. "I told them to begone."

She was greatly relieved. "I thank you."

"It is I who must thank you. You've shown me what
my purpose is, the function which the Fates ordained for
me. Now you must also follow what the Fates have set
you to."

He hurriedly searched the shelves which lined one side
of the room, opening containers and boxes and looking
behind books and scrolls. At last he drew a jewelry box
of plain cherry wood from one of the upper shelves, blew
off the dust, opened it, and removed a ring. He held it
up and approached Bessina. It was a plain ring but was
made of the purest burnished gold; the surface reflected
the forge's light eerily. She held out her hand as if
entranced, and he dropped the ring into her palm. It was
heavy and cold. But though it was obviously of great
value, she could see nothing special about it. She gazed
up at him, nonplussed.

His eyes glittered in his time-scribed face as he spoke. "Do you know how to read the language of the Empire?"

"All noble maidens learn that mode of speech."

He pointed toward the ring. "Then look in it and read."

She examined the ring closely, found an inscription circling one edge in tiny letters, hesitated, then began to read. "I, Parthelon, by all the gods' good grace, am Emperor across the Thlassa Mey." Her words stumbled as she finished her translation. "My powers issue from the deities; when evil threatens, I shall speak of them." The ring was ancient indeed, a possession of Parthelon the Great, and its worth was beyond imagining. "Where did you get it?"

He impatiently waved the question off. "It was given unto me. Do you know Sparth's Head Castle? Could you find the place?"

"It's somewhere west of here, upon the coast."

"Indeed. It stands upon a craggy cliff, all tumbled down, its heyday long gone by. The stream which flows below this convent, follow that, then follow down the Tanguine River to Verdast. Some leagues northwest of there, the ancient castle stands, its rotting towers gazing down upon the Thlassa Mey." He took the ring from her and placed it onto the middle finger of her left hand with great gravity. "You now must bear this ring unto that place."

"Cannot you bear it? I have told you how my father lies in Lothar's castle keep. I first must go to him."

"There is no time." The old man's voice was urgent and his eyes flashed in the firelight. "Who knows the schedule that the Fates require? You first must bear the ring unto its goal and then await whatever may transpire. As to your father, seek you not for him, for Pomfract Castle's donjons hold him not. Your father is dead as winter's skies."

His words struck Bessina like a blow. She leaned forward, placed her hand in her palms, and wept. She wept for a long time while he watched. The tears flowed without stopping, like blood from an open wound.

He allowed the tears to wash the grief out of her for

a long interval before he spoke. "Child," he said. "Did you know your father?"

"Certainly. We lived together ten and seven years and all that time I loved him from my soul. He meant the world to me and I to him, and now the King has sent him to his grave." Again she burst into tears and her sobbing filled the chamber while the soothsayer watched her silently. But she was young and strong and she would survive; she would go on. She raised her head, wiped her eyes with her sleeve, and gazed at the man who had given her the hard news. "The ring is yours. Why did you never take it to the destination you describe?"

He sighed. "My part is played. I see my role was but as caller for the steps you now must dance. My guess is that a month will find my bones a'moldering beneath the stitching of a shroud." He stood. "You cannot travel in the robes you wear, nor on your injured ankle. I shall keep you in my house until tomorrow night and send my servant to a clothier's shop to purchase garments as you may require. Now we must go from this small chamber's glare for all the Fates—the Moirae—fly tonight within these walls and strip the essence of our very lives."

He grasped her by the arm. His hands had become colder than ever; they had turned clammy and unpleasant. Had he told her the truth or had his words been the ravings of a madman? Had the King already had her father put to death? Why? Count Clauvis had committed no crime. Her head buzzed with questions and griefs, but in the center of her being she could not doubt the soothsayer's word; she had to do the thing he had told her to do.

As she reached the doorway, she turned to take one last glance at the mystical chamber and saw something lying in one corner. She did not scream, but she did gasp and put a hand to her mouth—the hand which bore the ring of Parthelon. Peristeras followed her gaze and his face assumed an expression of indescribable despair. Still, her emotions were as complex as his and over all lay the knowledge that he was not a madman, that the Moirae did, indeed, lurk in the chamber. She had to go to Sparth's

Head Castle; her father was dead. The soothsayer's shaggy alter ego, the canine-fanged familiar, which had watched him say his last sooth and had aided him in who could know what way, lay below its platform, dead as a hammer.

Chapter Eleven:
Wine and Fire

WHEN PALAMON RECOVERED from the blow to his head, he found himself bound securely and tied to the ship's railing. He assumed Flin was dead; the young warrior had been swept over the side by the swirling battle and had not appeared again. And all the men who had been brave enough to aid in the defense were dead; those who had not been killed during the fray had been butchered by the victors. They had paid a grievous price for listening to Palamon. The leader of the corsairs approached the tall prince and leered down into his face, a picture of villainy with a scraggly beard, earring, and stringy, greasy hair. He looked no different from the other corsairs; he was wearing the same leather breastplate as many of the others, and the same longsword was slapping at his hip. But there was an air of leadership about him, both in his manner and in the way his mates acted towards him. "I see you're with us again," he said. "You must be a strong man—as hard as that fellow hit you, I thought you were done in for sure."

Palamon's head still ached. "The blow was hard enough."

"'Twas not." Hrusk interrupted. "I've a half dozen good men dead because you wouldn't yield to my wisdom. And was the result any better?"

"Indeed it wasn't," the pirate chieftain said. "But they gave a good account of themselves." He turned to Palamon. "*You* gave a good account of yourself. There's a deal less men to share the booty with, I'll own to that. It's going to be a pity to have to kill you in the end."

Palamon smiled dryly, then Hrusk spoke again, in a more conciliatory tone. "You might not want to do that. He's a noble in his own land and there must be people in Carea or somewhere else who'd pay a good ransom for him." He looked at Palamon. "If I manage to talk them into sparing your life, my Lord, please make a note of it."

"The note is made," Palamon said. "And I suppose I must forget, forgive, and pardon other acts."

Hrusk looked uncomfortable but the conversation was interrupted. The raiders had been combing through the ship, examining the contents of the hold, and exploring the sterncastle. Now two of them appeared, forcing along before them Aelia and Chroma, who struggled each step of the way. "Look what we've got here, Master Drakon. There be women aboard this scow."

The raider chieftain rose and surveyed the two females. Predictably, Aelia stood like a queen and glared back at him; Chroma also stood, but her head was bowed and her eyes were clamped shut. Drakon eyed them like prey or like so many cattle at an auction. "Lovely ladies you are, though you're lovely in different ways. Are you connected to this fighter here?" He jerked his elbow toward Palamon.

"That warrior is Carea's noble Prince and heir unto the throne," Aelia said. "Release him now and you'll not come to harm for all your crimes. But harm his little finger and you'll find your cruel life ended by such might as you cannot begin to understand."

Drakon laughed. "He may be a noble but he's no Prince

of Carea. They're all dead years ago—everyone knows that."

This time it was Palamon who laughed until the sound of his mirth caused the raider's chieftain to turn his head. "You're wise in all your doubts," the tall prince said. "The title 'Prince' has earned my disbelief as well as yours." He chuckled again as he made the statement.

Drakon stared at him, nonplussed. "You wear pretty armor and you carry a pretty sword, which I plan to keep, by the way. So let's say you're someone important." He pondered awhile. "Whoever you be, you'll keep until I decide what to do with you."

"Another wise decision," Palamon said.

Drakon placed his hands on his hips and looked down at the *Spada Korrigaine*, which lay on the deck beside the tall prince. "That's a lovely weapon," he observed. "From the look of it, it's too heavy for the kind of work I do—but I plan to keep it all the same, just to show it to my friends. It would look nice, wouldn't it?"

He reached down and grasped the mystic blade. His grimy fingers wrapped about the haft. But his smile disappeared, replaced by a look of shock and pain. The sword's handle had become red-hot; the air was full of Drakon's cry as he cast the weapon away. "By all the gods, this is witchcraft." He clenched his teeth and rubbed his burned palms together as he glared at Palamon. "You should have warned me about that."

Palamon said nothing, but Aelia was defiant. "So now you see you are not even fit to hold the sword of him you've tethered. If you fear the gods, then you will set us free."

Drakon glared back at her. "I don't fear anything and I don't forget things, either." He was about to say more but he was interrupted by another of the raiders, who scuttled up from the hold. "Jewels. Jewels, gold, wine. There are butts of wine down there and two chests bearing all the coin and jewels a man could want."

A great cheer erupted from the throats of the corsairs within earshot, and Drakon seemed to put away his thoughts of pain and anger, at least for the moment. "Gold, you say? And jewels?"

"Enough for a king's ransom."

There had, indeed, been two casks of fine Carean wine loaded on for transport; that plainly filled the corsairs with ecstasy. "Then fetch up some of that wine," Drakon cried. "Here's cause for a celebration; we have hostages and gold and pretty women, all in one throw." He turned and looked down at Palamon. "This might buy you your life, warrior." Then he faced his men once again. "Hear me, you great lot of rich men, you scum-crawlers and whoreson dogs. Fetch skins, fetch up a draught or two of that wine. Is it a good vintage, do you say?"

"We haven't broken it open."

"Then break it open, fool. Heave it up to the deck and we'll be into it."

"The butt's too heavy to lift."

Drakon laughed a great laugh, his mood much changed since he had learned of the precious booty. "Then break out the cargo boom. We'll have a butt up on deck and we'll see what's in it." He turned to Palamon again. "You get more pleasant to look at by the moment. You made us pay dearly for this prize, by my faith, but it sounds as if it's worth the payment."

"What about me?" Hrusk asked. "It was my cargo."

Drakon hardly bothered to grunt a reply as one of the butts of wine was lifted onto the deck. Men clambered over the wooden container and knocked off the top in a trice, although they were wonderfully careful not to damage the cask in any other way. Then they became like children bobbing for apples as they dipped their faces in and sucked heady draughts of the dark brew. Drakon himself quaffed deeply, then turned to one of the other corsairs while liquid dribbled from his jaws and stained the leather of his breastplate. "Take those two women below. I don't want them touched."

For their parts, Aelia and Chroma seemed glad enough to leave the deck, although Aelia gazed with concern at Palamon as she was hauled away. In the eyes of both women lay the knowledge that they were in peril of losing more than simple life and limb.

The raider chieftain approached the butt once more, shoved another man away from the side of it, and drank again. Then he straightened, shook his head, and pierced the shipmaster with a malevolent stare. "As for you, I heard your question. You're a scurvy coward, you are. This knight risked his life to save your cargo for you and your gratitude was to knock him in the head. I've served under men like you; you're a scurvy, louse-picking, lizard-eating fragment of a man and you've no more honesty than the lowest piece of scum in my crew—and a sight less honor. I know your kind."

"For all of that, it would have been the same if I'd never hit him," Hrusk replied. "And you'd have more men dead."

"You make me sick," the chieftain said, drinking again before he continued. "But you'll not be killed, nor the rest of your crew. Those who want to join me, by the gods, let them do it—that would be a more respectable life than sailing with you. As for the rest, I'll think of something to do."

Hrusk turned away sullenly, his ring of keys clinking at the small of his back; it was plain to see he was not satisfied by the way things were going. Still, he had no choice but to accept matters for the time being. And the drinking continued. Palamon could tell the level of wine in the butt by the effort it took for each man to reach it with his lip. He was amazed by the rate at which the level declined. The raiders were draining the barrel at an astounding pace.

The corsairs carried the treasure aboard their own ship, then they all made their way back to the roundship to join in the drinking. Soon they all had clustered about the wine butt. As the darkness became complete, they lighted lanterns and the roundship's crewmen stood about glumly as the victors traded loud songs and long stories. Weapons were occasionally drawn—the corsairs were the only ones who still had any—and they made threatening gestures at the crewmen.

All at once, Drakon turned on Hrusk. "I've reached a decision, bootlicker. Do you know what it is?"

The shipmaster shook his head.

"You'll find out soon enough." Drakon said, then shouted at his own men in a raucous voice. "Listen to me, you drunken rats, and man the boom again. Unship the longboat and heave it over the side. Look hearty, now, and show these mules how free men can work when they've a mind to."

Drakon's men fell to their task in drunken disorder. After repeated tries, they made a line from the boom fast to the longboat and lifted it free of the deck, passing it over Palamon's head on its journey outboard. So haphazard was the handling that he feared it would fall and crush him; but by some miracle, they did manage to complete the process with few mishaps. Once the ship's boat had been hung out over the side, the line was released and the little craft fell with a great splash. Drakon looked over the rail and beamed. "Perfect. Never a hitch." He turned to breathe drunkenly into Hrusk's face and said, "Aren't you jealous?"

"What are you doing with my longboat?"

"I just put it over the side, you idiot, and now I'm going to put you into it." Drakon pushed the shipmaster to one side and walked unevenly toward the center of the deck. "Listen to me, all you who serve aboard this scow. Join my crew and you'll see adventure and good times all the days of your lives. There's nothing to what we do. You show a little pluck and put these Hrusks and nobles into their places and get enough loot for ten men just by doing what you're doing now for nothing. Who'll join?"

A few men raised their hands and stepped uncertainly away from their fellows. "Bravo," the chieftain shouted. "You men have oak in your keels. That sets you apart from all these pine-planked lubbers I see here."

Hrusk touched his shoulder. "What have you done to my longboat?"

Drakon turned and leered down at him. "I told you. I'm going to put you and the rest of your scurvy bags of flesh into it."

"You can't do that. I cooperated with you."

"Oh, can't I?" Drakon leered drunkenly at the ship-master, then he made a lightning move and grasped the smaller man by the sleeves. He laughed like a wildman as he hurtled toward the rail, hauling Hrusk with him, then he stopped, lifted the startled shipmaster from his feet, and hurled him into empty space. The shipmaster screamed as he plunged into the darkness; the sound was cut short by a splash.

Drakon laughed insanely. "He leaps into the brine like a great fish. Now come, my hearty men. Let's have them all off the deck. Into the sea with them. They're just little seal pups and they belong in the water." Excited by his own words, he pounced on two more seamen and collared them both at once. He sent them after their commander with superhuman strength, nearly losing himself over the rail in the process. Screams mixed with hoarse cries all across the ship as men hurled other men into the waiting waters below. One man struggled too fiercely against his fate and was cut down, after which the corpse was sent plunging among the other victims. The corsairs roared with laughter. One of them lost his balance and fell over the side himself, a writhing mass of arms and legs that had to be fished out of the water. Drakon presided over the insanity, his arms raised in the lamplight as the yellow glow reflected off his coarse, bearded features and made him look like a demon conducting an insane symphony in some Tartarus.

Palamon watched silently. He had seen many things in his lifetime, but nothing to exceed this. Would the corsairs send him flying after the crewmen? If they tried, the attempt would cost at least some of them their lives. But Drakon no longer seemed to notice the tall Prince; he bent over the wine butt again and bathed his face the way a peasant would bathe at a stream. When he straightened once more, his leather cuirass and breeches were soaked. "Let's have more. You say there's another butt of this stuff below? By the gods let's have it up here. Step lively, you wriggling worms."

And so the night went. Drakon seemed to have forgotten his earlier anger over the *Spada Korrigaine*. So great was the drinking that went on, Palamon nursed a hope the corsairs would collapse of their own drunkenness. But that was not to be; their tolerance for the dark potion was amazing. They partied and reveled far into the night, dancing, singing, and fighting beneath the swaying lanterns, making the roundship's deck rock as the two vessels drifted together across the Thlassa Mey.

Drakon seemed to drink twice as much as any of the others; his intake was so great that he did collapse at last. With roars of laughter, a brace of his fellows fetched up a wooden bucket filled with seawater and doused him with it. He coughed and sputtered into wakefulness, shook wine and water out of his hair and whiskers, and looked about with wild eyes. After an instant, his drunken laughter joined with that of his crewmen and his eyes lit on Palamon, who still sat bound a few cubits away.

He studied the tall Prince's face and a thick-lipped smile crept across his soggy features. "You don't like our party, do you? You don't think it's proper."

"My thoughts bear not. Your party may go on."

"Do you think the wine's a good thing? Maybe you hope we'll all drink ourselves silly and then go and drown ourselves like those sea-slugs we threw over the side." Drakon's words slurred into laughter once more, then he went on. "You can give up that hope. Any man of my crew can drink till dawn and still take on any two men like the ones you led. You may as well get a good night's rest because you're going no place except back to Vouil to be held for ransom."

"I thank you for your kind advice," Palamon said. "My mind may now relax; my certain fate precludes escape attempts."

Drakon laughed uproariously. "You see it then? You're a wise man." He crawled toward Palamon and patted him on the shoulder. "You're a wise man," he repeated, then smiled grandly. "See? I can tell a wise man when I see him and I've forgiven you for letting me sizzle my fingers on that witch's sword of yours. But you know a ransom is safer than more fighting, don't you? We'll ransom you and your two ladies to the proper notables when the time comes, and then you'll be none the worse for wear. That's good business, isn't it?"

"Most excellent," Palamon replied.

"Ah, they're both noble pieces, those women of yours." He peered at the tall knight with a sly expression. "Mind you, the young one isn't for me, not yet, at least. Hasn't had time to develop. But the other one, I bet she's a wild one when her hair's down. Is she your wife? I'd wager you know things about her other men would give this nose and these fingers to know." Drakon rubbed his nose clumsily as he spoke.

Palamon did not answer. The raider chieftain slumped against the rail and stared dreamily up at the mast as he rubbed his burned hands together. "I'd wager my share of the loot that she's a real mattress-shredder." He inclined his head toward Palamon and looked into the tall Prince's eyes. What he was looking for, Palamon could not begin to guess. Palamon could only hope the two women would not be made to pay for the prank the *Spada Korrigaine* had played earlier. Then Drakon's voice became crafty as he spoke again. "The young one's a virgin, I suppose."

Again, Palamon did not reply. There were no safe answers to that question.

Drakon stood and stretched, reeling a bit as he wiped wine and water from his clothing. "Maidenheads are money," he said, then repeated the words over and over in a kind of singsong chant. "Maidenheads are money, maidenheads are money." Then he finished with, "It's true, you know. A virgin is not to be touched. It spoils the value." Then he moved away, walking unsteadily aft.

There was no mistaking his direction. He was walking toward the sterncastle. Palamon did not know for sure what his intentions were but there was no mistaking his general frame of mind. The Prince had to free himself! He frantically strained against his bonds but to no avail. He was not sure where Drakon had thrown the *Spada Korrigaine*, though he had heard it land somewhere aft of him. He whispered the mystical weapon's name and he heard it slide across the deck, propelled by its own mysterious powers. The weapon's pommel rested against his fingertips. But try as he might, he could make no use of the sword with his hands bound behind his back.

Lady Aelia and the maiden Chroma waited in the darkness of one of the tiny cabins, whispering to one another through the murk. They both started as they heard a crash; someone was trying to get into the little chamber and he had not even bothered to open the door. There was another crash; the flimsy obstacle gave way and they saw before them the chieftain of the corsairs, holding a lantern, grinning in the doorway, weaving foolishly with the slight rocking of the vessel.

"What do you want?" Aelia demanded.

"What do you think I want? I want you." Drakon set the lantern down and reached clumsily for her. She tried to spin away but he caught her mantle in one hand and drew her toward him, tearing the material.

"You filthy, stinking, wine-besotted cur," Aelia snarled as she struggled in his grasp. "I'd never let you touch my mongrel dog, much less possess the favors you desire."

He was a powerful man; his arms crushed her to him, squeezed the breath from her as he kissed her savagely. She managed to free one hand and her nails raked his face, drawing blood while she kicked vainly at him. But to her disappointment, the only reaction she got was a drunken laugh. He did not even acknowledge the pain, although he did seem to recognize the attempt. "Oh, you're a bed-splitter, I can see that. We haven't got your little mongrel dog, so I'm just going to have to touch you. I'm going to touch you a lot." He shoved her toward the companionway with a grunt, then laughed again as he strode after her.

There was no escaping his iron grasp. Aelia staggered onto the vessel's deck, still trying to struggle as she glanced about. There was little to be seen that would offer encouragement; the deck was filled with reveling corsairs and Palamon was against the rail, struggling against his bonds like a madman. For an instant their eyes met, and the anguish she saw in his features clutched her soul.

But there was no time for that. Drakon dragged her

toward the roundship's rail and she realized that he intended to take her onto his own deserted vessel. Perhaps that was as well. There was no one to help her here. If she had to suffer the ravages of his body, at least there would not be the additional shame of suffering such humiliation before others. But that would not change the humiliation itself. Already his hand was exploring the front of her robe, caressing, pinching, and fondling. His bearded cheek rubbed against her face like some torturer's implement. His touch was a disgrace, his grin an assault, and his breath a pestilence.

She screamed. She had not wanted to give him that satisfaction; she had resolved not to scream or weep or make any sound, no matter what happened, but she could not keep herself from it, once and then again. She screamed and writhed and danced to escape his ravaging fingers as he dragged her toward his own vessel.

Then something happened which stopped her struggles and caused him to abandon his attack. There was a great whooshing sound, like a wind rushing out of a cave, and a wall of flame erupted from Drakon's ship. There came a gentle lurching sensation at the same time; the lines had parted which held the two vessels together. The burning galley began to drift away and the flames shot out of it, lighting the scene like a thousand torches.

Drunk though they were, the corsairs recognized the danger. They rushed across the deck shouting alarms and contrary instructions; many plunged into the sea while trying to leap to the departing vessel.

As for Drakon, he had paused in his fleshly pursuits. He seemed to shake off the effects of the wine as he stared at his flaming ship. Aelia allowed herself the hope that he would release her to plunge after the stricken vessel, but that hope was a forlorn one. Drakon grunted as he lifted her in thick arms. He snatched her from her feet with a cry, dashed across the deck, and launched them both into the void between the two ships.

As for Palamon, all he could do was watch in horror as the two of them disappeared into the darkness. What was the raider chieftain doing? Was he killing them both in his drunkenness? The Prince struggled against his bonds insanely, clenched his teeth, strained, gasped with exertion as he chafed his arms until they were raw. But the cords held. And as the moments passed away, he realized it did not matter anymore; if Aelia were going to drown, she already was dead.

Palamon struggled on while the last of the corsairs scurried about the decks in confusion. Some leaped after their ship to try to save it from the billowing flames; others leaped because their fellows had leaped. A pair of beefy men hauled poor Chroma screaming from the sterncastle, cast her over the side, and leaped in after her, a sight which caused Palamon to begin his struggles all over again.

At last he was by himself on the deck, listening to the cries which floated up from the waters below him as well as the shouts from those who had reached their vessel. How many would drown or burn before morning? There had to be some who could not swim, not to mention others too besotted to cross the widening gap between the two ships. Would they be able to douse the flames before their vessel burned to the waterline? Those were hard questions, not because of the raiders' deaths they encompassed, but because the fate of the corsairs was now linked to the fates of the two women. What would become of them?

Then he had to think of himself. All the corsairs had not returned to their own vessel after all; there was one left, a dark, rangy fellow, who advanced on Palamon with a drawn dagger. His eyes were blazing and intent, like the eyes of a cat, and Palamon struggled helplessly in his bonds as the fellow came toward him.

All his struggles accomplished nothing, so Palamon waited for the blow, gazing at the fellow with a steady eye. But even as he watched, another head rose up behind the head of the assassin; a pair of hands clutched the man's shoulders and whirled him about. It was Flin, of all people. Flin, whom Palamon had thought killed when he had been swept over the side by the fighting. That explained the mysterious fire and the parting of the lines which had held the two vessels together.

Flin had no weapon but he struck the corsair a mighty blow, knocking him down, rolling him into the scuppers. Then he leaped to the *Spada Korrigaine* and grasped the handle. Palamon winced, expecting him to scream and let go, but Flin only leaped toward his opponent. He seemed to feel no pain at all; the great sword plainly took him as a friend. Though he could not wield it with Palamon's expertise, he performed well enough; the blade tore into the man's neck like an executioner's axe. The struggle was over.

Flin glanced about, set down the great weapon, and leaped to Palamon's side. "They've all gone, then," he said as he cut the tall prince's bonds. "The ruse worked better than I'd hoped." He helped Palamon up, then gestured toward the two-handed sword he had borrowed. "That's a very nice weapon, by the way. Very light. I thank you for the use of it."

Palamon smiled dryly. "Think nothing of it. I am very pleased it proved to be as useful as it did."

"I'm glad there was something lying about," Flin said. "I thought there'd be a neck or two to hack at before we got completely free of their company. Are you sure that fellow was the last one? Are they all gone?"

"They are. The women, too."

Flin's face fell. "The women? That's bad. I had hoped for better. I'd gladly have fought for the women."

"They bore them screaming to the deck, in hopes of taking liberties with them." Palamon grimaced as he rubbed his bleeding wrists. "Just then, the flames shot up. They all pursued their craft by leaping pell-mell to the shadowed waves, and with them cast my Aelia and the maid, poor Chroma. Whether life or death awaits the two of them's unknown to me. Oh, curse me for a coward! Rather than be captured and allow their capture, too, I should have let the corsairs hack my bones to dust."

Flin cast a surprised glance at Palamon. "What did you have to say about it? Hrusk knocked you out. It's pretty hard to fight when your skull's been bashed in with a timber, I should think."

Palamon glanced into Flin's face, then turned and staggered to the far rail. The corsair's galley had drifted away from the roundship, a horrible inferno of blazing rigging and wood; it glowed in the distance like a huge lantern. But it was not blazing the way it had; even as he watched, the flames flickered and died away, leaving only a moonlit horizon between himself and the careless sky. Had the ship burned or sunk or was it floating on with Aelia and Chroma aboard? Palamon stared into the emptiness. "Oh, Aelia, I will find you, come what may, to take you in my arms with bursting heart or lay your form to rest, washed by my tears."

Chapter Twelve:
The Empty Sea

PALAMON LEANED AGAINST the vessel's rail for a long time. It was hard to gather himself together. When at last he turned back to Flin, he saw the young warrior's smile had disappeared.

"I'm very sorry," Flin said. "Was she your wife?"

"No, she is not my wife. And Chroma's not our daughter. We were playing roles; we sought fair Berengeria, Carea's high Princess, a noble maid."

Flin looked confused. "Then what were you doing on this ship? The only things you could find on this hulk would be rats, lice, and welts."

Palamon smiled grimly. "Indeed, that seems as true as any word that's handed down by priest or oracle. For all of that, the tale is tangled up and far too long to lay before you now. This vessel must be made to take us to the Isle of Kolpos."

"That's a hard order for two men. And the wind has changed, too."

Flin was right, of course; it was a hard order. But if they did not act, the present wind would only blow them toward the southeast shores of the Thlassa Mey, where nothing but evil awaited them. Palamon clapped Flin on the back to get him moving, but they could adjust the vessel's square rigging only a little. Still, after a great deal of sweating and hauling on lines, they did manage to bring the clumsy mainsail a little closer to the wind. Then Palamon grasped the tiller and hauled on it to bring the ship around, to place the southern axis at his right hand so that he would be headed east. The vessel hardly responded at all; it would be a long, arduous task, this sailing. All he could do was cling to the tiller and hope for the best.

For his part, Flin tumbled below to the vessel's tiny galley to look for food in the officers' stores. That was one of the few benefits of seeing the vessel laid waste by raiders—there was plenty left to eat. If many of the officers had made it to the ship's longboat, and if they were still in sight by morning, things would grow troublesome—but for the time being, Flin would eat well. And so would his noble commander, for Flin had put himself at Palamon's disposal ever since the tall knight had freed him from the lash. He found roast lamb, bread, and cups, which he brought to the deck. There they supped on what he had found, washing it down with what was left of the wine brought on deck by the departed corsairs. After that, Flin felt better and noted that Palamon's spirits also seemed improved. Then, on orders from the older man, he returned to one of the officers' berths to sleep and await a summons. If nothing else, at least the day had been interesting.

Palamon stood at the tiller far into the night, staring at the stars, seeking the horizon. The night became clear and cold; the stars stared back at him as if painted onto the dark canopy above. And the ship barely responded to the tiller. It would be a long voyage; the vessel was built like any of its sisters, which meant it could do little more than sail directly before a breeze, even with a full crew. Palamon could not even be sure they were near the course Hrusk had charted at the beginning of the day. But he stared into the darkness and did what he could to direct the clumsy vessel toward Kolpos.

Palamon and Flin took turns at the tiller through the night, holding the ship's head as close as they could to the right course. When the sun rose, they both searched the horizons for some sign of land, but there was nothing to be seen except a red sun, a cloud-spattered sky, and an eternity of dancing waves. There was no land, and there were no other vessels.

Palamon frowned and glanced at his younger companion. "The longboat and the corsairs both have moved beyond the slight circumference of vision. Strange to say, this feeble, fickle breeze has borne apart the three craft, which all began their journeys from the self-same point."

"They might not be so far away. I'll climb the mast and look about." Flin vaulted into the shrouds and made the long climb to the vessel's dilapidated crow's nest, where he lingered for a long time, clinging to the mast and sweeping back and forth with the motion of the ship as he examined the horizons. Finally he shouted down, "I can see a ship."

"Which way?"

"Far to the northeast. It might be them."

"The corsairs or the officers?"

Flin paused. "The corsairs and your two women friends. It's too big to be the other boat and if there was a sail, I'd be able to see it. It must be them."

Palamon gripped the tiller anxiously. "What think you? Might we overhaul their craft? We have a sail; I saw their mast consumed by leaping flames."

Flin stared at the horizon for a long time before he replied. Then he shook his head; the motion was practically invisible from the deck. "They must have manned the oars. They're moving away at a steady pace and I can hardly see them now."

"Ah, curse them. Then enough survived the night to man their vessel, taking it away and with it both the women in my charge. Oh, Aelia, would that I could speak to you and ease my soul of many aimless fears."

Flin climbed down toward the deck. When he had reached a point three or four cubits above the oak timbers, he vaulted the rest of the way, rolling as he landed and popping to his feet before Palamon like some child's toy. He smiled as he spoke to the older man. "What news there is, is good. They must have been able to douse the fire; therefore your Aelia and Chroma might still be alive." He shrugged. "At least they weren't drunk."

Palamon remembered words spoken by Aelia a long time ago. Actually it had only been a few months but so many events had taken place since then that it seemed an eternity—at least a lifetime. "All those can swim who hail from Artos' shores." He barely whispered the words, as if they were something out of a dimly remembered play.

Flin looked at him. "Say what?"

Palamon smiled and shook his head. "It's nothing, though perhaps your words are true. And I've the right to hope that Aelia had as good a chance as any of those rogues to reach the refuge of the galley's decks. But Chroma's fate still weighs upon my soul."

Flin looked deeply into Palamon's eyes. The tall knight turned away from the younger man's stare; the fading of his smile indicated his agitation. But Flin was happy enough. "You're a human being," he said. "I can see in your face the real thoughts behind all your words, you know. By the look in your eyes when you mention your Aelia, I'd almost wager you could fly across these dimpled waves to her. You say she's not your wife; then is she your mistress?"

Palamon's expression dissolved into laughter. It was a picture so ghastly and insulting that it was funny; he could hardly picture Aelia as anyone's mistress. "My mistress? There's a thought that's strange and new. No, she is not my mistress, by my faith, nor wife, nor relative of any kind. We've known each other less than one full year and in that space have argued more than once."

"But you still love her."

Palamon shook his head and became serious. "I thought I knew that word and all it meant not very long ago. But now I find it is a term all nebulous and quaint and none may understand the realms beneath its sway."

"What do you mean?"

"I'd tell you if I knew."

Flin's eyes twinkled as if he were enjoying the conversation more than Palamon. He stepped back a pace or two and beamed. "I know all about love. It's the most pleasant pastime ever devised for recreation and improvement of the soul. It turns your mouth into an instrument of beautiful rhymes and music, it turns armor and weapons into the finest plumage since the peacock, and, if all goes well, it turns sweat into ambrosia."

"You love for your amusement, then?"

"I do."

Palamon nodded, then smiled with little mirth. "I tell you love was not among the games that I was taught while still an eager youth. When I at last found love, it wasn't by my choice and then my love turned out to be a sin. You say I love again; perhaps it's so. The more I see of love, the less I know."

"What's there to know?" Flin danced away a few steps, his feet bearing him lightly across the deck as if the very topic had lightened him, freed him of the earth's grip. He spread his arms, turned, and faced Palamon. "You woo a maid, you worship her perfection," he said, then added, "All maids are perfect in their own way, you know. But as I say, you woo her, you worship her, you pursue her, you tell her many fine things, all of which are true, at least when you say them. If she responds in kind, you love her. If she doesn't respond, you don't love her—so much the worse for her. But in most cases she does respond and as long as you love her, you live a life of music, joy, and bliss. That goes on for a fortnight or a month or two months; in either event, the next season will find you loving another."

The joy of Flin's youthful philosophy could not help but warm Palamon's expression. "With what shall she be left when you depart?"

Flin answered easily and carelessly. "Why, she's left with the wonderful memory that she once deserved a proper lover and she was once properly loved. And that's a joy she can carry with her into whatever marriage her father makes for her. After all, there's no love in marriage, you know. Husbands don't know how to love; only lovers know how to love."

Flin seemed so full of the elixir of life that no unbiased person could condemn him. Palamon's only answer was a short one: "Ah."

"Therefore, I tell you that love is a game, the simplest and most pleasant of all games, and even if you're not sure of your love for this Aelia, you should still love her for the practice. After we've saved her life—which we shall surely do in good time—you can either forget her and pursue another or you can go on loving her." He looked at Palamon with the air of a man sharing a great secret. "You always have a better chance with a woman after you've saved her life, you know."

Palamon looked at Flin for a long time, studying, never revealing the thoughts that lay behind his smile. At last he spoke. "And yet you told me two short days ago you loved the maid Bessina, daughter of the Count of Galliardy. You risked your life in order to return unto her arms. In this case you have broken your own rules."

Now it was Flin's turn to hesitate. He made a thoughtful sound, the same sound Palamon had made an instant before: "Ah."

"So by your own example, all the things you say concerning love are proven false."

"No, they're not."

Palamon tilted his head a bit, his smile playing about the corners of his mouth. "Indeed?"

"Certainly." Flin mused for a moment, then folded his arms behind his back like a philosopher postulating a theory. "My own case proves nothing simply because it's an exception. After all, there's no maiden in the world who can compare to my Bessina; the rules that apply to all the others can never apply to her because she's unique and shines as far above any other maiden as a goddess. It's as simple as a kiss."

Palamon nodded. "It doubtless is as simple as a kiss."

Flin paused again. "But your mind really is full of this Aelia of yours, true?"

Palamon shrugged. "Were I to have the past the way

I'd wish, I'd not have had her risk her life with me upon this mission."

"Your mission to find your Princess?"

Palamon studied Flin. How much did he really know about the dashing young warrior? Flin had shown his reliability; he had set fire to the corsairs' vessel and had saved Palamon's life. Besides, how far could any story travel from the decks of the deserted roundship? And even if it did, what could Alyubol or Lothar the Pale learn that they did not already know? After a silence, Palamon cleared his throat and began to speak.

He told the younger man of Alyubol's hatred for Berevald and of the deaths or loss of Berevald's five children, of which Palamon himself was the eldest. He told of the capture of Berengeria and the escape from Pomfract Castle in Buerdaunt and how he, Ursid, and Aelia had made the perilous journey with her to her homeland. And he finished by telling how Berengeria and Ursid, nephew to Lothar the Pale, had once again been captured by Alyubol's agents, prompting the present mission.

When the tale was done, there could be no doubt it had captured Flin's imagination. "By the very gods," he exclaimed. "Such a life you've lived, you and your sister and this Aelia I've barely met. These are the things that minstrels make songs of, the kinds of tales bards tell when they enchant ears at hearths and firesides in palaces across the world. It's the stuff legends are made from."

"Indeed," Palamon said dryly. "But if our lives are fable's meat, it is an honor which I gladly would forgo."

They talked a long time. They talked of things large and small. They observed one another and grew accustomed to each other's manners and movements. Palamon found Flin to be full of the charm and grace of youth; besides, the young warrior had proven his valor and his sometimes naive enthusiasm was pleasant to behold. And among other things, Flin told the older knight of the women he had known, doing it in such an unassuming, pleasant manner that it caused neither rancor nor distaste.

There could be no doubt—to Flin, success in love came as easily and naturally as success at angling or with the dice. He dealt with his own conquests casually and mentioned them only in passing, as if love was indeed the simplest and most pleasant of pastimes, something to be anticipated, enjoyed, and finished with all the empty good humor of a day on the tilting grounds. Still, Palamon noticed something interesting in all this; all he needed to do was insert the name of Bessina into the conversation and Flin would stumble and pause to rearrange his thoughts. The change was always slight but it was there. She did not fit into the young warrior's scheme of things; she was a disease from which he seemed to wish no cure.

At one point, Flin turned the strategy against Palamon. With a sly look in his eyes, he said, "But what of this Lady Aelia? You tell me you don't know of love, that it's an unknown quantity to you. But I can see things in your eyes which deny every word. I'll tell you this—while you may be a stranger to love, it's no stranger to you."

Palamon considered that statement, then he smiled and shrugged. "The feelings which she stirs are like a cloud of butterflies and hummingbirds and moths. They eddy through my soul without a pause, and what I make of them I cannot say."

"Who was this love you spoke of once? You told me something about a love that turned into a sin—I can't imagine love and sin going together. Tell me about it."

Palamon's smile soured a bit; the tiniest corner of his mouth curled unpleasantly. "'Twas nothing."

"'Twas something, or you'd not have mentioned it."

"Perhaps."

Flin's gaze was full of mixed respect and amusement. "For all your prowess at battle, that prowess doesn't extend to the ballroom and the garden and the boudoir, does it? If I asked you about tournaments, you'd tell me of your victories like another man describing his shoes. Can you deny it?"

Palamon shrugged.

Flin smiled happily as he spoke and thought. "It's so and we both know it. But it's also true that the conquest of a woman's heart is a far easier and less dangerous goal than victory in tournament or on the field of honor."

"There are no easy victories."

"You think too much. You may be wiser than me but still you think too much. You wouldn't need so much wisdom except for that."

Palamon burst out laughing. Flin's statement, airy and nonsensical though it was, did contain a sort of mad truth; it helped break the tension which bound the tall Prince's insides. "Indeed, indeed, it's true. I think too much."

"And you think about love?"

Palamon shrugged. "Some questions sometimes pop into my brain."

"So there it is. You can't ask questions about love. You have to act."

"As I have said, I know not what is love, and even if I knew, it's not assured that I would find it pleasant to my taste. This conversation drags."

Flin put up his suntanned arms. "No, no. Either you're in love or you're not, and since you're a man and the normal state of any man is to be in love with someone, I say you are. You don't seem to be the type to be in love with yourself, so you must be in love with a maiden, namely this Aelia, this slender, willful woman. You're in a bad way because you're in love without knowing it."

Palamon sighed but did not respond. He watched Flin's ponderings and all he could do was shake his head.

All at once Flin stood and clapped his heads. "I have it. You have to write her a letter. You have to put down all your feelings." He leaped toward the sterncastle, then paused to add another statement. "I warrant you've not told her how you feel. Don't answer, I know you haven't. A few women will bring their love to you and all you have to do is smile and agree and accept the gift. But it's not that way with many. You can't woo a maiden without telling her you love her; for all your wisdom, you've overlooked that detail."

Then Flin vanished into the sterncastle, to return a moment later with ink, a quill, and a page torn from the vessel's log. "You have to write a letter to your Aelia and tell her all your feelings. You see, since I'm comfortable with maidens, I have no need of writing any more than a bird needs a ladder. But since you think so much, you need to write your thoughts down. When a fellow doesn't know what to do with all of his own thoughts, the first thing he'd better do is put them onto parchment. Write everything down and give her the letter; that lets you use all the best words. It's easy." Flin proffered him the writing materials.

Palamon sighed again. Were it not for Flin's natural charm, the youth's enthusiasm about helping Palamon's love life would have become impossibly taxing. As it was, the Prince extended a scar-tracked arm and allowed Flin to push the implements into his hand. He looked at them with little enthusiasm and turned the vial of ink in his fingers. His lips curled into a wry expression.

"Go ahead, write," Flin said. "Let me take the tiller for awhile and you can put down whatever comes into your head. That's the wondrous thing about letters—if you don't like what you've written, you tear it up and write it over. Spoken words go out untested to fly or fall without another chance."

Relinquishing the tiller, Palamon walked across the deck and threw himself down near the rail, eyeing the blank paper like a man contemplating a slime-crusted gutter which had to be cleaned. "Go ahead, write," he heard Flin's voice from behind him. The Prince drummed his fingers for a moment, then broke open the vial, dipped the quill, and tried to produce words.

He hardly knew where to begin; there were so many thoughts, so many questions, and so many doubts. For want of a better idea, he began to put lines down on the paper in the same form he used in offering prayers to his patron, Pallas. It was slow going. The thoughts emerged from the end of his pen with great difficulty; it was hard to make them align themselves in the proper meter, and they rhymed only after long thought and consideration. He formed them into a statement of fourteen lines directed toward Aelia, whose name he had scrawled at the top of the page.

He finally stopped and read over what he had written. What he read disgusted him; he had said nothing which could be of interest to anyone. He had put down doubts, questions, apprehensions, anything but the proper contents of a love letter. The entire project was a catastrophe. He read the piece over once more, then made a sour face and let it fall to the deck. How could something which took so long to produce say so little? It was shallow, it was unoriginal, and it was hardly a letter which would impress a woman like Aelia.

The breeze caught the piece of paper, carried it a little way, and deposited it on the deck midway between Flin and Palamon. Flin looked down at it, and curiosity lit up his features, but before he could succumb to the temptation to pick it up, the Prince rose, crossed the deck, and retrieved it himself. "Nay, nay, my lad," Palamon said. "It wasn't in our pact for you to read the missive I produced."

Flin nodded, smiling a bit guiltily as far as Palamon was concerned. "I'll admit I was curious. Was it a good letter?"

"'Twas offal."

"Then write another. I'll get you more paper if you'd like."

"No paper's needed; this is not a game which holds my interest." Palamon smiled dryly. "I'll keep this note to save me from the sin of hubris, should I sometime come to think myself too wise."

And the conversation ended. No urging by Flin would make Palamon reconsider; at last the young warrior dropped the subject. Besides, night fell, and darkness and appetite precluded further epistolary pursuits. The night was long and tedious, with little progress shown by stars or passing clouds. The wind strengthened but it still blew from the northwest. Their progress could only be slight and was probably in the wrong direction. The two men took turns manning the tiller throughout the night, doggedly keeping the ship's head pointed east in spite of their lack of progress.

When dawn finally cast her golden robes across the Thlassa Mey, it was Flin who stood at the tiller while Palamon slept restlessly. As the darkness transformed itself into the colors of the day, the horizon gradually became the dancing line which one would expect to see between sea and sky. But in one place that line was interrupted; off the vessel's starboard side lay a jagged strip, lighter in color than the sea. "Land," Flin shouted. "I see land off to the south. We've arrived someplace."

He shouted again and Palamon responded. "Is it Kolpos?"

"I don't think so. It's in the wrong direction."

Palamon rushed to the deck and peered anxiously over the rail. As he looked at the southern horizon, his face fell. "Indeed, it's not. I know the land we've reached; one time before I viewed it from the sea. I know the contour of those sandy shores, the current, and the way the cliffs fall back. We've reached the Cauldron of the Stilchis, lad, from whose expanses no man may escape."

Chapter Thirteen:
Bessina's Journey

BESSINA AWOKE. THE first sensation she felt was the throbbing of her swollen ankle, though it was better than it had been the day before. She was lying in the loft of Peristeràs' house, in a cot with a straw mattress. The air was cold; the season's first hard frost had come and every breath she released hung before her, accenting the dark rafters overhead.

This was to be her day of rest before she would start out for Sparth's Head Castle. Peristeras had told her more than once that her role was to remain abed, to let her ankle heal as much as possible before evening. Then she would have to leave.

So she snuggled beneath the covers, allowing them to protect her from the chill autumn air the way the womb protects the baby. She had not been so comfortable since before the King's knights had sacked her father's castle— and taken him to his doom; that thought ended her pleasure. Her father was dead. The thought assaulted her, overwhelmed her, made her sick and weak. She had loved her father—every daughter loved her father—and she would have found a way to obtain his freedom if he had been allowed to live. She was filled with emptiness; her body ached with the loss.

She pulled her right hand from beneath the coverlet and examined the ring Peristeras had given her the night before. It was mute; it held no comfort for her. She read the inscription: "I, Parthelon, by all the gods' good grace, am Emperor across the Thlassa Mey. My powers issue from the deities; when evil threatens, I shall speak for them." The ring was ancient, priceless; she had no idea how Peristeras could have come by it. He had to have total faith in his sooth to part with such a valuable artifact, to give it to a stranger. But she did not feel as if fate had singled her out for anything. She felt lonely, uprooted, pursued, but in no way magical or even special.

Her thoughts were interrupted by the sound of someone working in the garden. Curious, she sat up on the edge of the cot, then hopped toward the little window which admitted all the light that managed to find its way into the loft. The pane of glass was thick and crudely blown, but she was able to make out the figure of Omo the servant. He was wearing a heavy fur robe and was digging a hole.

Her mind returned to the evening before and the old man's familiar or demon or angel or whatever it had been; his op, he had called it. It had died. The Moirae filling the cellar room had been too much for it, it seemed, or— what had the soothsayer's words been—had it simply fulfilled its mission?

As she watched, the mute servant climbed from the hole and Peristeras bore from the cottage the dark form which had so terrified her. There was no terror to it now; whatever spirit it had contained had departed with the life force. While she watched, the elderly man passed the creature to Omo, who gently laid it to rest. Then the mute picked up the spade to fill in the hole. There was no ceremony, no words, only an interval of silence; it was as if a mere pet had died and been disposed of. The old man did not stay to watch the burial. He sighed once and turned toward the cottage. A moment later she could hear him climbing the ladder toward the loft.

"Good morning," he said to her as his head appeared above the rough pine flooring. Then his face turned grave as he saw her standing beside the window. "That is not a wise pursuit. Your ankle ne'er shall mend if walked upon."

"I'm sorry. But I've put no pressure on it." To demonstrate, she hopped one-legged back to the cot and sat down. She was no longer afraid of him; he hardly seemed the same man who had toyed with the supernatural only a few hours before. In fact, the change which had come over him was disturbing. He seemed small, shrunken, and dried up; he looked as if death was upon him, as if he should hardly even be able to stand. Her mouth was stopped by the sight of him, although she finally did manage to produce some words. "You look unwell this morning."

"The Moirae have withdrawn their strengths from me. My power's gone and life will follow it; I'm like the silver salmon which has spent his mystic strength and beauty to ascend the torrent. Once he spreads his seed, his destiny's fulfilled, and all the prowess falls away. He rots the while he swims, his body dies, his flesh deserts him, though he clings to life; it putrifies while still upon his bones. He slips into an eddy by the shore and welcomes death. So shall it be for me.

"You do not know the power of the Fates. They have manipulated your green life the way five digits operate a glove. Your life and mine, the green and brown, are brought together to a single end—to save the world from evil's conquest. You will play the crucial role, you and the ring."

It was a frightening and troubling speech. Bessina did not like the thought of being a pawn of the Moirae, some tool of the Fates. She was Bessina, only Bessina, no more and no less. "But what's the consequence of this one ring?"

The soothsayer hesitated; the conversation was visibly draining him. "I cannot say for sure. The legends say three artifacts were placed into the hands of Parthelon by the three virgin goddesses we know as Pallas, Hestia, and Actaea, who rule the soul, the home, the verdant world. That ring is one of those three artifacts. Some horrid evil threatens to arise, although my scrying does not specify its nature. I had long suspected it and knew that I would somehow play a part in its defeat. But you are bound up by the Fates still more than I, although you do not take your sustenance from them." He paused again. Bessina could see the sweat glistening on his forehead.

"But I digress," he went on. "The ring must be returned to Sparth's Head Castle to be joined with both the other mystic treasures. That's your role. And when you've finished with that journey, then you shall be told just who and what you are."

"And what of you?"

He shook his head. "I do not matter, for I doubt that I shall see two sunsets more. My role is played—I kept the artifact and passed it to its chosen courier."

The thought of the soothsayer's death filled Bessina with infinite sadness. Indeed, he was like the beautiful, mystical creature he had described; life was deserting him before her very eyes. There was too much death in the world. Her face fell and she stifled a sob.

He smiled, plainly touched by her display of emotion. "You need not grieve for me; I've lived the span of more than one full life. The point to which we must address our thoughts is that you must reach Sparth's Head Castle soon, and with that ring in your possession." He pointed to Bessina's right hand.

She glanced down at the bauble once more. "Indeed, and how much time remains to me?"

"Two days, a week, two weeks, I do not know," he said. "The only course is that you get there soon and then remain until it comes to pass."

"What comes to pass?"

"I do not know." With that he left her. The servant brought her breakfast, then was sent to the village to buy the items she would need for her journey. When evening came she dined once more, dressed in the heavy traveling gown and cape that had been purchased for her, and accepted a satchel full of biscuits, dried meat, a flask of wine, and other items she might need. With a sad expression, the soothsayer also handed her a small dagger, the blade of which slid back into the ornate handle and secured with a clasp. "I hope the need for this does not arise," he said. "But still one must prepare for what might come. You are a strong young maid; it's to be hoped your heart is stout."

"I think it is," she said, hesitating to leave him. But she knew she had to begin her journey. He knelt and prayed for her soul and her success. He invoked Hestia, Pallas, and Actaea, virgin goddesses of the heart, the soul, and the forest, along with the rest of the accepted deities. Then he placed his hands about her hands and gazed for a moment into her striking green eyes. "The gods be with you," he said. "I shall pray for you from now until the final moments."

She thanked him, then turned and walked into the darkness. She took the path which led from the cottage door and favored her injured ankle by leaning all she could on her walking staff. She felt alone, more alone than she had ever felt in her life, even more alone than she had felt when the King's soldiers had hauled her from her quarters in the middle of the night. That had been a long night, indeed, and though only a few days had passed since then, she felt as if she had been an orphan for ages.

And this night would also be a long night; the first twinges from her sprain told her that much. But she hurried along as quickly as she could, away from the Douzainium and toward the little village of Cos, which stood dark and quiet beneath the sympathetic stars. A road—or path, rather—paralleled the stream through the village and beyond, but she avoided the village itself, returning to the beaten track only once she was safely past the last dwelling. She did not want to meet anyone who might delay her pilgrimage.

Her progress slowed as the night wore on; her ankle swelled up and each step became an ordeal. She paused and rewrapped the injured member in the darkness but that only helped a little. At last she had to stop. The agony of each step would let her go no farther.

She was a couple of leagues from the cottage by this time, far enough from any byways to avoid detection. She found a sleeping place in the midst of a clump of bramble bushes, pulled her cape about her shoulders, and closed her eyes. After what seemed to be a long time, she drifted into a fitful sleep.

She awoke several times; each time she looked about to see that the sky was still star-spangled and dark and that the bushes were still draped in shadow. Then she slept once more. But at last she awoke to the sounds of small birds twittering. Day had come; hoarfrost covered the grass and bushes and there were even patches of it on her cape. She shivered and cursed the cold, and she would have lit a small fire if the stiffness in her joints had not kept her from such an enterprise.

It was all madness. The journey through unfamiliar forests and along unknown roads to a place she had only heard of was the height of folly, all done at the behest of an eccentric old man, ecclesiastic though he might have been. For that matter, no prudent woman would travel anywhere across the Greenlands alone. The rolling grass-lands and forests were infested by more than their share of brigands, bandits, and highwaymen. The greatest among these was Flin's own Red Company, a militia of dis-charged knights and unemployed mercenaries which was more powerful than the armies of some Counts. They even held castles and extracted rents from the tenants of the occupied lands. Still, she did not fear the Red Company. Even renegade knights had their sense of gallantry, and besides, she knew her relationship with dashing Flin would make his companions her allies. Perhaps he was already back with them and awaiting his chance to rejoin her; that thought made her tingle.

But the highwaymen were less gallant. She would have to avoid them. Peristeras had given her a purse full of gold and silver; once she had traveled a suitable distance, she could at least hope to purchase lodging each night. That would minimize the risk of attack. But that lay in

the future; for now, legal authority was as much a threat
to her freedom as any outlaw.

She lay beneath her cape with her head barely sticking
out, wondering how she had begun such a trek. She
watched her breath float out on the autumn morning's air,
then fade away like a maiden's dreams; she really was
insane to be taking such a journey. She clasped the dark-
dyed wool to her and, as she did so, she felt the ring. It
soothed her; it was the only real reason she had for her
actions now, the link between Peristeras' visions and the
real world.

All at once she heard something. It was not the birds
or squirrels, for they had all become silent. It was the
sound of feet treading through the leafstrewn forest. Half
the summer quota of leaves still remained on the bramble bushes which surrounded her—but the footsteps
approached and she felt as naked as a man standing before
a gibbet.

Two sets of feet were making the footsteps; even though
she did not dare look, she could tell that much by the
sounds of the crunching leaves. She tried to be as silent
as a fawn as she reached for her dagger, pulled it from
her girdle, and extended the blade. They would not take
her without a struggle. Then she thought about the ring;
they could take her coin, her food, whatever, but she
could not give up the ring. She took it off, held it in her
hand, and pondered. Should she place it in her girdle?
No, they would find it there and it might encourage them
to search further.

She lay silently, feeling vulnerable and alone, listening
as the footsteps stopped. Then she heard a voice, a man's
voice. "Where can they be? We were supposed to meet
them below Hades' Spire."

"Maybe they're not here yet," the second voice said.

"I hope the provost didn't catch them."

"That's impossible." The second voice was indignant.
"He's not smart enough to catch them, or us, or any of
the band."

"I hope." There was a pause, then the first voice made

an exclamation. "There. Over there, I saw something move."

Bessina stared at the ring for less than an instant. Then, acting on impulse, she popped it into her mouth, gagged a couple of times, and swallowed. Waves of pain and nausea flowed from it as it forced its way down her gullet. She gasped with the sensation, which was made all the more horrible by the certain knowledge that a rough hand was about to seize her by the hair and yank her to her feet.

But the hand did not come. The footsteps moved away, down the slope toward the stream, and she heard shouting. "Halloa, halloa, Theudo. We're well-met."

There were more voices, more footsteps, then the entire band moved away until Bessina could hear no more. But she still lay silently, thanking the gods for allowing her to remain hidden, swallowing against the agony which flamed along her throat, cursing herself for her panic-prompted folly. Had she poisoned herself? Would she ever be able to eat a normal meal again? Would the ring pass through her body or would it remain inside her, corrupting her from within as punishment for mistreating Parthelon's treasured artifact?

She would have given anything for a drink; a drink would at least have made her throat feel better. But she did not dare move. There were at least four men in the party—more than enough to overcome one maiden with a dagger—and she did not know how far away they had gone. So she lay on the cold, leafy ground, swallowed, and listened. After an eternity, she summoned the courage to peek out of her hiding place. Gone were thoughts of the cold air and the stiffness of her joints; she was poised, ready for action. However many there were, they would not take her without a struggle.

But there was no one to be seen; the forest was as empty as a cathedral on the morning after the sabbath. A stone pinacle, doubtless the "Hades' Spire" one of them had mentioned, jutted up on the far side of a nearby stream but all the voices had gone. They had surely been robbers; after all, they had discussed being apprehended by the provost of the district. She rose to her knees and fetched the wine flask from her satchel; there could be no better time than the present to sample its contents.

She gulped down the flame-colored liquid and each swallow both soothed and nettled the path the ring had taken. The wine filled her with warmth that was followed by a heady giddiness, and she sent after it a couple of biscuits which also went down with much pain, though less than she had feared. That was the extent of her breakfast; she avoided the dried meat.

Then she rose, shouldered the sachel, grasped her walking stick, and set out. Her ankle throbbed more than it had the day before but she could see the ground now that it was daylight. She was able to use her staff to its full advantage, allowing it to support her with such growing skill that before long she was hardly placing any weight at all on her injury.

As the sun climbed above the trees to the east, her spirits rose with it. The chill went from the air, the stream danced and sparkled downhill from her. Breezes made the fallen leaves caper at her feet. The sky was clear and blue; it had become a glorious autumn day. Her journey no longer seemed as hopeless or as purposeless as it had seemed earlier.

There was no telling which way the bandits had traveled; after all, she had never even dared take a peek at them. But that would not matter. Whether on foot or on horseback, there was no reason they should not easily outdistance her, which meant they were no longer to be feared. With all the resiliency of her seventeen summers, she began to recover from the shocks of the last week. She was on a mission approved by a soothsayer, the autumn day was fresh and beautiful, and she felt like whistling a tune. If only she could have had her father and Flin beside her, reconciled to one another, the world would have been perfect.

By noon the exertion of her walk had caused her to break into a sweat. She looked down at the stream with covetous eyes; a drink of that crystal-clear water would be most welcome. Ahead of her the forest was thick and heavy all the way to the streamside; what better place could there be to stop, drink, and rest awhile?

So she did. She sat on a flat rock, unwrapped her ankle, and allowed the sweaty skin to kiss the air for awhile before she rewrapped it again. Then she stretched out her legs, sighed, and eyed the water. At last she knelt upon a stone and cupped her hands to draw the sweet liquid to her mouth. She drank several handfuls, swallowing the stream water with joy as it swept away the soreness in her throat. Then above the sound of the scurrying waters, she heard another sound.

"Is the water good to drink?"

Chapter Fourteen:
Bandits

STARTLED, BESSINA LOOKED up to see a rough young man gazing at her, his features twisted into an ugly smirk. His beard was short but untrimmed, his clothing was ragged and worn from hard usage, and a longsword glinted in the hanger at his waist. There could be no doubt he was a bandit. Her stomach shriveled to a little ball and her pulse raced; she leaped to her feet and tried to run from the fellow, reaching for her dagger as she went.

But her injured ankle betrayed her. She fell with a shriek, sent the water flying, and bruised herself against sharp stones as she landed. The man was on her like a spider, pinning her down and groping for her hands. Even as she touched the hilt of her dagger, he pulled her hand outside her cape and twisted it behind her back. "Alan," he cried. "Theudo, Scrugg, come and see what I've caught."

He was strong and heavy for all his ragged appearance; it was all Bessina could do to keep her nostrils above water. Her greatest efforts could not begin to dislodge him. She heard the sounds of feet crashing through the

146

brush above the stream, then another voice answered her captor's shout.

"A girl. You've caught a girl. Don't just lie there on top of her, lad; bring her up here and we'll have a look at her."

"I'd do it, but she's struggling like a lynx. She'll tear my eyes out if I let her up."

The other laughed a rough-edged cackle. "Alan, get down there and give him a hand. We don't want her to hurt him."

There was more splashing, a second pair of hands grasped Bessina's free arm, and she was jerked to her feet, half drowned and raining water. They hauled her to the bank. There were four of them, all of them ragged and nasty looking. The leader was the oldest; in fact he was as old as her father.

That worthy looked her up and down and whistled. "A rare bird have we here. I've seen sunsets, clear lakes, and firesides, lass, but if I were a minstrel I'd earn my bread by singing about your face forever. As sure as my name's Theudo, I'd have plowed a field and stayed home all my days if my woman had had a tenth of your beauty." The wonder in his eyes relaxed as he smiled. "These lads of mine, they're too young to appreciate a looker like you. That's too bad. But business is business for all that. Let's have her purse, Scrugg. Look lively, now."

The fourth bandit stepped forward, beaming at his task. For all of Theudo's words about how only he appreciated her beauty, Bessina knew the young man before her at least appreciated the opportunity. His hands fumbled here and there for an eternity before they settled on the purse Peristeras had given her. After further orders from the leader, Scrugg removed the little pouch from her girdle. But his preoccupation with her curves had produced one good result; he had neglected to search her carefully and her dagger remained concealed upon her person.

Theudo beamed as Scrugg showed him the purse. "Ah, a nice little prize. Heavy? That's good. But let's get her up to the camp so we can count coin and see what we want to do with her." He turned and started up the hill, picking up her satchel as he went.

The other two released her but they drew their long-swords as a silent warning for her not to attempt escape. As a matter of fact, flight was out of the question; she had all she could do even to walk. "I know what I want to do with her," the youngest one said, the one who had seen her first. "You three divide the purse; I just want her."

"Now don't let's be hasty," Theudo said with a snicker. "You wouldn't have thought more of her than any village tearsheet if I hadn't mentioned it first. Now you want to put on airs. By the gods, I'm sorry I said anything."

"We can all have her together," another offered. "Then when we're tired of her, we can set her free."

"Or kill her," the last man chortled.

They reached the camp; a fire burned, a pair of horses nuzzled the grass, and blankets and cooking utensils littered the ground. The leader turned and raised a hand. "The first thing you'll do is bind her. The second is listen to me before I have to knock some heads together." He paused while Alan rummaged through a bag for a length of cord and bound Bessina's wrists behind her back. "Let's talk to her a bit. What's your name, lass? What's the reason you're traveling alone in these forests? Don't you know it's dangerous?"

Bessina could barely force a reply. "I'm on a pilgrimage."

"To where?"

Bessina hesitated, wondering if she should explain her mission to such men. She was glad she had swallowed the ring; at least they could not take that from her, short of killing her and ripping her open. She shrugged, sighed, then spoke. "To Sparth's Head Castle."

Theudo waved a hand. "You don't want to go there; they say the place is haunted. That was the refuge of the Great Emperor, after all, and it's said his ghost still wanders the battlements and sings in the galleries. No more of that. Where do you come from?"

"The refuge, the Douzainium."

The four of them exchanged glances. "A virgin, then," Alan said with a smile.

"Not necessarily," Theudo replied. "There's many a wench in there that gave her favors easily enough before she got religion. But for all that, I doubt this lass is one of them. She's well-spoken and you can tell she's a lady just by her words. And we all know she's a beauty." He pondered silently a moment, then spoke again. "But open the purse and pour it onto the ground. Let's see what she carries."

It was done in an instant; they ripped the little leather pouch open and threw the gold and silver coins onto the ground. Each coin shone a different shade in the sunlight. There was no fortune, but it was a large enough sum, and the four of them exchanged whistles. "Well, well," Theudo said. "We've done a good day's work already."

Meticulously, with the air of a man who could barely count but who could still do better than his fellows, he crouched over the coins and divided the loot between the four of them; each took a share without grumbling. Then he stood again and rubbed his beard while he pondered Bessina. "We've done a good day's work. We have done that. But I think you're worth a deal more yourself than this purse you carry. There are men in this land, rich men, who would pay for your company."

Scrugg laughed. "We can't start a bagnio with just one woman, Theudo. Besides, that's not our line of work."

"You don't understand me, you idiot. I'm not talking about making her into a trull; she's more valuable going to a single customer who has a lot of money." He looked at Bessina again. "Where does your family come from?"

"I'm the daughter of the Count of Galliardy."

Theudo's face fell and the breath whooshed between his chapped lips. "I don't know whether to believe that or not. Would he pay a ransom for you, I wonder? If he's so fond of you, what were you doing at the Douzainium?"

Bessina hesitated. It seemed as if the stupid questions would go on forever. "My father's dead, for he was murdered by the King and royal bailiff of Buerdaunt."

"Then you're an orphan." Theudo clapped his hands

and laughed. "Or as good as one, at any rate. I still don't know whether I believe you but it doesn't matter. An overthrown Count's no good for a ransom; his money's already subscribed. I still like my first plan." He was speaking to his fellows more than to Bessina by this time. "I know a trader in the city. He doesn't deal in leather goods or clocks or wool or linen; he deals in information. If I don't miss my guess we can take her with us and sell her for enough to keep us comfortable for a long time." He looked back at Bessina. "How would you like to live in a palace again, Countess?"

Bessina did not reply; she could only glare.

"She doesn't seem pleased. If a palace doesn't attract her, maybe she's telling the truth. In any event we'd better be off, lads. Break up this pitiful camp and we'll be on our way to make our fortune."

And so it was done; the vagabonds swept up their few possessions, heaved the goods onto their two horses, and set off. It quickly became obvious that Bessina's injury would hamper them, so they placed her astride one of their mounts, tied her hands behind her back more tightly than ever, and continued their journey. They traveled quickly, considering two of them had to walk. Bessina could not tell their destination; the country through which they passed was wild and unfamiliar and they kept away from all roads and settlements. After a day and a night, Theudo left them; he climbed onto a horse with terrible threats against any of the band who disturbed the prisoner during his absence. The night which followed was not an easy one for Bessina. Despite their leader's warning, the three men took all the liberties they dared, sometimes in the guise of jokes, sometimes with cruel insolence. It was awful. But during the same night Bessina regained the ring of Parthelon, not without a good deal of fear and suffering, cleaned it, and tucked it into her girdle to hide it as well as she could beneath the thick cloth.

By morning she was more exhausted than she had been when the night had begun. It was with relief that she saw Theudo returning through the trees, singing at the top of his lungs, carrying a quantity of provisions. He dismounted and it was instantly plain that he was drunk: he was roaring drunk, enthusiastically drunk, and brimming with prophesies of the wealth they would gain by selling the captive. "Then where is it?" demanded the thief called Alan. "Show us some of the money."

"You blind knave, I don't have it yet. I haven't a farthing. I had to pay a commission for the information I have. But don't fear. The money'll be there, though we have to travel to get it." He looked serious. "You haven't touched the girl?"

The three filled the air with their protestations. They appeared to fear Theudo even when he was in his cups.

"That's good," he said. "She's too valuable to be trifled with by the likes of you." He continued with his plan and his voice grew ever lower as the liquor of avarice gradually displaced the cheap wine in his bloodstream. Bessina listened hard but she could not make out all he was saying. All she could understand was that he had found a man in another city who catered to the whims of some of the highest nobility in the land. "A hundred talents in gold," Theudo's voice rose as he named the sum; Bessina had no difficulty understanding that part of his tale. The talk dragged on, accompanied by exclamations, oaths, or simple drunken giggles as Theudo shared his wine flask along with his wisdom. His faith in his own ability to contact the noble procurer was absolute; he and his companions all seemed sure their fortunes had been made.

They broke camp and traveled in a southerly direction, moving by night as the lands they crossed became ever more thickly settled. Days passed. At least they began to treat Bessina with more respect than they had shown before her value had gone up; no more hands casually rested in intimate positions, no more bodies pressed against hers. She was treated as a valuable cargo; the change was startling and pleasant. The brigands became so concerned with preserving her value that they treated her almost with the deference of attendants, which was very good; she had no difficulty holding onto her secret dagger and her ring, both of which she kept tucked safely away in her clothing. And the less she was mauled and handled, she knew, the greater were her chances of retaining both possessions.

They camped beside a stream before dawn one morning and, to Bessina's surprise, the four men bathed. She rubbed her fingers along her grimy arms and watched jealously as they washed layers of filth into the stream, cleaned their clothes, and Theudo even produced a new jerkin from one of the bags. It was all done amid considerable joking and good humor. Finally, long after sunup, the leader departed.

He returned in the afternoon and this time Bessina was left completely out of their councils; there was no doubt something big was up. The camp filled up with a strange tension, as if her captors were dealing with forces that were both mysterious and frightening to them. For her part, Bessina's spirits sank ever lower. At least she still had her dagger; if the den of depravity into which she was being cast became too horrible to bear, the dagger would provide the ultimate answer—if only she would have the courage to use it.

The sun descended behind the trees; golden threads of twilight filtered through the brigand camp. Alan, the youngest outlaw, was standing sentry duty. Bessina sighed; she was nearly dozing. Then a high-pitched whistle caused her to lift her head. Theudo stood and looked toward the west, then signaled the other men to rise also. "They're coming," he said.

Someone was indeed coming. Alan appeared first, whispered to the others, and pointed back the way he had come. Then a party entered the clearing. A dozen stout men bore a pair of litters, though Bessina could tell from the way they moved that one litter was empty. They were hard-eyed men; they carried weapons and stared at the brigands with stern expressions and superior gazes as they lowered their burdens.

There was a stirring at the curtains of the heavier litter and a figure emerged wearing a black robe, the hood of which covered his face with shadow. And not with shadow only; on looking more closely, Bessina could see the stranger also wore a veil across his face. His jealousy of his identity was obvious.

Theudo gestured sheepishly toward Bessina, hardly daring to meet the gaze of the newcomer. "There she is, and a beauty to look upon, isn't she? She's a bit dirty from the travel, I grant that. We would have had her wash up but we were afraid to leave her to herself, you know."

"I understand." The stranger's voice was cultured, level, although a bit too high-pitched. And there was something strangely familiar about it, something Bessina could not place. She shrank before him as he approached. "It seems unwise to give a richly feathered warbler such as this undue encouragement to spread her wings and risk her beauty in adventurous flight. Her kind was meant for keeping within doors and far from injury or blemish."

Bessina felt as if she were lying naked before the man, as if the invisible eyes had the power to peer through her clothing as easily as normal eyes through a bottle. She unconsciously covered herself by folding her arms, even though she was still fully dressed. Ever since she had been a girl, she had taken pride in a beauty which had been remarked across the countryside. Even when she had been in her early teens, she had listened and laughed joyously at tales which came back to her about peasants claiming her hair could set a man's flesh aflame with one touch or that her green eyes could devour a man's soul as easily as a child eating a wafer. She had laughed at such stories, but she had also taken hidden pleasure in them and had done nothing to quell them. Now she wished she had been born awash in a sea of warts, if that could have removed the shrouded gaze from her.

To her relief, he finally turned away and spoke to Theudo. "Now, to callous facts," he said, folding his arms and gazing at the bandit leader. "How many talents do you seek to gain by yielding up this precious creature to my care?"

Theudo shrugged uneasily. "Indeed, indeed, my Lord, she's a great beauty. We took great risks in capturing her and went to a lot of trouble to bring her here. We think she's worth at least..." He shrugged, spread his hands, cleared his throat. "A hundred and fifty talents?"

One of the other bandits whistled but the dark-robed man did not seem taken aback. "The sum is not beyond considering; still, I doubt you really have the need for such enormous wealth. This maid is far too fair for us to haggle o'er her buying price as if she were a goat or sporting wench. A hundred talents will I let you have, or none, for I can take her by main strength. The choice is yours."

Theudo quailed before the hooded man's cool, high-pitched voice. But a hundred talents was a great sum; he was obviously pleased by it and afraid of what might happen if he tried to bargain further. He beamed stupidly and gazed more at the ground than at the stranger; then he laughed a self-conscious laugh. "I suppose you're right. We're all poor farm boys, really, and I'm sure we might not know what to do if you paid us too much..."

The stranger silently interrupted Theudo by pulling a heavy purse from the folds of his robe and casting it at the outlaw's feet. While the brigands clustered about their leader, the dark lord approached Bessina and offered a gloved hand. "Now rise you up, my maid; you have no cause for fear. I say your hands shall not be bound; I'll not restrict your limbs in any way. You shall be borne within that litter's shade as if you were a monarch's only daughter. Still, you must remember that you *are* my property; should you attempt escape, your punishment will be severe, indeed. Tell me you understand."

Bessina nodded silently. There was a sinister note in his words which drove to her marrow the realization that he would not hesitate to carry out his thinly veiled threat. She pulled her robes tightly about her as he escorted her to the litter, then she climbed in, glad to be hidden from his view. What was she to do? That decision rested on what she would find at the other end of her journey. Perhaps she could still escape to find the destiny prophesied by Peristeras. And what was more important for the moment, there might also be hope that the sinister purchaser was simply an agent for another, that he had not procured her for his own amusement.

She heard him climb into his own litter and issue a single word of command. "Go." She was lifted up, she felt her litter turn, then a gentle bouncing commenced. She did not even dare peek out; she knew that. She had to lie within the darkness of the litter without any idea of where she was going.

But the sensation of the ride was a pleasant one for the time being; she was rocked gently along, the litter's frame creaked a soft music into her ears, the curtains swayed and rustled, and the lush velvet cushions beckoned her ever more deeply into their softness. There was no telling the passage of time. She became weary and sleep summoned her to its sympathetic bosom.

She did not know how long she slept but when she awoke, it was to the sensation of the litter being set down; she heard voices, the sounds of departing feet, then the sound of a chamber door closing. She did not open the curtains before her; she waited for her purchaser to pull them back, clenching her teeth in anticipation of that moment. And at last it came. She heard the scuffing of slippers, then a hand touched the lush material and swept it away, revealing to her the chamber to which she had been brought.

It was a room of great luxury. Thick carpets decorated the floor, and the walls were covered by tapestries of embroidered cloth of gold as lavish as anything she had ever seen. A pair of servants stood before her bearing torches, and between them stood the dark-robed man. He extended his hand to help her from the litter. "I welcome you into your new abode."

She stood unsteadily and looked about. She was in a sitting room; couches and chairs stood on the lush carpets, their fine leather upholstery shining in the torchlight. A blaze roared in a deep fireplace, and before her stood a small table laid with tasty viands, the like of which she had not seen since she had been torn from her father's castle.

But her eyes passed over such things, for she was

looking at the man who had brought her there. He had stepped back, removed the veil, and thrown aside the hood of his robe; he now stood gazing at her with a smile that conveyed both lust and a sense of smugness. And she recognized him with horror.

He was Gymon, the bailiff of Pomfract Castle, adviser to King Lothar the Pale.

Chapter Fifteen:
Vouil

IT TOOK DAYS for the corsairs' crippled vessel to reach the encampment near Vouil; Aelia's voyage with them was rough and troubling. She and Chroma were hauled onto the corsairs' cripped vessel, shoved into the dank, narrow hold, and left there for what seemed an eternity. They spoke little; the hold was too filled with the noises of the firefighting above.

The raiders managed to save their vessel, but that hardly lessened the ordeal suffered by the two women. Each time their tiny prison was opened, they were faced by lewd remarks, obscene gestures, and leering faces. Drakon was the worst. The man's hands constantly fastened themselves to Aelia like gnats to syrup. And Chroma fared little better; while Aelia was vexed, the young maiden was terrified.

The raiders struck out for their home base of Vouil, on the eastern end of the Thlassa Mey. It was a hard voyage, because their vessel had been dismasted by the fire. On the second day, they put in at the Dark Capes for water. Aelia was beside herself with concern; the Dark

Capes concealed Alyubol's castle. She had no way of defending herself against the mad wizard if by chance they should meet.

But she was amazed to find he had gone. His castle of salt blocks had fallen to pieces and he had disappeared without a trace. She also learned that the corsairs of the Thlassa Mey had performed many errands for him, which helped explain his grip on the broad sea's traffic and politics.

To what place had he disappeared? Had he died? Was he plotting new villainies? There were no answers to be found at the Dark Capes; Aelia and Chroma had to return to the hold as their captors set off on the last leg of their journey. The constant creaking of the oarlocks overhead became music to lull the two women to sleep, a background for all their conversation, and a chamber melody to accompany their dining. But Aelia also knew that each stroke carried them nearer the corsairs' base and with it, more advances by the raider's amorous leader. The very thought of facing Drakon again made her shudder.

But thinking of such things did little good. Days passed and they heard the sounds of men scurrying across the deck, followed by a course change. Then there was a jolt; the vessel had been grounded. They had reached the beach west of the open city of Vouil. The hatch flew open and the two of them were hauled up to the deck. "We've landed," a crewman said to them. "We need to pull the ship onto the beach for repairs, so we want you and all the other movable goods off."

Aelia sighed with relief to see that Drakon was not present, then looked about at the flat stretch of sandy beach which extended both ways from their landing. The dense brush and scrub forest stopped a hundred cubits from the water's edge, chopped off abruptly like a peasant's hair, and a quarter of a league away stood a high timber stockade, the wall around the boisterous town of Vouil. There were two other ships unloading on the beach, both dragged up onto the sand between the corsairs' vessel and the town. "This is a busy place," Aelia said.

"It's busy all the time," another man responded. "But

this is something unusual. You don't usually see two ships unloading at once, let alone three."

"I see," Aelia said quietly, relieved that at least some of the corsairs could carry on a decent conversation. "And all the goods go to the town?"

"They do. There are shoreside traders there who buy all we have. They're as crooked as old grapevines; that's why we don't land there. We land out here on the beach so we can keep an eye on our booty. Besides that, the local authorities don't give us as much trouble if we lie out here; that way they can say they're keeping us murderous rascals out of their city. They reserve their wharves for the honest traders who stop here to buy the goods we've stolen." He laughed. "We're all thieves, you see. The merchants are, the masters of of the merchantmen who land there are, and we also are. But we're the only ones who get called thieves."

"And I suppose we sleep aboard the ship?"

He shrugged. "Who knows? Some of the men sleep aboard, some make camp on the beach, some spend their gold for rooms, wine, and women in town. You two'll sleep wherever Drakon tells you to sleep—but you'd best get to carrying gear or we'll all get a dressing down."

Aelia and Chroma began their labors while the fellow's words settled in Aelia's soul like frost on damp ground. Indeed, they would sleep where Drakon told them to sleep. The fellow had spoken the words without malice, but the chilling truth in them was by itself a reminder of the seriousness of their position. Meanwhile, they could deal with the task at hand, unloading cargo and equipment from the damaged ship. Since the raiding voyage had plainly been a short one, there was little cargo to remove; still, there were many other items. Damaged rowing benches, oars, cooking equipment, the bow, and stern ornaments, all were taken off the vessel to lighten it and allow it to be dragged onto the beach.

They had almost finished when Aelia saw a man riding toward them; he sat so awkwardly astride his horse, it was plain he had spent more time afloat than in the saddle. It was Drakon, returned from his business in Vouil. He slowed his mount and walked it alongside Aelia, looking down at her as she carried an armload of cooking utensils. "You women are good workers," he said. "Maybe I should keep you and let the rest of my men go."

"Perhaps," she said. She was determined not to be hostile. The scars her nails had put on him days before were dark and festered, and she knew both she and Chroma would pay for any more open resistance. "But where did you come by the horse?"

"I borrowed it. I've been spending our booty; I had to make arrangements to get timber for a mast, sailcloth, all that sort of thing, and my business is worth the loan of a horse. I can't stay long, but I want to have a talk with you when I get back."

Aelia looked up at him and dumped her load near a growing pile of items removed from the vessel. "Yes, I suppose."

She turned back toward the ship, toward her weary rounds of lifting, carrying, and discarding equipment. Drakon climbed down from his mount, tied its reins to a rowing bench, and walked rapidly after her, his sword and dagger slapping his thighs as he went. He caught up with her and walked beside her for a few cubits, then his hand shot out and his fingers wrapped around her arm to turn her. "I don't need to ask again," he said. "If I were some men, you'd be missing teeth by now."

Aelia lowered her face; her mouth was pressed into a tight line. "Yes."

"Then you know what I'm talking about. So what's your answer?"

She hesitated. "Perhaps."

He shook his head, grasped her by both shoulders, and looked down at her. His eyes were bright slits. "There's no 'perhaps' any more. Does it happen tonight?"

She turned her gaze away from him and toward the ship, toward the trees, toward anything. She had withstood him for days but would it happen when night came? Would she be able to delay him or would evening bring an end to her resistance? She knew one thing for sure—

the battle was not over. Simple talking about surrender did not mean she had given up.

He threw his arms about her waist and pulled her to him, squeezing the air from her, patting her playfully on the hip. "I'll get us a room in the town. You'll never have to lift another hand as long as you stay on these shores."

"And Chroma? Is she free from labor, too?"

His smile faded for only an instant, then returned. "Why I let you bargain with me I don't know. I suppose she can stay with you or whatever you want. You bargain like a pawnbroker."

Drakon continued to gaze down at her. "We should go into the trees right now." He caught her hand in a grip that was like iron and pulled her up the beach behind him as he started toward the nearby forest.

Aelia cringed away. She could not go to the trees with him; she could not stand the thought of his touch. But then they were interrupted by a sound from those trees a hundred cubits away, a hoarse shout which came from dozens of throats. "We serve the holy Maiden; fight or yield."

Drakon whirled toward the sound as a line of great war-horses thundered out of the forest. Astride them rode men wearing great basinets, greenish-gold hauberks, and flowing capes; each man wielded a heavy sword or mace, a flail or a morning star. They galloped across the beach and fell upon corsairs from all three vessels, splitting skulls and hewing arms and legs.

There was no place to hide from the onslaught; the only choice was to fight or be taken. Drakon turned toward the oncoming knights. He brought his sword hissing from its sheath while Aelia sought Chroma with her eyes; the maiden was a ship's length away, her face turned toward the developing battle. Many of the corsairs had drawn their weapons and were making a hot contest of it, for they outnumbered the attackers by many times. But they were paying no heed to prisoners, so Aelia cried out Chroma's name and shouted when the maiden turned. "Sweet Chroma, run, seek refuge in the trees where none will find you."

Chroma reacted like a person startled from a trance. When she glanced about and saw that all her captors were either fleeing or drawing weapons, she dashed toward the forest. Aelia tried to run after her but a hand struck her shoulder and tumbled her into the sand.

"Not so fast, my princess," Drakon said with a snarl. "I've won you fair and square; stay and watch what happens before you fly." He jerked her to her feet and dragged her toward the bow of his own vessel.

Aelia saw one of the knights in particular. A tall fellow on a glistening black steed struck right and left with a mace, flattening some of the corsairs and sending others scurrying before him like mice before a housewife's broom. Her heart leaped; he had seen her. He broke through the defense hastily thrown up by the raiders, then sent the sand spraying as he galloped toward the two of them, reined his animal to a sliding halt, and aimed a deadly blow at Drakon's head.

But Drakon used the vessel's hull to what advantage he could, avoided the blow, then circled the horse and tried to reach the knight's left side. The animal was too well-trained to allow such a maneuver but it was a small advantage under the circumstances.

Drakon was an able fighter. All at once he slid in beneath the knight's guard and deftly shoved his blade between the horse's ribs. The animal screamed and reared; the knight had to fly from the saddle to keep the beast from falling on top of him.

At the same time, Aelia saw her opportunity. As the raider chieftain delivered the blow, she ran toward the trees. But she was too hasty; her foot struck a piece of driftwood and she fell. All she could do was lift her head to watch the knight recover, attack furiously, and bring his weapon down on Drakon's shoulder. "That's for my horse," he cried as the chieftain reeled backward. The mace fell again, this time fatally on the side of Drakon's head, crushing bone and sending the blood flying. "And that's for this poor woman whom you hold." Drakon swayed, bled, then toppled like a tower to lie on top of Aelia in the sand.

There was blood everywhere. It had spattered onto Aelia's hands and onto her face; her gown was drenched by it. But she had no time for blood; she had to escape, to flee and find Chroma. Gasping, almost hysterical in her need to get away, she writhed from beneath the bleeding corpse and scrambled to her feet, turning toward the forest for the third time.

But an iron-gloved hand caught her by the shoulder. "How now, good woman, you have seen a sight. You watched my vengeance for my courser's loss and now you seek to run away from me." She was spun around by the combination of her haste and his grip and found herself face to face with him. "But fear me not," he said, still breathing hard from his fighting. "My mission's to do good. I must fight on until this filthy band is slain or captured and their ships are burned. Now we will harry them unto the point they cannot pose a threat to you or others, at least not for awhile. But can you see that tallest tree straight south?" He pointed toward a beech tree which rose higher than the others. "Make haste for it, for that is where we've camped two solid days, a'waiting for the time our strike would wreak most havoc. Get you there among my people and then ask for squire Prombard."

He gave Aelia a little shove and she sprinted across the sand toward the place he had indicated. She did not pause to see him battle on, or to watch his poor slain horse, still kicking helplessly in the sand. Her gown caught at her feet like demon hands as she ran, slowing her down and tiring her. Her chest burned from exertion, even before she had reached the woods; by the time she had run along the edge of the trees for a way, she felt as if her eyes were about to burst from her face.

"Chroma," she called. "Chroma, Chroma." At length the maiden answered from behind a clump of brush, then appeared, tears of relief moistening her cheeks. Aelia sagged against her and tried to catch her breath. "The knights have left their camp not far from here. If we can reach it, then we shall be safe."

They made their way toward the place, slipping carefully through the underbrush because Aelia wanted a peek at the encampment before she would offer Chroma and herself up to the occupants. And all the time, the sound of battle rang from the beach. The place was difficult to find, even though the knight had given Aelia its location; the men who had planned the attack had concealed their base well. At last, however, Aelia sighted movement between the shrubbery and the trunks of the trees; there was a glimmer of armor or the dancing of a bit of cloth. The two women approached and emerged into a cunningly concealed clearing guarded by several dozen armed youths. There were no tents or pavilions; the compressed grass across the space showed the warriors had slept on the open ground, which was unusual for knights of the heavy horse. Supplies and lances were stacked at one side of the clearing, because the lances were too cumbersome for battle against the mobile marauders.

"Halt," a voice cried. "Move slowly from behind concealing shrubs and show yourselves to us. Be you not foes, you shall find hospitality enough."

"We're prisoners, escaped from pirate hands," Aelia said as she and Chroma followed the orders given them. "I wish to speak unto a squire whose name is Prombard, for his master sent us here."

Many young warriors knelt with their weapons and gazed silently between the trees. One of them, a tall, strapping lad with flaxen hair, stood and addressed the two women. "My name is Prombard," he said. "I serve the Knight Sir Phebos. Tell what tidings you may bring; he only left to fight the foe a blink of time ago." The young man's concern showed in his face.

"Your worries may be eased. He killed the man who held me captive, though his horse was slain. He sent me to this refuge."

She was interrupted by a shout from the tall beech which spread its limbs over the clearing. "The ships are burning. Victory is ours; the terrors of the sealanes all are slain or fled or now are captives rounded up. The signal has been given; twenty men are needed to escort the captives back and aid our wounded."

A group of the young men moved quickly into the trees

with those words and was gone. Aelia watched them go with interest but Prombard was not among them. "I must say this," she said. "I find these actions to be planned with care and wit."

"Our actions always are, when possible," Prombard said, taking the compliment in stride. "Our teachings tell us bravery is dead without both wit and honor. So it is."

Even as the two of them talked, knights began to return from the battle, riding their horses into the clearing or leading their animals or walking if they had lost their mounts entirely. Some were limping, some were nursing bloody wounds, and some were unharmed; the most grievously injured had not yet been brought back. One knight broke off from his fellows, beamed, and shook a left hand which was bleeding from a cut across the back of the wrist. He gazed upon Prombard and the two women. "A worthwhile scrimmage; I've a little cut, we lost one man, and others have their hurts. But still the Maiden's served. This filthy pit is scoured now and thus it shall remain. The town of Vouil, deprived of all its ill-got commerce, soon shall have to find more honest roads to reach prosperity."

Then he paused and looked at the younger man. "Alas, my lad, my gallant horse is slain."

"So I was told," Prombard said. "But still you have survived and thus my heart beats gladly in my breast."

Sir Phebos touched the youth on the shoulder, then turned toward the two women. "I see you reached our camp. Are you unharmed?"

Aelia was slow to respond. There were hurts to the body and there were hurts to the soul; neither she nor Chroma had been harmed physically, but it would take them many days to recover from their captivity. And there was something more than that stopping her tongue—in the heat and horror of the battle, she had not observed the Knight carefully, nor any of his fellows. Now there was no mistaking the symbol painted on his shield or embroidered into his cloak: the two gray eyes of the holy Maiden, the patron of honor, wisdom, and warriors, the virgin goddess Pallas. There was no mistaking the greenish-

gold chain mail worn by each Knight, hauberks renowned
for both lightness and strength. Her mouth fell open and
she tried to stammer an answer. She and Chroma had
been rescued by a company of the Knights of Pallas. She
stared at the Knight who had saved her. Her emotions
mixed strangely as he called for Prombard to bring him
a stool and to begin dressing his wound. After all, she
was tied to the Knights of Pallas in a unique way—that
order had expelled Palamon long before she had met him.

Chapter Sixteen:
Knights of Pallas

AELIA AND CHROMA had been rescued by a company of Knights of Pallas, the noblest of the knightly orders on the banks of the Thlassa Mey. Many applied for admittance to the Knights of Pallas and few were accepted; Aelia knew that. And those who did become members of the order had to meet the most rigorous standards; they had to maintain their celibacy as long as they were members, they had to keep themselves spotlessly clean, they had to pray as regularly as the most devout monks, and they had to be fearless in battle.

Palamon had been cast from the Knights of Pallas; he admitted the crime of fornication and had been expelled, a disgrace to the order and the holy Maiden. The rub was that Palamon had never committed the act for which he had been punished. He was still pure as mercury—Aelia had witnessed the proof. He had admitted the act simply to protect a poor country maiden from wrathful villagers. But he had been expelled all the same; he had been degraded and now Aelia had to face men who had likely witnessed the Prince's humiliation.

As for Sir Phebos, he was the picture of the noble Knight of Pallas, fresh from victory over evil, as he removed the gauntlet from his damaged hand and allowed Prombard to bandage it. After a moment he bade the two women tell of their experiences.

Aelia and Chroma related to him how they had fallen into the hands of Drakon and the corsairs, though Aelia was careful never to mention Palamon. After all, since Palamon had fallen from the ranks of the Knights of Pallas, she did not care to bring his ordeal up or to have it brought up by another. She allowed Chroma to tell the bulk of the story, which was not difficult; the maiden waxed into a pleasant and talkative mood as she grasped the fact that she had been rescued and that her life and honor were no longer in danger. She cast away the shadow of the last days with the resiliency of her youth.

For Aelia's part, she was fascinated by all that went on about her. Her eyes missed nothing. The air was filled with accounts of the fray, the clatter of armor being removed, and the moans of the wounded Knights and prisoners who were being bound for transport to the authorities. There was also the excited babble among the squires who were tending the less severely wounded, putting the camp back in order, and preparing the evening's repast.

That was augmented by the arrival of a large baggage train. It had evidently waited at a distance and now bore the posts, colorful canvases, and fittings for the pavilions and sleeping tents. The squires and younger Knights set about the task of pitching a full camp the same way they seemed to deal with their other tasks—with competence, enthusiasm, and skill. And in the midst of all the hubbub stood a single, elderly man, marked by a towering crest on the helmet he held under one arm. The crest was made of huge plumes which bobbed and swayed as he issued orders and instructions. He was the Field Master, the senior Knight in charge of the expedition.

But most fascinating of all was the legendary "laying on of hands," the mystical rite by which the Knights healed their most severely wounded brothers. There were three such patients, each administered to by a senior Knight who prayed devoutly, meditated, and then pressed his fingers against the wounded man in symbolic patterns. It was fascinating and engrossing, a sight few outside the order were ever allowed to see.

But Aelia had seen it once before. She had watched Palamon heal Ursid, the young Buerdic prince, of terrible wounds, greatly weakening himself in the process. Thus, despite the fact that he had been cast from the Knights of Pallas, Palamon still possessed the mystic power to heal, which could be given or taken away only by the holy Maiden herself. He had not committed the crime for which he had been condemned, and his patron, who knew all things, had not punished him for a villainy he had not performed. But he had been scourged by his fellows.

After healing the wounds of their injured brothers, the three Knights who had performed the miracles were taken to cots and given wine to help them rest and recuperate from the strain of their ministrations. So it had been with Palamon after he had healed Ursid and proved that he had been expelled for a trespass he had never committed. The unfairness of it all agitated her enormously, the knowledge that her gallant Prince, who even now was in danger or dead, had been cast from the ranks of her present hosts.

She looked back at Sir Phebos and saw that he was studying her. "My pardon, madam," he said. "I could not ignore the look upon your countenance. For one who has so lately been released from vicious corsairs' clutches, your elation's muted, by my troth."

She tried to smile. "I must apologize, my noble sir, for letting my attention wander so. I've never in my life seen such a host of Knights of Pallas in a single place. In fact, in all my life I've met just one."

"Well, then," Sir Phebos said with the air of one who had now had all his questions answered. He played no part better than that of a genial host. He was heavily muscled for his height, and a bandage covered his hand, but she could picture him more easily as a franklin in a large country house or as the host at a banquet than as a knight who had just risked his life. She suspected he was trying to draw her out and make her feel more at home with the troupe of holy warriors. "But tell me, then," he said, "what might have been the name of this one noble brother whom you knew?"

Aelia hesitated and bit her lip. The question was friendly enough, but it gave her no comfort. She had no desire to name Palamon and she knew no other Knights.

She was rescued from her little dilemma by a call from the Field Master, or rather from that leader's squire. The young man's voice rang through the glade with a clarity and purity of pitch which left no doubt why he had been chosen for his position. "Now gather 'round us, brothers. It is time we offered thanks for what we have achieved. This victory at arms would not have come without the strength and guidance of our Liege, our patron, Pallas. Come away from all your tasks awhile and let us stand together to give thanks and pledge ourselves once more unto her service."

Sir Phebos moved toward the center of the clearing, gesturing that Aelia and Chroma should accompany him. Once more Aelia hesitated. "Perhaps I should not taint the sanctity of your devotion with my presence."

"Come," he said. "Whoever you may be, come pray with us."

Aelia did not refuse. However ill-at-ease she might feel among the holy warriors, it was not fitting that she refuse to share their devotion. The gods did deserve thanks, so she accompanied Sir Phebos and Prombard to the center of the clearing.

The Knights and their squires bowed their heads and the Field Master began the prayer in a solemn tone. For her part, Aelia offered a silent word to Hestia. Then, when thanks had been given, every Knight fell to his knees and the air was filled with the jumble of low voices as each one offered his own word of thanks to the holy Maiden. Aelia could not help noticing the form taken by each prayer she could hear.

They were all spoken as short poems, the same as the prayers she had heard Palamon utter during their time together. The glade filled with a magnetic quiet, a sense of brotherhood that was remarkable. How it must have pained Palamon to be driven from such ranks! That thought racked her with a whole new poignancy. Her fingertips passed silently to her mouth and her eyes filled with moisture as the realization swept over her. How it must have hurt when he had been cast out. How it must have hurt.

The moment was quickly over. As the sun sank toward the trees and yellow and red leaves rattled in the day's last cold breeze, the solemn air that had filled the glade gave way to celebration. The raising of the tents was completed, a great fire was built, and an ox was produced from one of the supply wagons. There were shouts and commands, then a body of enthusiastic squires skewered it as easily as a farmer's wife would have spitted a squirrel. They began roasting the ox; dripping grease made the fire blaze up over and again.

The squires ranged in age from their early teens to a few past the age of twenty. They competed and argued gamely over the honor of turning the beast while many of the Knights watched them, laughing or quietly chatting in front of their tents or in the circle of light cast by the blaze itself.

Prombard joined the youthful crew roasting the ox, but Sir Phebos took Aelia and Chroma with him to greet the Field Master. "My good Sir Pompau," Sir Phebos said with an air of deference. "These poor ladies had been seized and held as prisoners aboard the ship we burned upon the beach today. Their tale is harrowing, as well you might expect."

"I find that statement easy to believe," Sir Pompau said. He bowed to the two women, exchanged pleasantries with them, and invited them and Sir Phebos to take dinner with him in the main pavilion. He also gave instructions that a tent be placed at the women's disposal and materials provided for them to bathe and freshen themselves in privacy. Then, having proven himself as gracious a host as Sir Phebos, he left them with an apology. "I must attend the prisoners. It is my most unpleasant task to sit and judge them, to decide their destinies. It's not a task I love. Excuse me, please."

At dinner that evening, Aelia and Chroma were given places as guests at Sir Pompau's left hand while Sir Phebos, as their rescuer, and Prombard, as his squire, were seated beyond them. Aelia looked about her all the while the meal was going on. It was a sedate affair as victory dinners tended to go; there was no drunkenness, no loud jesting. The conversation was polite and reserved, and the only shouting and loud laughter came from the younger squires who were eating their dinners in a circle around the bonfire. Had it not been for her cares about Palamon and Berengeria, she could have felt quite comfortable.

Sir Pompau listened gravely as Aelia told him her story, but she did not mention Palamon's name. She said only that she had been on a diplomatic mission with Beredoric, the prince of Carea, for that had been Palamon's given name before he had become a Knight of Pallas.

Sir Pompau raised his eyebrows. "Indeed, my Lady. I have heard the news the Prince had been returned. A host of years went by while he was mourned for dead. But tell me, for I yearn to know, where was he all those years he went unseen? Why, I was just a youth when I first heard he'd vanished from the court of Carea and now I have white whiskers on my chin. What was his tale for all that unknown time?"

Aelia hesitated. When she finally spoke, it was with a soft, firm voice. "I have no wish to flaunt my Prince's name upon his former comrades, goodly Knight, but neither do I have the low desire to hide that name. In faith, then, I must say there's every chance you've met him without e'er suspecting it. He passed those years within the very walls of Pallas' Fastness, for he was a Knight."

The Field Master's eyebrows lifted but he smiled politely. "That comes as a surprise. We have no Knight named Beredoric, madam. I believe if one among our rank were made a Prince, it would not be a secret to us all."

Aelia felt herself coloring before his expression. But she had come this far; there was no room for flinching. "I speak the truth. It was some years ago he left your hallowed ranks. He then was known to all as Palamon."

"The gods. It is not so." Sir Pompau looked as if she

had struck him across the face. His mouth worked, and his complexion darkened. A stunned silence spread through the tent, sweeping the length of the U-shaped dining table and spreading like a pox to the younger Knights and squires. Sir Phebos became as pale as a ghost.

For his own part, Sir Pompau regained his composure and became once again the gracious host. "I should be pleased that Palamon has had such fortune and in truth, I wish him well. I do not doubt that he has paid enough for any errors he committed while he served the Maiden. I say that every Knight within our ranks should bow to him for his good fortune. And Sir Phebos, I believe, once served with him."

For all the graciousness of the words, Aelia could not mistake the coolness with which they had been delivered. And there was also no mistaking the fact that her host had been careful not to place the title 'sir' before Palamon's name; it was the first time during the evening that he had failed to use that title when speaking of a Knight of Pallas, past or present.

As for Sir Phebos, he sounded as if he were about to choke on his words. "Indeed, Sir Palamon instructed me. I was his squire before he was expelled."

With the sound of the word "expelled," the tent became even quieter, if such a thing could have been possible. Prombard gazed at Aelia in stony silence.

At last the meal went on, although she could not ignore the air of tension which hung over it. Neither Sir Pompau nor any of the other Knights engaged Aelia as freely in conversation as they had before. Even so, she was glad she had made the revelation. Palamon—Sir Palamon— was a good man and true. He had suffered unjustly and it was with a feeling of stubborn pride that she had mentioned his name and would mention it again.

As the evening wore on, Sir Pompau once more warmed in his attitude toward the two rescued women, although it appeared to be more from his instinct for civility than the friendship he had shown earlier. After the meal ended, several Knights accompanied the two women to their tent. Sir Pompau took their hands and wished them a pleasant night's slumber. "I must suspect that this night is the first in several that might afford to you the hope of pleasant dreams."

Aelia shook her head. "Alas, good Sir, I doubt that I shall sleep, though Chroma's part of this adventure's over. My Prince and Princess are now both lost; my duty is to find them if I can."

Sir Pompau nodded. "Ah, yes. The Prince." But this time he did not betray his feelings. He wished them a good night once more, then made a quick departure.

The two women sat up and talked—but they were both too weary to talk long. Soon, they both fell silent. It took a long time for Aelia to fall asleep; she lay upon her cot with her eyes closed while she listened to the occasional sigh of Chroma's slumber in the darkness. But Palamon was Aelia's companion even more than the young maiden who slept only cubits away. Aelia could see him in his armor, his greenish-gold chain mail, looking like any of the other Knights sleeping in the tents around her. He would have fitted in with this company the way one well-bred stallion blended in with a stable of such steeds, except for that ceremony which had taken place all those years ago.

Would she ever see him again? Would she ever see his sister, Berengeria? There was no way she could answer either of those questions; all she could do was hope for the best and try to go to sleep.

Even when she did fall asleep, the sleep was a restless one. She had a dream. She lay in a twilit chamber with tapestries hanging thickly on the walls. She was lying on a stone altar and her eyes were shut, though that seemed to make no difference. The light was dim but she had a sense of all that happened about her. A tripod stood beside her; coals glowed crimson in the brazier it held, and a sibyl extended her arms over Aelia's body. The dream-priestess began chanting: "The question must be asked. The question must be asked." The words were repeated over and over.

The phrase echoed endlessly through the dream chapel. "The question must be asked." The chanting was disconcerting but the overall feeling within the dream was of comfort and satisfaction. And there was something more; Aelia could sense it. Each wall was hidden by thick tapestries, except for the wall at her feet, which was hung with a simple drapery, a light-colored arras made of silk. With her senses in their heightened state, Aelia could tell there was unnatural movement to the fabric; there was a presence behind it and Aelia could feel herself being watched.

But she could not stir; she could not speak or open her eyes or respond in any way. That remained her condition until she drifted from the dream-vision off into a deeper sleep which was filled with thoughts of Palamon. The dreams were vivid; she could almost smell the sweat of his horse, but she awoke to find herself refreshed and the cloth of the tent bright with the new day.

The two women rose and Sir Pompau met them before his pavilion. "The day has come and duty beckons us. We must return to our own halls, and you must go back to your land. I've volunteers who shall escort you on your journey."

The clearing was again filled with the hubbub of Knights, squires, and attendants, preparing gear, bundling up equipment, and repairing weapons and armor. Tents were already being taken down and loaded onto the mules of the baggage train. But Aelia could not return to Carea to tell Berevald of the mission's failure; what would the old King do at the news that both his children were lost to him? She bowed her head and spoke quietly. "For all your kindness, sir, I must decline. While Lady Chroma yearns to go that way, for my own part I'd travel to Buerdaunt. I've every reason to suspect my Princess has again been clamped within the grasp of Lothar. I would take her from that place or at the least, endure captivity along with her. Therefore, a horse and some supplies are all I ask."

Sir Pompau looked grave. "And what of Palamon, who has become Prince Beredoric? Is there some chance that he might come upon the scene to lend support?"

Aelia did not like the question. "I have no way of finding out his fate. E'en so, for all the hate you bear for him, I know he is as good and true a knight as ever couched a lance. If he survives and has the capability of travel, we'll meet within the cranks of old Buerdaunt, for he will keep his quest the same as I."

"Though that may be the case, I fear for you," Sir Pompau said. "One woman, all alone in broad Buerdaunt, is scarce a match for armies of a king."

"She needn't go alone." The voice that boomed out from behind Aelia belonged to Sir Phebos. He stood with a group of Knights who had evidently volunteered to accompany the two women to Carea; she should have expected that. "Her quest is just," he said. "Our laws allow a Knight to ride in aid of kidnap victims or in any case where cruel extortion's practiced. I wish to ride beside her to Buerdaunt."

"You know our statutes well," Sir Pompau said. "Still, bear in mind that this is a dispute between two kings; disputes of state do not concern the Knights."

"And yet I may fare forth in such a case, although it's my decision, mine alone."

"So say our laws. A Knight may volunteer for such a mission, but he rides alone without the sanction of his order. Is that what you now want to do?"

Sir Phebos nodded.

"We cannot help you if it comes to blows."

"That's my decision, sir."

"I'll also ride." This voice belonged to Prombard. "Sir Phebos is my mentor and my friend, and if he sees the need to hazard his own life for such a cause, I also shall."

Sir Phebos shook his head. "Ah, nay, my lad. I'll not have you along. This quest is dangerous and I'll not have your life and future in this order's ranks upon my conscience if by chance we fall."

Prombard looked disappointed; his features fell and his mouth narrowed, but Sir Pompau agreed with the elder warrior. "Sir Phebos' words are true; his thoughts befit fair Pallas' noble Knights. But still this matter's not beyond our aid until he crosses onto lands held fief by Lothar and Buerdaunt—for only then must he ride on alone. I give permission to a brace of Knights and their attendants to accompany you, Sir Phebos, with young Prombard here, until you reach the hills which cast their shade upon the River Priscus and Buerdaunt. Then they must leave your company and you and Lady Aelia must ride alone. This is the limit of the aid I may extend before I breach our laws."

Aelia bowed her head before the Field Master. It was a considerable offer; at least it would see her up to the shadow of Buerdaunt's gate. She and Sir Phebos would have greatly improved chances of success for that. And so it was decided. Two more volunteers came forward, along with their squires and attendants. Aelia bade Chroma a tearful farewell. The party which set out numbered a dozen men, along with extra horses. It was a formidable body and it eliminated any worry Aelia might have harbored about being attacked by roving bands of outlaws. The Knights of Pallas with their shining hauberks, their excellent horses, and their unmistakable banners, formed a company with which few would dare trifle for all its small size.

They set out, rode south along the hills overlooking Sparth's Head Castle, and then on to Verdast, where they purchased lodging for the night. Although such a company of warriors caused some raised eyebrows, no one was brave or reckless enough to ask their business. They ate their suppers, slept the night out, and went on the following morning.

To Aelia's surprise, her strange dream repeated itself that night. It was all the same; the dream chapel was the same, the brazier was the same, and the sibyl was the same. The unseen presence watched from behind the arras, just as before. The only change was a second phrase which flowed from the sibyl's mouth at the same time as the first: "Consent shall then be given. Consent shall then be given."

"The question must be asked, consent shall then be given."

Then Aelia drifted into quiet slumber. She pondered the dream in the morning but there was no time to give it long consideration. She and her escort had to prepare to take to the road once more.

They camped within the broad embrace of the Greenlands the next night, and a day later they reached the range of hills which marked the boundary of the lands ruled by Lothar the Pale. There the Knights parted company with manly embraces and slapping of backs. The farewell between Sir Phebos and his squire, Prombard, was especially touching; each swore he would return to the company of the other. Tears were shed by both men, Sir Phebos avowed he would be proud to serve with Prombard again, and Prombard said the same. Then the company turned and the riders went back the way they had come. The sound of the horse's hooves and the clatter of harnesses and accouterments could be heard for a long time, fading into the distance.

Aelia and Sir Phebos did not pause to listen, however. They glanced at one another, Aelia thanked him for his help, and they nudged their horses toward Buerdaunt and whatever the Fates held in store for them.

Chapter Seventeen:
The Black Cones

IN SPITE OF all Palamon or Flin could do, autumn's golden winds pushed their roundship toward the Cauldron of the Stilchis without respite or mercy; they were only two in number and there was no way they could stop the vessel from being grounded. The seas were high, the tide was at flood, and soon each wave was driving the ship farther onto the sand.

They struggled until midday but there was no hope; the vessel would never sail again. What was worse, Carea's battle fleet would soon sail to blockade Buerdaunt's harbor. Palamon had to find Berengeria before that could happen, which meant they had no time to wait for developments.

It was a bad situation; the Cauldron of the Stilchis was a wasteland which stretched along the coast for dozens of leagues and inland farther than any man knew. It was a great valley, lifeless as the inside of a furnace and surrounded by unscalable cliffs. All that lived there were the fish in the Stilchis River itself. Everything else was cinders, ash, and blowing sand. Men so shunned the region that if Flin and Palamon waited for rescue, they would surely die. So they would have to walk.

Travel to the south was impossible. The deep waters of the Stilchis waited for them only a league or two away, as impenetrable an obstacle as the highest wall. They also did not dare venture inland, Palamon knew. The sheer cliffs which formed the boundaries of the Cauldron of the Stilchis rose up practically at the water's edge; only by keeping to the shore did they have any hope of skirting the barrier. So their course was decided; they would travel north to beard Lothar the Pale in his own den. They would hug the coast and try to enter Buerdaunt incognito, though the danger would not be much reduced by that.

So they fashioned backpacks out of canvas and packed rope, food, wineskins, and everything which looked useful. Then they climbed over the ship's teetering rail and started out, Palamon wearing his gleaming hauberk, Flin armored only in an iron-studded leather jerkin he had peeled from one of the dead corsairs.

There was much driftwood left along the shore by the waves. Late that afternoon, they found a sea-tangled cluster of such logs in the lee of a dark promontory. They stopped there for the night. They built a fire and heated boiled haricot beans they had brought from the ship's stores. They were able to make a fair meal out of what they had; then they sat in silence and watched the fire burn down while they listened to the cold wind that was sweeping over their stone shelter.

The future held many challenges. Still, Palamon's mind was not on that. His thoughts were filled with the image of Aelia being hauled over the ship's rail by the corsairs' chieftain. Where was she now? Was she dead? Had the raiders used her as their plaything and then discarded her? Had she even survived the swim to their vessel? His hopes were fastened on that phrase he remembered from another time, which she had spoken not far from where he now sat. "All those swim well who hail from Artos' shores." He clung to that single phrase as if it were a holy relic.

His mind still refused to comprehend the fact that Aelia

was the bride selected by Pallas; it was impossible to picture her in that role. But that was a question for the future to answer; he had traveled far with her and he could not keep from grimacing at the thought of her in the hands of the raiders. It all formed an interesting question; if she had been selected by the holy Maiden, did that mean Aelia's survival was certain, ordained by the gods, or did it mean that Palamon had let her go to her death through his own carelessness, thereby foiling the Maiden's intentions and offending the gods? It all came to the same thing; he never should have allowed either of the women to accompany him on a dangerous mission.

Flin's head turned and the younger man watched Palamon in the firelight. "You still worry about your woman friend—your two women friends—don't you?"

"Perhaps."

"It won't help for you to worry about her, you know. If she's as crafty as you say she is, she'll fare well enough."

"Both she and Chroma face the dangers of the sea as well as brigands. There's no craft that ever might dissuade the salty waters as they close above one's struggling form."

"How much good can you do her by fretting?" Flin said incredulously.

"Her life—their lives—will ever be upon my conscience if they've suffered any harm."

Flin shook his head. "You're hopeless. You can't do her a bit of good from here and there's no sense in mourning her until you know there's something to mourn. She'll find a way to get by, the same as we have. Besides, a man fares best if he doesn't have a conscience. You may be a great warrior but you're faced with the unlovely prospect of being a rather second-class lover. You'll never win your Aelia's hand with the kind of attitude you've got; she'll never put up with it."

Flin never ceased to amaze Palamon. His sympathy was real enough, Palamon could tell, but he did not seem to understand the situation. The dangers which faced Aelia and Chroma were of no more account to him than the dangers which he and Palamon faced in trying to walk out of the Cauldron of the Stilchis. His attitude was either refreshing or brainless, but it was hard to decide which.

"You are a boon companion, I'll admit," Palamon said. "Though whether I should smile at all your words or thrash you for your thoughtless pleasantries is far too hard a question. As for love, we've talked of that too much already; all I say is this—if you claim knowledge of my love for Lady Aelia, you have insights quite unknown to me. If what I feel for her is love, it differs much from what I've known as such before."

"Oh, you love her," Flin said. "I've watched you for days and there's no doubt about that. You just haven't found it out yet. You will sooner or later, though what you're going to do about it is beyond me. You're as helpless in front of a maiden as a toad in front of a snake; I've really never seen anything like it. She won't come to you, you know. You're going to have to pursue her when the time comes.

"I've seen women like her before. Very classy, I'll say that for her. When the Fates bring you back together—and they will, just the same as they'll bring Bessina and me together—you'll have to run after her from pillar to post to win her. You'd better get all this thinking business out of the way by that time. That's what my father told me once. He told me never to let thinking stand between myself and a woman. If they want to be chased, chase them. Don't think about it."

Palamon nearly laughed. The picture of him pursuing any woman, even one who might be a bride selected by the Maiden, was too ludicrous to be taken seriously. He wondered if Flin would have spoken of Aelia that way if he had known she was a priestess of Hestia.

As the fire died away, they pulled their canvas cloaks over themselves for protection from the chill sea wind. It was hard to sleep in the cold wasteland with the waves crashing onto the sand only a few cubits away; both men were awake long before the pink glow of dawn could paint the horizon ahead of them. As soon as it was light enough to walk without stumbling, they were on their way. As they moved up the coastline, Palamon hoped there was still time to locate Aelia and Berengeria before Carea's galleys could sail and set off a horrible chain of events.

They stayed close to the beach as they labored up the shoulder of a great, grim, cone-shaped mountain. Their path led across cinders. Below them the mountain's northern slope was truncated by the sea. Palamon recognized the smoking peak, along with others in the distance, each one topped by dark clouds of unknown gases. He and Flin were traversing one of the Mountains of the Moon. Palamon had heard many chilling tales of those grim peaks; still, the peak they were passing did not look any more sinister or unpleasant than any other part of the forbidden basin.

Their path caused them to turn away from the line of the breaking sea. The going was slow; the slope was composed of nothing solid. There were only porous rocks and ash of various sizes which seemed to absorb all the sun's heat, even on this brisk autumn day. Walking became painful as ankles and feet protested the constant slope and irregular footing.

They could see the peak looming in the center of the mountain, placed as evenly as the center of the little pile of sand which forms at the bottom of an hourglass. Occasionally the rocks would tremble; the mountain seemed to pulse with a life of its own and the cloud above the peak hovered in the chill air like a vapor of respiration.

As the morning dragged along its course and noon came, they started down the peak's eastern slope. The sun was at their backs now, and huge, basalt blocks cast strange shadows across the cinders above them. Then, from behind them, they heard a sound that was different from anything they had heard before. It was the sound of loose stones shifting, a great many loose stones. Flin stopped and looked about. "What was that?"

Palamon had no reply. There was no sign of life, but behind them one of the boulders had moved. It was a tall, cone-shaped stone and it had slid toward the path they had followed. "Perhaps this mountain shifts e'en as we walk. We must be on our way."

They hurried even more. It would be a hard fate to be

crushed by some rolling block of stone in the midst of the wilderness. But a strange vibration assailed their ears, a sort of harsh puffing sound from behind and above them, and they turned again. The cone-shaped block they had noticed before was even closer to them than it had been, even though they had walked several cubits. Palamon was nonplussed. He and Flin glanced at one another's sweat-soaked faces.

Suddenly a dark hole opened in the sloping mountain side before them, and the loose black stones shifted and slid inward like the sand about an ant lion's trap. Out of the funnel-shaped opening rose a conical stone mass exactly like the one they had seen behind them. But it moved; it huffed and puffed, its surface so hot the air rose from it in shimmering waves. The top of the cone pivoted and the two travelers could see a single opening toward the top, an opening which led to a molten interior that seethed red with heat.

Palamon caught Flin and pulled the younger warrior back with him. "It is a pyrothere. I've heard the tales of creatures such as this, although I never have believed a word until this moment."

The thing was a molten horror twice the height of a tall man; there was no sense in seeking combat with it. But the one behind them had been moving, following them. It reached forth, and tentacles materialized from its dark surface, the way a waterspout would drop out of a cloud. They scrambled away and nearly fell as they rushed head-long down the slope. But there was no escape. From another opening downhill came a third apparition, which rose and moved toward them, as relentless and implacable as fate.

The pyrotheres pursued them with loud sounds, the grumbling and sliding of shifting stone. More appeared behind the first three; there were a half dozen of them in all.

"By all the gods," Flin said. "These are nasty monsters we've found."

"There does not seem to be a clear escape," Palamon replied as his fingers settled onto the hilt of the *Spada*

Korrigaine, his two-handed sword. "We'll stand and fight and hope the mighty gods look down upon the fray with sympathy."

Flin also drew his sword and he and Palamon moved back-to-back as they faced the shambling piles of stone. Broad bases rippled across the mountain's slope, and tentacles bulged from conical surfaces. Flin lunged toward one and swung at an extended member, but he had little success; his blade clanged against the stone and rebounded with a huge nick in the edge. He cursed, then leaped forward, using his speed to duck under the pyrothere's reach, and tried to push it off balance. But that was a hopeless strategy; the mobile mountain's base was too broad. Flin jerked away from it, nursing scorched hands.

Palamon fared better. With a cry invoking the holy Maiden's aid, he also aimed a blow at one of the tentacles reaching for him. There was a crunch and a hiss as his mystic blade sheared through stone and cut away the target, which fell and shattered like a piece of crockery. But the creature did not even seem to notice. Another tentacle formed to replace the first one and the conflict continued. Palamon leaped closer, hacked away more swaying members, and tried to reach the flaming inferno hole which seemed to be the pyrothere's eye. To his surprise, he succeeded; the *Spada Korrigaine* pierced the seething well and the creature from the volcano writhed violently, steam screaming from its depths. Then it stood motionless and dead, but Palamon was too busy with another to notice.

One of the cones grabbed Flin, but Palamon managed to hack him from its grip. The young warrior fell with a thud which knocked the air from him. Then he lay in the center of the mêlée, still bound by stone tentacles; there was no chance to set him free.

Palamon felt himself grasped from behind; the tentacle clattered against his armor and tore his outer tunic to shreds. He was able to twist and carve deeply into the creature's stone surface but he paid a high price. There was too much substance there for him to cut through it all in one blow; the blade of his sword stuck fast and the handle twisted from Palamon's hands as the pyrothere lurched. He was weaponless.

He was also helpless. He struggled in the hot grasp and he tried to batter the creature with his bare hands, but the only result was skin lacerated as if he had been juggling clinkers. The only consolation as he watched another monster scoop Flin up was that the tentacles were not as hot as the creature's interior; the heat was all he could stand, but no more than that.

The pyrotheres carried their captives up along the smoky slopes of cinders and tailings toward the place where the mountain's top was hidden in vapor. As they made their way into the fog, a great opening appeared in the mountainside, a cave which belched hot air and sulfurous fumes. Flin had revived and Palamon watched the younger man gag as he was carried toward the entrance. Palamon was not doing much better; the rotten-egg smell was terrible.

Suddenly all the cone-shaped pyrotheres paused. They stopped simultaneously, like a pack of dogs which had heard the master's whistle. The flaming eyes shifted as the creatures turned; Palamon was impressed at the way their attitudes matched those of listening animals. Then they began to move away from the tunnel mouth. That was a relief to the tortured lungs of the two captives, and Flin even regained his breath enough to shout to Palamon. "Can you reach your sword? It bobs just above your head."

"I cannot free my arms for such a task." Palamon knew the weapon's loyalty to him was so great he could probably call it to his grasp—but what good would that do when his arms were pinned to his sides? Besides, there was no way he could be certain that the weapon could wrench itself free. That was why he waited; he could call the sword if the creatures actually started down the foreboding tunnel, but not before.

The cone-shaped monsters moved along slowly, aimless for a moment; then the two which held the warriors began to make their way back down the mountain's slope. The others started after them, but had gone only a few cubits when they halted again, and the ones bearing Flin and Palamon went on alone.

"By Tyche's dice," Flin said. "I wonder what they're doing. We seem to be headed south."

"Indeed, we do," Palamon said.

"Maybe they've changed their minds."

Palamon smiled grimly. "We do not even know that they have minds to change. Have you attempted to break free?"

"I can't. I'm caught as tightly as a rabbit in a net." Flin kicked a bit to lend emphasis to his words. "I only wish I could match the love this fellow bears me."

Palamon noted the younger man's forced humor. "I fear its love will grow too hot by far." But there was something else in his mind, something that gave him a sliver of hope. The ancient sage Reovalis lived on the south shore of the Stilchis, several leagues away. Could he be rescuing them? Had he viewed their plight through his mystical powers and was he calling the lava creatures away from their lair? There was no quick answer to such questions, but the two stony cones had not shown any desire to go south before they had paused at the mouth of the sulfurous tunnel. "Perhaps there's hope," he said. "Perhaps there may be hope."

"What makes you think that? This seems to be a tight little knot, even for our nimble fingers."

"I cannot say for sure. My reasons are as tenuous as cobwebs in a gale. But even so, I tell you to have hope."

Flin laughed. "I don't seem to know all you know but you needn't worry. I'm sure the gods wouldn't allow us to get this far only to let us be cooked by these walking furnaces."

Palamon smiled but did not reply. No man could be sure of what the gods would and would not allow, and the mighty Moirae, who controlled the destinies of even the gods, could be as perverse as the most demented child. No, he could not maintain Flin's confidence. Even so, they seemed to be safe for the time being. The creatures moved with surprising swiftness, their circular bases undulating over the sliding stones. There was enough breeze to cool the two men, and progress was steady toward the south. Palamon grew stiff in his captor's grasp, but it was so tight that he could not even struggle, so he endured the journey even as Flin was enduring it.

The strange beings covered ground steadily; the dark cone of the mountain fell away behind them and they traveled across the cinder-covered floor of the Cauldron of the Stilchis. Ravines which had lain hidden ahead of them opened up and the pyrotheres dropped along the descending bottom of one of them, following its course toward the Stilchis itself.

The sun sank; the sky began to grow dark. The holes the creatures used as eyes, the ugly, flaming pits a cubit or so from the tops of the cones, became livid in the gathering darkness and Palamon could even notice an occasional glimmer of red through cracks in the black slag which covered the things the way scales covered reptiles. And the heat rolled off them. They had to be molten stone inside; they were formed of the molten stuff of the volcanoes they had left behind.

At length the two men found themselves beside the Stilchis itself as the last rays of the dying sun turned the broad, roiling waters a pale blue. Palamon had passed this way only months ago, but it was too dark to tell exactly where they were. He only knew they were downstream from the very deepest gorges. By craning his neck, he was able to see a pinpoint of light on the far shore. Did an ancient temple, huge and decaying, stand atop the far cliff? It was hard to be sure, but it seemed likely.

The two stone beings entered the water without hesitation, moving as if they were still on dry land; their round, flat bases carried them the way a snail's foot carries it across the sea bottom. But these were not snails; the instant the pyrotheres touched the autumn-chilled water there came a violent hissing. Huge clouds of steam belched up where stone and water met, nearly suffocating the two captives. Pieces began to break off the pyrotheres and plummet into the river's murk.

But the strange creatures kept on, into the deepest waters; their stony tentacles lifted the two men and barely kept them clear of the river's bosom. As they went on, the water became too deep for that to keep Flin and Palamon dry. The channel was deep; the flood surged over the captives' heads and they were hauled down among the heaving waters. Each held his breath to keep from being drowned, fighting the liquid element too totally to be able to pray or even to think.

It seemed an eternity before Palamon's head broke the surface again; he coughed and gagged, spat the muddy water from his mouth, and blew it from his nose. From the sounds behind him, he was sure that Flin was doing the same. And he noticed something else; the tentacles which held him had become as cold as clay. He could no longer feel the creature's heat welling past him. Something was wrong. The chill of the water was hurting the two creatures. They were both moving more slowly; larger pieces were breaking free, falling into the water. Palamon was not even sure the things would be able to make it all the way to the far shore, even though there were only a few cubits to go.

And Palamon's heart leaped. Two figures stood on the beach ahead of him, dimly lit by the torch the smaller figure was holding. One was a man, shielded from the autumn cold by wool robes, his head covered and hidden from view. Next to him stood the hulking figure of Usmu, Reovalis' conjured flesh servant. Usmu's wolf face was dimly visible, and he was still bearing the great axe Palamon had seen him carry when they had last parted. So it had indeed been Reovalis who had caused the two moving mountains to forsake their original design and bear the men to the Library of the Polonians.

Such transport had cost the pyrotheres dearly, that was certain. The water had chilled their internal mechanisms so much they could hardly move, even though they had nearly reached the shore. Palamon looked down. The flaming red pit which had been the creature's eye had become a pale gray. Even as Palamon watched, all color vanished. The orifice winked out, turning black as a cave in Hades, and the creature stopped moving. It had been destroyed by the cold water.

"Now Usmu, release them. First Palamon, then his young friend. Your axe will crash easily through those stone tentacles. Go."

At that urging, the flesh servant waded toward the stone creature which still held Palamon. The tentacles had been the first part of the pyrothere to expire for want of heat, it seemed; it had never been able to lower him after carrying him through the deepest part of the river. While Palamon watched, Usmu waded out until the water was to his chin. The flesh servant swung the battle axe and there was the sound of splintering stone as the tentacles were smashed to bits. Palamon dropped into the water, bouncing off the side of the pyrothere as he came down, but he was grasped roughly by his arm and he felt himself being dragged toward the shore. It was no gentle rescue, that was certain; Usmu had never been one to stand on ceremony.

It was only instants before he felt the sandy beach beneath his feet. He struggled to stand as Usmu pulled him from the water. The river was cold and he shivered while he wiped the water from his face and coughed it from his throat. But he was stopped short by another order. "Now quickly, the rag and the rope. Stop his mouth up before he can speak; bind him up and then fetch his companion, to bind in his turn."

Palamon was astonished as the lightning-fast paws of the flesh servant grasped him, gagged him, then bound him as easily as the hands of a nurse swaddling a baby. He looked up and his heart sank like a lead ball in a pitcher of wine.

Now he was able to make out the features of the man directing the flesh servant, features which had been hidden inside the hooded woolen robe. Palamon had seen that face before; it was stamped indelibly into his memory, along with the other face which it served. It was not Reovalis. Palamon found himself looking into the grinning face of Navron, Alyubol's minion and loyal servant.

Chapter Eighteen:
Pomfract Castle

BESSINA FELT SHOCK and surprise when she recognized Gymon. The last time she had seen him, he had stood beside the King as both men had condemned her father; to look at him now emptied the blood from her face. Her father had been alive and Count of Galliardy then; now there was no knowing where he was. Was he buried in a potter's field? Had he been burned or cast into the sea? One thing was certain—Gymon and Lothar the Pale were his murderers.

But Gymon was not concerned by the hardness of her expression. He smiled, finished removing his hooded cloak, then threw the garment carelessly onto a couch. It was strange. For all the power he held over her—and she did not doubt for a moment that it was the power of life and death—he was no longer awesome; he was not as frightening as he had been before he had revealed himself. For all his cunning and his designs on her, Gymon was physically unimpressive. His eyes were a watery, washed-out blue, and white traced his orange hair and scraggly beard. He was no taller than she was and the sunken chest beneath his doublet made him look like a victim of his own donjons. His appearance was actually laughable. It left her with a strangely relaxed feeling, in spite of her hatred for him.

His eyes fondled her for a moment; then he bent to pour wine into two goblets, lifted one to his lips, and offered her the other. She sipped the liquid; it was warm and sweet, fine spiced wine and a welcome change from the water she had been drinking for days. She felt the beginning of a warm glow spread through her as she took another sip.

He sat down on a campaign chair without taking his eyes from her; the longer he smiled at her, the less the expression meant. "You may remove your traveling robe, my child." He gestured toward the fire that was leaping and crackling in the chamber's great fireplace. "It's warm enough in here. Do you know where you are?"

Bessina put down her goblet and loosened the cord which held her outer robe in place. Since he no longer made her feel naked and vulnerable, she lifted the heavy garment over her head and let it fall to the floor; she was more comfortable wearing a light gown. "I must be in Buerdaunt," she said coolly.

"You're quite correct. You're in a tower chamber I've arranged in Pomfract Castle. I am bailiff here and what I wish to happen in this place will always come to pass. Now let me see; the viands on this table tempt the tongue but I suspect that you have need of food a bit more nourishing." He rose, spoke to one of four servants who were holding torches along the walls, then watched the fellow leave. As the door closed behind the servant, Gymon turned back to Bessina with a smile. "Some supper shall be brought," he said. "Perhaps you'd like to see the chambers I've arranged for you."

Bessina shrugged wearily. Gymon was ugly and hateful and she did not want to look at him. "I'm tired. I'd rather sleep."

"The time for bed is later, though the room which serves that purpose is a lovely one." He took her by the hand and pulled her into another chamber. There were no servants in this room; there was only the feeble light thrown by another, smaller fireplace.

Bessina did not like the touch of Gymon's hand; it was cold, moist, and unpleasant. She tried to pull from his grasp but his fingers were like iron. And she shuddered at the sight of the great, canopied bed which occupied most of the wall opposite the fireplace. If she had nursed any doubts about his intentions, the sight of the bed certainly dispelled them. She had no respect for him and she hated his touch; but even though he was ridiculous, the prospect of his caresses was frightening, horrible. The moisture of his grip soaked into her skin; even after he released her, she felt as if she would have to wipe her hands for hours before they would ever feel dry.

For his part, Gymon seemed to be in a grand mood. He strode to the outside wall of the chamber, swept a tapestry aside, and revealed a shuttered window. He withdrew a ring of keys from his doublet, unlocked the shutters, threw them back, and summoned her. "Come here and see the world I give to you."

She reluctantly did so. The glass which formed the windowpanes was clear and without impurities; she could feel its coolness as she bent toward it. It was a cold night. She felt even colder as she looked down. Gymon had not lied when he had told her she occupied one of the highest towers in the castle. The light flooding out the window touched nothing except air. Far away, she could see lights from windows in other towers but none of them was as high as the one she peered from.

Pomfract Castle was a huge, sprawling citadel; she could not make out its full outline in the darkness. Below the window jutted a narrow stone ledge which probably had been used to support scaffolding when the place had first been built; below that, a dozen empty fathoms separated her from the swinging lanterns of guardsmen who paced the crenellated walls. Beyond the walls she saw what she guessed was the bay, judging from the slowly swaying ships' lanterns in the harbor.

Her heart sank; she was as alone as if she had been imprisoned in the middle of the sky. There could be no doubt that Gymon had placed her exactly where he wanted her; she saw him smile as he watched her expression. He gestured toward the great bed. "Sit down."

She would not sit on the bed; she folded her arms and walked quickly into the other chamber. She could not really feel afraid of the man; he cut a comical figure as he followed her through the doorway. But he was horrible and repulsive and the suite in the sky, with all its ornate and luxurious trappings, made her feel as if her insides had been turned to lead. She sat down heavily before the tray of sweet-smelling viands, though she was not hungry.

Gymon stood before her, his hands clasped behind his back. "You should appreciate what I have done for you. I'm sure you know your beauty fires the blood—I have no doubt you've heard that many times. The gods know that my youth is long gone by, but you impart to me the urge to act as I've not acted since . . ." He shrugged. "The hair of both of us is red, you know, and that implies a soul that's full of passion. But my hair has more of orange, a clownish color which men jest about." He lifted an eyebrow. "Though not, of course, when I am present. But—oh!—your auburn locks so deep and glossy, and your limpid eyes, your soft and satin skin—they make my flesh crawl with desire for you."

Bessina cast her eyes down and rested her forehead on her fingertips. The worst torture imaginable was having to listen to his words. They made her flesh crawl, but not in the way he had meant.

"I see that you dislike my flattery; it's not, you know. Each word is true as from a sibyl's lips. Besides, your beauty saved your life. Those robbers who accosted you might well have slit your throat or issued you the fate that's worse than death if your great beauty had not promised them a greater profit than their lust could match."

She coldly looked up at him, the man who had taken her father from her. "What makes you think their touch offends me more than yours?"

His expression did not even waver. "You do not know the lengths to which I went to get you here, the setbacks I endured, the risks I took. I shall not speak of love. Your body's all the virtue you will need to please me well. I've moved the earth for you, you simple girl. I doubt you have the mind to comprehend the things I've done."

Bessina did not respond. She sat and stared at him, her eyes smoldering with hatred; she hated his manner nearly as much as what he had done to her father.

"I doubt you can recall the day we met," he said. "Your father played the host to many men as pale King Lothar made his way across our realm. 'Twas—let me think— two years ago. But even then, although you were a bud just newly blossomed, you had such a look about you I decided then and there you'd grace my bed. Whatever hindrances stood in my path, I'd overcome them to secure your favors." His tone was hardly that of a lover; he spoke with the manner of a man showing off a new horse, explaining a *fait accompli*. It made Bessina grimace. He already considered her his safely won prize.

But he went on without heeding her expression. "I thought there was a chance of buying you out of her father's hands for some great dowry. But alas, 'twas not to be. Your chamberlain, Lord Crecche, had started that road first; I couldn't overtake him for the prize. So I decided force would serve my ends. If Clauvis would not let you be my bride, I'd tear him from his place and have you anyway."

He refilled his goblet, then continued his harangue. "Old Crecche had reached the Count before me and had offered bribes to win your hand for gold. I could have done that if I'd started sooner. But very well. I have Pale Lothar's ear; what I cannot acquire by bribery, I have the means to seize by simple force. I had to turn the King against the Count, but how to do it? Faith, it wasn't hard; the taxes levied on fair Galliardy were in arrears—and by adjusting entry dates in ledgers in the royal treasury, I made them more so. Still, a catalyst was needed to insure the King's reaction be as fierce as I thought necessary. Do you know the thing I did?"

Besinna shook her head. Her expression had turned to stone.

"I hired a lone assassin to assault the King as he returned

from hunting. I had never let the fellow see my face and I would be beside the King, well knowing what would come. Therefore I would be able to prevent the deed from being brought to its fruition. I didn't want the King to die, you see, I wanted him enraged. The murderer could never recognize me and besides, I saw him dead before he could confess who urged him to the crime. It all went perfectly. Pale Lothar in his fury turned with ease onto the trail I'd mapped for him."

Bessina gasped. Such treachery was beyond belief. "You beast."

"No, not a beast, my treasure. I'm a man with subtle ways of sealing up your fate. But Lothar is not foolish— I soon found that he had reasons all his own to take your father's Castle Gnoffe. And when 'twas done, he sent you to the refuge, for he knew that I had yearnings for your tender flesh." He drank off the last of his wine. "They say the gods will help a man who strives to gain an end, and so they have helped me; when you escaped and robbers snatched you up, the very Fates conspired to bring you here. And so you came; you're more within my grasp than if your father had accepted my proposal for your hand. Myself and you and some few silent servants e'er shall know that you are in this tower. You're my pet, my lovely captive bird, my plaything. You will live in comfort, with your wants all satisfied. Do you know what you'll give me in return?"

"It's very obvious."

"Indeed." He extended an arm and picked up an exquisitely carved vase. "I love collecting treasures, girl; they symbolize my growing status. You are now the chief among them." He put the vase down, approached her, caressed her cheek. His touch was a violation and she turned away from it.

He plainly expected that reaction; he reached out, grasped her shoulder, and forced her to face him. Her disgust and anger overcame her and she responded violently. She slapped him hard and when he grasped her wrist she tried to claw at him with her free hand. The struggle was a short one; a pair of the servants caught her arms and twisted them behind her back. She struggled and panted but she could not move. "You fiend," she shouted.

They were interrupted by a double knock at the chamber's massive wooden door. Since all the servants were occupied, Gymon stepped to the portal and opened it himself. Two female attendants bore platters of steaming food. "Take that away," Bessina cried. "I have no urge to eat before a fiend the likes of you."

Gymon smiled as he lifted a cover and tasted the dish beneath it. "That is a pity. Still, it's said wild fawns do not eat well when in captivity. I'll have to gain my satisfaction quickly, in a day or two, before you start to waste away and lose your lovely curves." He directed the two women to set the platters down and retire. "But it would be a pity if you starved, for me and you as well. Life's much too sweet for you to cast it off because of some slight inconvenience I put you to. Not every maid would weep for you, my dear."

It was as if he were deliberately baiting her, sure of the hold he had on her. Bessina was beside herself with anger and loathing. "I hardly have the words with which to name your qualities. You have the gall and smug, offensive manner of foul creatures not yet classified by language. Do you think I'd step into your arms all cheerfully and be your concubine? Why, dogs have more to recommend them to my bed than you. An op has features more well-formed than yours; a serpent has a far more pleasing eye. Your arms compare to my true lover's arms as some reflection off a muddy pool and I am sure your legs are only fit to scratch some barnyard's dirt, well-matched with all the other chickens' legs." She paused for breath, having used all the insults she could conceive on such short notice. But she had more vitriol to pour out and she did not hesitate. "Besides, how can you be so crass to think that I could ever bear your touch when I hold you responsible in full for my poor father's death?"

Gymon was not troubled by Bessina's insults; his interest seemed piqued by them rather than dampened. Only the statement about Bessina's father seemed to set him back at all. "Your father's death?" He paused for an instant, then smiled once more, his eyes probing her features in a way she had not expected. "Why should you be offended by his death? The way you fought with him, I should have thought you would have thanked the man who rid you of his presence."

His response gave pause to Bessina's anger. It was true, of course; all her life she and her father had quarreled, bickered, and fought. Count Clauvis had oppressed her and she had rebelled. But that had been a different matter; she herself would not have believed the way she grieved at his loss. A quarrel or two could never lessen the love between father and daughter. "You have no human sensibility or you would know a daughter's feelings for her father do not change when there is strife. I loved him much. I would have killed or died for him and he for me. The love I bear my Flin wedged us apart, but still the love of fathers for their girls and daughters for their fathers is a thing the Fates themselves decree. And you who snuffed him out now seek my touch; I'd let the dogs rip all the bleeding flesh from off my ivory bones before I'd yield to you, you murderous scum."

"Indeed?" His smile became incredulous. "I thought you'd want him dead."

Bessina burst into impotent tears; his very words were a crime. "I'd never think such thoughts. He was my father."

"Who would have thought? One cannot predict the muddled workings of the female brain. So tell me, most surprising maiden, what things would you do to have your father's life restored to him?"

She turned away from him, still sobbing. "Go take your pleasure elsewhere. Taunt me not."

"I'd never think of taunting you. In fact, I'll take you to your father if you wish."

"So I can mourn the corpse you made of him?"

He shook his head. "So you might speak with him. He's still alive."

Bessina was stunned; disbelief warred with hope. "He cannot be alive. The news I heard makes that impossible."

Gymon shrugged. "Your news is false. It's all the same

to me, but if you'd like to go to him, I offer you the chance."

She hesitated. Was he playing a trick on her?

He lifted his cape and thrust it toward her. "Put on this wrap to keep your form concealed and we will go to see whose word is false. You may not have the cause to hate me that you think you have."

Bessina held back a moment, then took the heavy robe from him. What reason would he have to lie about such a thing? He had to know she would never yield herself to him willingly in any case. He was repulsive, awful; even in the benevolent moment of offering to take her to her father, he cut a figure that was both ridiculous and disgusting. As she put on the robe, she noticed that it actually fit her quite well; the bailiff's body was scrawny; he was smaller than she, though she was not a large woman.

He ordered a servant to bring a torch, then they left the chamber. They passed down endless flights of stone stairs offset by short stretches of level corridor, until they reached a long, gloomy hall. Then they paused, and Gymon told her to turn her eyes away from him. When he allowed her to look once more, they were standing before a secret doorway.

He stepped through, then extended his hand to take hers; his touch made her want to recoil. Whether her father was dead or alive, she hated this man who held her in his loathsome grip. But the servant stepped through behind them, the panel slid shut at their heels, and they went on their way.

"The hallways leading to the catacombs are watched," Gymon said. "And I have no desire that you be seen or even that some people know that I have undue interest in a prisoner. This keep is laced with secret corridors which no one but myself has knowledge of; thus I go undetected."

The passage wound crazily downward; Bessina had no idea where they might be going. There was dust everywhere, although it had been disturbed so much she suspected the passage was Gymon's regular thoroughfare. Ever so often she would see a glimmer of light through a

crack between the stones or hear the mutter of voices.
The secret route apparently served many occupied chambers.

Gymon paused and a smile lifted his features, making
him look like an evil pixie. "This chamber which we pass
would interest you. A maiden's kept within; I know her
name, although I have not seen her for myself. She's a
Princess, a hostage here. Though she escaped us once,
the King has sworn he'll see her buried rather than allow
her ever to return to her own shores. The story's interesting but there's no time." He crooked his finger at the
servant and they went on.

The passage became more twisted and irregular than
ever; the dust and the flickering torchlight made Bessina's
eyes smart long before they reached their destination. But
at last they did stop. Gymon paused, gestured for her to
turn away, then opened another portal which revealed a
broad, low-ceilinged chamber.

A chill crept through her as he beckoned her into the
large chamber and she was reminded of that time—it
seemed as if it had been aeons ago—when her father had
taken her to see the prisoner below Castle Gnoffe. She
was in such a chamber now, a torture chamber. But this
one was even more horrifying than the other.

The place was well kept up and still in use; it was clean
and neat, and the broad, flagstoned floor was dotted with
the most modern instruments of persuasion. There was
not a speck of dust anywhere. Polished steel and oiled
leather gleamed, the floor was worn from the endless
treading of feet, and the sickening smells of blood and
burned flesh invaded her nostrils, no matter how she held
her breath or snorted to keep them out. She saw racks,
spiked tables, stocks, all kinds of machines for pressing
and for breaking bones, pincers for ripping out fingernails,
and braziers for heating irons. The chamber was empty,
but even standing in it made her shudder violently.

Noticing her reaction, Gymon took the time to escort
her to one of the tables. He placed her hand atop one of
the oiled leather straps which would hold a body down
while that particular form of torment was being applied.

He produced a rosewood box from beneath the table and opened it for her; it was full of long needles, some straight, some curved or even hooked. Each one was carefully housed in its own compartment. "The body is an instrument of music, or at least that is the saying of the provost. Yes, he is a virtuoso at his craft; his ingenuity at this, his art and love, can scarcely be believed. I must admit that he produces sounds out of the lips of humans one would think could not be made by vocal cords."

He observed her reaction. Then he put the box away, took her hand once more, and beckoned the servant to follow them. "We must move on. These sights, though interesting, delay us from the object of our journey." They crossed the chamber cautiously; beneath a torch she could see a man sleeping with his head upon a desk. Gymon smiled and gestured toward the sleeper. "I gained him his appointment. It's quite convenient for the guard to be a man who sleeps the boring hours away; I do not like my travels to be watched. But make no noise, for he does not sleep soundly."

They hurried along until they had reached an angle in the chamber's irregular wall. Then they proceeded more easily until the bailiff stopped before an iron-barred door. He gestured for Bessina to look through. She obeyed, still trembling. What she saw inside made her catch her breath.

It was her father. The beard had been shaved away; he lay on a wooden pallet covered with filthy straw and wore only a loincloth, but there was no mistaking Count Clauvis' form and face. Tears rushed to her eyes. Even in the torch's irregular light, she could see he had been horribly abused; bruises and scars speckled his chest and legs, his lips were horribly puffed, and the ends of some fingers were bloody and raw. It was the scene at Castle Gnoffe all over again, except this time it was her father she saw in the midst of agony.

She felt her knees buckle; the bailiff and the servant had to catch her to keep her from collapsing. She had thought her father dead. Now she found him alive but in a lair of horror. She was not sure which was worse. Once more she saw in her mind's eye the man she had watched

breathe his last in the donjons below Castle Gnoffe. Would
her father end the same way, grown prematurely ancient,
deformed, and hardly human? She could not bear the
thought; she wept and reached for support, any kind of
support. Her hands touched Gymon. He was less than a
man and more than a monster; he had made these things
happen, but in her moment of weakness, it did not matter.
She laid her head on his shoulder and sobbed. He patted
her back softly while motioning for the newly awakened
guard not to interfere.

"I want to speak with him," she said through her tears.
"Although it be for just an instant, I must wish him well."

But Gymon laughed softly and pushed her away from
the iron door. "Alas, that cannot be, my haughty maid.
You have insulted me and called me names and now it's
time for you to understand the rules which guide the game
I play with you. The maiden who looks down her nose
at me does not receive each gift for which she pleads."

He threw a hand across her mouth and together he and
the servant hauled her from the chamber. "Besides," he
said with a smile. "This sleep is all the refuge he's allowed;
it is his recreation and his medicine, so why disturb him
in the night? It's possible that he would not desire to speak
to you."

His words and the sight of her father's misery were
the most vicious punishment Bessina could imagine; she
felt herself being drawn toward the pit of despair. She
looked at the bailiff with pleading eyes. "Please, might I
see him at some other time?"

Gymon's smile was subtle, meaningful. "That will
depend on you." He took her by the arm and led her along
a broad corridor. She was so dazed by what she had seen
that she hardly noticed the route they took back to the
tower chamber.

When they reached her rooms, she noticed the air was
filled by the aroma of the food which had been brought
for her; the smell was sickening after the lingering airs
which had filled the torture chamber. The carefully prepared dishes were cold but it did not matter; she could
not have eaten anyway.

She sank into one of the couches, holding her hand before her eyes, her fingers resting on her temples. Gymon stood before her and placed a hand on her shoulder, but she shrugged it away. Her moment of weakness in the torture chamber had passed, although she was still badly shaken. His cruelty there had taught her she dared never be weak before him again.

But he was relentless. "What would you do to see your father saved?"

She gave a short, very bitter laugh. "I know the thing you want. Have you no soul?"

He laughed back at her, then scratched his scragglebearded chin. "What value has a soul in coin of realm? What does it weigh and what's the price per pound? You're doubtless right; I have no soul, nor do I need one for the business that I do." He strolled toward the chamber's door and turned to look back at her, still smiling. "I do not need your love, nor do I want it. Still, I'll have your body till I gorge on all the sweetness of its luscious warmth. It's your commodity but do not try to bargain with me; I will offer this—if you will yield to me all willingly, your father shall be exiled to the province called Laurons. His skin shall not be made to bear the marks of any further torture. But refuse and you shall watch him writhe his life away beneath the hands of men who'll make his pain a work of art. And then I'll have you anyway. Three days is all the time I give you to decide." With that, he winked and left.

The question before Bessina was a simple one, really; three days was all the time left for her to live the life of a human being. She buried her face in her hands and sobbed, and words crept out between her tears. "Oh, Flin, my Flin, wherever you may be, forgive me for the act I must commit."

Chapter Nineteen:
Two Intruders

AELIA AND SIR Phebos rode on toward Buerdaunt long after darkness had fallen. They rode slowly, taking care that no unsuspected eye might see them. They were in no hurry, after all; the later the hour when they made their attempt to slip into the city, the better it would be for them.

They saw no one. They stayed far to the north of the city, both to avoid the great inland gate and also because the forest rolled down close to the wall along this side of the valley. They rode quietly and cautiously, their horses striding through fallen leaves which had been soaked into a mushy carpet by recent rains. To their delight, they found a brushy area amid some trees shortly after leaving the road. The place looked as if it was seldom visited by men, which made it ideal for their purposes.

They dismounted and hobbled their horses. They had discussed it all earlier; their plan was ready to execute. Aelia removed her traveling cloak and handed it to Sir Phebos. The gown she wore beneath the cloak was plain and very worn but that made it all the better for her purposes; as for the cloak, Sir Phebos would wear it. He had balked at the thought of trying to enter the city without the hauberk which marked him as a Knight of Pallas—but he did not refuse Aelia's offer of the cloak to cover the hauberk. She was tall for a woman, almost as tall as he was, but she was thin; the cloak would not begin to encompass his shoulders. He had to tear it in several places to make it fit, which did no harm. In fact it added to the impression they were trying to create.

Aelia mussed her hair, rubbed dirt in it, stirred it until she looked as if she were wearing a bird's nest on top of her head. Then she did the same for Sir Phebos. He made a sour face at such treatment; as a Knight of Pallas he did not like being filthy, however necessary it might be. Still, he allowed himself to be mussed.

He hid his heavy-headed mace beneath his clothing and stuffed his helmet beneath a half-eaten loaf of bread in a burlap bag they had brought for the purpose. Then, as a final touch, Aelia produced from her saddlebag a goatskin filled with cheap wine. Sir Phebos could hardly stifle his laughter as she poured some of the dark liquid into her hand and flicked it onto his clothing. "My troth. You have an eye for details, Madam; we'll smell as if we'd been carousing for a day or two, at least."

She smiled back at him. "We have to smell the part as well as look it: you, a well-worn knight of lowly bearing, me, a trollop from the waterfront. We've been outside the gates to have our tryst."

He touched her hair, which she had made as frizzy as an eccentric mind. "It's wonderful. Just wonderful."

"Indeed," she said. "I'd not look in a mirror, were I you; you'd find you look no better than myself. You bear the goatskin, I will hang upon your arm, and we will go a-walking toward the town. I know the gate I want to enter by; Buerdaunt was prison to me once before. I know its streets, I know a goodly pack of beggars and informers, and I know the passage which I hope will lead us to my Berengeria." They started down the slope, making their way carefully through the brush in the darkness. Once they had reached open meadow, Aelia stopped him and took the goatskin. She swallowed a short draught. "The image must be finished. Thus, our breath must be as rank as wind from dogs' behinds."

He looked at her and marveled. "You are a wondrous woman. From the way that I saw you conduct yourself when we first met, I'd never have imagined such a change in dress, in manner, or in speech. You look as if you might have lived in gutters all your life and sound the part and smell it, by my troth."

"And I'm a priestess, too." Her mouth twisted into an interesting expression as she gave the goatskin back to him. "I've had to learn all sorts of roles throughout my life. When one cares for the Princess of Carea, one quickly finds she must do more then tend to matin prayers and advise which gown goes best with silver earrings."

"So I see." They became silent. They could see a spot of light relieving the darkness of the city's wall, and that was enough to reveal their destination. It was a small pedestrian gate, not tended by the ablest guards. It was used mainly by tradesmen who kept a goat or a cow or two and wished to have them herded outside the city by a boy hired for the purpose. As such, it was hardly ever used, except first thing in the morning and late in the afternoon.

As they approached, Aelia surprised Sir Phebos by clasping his left arm with both her hands. She hung onto him, leaned against him, and began to hum drunkenly. She had become the image of a slatternly trull; she looked no more an agent for the Carean throne than a flea would resemble a butterfly.

They approached the portal at a steady, though weaving, pace. When they came within earshot, Aelia began to sing; she started out softly at first, then put more force behind her notes. It was an odd strain, a lullaby she might have learned as a girl, or a song a trollop might sing while dreaming of days when the world had been pure and clean and she had been one with it. But as they closed within a few cubits of the gate, the guard signaled them to a halt. She stopped stock-still, then tore herself from his grasp and saluted the guard drunkenly, her lower lip shoved into

a vacuous pout. Then she began to sing a different song
for the guard's benefit:

> "Oh, I didn't raise my boy to be a soldier.
> I brought him up to drink and whore
> And do the things that soldiers do.
> I taught him to use loaded dice
> And keep a razor in his shoe.
> But he is still respectable,
> At least when you compare him to
> All guttersnipes who stoop to being soldiers."

She paused as she watched the reaction produced by
her words. There were two guards and they smiled at her
the way one would smile when watching someone make
a particular ass of himself. "I think you like my singing,"
she said, letting her voice crack. "Then I have another
verse I'll give you all for free." And she began again:

> "Oh, I'd never let my boy become a soldier.
> I know he's far too sensitive.
> He'll stay at home and beat his wife.
> He couldn't bear to eat the food.
> I've told him how you need a knife
> To slay the beetles in your drawers
> So he could never stand the life
> That he would have to live to be a soldier."

One of the guardsmen scowled and told Aelia to stop.
"By the gods, woman, haven't you any pity for the poor
souls who have to listen to that caterwauling?"

Aelia scowled. "What's that to you?"

"We're among them. Why are you out at such an hour?"

"We've just been walking," Sir Phebos said.

"This is an odd place to go walking," the guard said.

> "Oh, my boy would never make it as a soldier.
> He'd wear big holes in both his shoes.
> He doesn't like to walk or fight . . ."

The same guard silenced Aelia again, at which she looked very offended. But she waited for the other guard to repeat his question. "Why are you here instead of home in bed?"

Sir Phebos did his best to look embarrassed and Aelia broke in once more. "At home there's someone *in* the bed. 'Twould be a little nasty getting three of us into a single bed." She snickered at her own joke. "It's broken down already."

"We'd like to pass the gate," said Sir Phebos, looking nervous and ashamed. "You see, she's not my wife." He allowed his voice to trail off into an awkward whisper.

The guard who had been doing most of the speaking burst into laughter. "And no wonder. Who'd marry her?"

"Who'd marry you?" Aelia snapped.

The guard began to reply but Aelia interrupted him with another verse of her song:

"No one in her right mind would wed a soldier.
They're not much good for anything.
Except to transport sweat and bugs.
A strumpet never touches one,
That is if she cares whom she hugs.
They're always out a'killing folk
And when they're not they're squeezing dugs.
There's nothing quite as useless as a soldier."

The second guard was laughing very hard by now, which only hindered the first in keeping some kind of order. It was made all the more ludicrous as Sir Phebos tried to still his female partner. He was playing his part nearly as well as she was playing hers, acting out the role of a man who simply wished to get his paramour back home with as little embarrassment as possible. At last the guard managed to make himself heard, although he had already surrendered the point of whether to admit the two into the city. "I'll need to have your names before I can let you pass."

"Sir Standoff is his name," Aelia interrupted once more. "He makes his house wherever his horse falls to sleep."

"And where do you make yours?"

"I am the mistress of the Silver Knight, as good and clean an inn..."

"And where's your husband, madam? Do you have one?"

At the mention of the word 'husband,' Aelia lapsed into a sorry, besotted picture of drunken remorse and lost innocence. "I tell you he's as good and fair a man as ever asked the hand of woman. He cares for me as if I were a queen and never asks for nothing in return."

The guard was dumbfounded while his companion became practically hysterical. "Then what are you doing with this worn-out knight?" he asked.

There was a pause. "My husband's gone a bit of... well, you might say that he's softened his age. He's not the man he used to be. This fellow here's a fine, upstanding man."

Both guards sputtered into raucous laughter while Aelia glared at the two of them. "Then laugh at me, why don't you? I've worked hard for all my days; a woman such as me deserves a little pleasure now and then." Tears began to flow convincingly. "You'd pet a faithful dog if he worked hard to guard your door. And if your family cat kept out the rats, then she'd deserve to have her backside stroked a little. You left wives a'crying in their beds to come and stand about to serve no purpose but to pass the time by telling lies. Stop laughing, now. Piss on the lot of you, you'll never understand."

Even as Aelia spoke, the guards shoved both her and Sir Phebos through the gate. "Go to your homes and get some sleep, both of you, before we have you arrested."

Aelia and Sir Phebos went willingly enough. As they weaved out of the guardsmen's sight, she began another verse of her song but she allowed it to trail off and dropped it completely as they walked along. The look of stupor dropped from her face; they were past the gate and loose in Buerdaunt, but they still had far to go before they could relax.

They made their way along tortuous streets toward the center of the city and the low, rounded hill where Pomfract Castle stood, dark and brooding beneath the watchful moon. "I've got to give you credit," Sir Phebos said. "You just played that part as well as could be—but I hope you have a better route out of this town than through the gate we passed by bluff. I doubt those guards will e'er forget us."

"If worse should come to worst, we needn't pass out of the town. I know of persons who would take a bribe to keep us from the public view; the main thing is to pierce the castle's walls and rescue Berengeria before King Berevald's great fleet makes sail. The time we have is almost gone: a fortnight was the space he gave to us to pry her free by our own means. When that much time has passed, the fighting starts."

"I see," Sir Phebos said.

"If Lothar keeps her hostage, she may die as soon as word is brought that there is war. Thus, we must have her stripped out of his hands and hidden someplace, though it's still in town."

"But still and all, your purposes would be best served if we could spirit her out of the town entirely. Is't not so?"

Aelia nodded. "Indeed."

They walked as quickly as they could without attracting attention. There were few people about, though they could never be sure who might be watching them unseen. The cobbled streets became steeper and the buildings became older as they moved toward the heart of the city. The hill they were climbing was full of ancient structures, and Pomfract Castle stood at the top of it; they could already make out the battlements which stood like dragon's teeth along the tops of the massive walls. That made them cautious. Pomfract Castle was the King's citadel; he slept in one of its chambers. That meant the area would be tightly patrolled by the night watch. They had to duck into dark doorways more than once to avoid being spotted and perhaps stopped, until such maneuvers became habit.

At last they reached a square surrounded by buildings

which appeared to be as old as time itself. There were huge old houses and shops, some of them four and five stories high, and there was a large temple which stood silent and dark as it faced the square. They were very close to the castle; its wall rose on the other side of a row of houses, fearful in its huge proximity. The walls towered against the moon, as massive and dark as evil itself.

The square was large, about a hundred cubits across, and in the middle stood a small stone structure, open on all four sides and covered by a thatched roof. They hid in a doorway for a moment. Aelia's eyes darted about the square, then she and Sir Phebos hurried to that stone structure and hid carefully in its shadows.

It was a well, an ancient well from the look and smell of it. Aelia looked about one more time, then stood and began cranking up the water bucket. Sir Phebos helped her. The well was deep and they had to stop a couple of times as footsteps sounded across the square, but the bucket thumped against the crossbar after a few moments.

Aelia gathered her skirts about her knees, clambered up the side of the well, then climbed astraddle of the bucket. She could not seat herself; she had to hold herself awkwardly with her feet on the bucket's rim as Sir Phebos let it down. "Now lower carefully," she said. "For I will have to feel with my free hand and I could miss the passage in the dark."

Sir Phebos did as she told him. He lowered the bucket steadily and carefully, listening to the creaks and groans, taking care not to let the handle slip from his grasp. He fed the rope into the blackness of the well's mouth for what seemed an eternity. Time became the enemy; at any moment, the rope could snap or he could be discovered at his task. Still, the rope held and no one came to investigate.

At last the tension on the rope eased; it moved away from the center of the well's dark mouth, then wriggled sluggishly. Aelia was shaking it from below. That meant she had found the tunnel, so he released the handle and allowed the vessel to drop to the water. The splash echoed dully.

Sir Phebos glanced one last time about the square, then climbed onto the side of the well, caught hold of the rope, and began to lower himself hand-over-hand into the musty darkness. That the rope had not snapped while bearing Aelia's weight was little encouragement; she weighed far less than he did. Still, he let himself down, his knees wrapped about the rope like a schoolboy's, his arm and shoulder muscles strained, his nostrils wrinkled at the smell of dampness and decay into which he was plunging. The circle formed by the night sky above him became no more than a pinprick.

"Take care, take care, you're almost here." Aelia's voice reassured him; then her hand caught his leg in the darkness, and she pulled him toward the side of the shaft. An instant later, he felt his foot touch solid stone. He released the rope and staggered as he regained his balance. They had arrived, but this tunnel at the bottom of the well was as black as the inside of a demon's bowels.

He felt the stone wall. It was cold and clammy; the stone was so ancient and soft it felt as if it might crumble at his touch. "So here we are," he said. "We've reached the tunnel as you said we would, and I no longer doubt your prior intelligence about this stronghold. If you tell me that this tunnel goes beneath the castle, then it does. How did you know of its existence?"

"When my dear Princess and I were held within that castle, I pursued all means to find out everything that I could learn of it. I had three years to study all its nooks and crannies and to listen to the tales of workmen and of servants. Workmen are the finest ones to ask if you would know the secrets of a place. I now possess more lore about this keep than Buerdaunt's King himself." They began to feel their way along the tunnel as she spoke, placing their hands against spiders' webs, clammy stones, and dank hollows where stones had fallen away. There was no other way for them to go. The tunnel was black, black as mortal sin, black as hatred, so black a person had to feel the wall to keep from losing his balance.

She added a word to her explanation. "This tunnel first was dug as an escape route ages past, and most of those who live within the castle do not know it's here. It's hardly traveled, since it's so unpleasant."

"That much is true," Sir Phebos said. "Were you, a woman, not to make your way as boldly as you do, I think I'd shirk. I'd flee this place and try to climb the walls of yonder castle as an easier route."

They inched their way. The air outside was cold, but the gelid atmosphere within the black passage was even colder; then the walls suddenly began to feel warm and dry. "We've reached the castle," Aelia said. "We're within a wall between two heated chambers."

Moments later, a glimmer showed between two stones, like a star against a dark sky. The two intruders' eyes had become so sensitive in the darkness that even such a tiny light was almost painful when they looked directly at it. While Sir Phebos waited, Aelia fumbled in the darkness until a sliding noise ushered in yet more light, a dazzling amount. They found themselves looking into an unoccupied chamber where a torch flickered in a wall sconce. There were more torches in a great bin along one wall and Aelia took two of them, lit one, then handed it to Sir Phebos. Then they returned to their secret passage.

The tunnel became a different world with the addition of the torch; it stretched ahead of them, curving away into a darkness formed of flickering shadows. It was not an inviting world; the stones glistened like insects' eyes with moisture and many had fallen from their places. Rats scurried before the intruders, their eyes glittering like evil stars in the torchlight.

"I'm trying to remember," Aelia said, "how to find the way up to our chambers. When we fled the castle, it was thus—two lefts, a right, a left, and then we reached the torch depository."

"This is how you left the castle this last spring?"

"Indeed it was." They came to a place where the tunnel divided. Both branches were low-ceilinged and restrictive; they would have to crawl to go either way. "To reach her we must now reverse the course; a right, a left, two rights, and we are there."

Before he would accompany her any farther, Sir Phebos

paused. While she held the torch, he doffed his tattered cloak, pulled his helmet from the bag he had kept tied to his belt, and became his old knightly self, his chain mail shining like a metallic galaxy in the torchlight. Then they were on their way once more, penetrating the rat- and roach-infested world beneath Pomfract Castle.

When they came to the tunnel's end, Aelia opened a panel gingerly and peered about for any sign of foot traffic. Like rats themselves, they scuttled along a length of corridor, into an alcove, and through another panel, into a different section of the labyrinth. Their torches were beginning to burn low as they came to a halt behind still another panel.

"We've reached our chamber," Aelia whispered. "This is where we once lived out a three-year span as prisoners of Lothar. I will see if luck is with us." With that she released the panel and peeked into the chamber beyond. All was dark, but the darkness was pierced by the soft sounds of sleeping.

Aelia looked puzzled. "Before, no person slept within except the two of us, her Highness and myself." She had Sir Phebos hold the torch higher, put her head a little farther into the chamber, then made a startled sound, withdrew, and slid the panel shut. Her face was ashen in the torchlight. "It's not the room. I see a raft of serving-maids serenely sleeping there." Her back rubbed against the rough stones as she sank into a sitting position, her face fallen and desperate.

Chapter Twenty:
Princess Berengeria

AELIA LOOKED AT Sir Phebos in anguish. If Berengeria was not in Pomfract Castle, where was she? Or had Aelia herself made a wrong turn and guided them to the wrong chamber? She sat and thought for a moment, then spoke. "I have to look again."

Sir Phebos protested. "We dare not operate the panel more, for fear of waking them."

"We have to take the chance. I want to see the way the chamber is configured; perhaps I'll find a key to what's amiss."

She opened the panel a crack, peered through it once more, then closed it again. "The room is right. I ought to know it well; I paced that same stone floor a thousand times—but all the furnishings are moved about and now it houses serving maids. Perhaps she sleeps within the other chamber of this suite. If so, we have no way to get to her except to cross this chamber first."

Sir Phebos frowned. "I could hold them all at bay while you seek farther. First, though, search your mind. Is there another place we ought to look? Once we appear before this flock of maids, the die is cast. We'll hardly have the time to probe this castle if she's not within."

"You're right. Why would they put her with the maids?" Aelia pondered for a time, then a subtle shift in her features revealed a new thought. "There is another room where she might be."

"Where's that?"

"If all the serving maids are sleeping here, then their old quarters are unoccupied." Aelia started along the tunnel again.

"But can you find that place?"

"I'm going to try." It was a gamble, a true shot in the dark. Still, darkness was the one thing they had in abundance in the tunnel, and they had the time to explore, as long as they stayed out of sight. They scurried about for what seemed to be ages; they backtracked more than once as Aelia sought the other chamber along the meanderings of the tunnel. At last they reached a panel which she said looked promising. She paused before it, hesitated, then looked back at her companion. "If I should choose amiss, then let them take me. Do not make a sound; perhaps you might escape in all good time."

Sir Phebos smiled but shook his head. "I am a Knight of Pallas, madam. We do not escape while others sacrifice themselves in our behalf."

"So be it." She made a sign with one hand, released the panel, and slid it back. Her face sagged as she peeked through, then the look changed to one of relief. She opened the panel all the way and revealed a tiny chamber where a shawl hung, along with a few gowns and some other articles of clothing. "We've come into the wardrobe," she whispered.

She began to climb through but Sir Phebos stopped her. "There may be danger," he told her. "Let me take the risk."

She shook her head. "You are a stranger. If this opening should be the pathway to my dear Princess, I'd never jeopardize her modesty by letting strange eyes fall upon her ere I'd seen that she was rightly gowned."

Sir Phebos' face wrinkled in the torchlight. To be

accused of posing any kind of threat to a maiden's modesty, even in such circumstances, was enough to annoy any Knight of Pallas. He spread his hands, plainly vexed. "I must apologize. You lead the way."

She climbed through and he climbed through after her, taking care to keep the torch's flame away from the garments in the wardrobe. Aelia crept to the tapestry which separated them from the outer chamber and drew it back. The space on the far side was dimly lit and she saw furnishings, chairs, couches, a table, and a curtained bed. Then her heart leaped. A young woman knelt beside the bed, lost in prayer. There was no mistaking the curve of the features and the amber hair, although the body had grown terribly thin. Aelia approached Berengeria silently.

Berengeria heard the older woman's approach and turned; her face lifted into an expression of surprise and delight and she uttered the beginning of a joyful cry. Then she caught herself and stifled the sound. "My Aelia," she whispered as she reached toward the older woman. "You have come. How I have missed your stout companionship."

They hugged one another and their shoulders shook silently; their cheeks nestled warmly together and their tears mixed. Aelia had no children; she was a priestess of Hestia. This maiden was the closest thing to her own child she had ever known, so she embraced Berengeria and they kissed once more. "You've grown so thin," Aelia said. "By all the loving gods, how could this happen? They've been starving you."

"This new imprisonment has been quite harsh," Berengeria said quietly while she threw a robe about her night-clothing. "There's been but little food and I have not seen daylight since I came here."

Something horrified Aelia even more than Berengeria's thinness; the younger woman had been chained. Aelia's gaze fell on the shackle about the maiden's ankle and the chain which bound her to a ring set into the stone floor. She caught her breath.

Berengeria answered Aelia's wordless question. "They thought I might escape—and they were right. They took

the cruel precaution of that chain, and so it is they lock
me to the floor whenever I am left alone. They know that
there are tunnels in the walls and they have no desire to
see me pass along them once again."

"The beasts. The vermin." Aelia fumed quietly but her
mind raced. Brawny Sir Phebos could smash the lock,
but would that alert the guards? It could not be risked.
She withdrew her slender dagger; perhaps the lock could
be picked.

"No, wait." Berengeria grasped Aelia's hand. "That
trick is useless if you've not been trained in such tech-
niques. I've tried with pins and knives and things. We
need more strength." She showed Aelia the scratches about
the keyhole.

"Your captors have the hearts of animals," Aelia said.
"But we are here and we will get you out; I have a stout
companion at my side. Come out, Sir Knight, her modesty's assured."

Berengeria's eyes brightened until they lit on Sir Phebos.
Then her face fell. "I'd thought you meant another," she
said.

Aelia nodded. "Palamon. I'll tell that tale once we have
gained escape. But now, Sir Phebos, can you break the
lock?"

"I think I can," he said. He had Berengeria recline so
that the heavy padlock lay on the floor, then he brought
his mace down on it twice. The lock sprang open beneath
the impact but the noise was enough to wake the dead.

"Now we must go," Aelia said. "We have no way of
knowing who has heard." She said no more about
Palamon's uncertain fate.

"You have a way to pass out of the town?"

"I do not know. But if we go with haste, perhaps we
might escape the city's walls."

Berengeria hugged the older woman, her face alight.
"I never should have doubted that you'd come." She
bounded toward the wardrobe, her robe flapping, until
she noticed the Knight of Pallas and paused. "I beg your
pardon, Sir. In times like these it's difficult to act all
properly."

"Think nothing of it," he said. "I quite understand."
Even so, he looked out of place with a young woman
standing before him in such informal dress.

Berengeria talked excitedly as they entered the wardrobe. "I knew that you could do it, although I am quite
surprised that Palamon did not accompany you upon your
quest. Where is he now?"

Aelia hesitated. "That tale would take long. I'll tell it
when we've cleared this place."

Berengeria looked up at her. "But by your voice's tone,
I fear for him."

"Please hurry though the panel. We've no time." Aelia
feared whatever ill fortune might bring. Had someone
heard them break the lock? Would guards investigate?
Her eyes urged the younger woman to hurry even more
than her tongue.

Berengeria moved toward the secret opening but she
still spoke of Palamon. "Although I do not like the tone
of voice with which you speak of him, I shall forbear from
doubtful thoughts; I hope the news of him shall not bring
consternation. Now to facts pertaining to our flight—I've
seen Ursid one time since we were taken from Carea.
'Twas a week since we were hauled into this castle's
depths. Pale Lothar had allowed him just that once to
speak to me. At any rate, his quarters are the same ones
he was living in when we first met."

"Why should that matter?"

"Why, we must rescue him."

"It was not planned to save each person in this sprawling keep. We have no time to seek Ursid."

"We must." Berengeria's expression pleaded with the
older woman. "In all the days I've rotted in this room
without the sight of tree or bird or flower, I've had the
time to ponder all that's passed. We treated him unfairly,
all of us. He risked his life for love of me and yet I knew
from the beginning I did not love him. His face is scarred
and he has lost his titles for his deeds, if not his life; for
as I said, I saw him only once."

Aelia shook her head, desperately interrupting the

younger woman. "That all may be. But still your loyalty
is to the throne. You first must save yourself."

"We'll all escape together. Palamon has taught me that
if one does not remain allied to principle, then thrones
mean nothing."

Aelia was shaken by the argument. This was not something she had planned for. Ursid's rescue could take a
long time. It could allow Lothar the Pale to discover the
escape and bottle them all inside Pomfract Castle's hidden
labyrinths like so many rats in a trap. And the argument
was based on principle; what a terrible time it was to
bring that up. There was no time for Aelia to argue; she
could only direct Berengeria, use the voice which had
once cajoled the maiden into taking medicine when she
had been a girl, or into attending to studies when she had
been an adolescent. "We have no further time. I'll not
have Palamon and all his past and principles prevent our
flight out of this keep and Lothar's claws. Please hurry
now, my child, so we can go."

Berengeria's eyes became hard as stone. "One thing
that I am not, alas, is that. My childhood ended in a private
room when some old fragment dredged up from the past
tore me apart from him I loved. Would that I could have
lived out all my life in childish ease, outside the glare of
life's great disappointments. No, I'm not a child and all
my acts must now be governed by my faith, my knowledge
of what things are right, as well as the example set before
me by great men." She threw herself into a corner of the
wardrobe. "If you cannot save both us prisoners, then
save yourselves. Go out the way you came. Ursid has
risked his life full oft for me—and nearly lost it, too. He
cannot be abandoned to the tortures of his King."

Aelia stared at the young woman. Berengeria had always
been willful, but what a dreadful time for that part of her
personality to come into play. Aelia and Sir Phebos could
drag her to the secret panel but they would never be able
to force her into the passage, if she refused to go. And if
they struggled, it would surely bring the guards. So Aelia
nodded wearily. "Then we shall do as you demand. Now
hurry, please, before the night is gone."

Berengeria became firm and businesslike. She hurried to the panel and all three of them climbed through the little opening, into the narrow, winding passages, with only the light of Sir Phebos' torch to guide them.

As Aelia remembered, Ursid had lived in a nearby suite a level below the rooms the two women had occupied. To reach the access point, they had to follow their passage to a garderobe shaft, descend a ladder, then pass along another tunnel until they reached their destination. They went as quickly as possible, although the descent down the ladder was slow and distasteful and took valuable time. Just as they were leaving the shaft, they heard a sound which chilled all their souls, even though it surprised none of them. The door to the little chamber at the top of the shaft opened with a bang and they could hear a voice bellowing. "She's disappeared. We'll search the castle. The Carean hostage isn't in her chambers." There was a scuffling sound in the garderobe—evidently it had been occupied—and they could hear the sound of pounding feet. Luckily, the commotion was moving upward, away from them.

They hurried on. The secret panel in Ursid's chamber was larger than the one in Berengeria's wardrobe had been. That was both good and bad; they could enter and leave without effort, but it was impossible to open the panel without everyone in the room seeing it. Aelia carefully inched it open. She breathed more easily as she found the bedchamber empty.

She gestured for the others to follow as she stepped into the room. It was dimly lit and a quick check of the curtained bed showed that it, too, was empty. But the three of them remained as silent as death. The tall oak door leading to the next chamber was ajar and voices flowed through the opening. There were men talking on the other side.

Aelia held her breath, tiptoed to the portal, then peeked through. Three men sat in campaign chairs; none of them looked in her direction. They were seated about a chess table; two were obviously playing the game while the third, who sat with only the back of his head visible, seemed to be watching.

"Good move, Malias," the third, unseen figure said. "Thus his knight will fall and with it his defense is badly mauled." The voice belonged to Ursid. They had found him.

Aelia turned to inform the others in the lowest whispers. The two guards would have to be dealt with but Ursid could indeed be taken from the castle quickly. They did not dare wait for better conditions. They burst through the door, Aelia drew her dagger and leaped toward one side of the chess table; Sir Phebos covered the other side.

The three men were astounded. One of them upset the chess table. He leaped to his feet, but a blow from Sir Phebos' mace sent him sprawling. The other saw the blow and became agreeable, though all he faced for the moment were Aelia's dagger and Berengeria's bare hands.

As for Ursid, his mouth hung open as he also stood. He had changed from the time Aelia had first known him. His face had become lean and purposeful, and his scars lay across his features like badges of honor. He appeared half-stunned by his rescue, but his clothing surprised Aelia as much as the rescuers had surprised him. He was dressed in a light cavalry uniform and he clasped a half-full wineglass. His imprisonment had not been as harsh as had Berengeria's.

Berengeria spoke first, addressing the guard who was still upright. "Now sir, you must keep very still. One word or move that's false and you shall lie beside your fellow."

"No, no, no," Ursid protested. "These men are friends; they will not harm our cause." He looked at the Princess. "My Berengeria, how can this be?"

Berengeria flinched at Ursid's use of the word 'my,' but she replied proudly. "As always, Aelia comes when there is need. But tell me, are these men your loyal friends? If so, they'll not be tied."

"They're true and faithful. I'll not be betrayed by either. I would trust them with my life."

"If they're not tied, that shall be what you do," Aelia observed dryly. "We've come to take you with us, if you wish to be released from your imprisonment. If they can help us, then so much the better."

Ursid stepped toward Berengeria. "Released from prison? You'd do that for me?"

As he spoke, the sound of voices and footsteps came from outside the chamber and someone pounded on the door. "The hostage has escaped. Open the door, the castle must be searched to the last stone."

They all stood as if turned into statues; they were trapped. But Ursid acted instantly. He leaped between Aelia and Berengeria and pushed one of his friends toward the portal. "Now let him speak to them," he said in a harsh whisper. "He'll stall them off. No other way can we prevent a search."

It was good advice. Aelia reluctantly watched the man walk toward the chamber's double doors and open one panel slightly. She hoped he was as true as Ursid had said he was, and that he was also gifted with potent powers of persuasion.

Chapter Twenty-one:
Gymon's Bargain

BESSINA LAY IN the big bed and awaited Gymon the bailiff. It had been three days since he had issued his ultimatum; now it was night and time for him to appear and collect the goods he had bargained for. The thought made her shudder.

Oddly enough, she had hardly seen him since that first night; in fact, he had appeared only once. It had been the morning after he had taken her to the donjons to see her father. He had entered her chamber, still smiling, still smug, and had asked if she desired entertainment.

She had been picking at her breakfast and she had looked up at him with suspicion clouding the clear emeralds of her eyes. She had spoken as coldly as possible. "What entertainment could you show to me?"

"A kind which might be educational." He had ordered the servants to dress her and had led her once more through secret passages known only to him, along dark corridors to that same awful chamber where men were broken and burned at the pleasure of the King.

The place filled her with the same horror as before; in

fact the sight of the tormentors and their victims made it even worse. Men in dark robes moved about, silent and demonlike, their faces hidden within their black hoods, their motions casting eerie shadows up into the vaults and groinings of the ceiling. It made the entire chamber look as if it had come alive; it was terrifying. She asked Gymon if she was to be tortured herself; he smiled and said that the marring of a body as perfect as hers would have been sacrilege.

But that was only a momentary relief. Two victims had been strapped down. Though Count Clauvis was not one of them, that made the process only marginally less dreadful to watch—and she was forced to watch it. While Gymon and his two servants held her, she had to observe the fiendish operation of the machines of pain.

The hooded torturers worked as precisely as surgeons, two operating on each of the prisoners. They silently turneds cranks, inserted and probed with needles, applied hot irons, and operated levers to horrible effect; the screams and groans of the victims filled Bessina's ears to bursting. It seemed a marvel that the stones themselves could have borne such sounds through the centuries without crumbling.

At one point, a wizened little man appeared from a room at the end of the chamber and questioned one of the bound figures in a voice barely audible for the groans. Then he shrugged and retired and it all began again. It went on and on; Bessina could still hear shrieks ringing in her ears. She begged to be taken away, she pleaded with Gymon, promised him his will if he would only take her back to her room. Oddly enough, he himself never mentioned his ultimatum and he only smiled at her pleading.

But he had finally brought her back to her tower. She had been left alone ever since, except for her servants. And when the sun had set, they had gently but firmly escorted her to the bedchamber, her own place of execution. The bed was as large as a sea and as soft as a swan's breast, but there was no comfort in that.

At first she had an idea; the door to her chamber opened

inward. She looked at it a moment, then pushed a chair against it. She added the other chair and, with some difficulty, the washstand. None of the items was very heavy; it was a futile gesture, a hopeless gesture, but it made her feel a little better.

She lay for a long time with the curtains open; the single torch which illuminated the chamber burned low, then flickered and went out, plunging her into darkness. And still he did not come. Her emotions seethed. She wished he would make his appearance and get the horror over with, but that wish was blunted by the empty hope that he might not come at all. Perhaps he had forgotten. Perhaps he had found another to distract him. Best of all, perhaps he had died.

She must have dozed because she could hear a clock chiming a late hour somewhere in the castle; the night was more than half over and the bailiff still had not come. Hope began to blossom; perhaps something really had happened to him. She pictured him dead of a stroke or of surfeit, pictured his funeral on a gray, drizzly day. They were reassuring images.

Then the images all faded, along with her hopes; she heard voices in the outer chamber and one of them belonged to Gymon. She was wide awake instantly and her blood turned to ice. Then someone tried the door to the bedchamber; it would not open because of the furniture she had stacked against it. She heard more voices, thumping sounds. Too late, she wished she had not barricaded the door as it relentlessly swung toward her.

The servants were pushing it open. It was not a great task, after all; she had not had much material to work with. Then Gymon stepped through. In one hand he bore a torch which cast an evil glow over him and the two men who looked through the door after him; in the other hand he carried a vessel of wine. His face was flushed and he was obviously agitated.

He strode to the wall sconce, removed the expired torch, and replaced it with the one he had brought. Then he ordered the servants to replenish the wood in the fireplace. He did not even seem to notice Bessina watching him. But once all preparations had been finished, he turned to the door and spoke to the two attendants. "This door shall not be opened till the morrow. If a man disturbs my pleasure ere that time, his death shall be unpleasant. Do you hear?"

The two nodded and withdrew. Gymon bolted the door and only then did he turn toward Bessina. She crossed her arms before her and shrank against the headboard of the bed. He smiled, but there was an evil glint in his eyes. "What did you think to gain by that?" He gestured toward the chairs and toilette stand where they had been shoved out of his way. Bessina had no reply. She could only look at him.

He sat on the edge of the bed and offered her the wine flask. She refused it. "It does not matter," he said. "We have all the time we need and you will soon forget what bothers you." His expression hardly ever changed. He was smug, sure of himself, and there was no reason for him not to be; after all, she was alone in a great castle and her father was in his power. She could do nothing against him. If she tried, he could wreak horrible vengeance on the man who had given her life; it was all perfect for him and horrible, dreamlike for her. She watched as he slowly removed his clothing. He allowed his slippers and leggings to fall to the floor with a soft thud, then removed his belt with its dagger and great key ring and dropped it on top of them. He pulled the dark robe off over his head, then his underclothing. Naked, he was a pink, splotchy apparition; it was a horrible display, repulsive and sickening.

The bed shifted beneath his weight; she could tell he was sitting and looking at her in the shadows. What was he thinking of her? What would anyone think of her? What did it matter? "I knew you'd see the light," he said. "You'll live quite well and come to love these meetings 'twixt ourselves."

But someone pounded on the door to the outer chamber. There was the sound of rapidly moving feet and then Bessina could hear an excited voice. "The hostage girl is missing. Summon him." There was more urgent speech, then someone pounded on the door of the chamber. "My Lord, come quick. The hostage from Carea's disappeared. The King demands your presence."

Gymon's head snapped toward the voice and Bessina heard him curse softly in the shadows. "Yes. Very well. I'll come to him at once. Do not disturb me till I've gotten dressed." He began dressing in haste; he seemed to have forgotten Bessina's presence completely, the way a child would forget a toy it had thrown down. The bed shook with his motions as he hurried to regarb himself.

Bessina watched him and felt more wretched than ever; her torture was being postponed but it would still come. And it seemed to mean no more to him than a sip of particularly good wine. She hated him. She would never have believed she could hate anyone so completely. She watched him and she seethed. All her misery and fear transformed into hatred; she wished him dead, she wished his living flesh would decay and fall from his bones.

As he pulled his gown back on and hastily straightened it, her hand slipped under the pillow which concealed her dagger. She wrapped her fingers around the handle. But her father's life hung in the balance if she opposed the bailiff. Besides, what could she really do with her little weapon? They were questions that had ceased to matter as she glared up at him, her fury doubled because she was helpless, because he was secure and comfortable in her helplessness. She dared not strike. But all other considerations faded before her hatred for the man who would soon ravish her, but who was now hardly even aware of her presence a cubit away from him. Her heart beat like timpani and she felt her breath quicken; nothing mattered except the sight of the horrible creature's blood.

Catlike, she pulled her dagger from its place and, before he could turn and prevent her, she buried it in his back as far as it would go. The breath hissed out of him like air out of a bellows; his hands flew up. He cursed her from between clenched teeth, then turned and hit her, his fist landing flush upon her cheek. The blow snapped her head about, made her ears ring, and dazed her. Then the horrible realization came to her that he had not even called the guard. She had hurt him but he was still sure of his mastery; he was going to punish her himself.

She recoiled in terror as he reached for her. He grasped her hair, pulled her from the bed to the floor, and knocked the wind from her as his blood spattered her face and neck. He kicked at her, but she still had the knife. She lashed upward in desperation, felt the blade strike home, withdrew it and struck again. He toppled and they struggled on the floor; she drove the blade in once more, and at last they both lay still. The panting was now all her own. She pulled herself away from him and looked down; he was still and silent, his death grin a reflection of the smirk she had come to hate. There was blood everywhere. She dropped the dagger and shrank away from him; horror had blended into horror. What had she done? She would surely die, and her father would surely die, both under the precise fingers of the torturers in that dreadful donjon chamber.

There was a sound from the other chamber; she turned and heard talking and laughter. The door was still bolted, but it would open at any moment, and then her crime would be discovered. She fell to her knees in helpless desperation, frantically looking about until her eyes fastened on the window. It was the window she had gazed from, but which was now barred by locked shutters.

A quick death by falling was preferable to death under torture. She knelt over the body, snatched the key ring, unlocked and flung wide the shutters, then stood and stared at the glass of the window. She bit the back of her hand; was this where it was to end? No more life, no more joy or laughter, no more father, no more Flin. Peristeras had said the Moirae were upon her and the Fates had set the course of her life. They were cruel Fates, then.

But she dared not weaken. She could not go back to that horrible chamber and face the provost and his minions and their terrible machines. She threw down the keys, faced the window, then clenched her teeth as she pushed against the leaded panes. They gave with a soft rasping sound, then fell away to smash on the walkway far below.

The cold air which rushed through the opening made her gasp as she climbed across the sill.

But then she hesitated; she looked down and her eye caught the stone projection she had noticed before, the ledge which had supported scaffolding during the castle's construction ages past. She could actually reach down and touch it with her foot; it was wide enough to stand on.

A desperate hope filled her; perhaps she was not to die, at least not right away. Her mind cleared and she scrambled back into the chamber, to return to the bailiff's body. He was a small, scrawny man and she had been able to wear his robe; now she would wear all his clothes. She quickly stripped his robe from him, put it on, put on his slippers, and buckled on his belt. She even donned his fur cap, breathlessly stuffing her hair up into it. Then, last of all, she snatched up his keys and both his and her daggers.

There was blood on the robe but there was nothing she could do about that; the material was dark and she hoped the stains would go unnoticed. Besides, if anyone came close enough to examine her that carefully, she was lost anyway. She looked at the door once more. At least Gymon had done her a great service through his threats against anyone who might intrude; she would have a little time to escape while the servants pondered his failure to appear.

Her heart raced; she climbed onto the narrow ledge and began to make her way around the outside of the tower. Perhaps her escape would only be a short one. Perhaps the ledge would be just as much a trap as the bedchamber had been, but she had taken the great step. Hurrying, afraid to look down, leaning against the breezes and vertigo which tried to pull her into emptiness, she pressed herself against the cold stone of the tower and inched along, moving her right foot, then her left, her right foot, then her left. She tested the footing with her toes constantly, always afraid there would be an end to her escape route. But the stones of the ledge held firm.

She came to a window, but it was shuttered on the inside. She did not try it; even if she broke the glass, the stout shutter would not yield. So she went on—right foot, left foot, right foot, left foot. The tower was huge and she inched her way more than halfway around it. Had the bailiff's body been discovered? She hoped the messengers who had come were as awed by his threats as the servants were.

She reached another window, looked in, and her heart leaped. There was no shutter on the other side. She grimaced as she kicked the glass in, then climbed through and found herself on a landing of the great staircase which traveled the height of the tower. There still was no hubbub from the chambers she had left, although she could hear shouting below her. Whoever the hostage was who had escaped, it was causing great concern.

She ran down the stairs, sometimes taking two steps at a time, stumbling, nearly falling. She kept her eyes open for hiding places in case someone appeared, but there was no one; the commotion was moving to another section of the castle.

Her father! There was a chance she could keep her father off the leather-bound tables. She had the bailiff's keys; perhaps one of them would fit the lock to her father's tiny cell. But how to get to the donjon? She knew the way, but many guardsmen stood between her and that fell chamber.

She made her way cautiously, hiding whenever she heard footsteps, wishing she had known how to get into the secret passages Gymon had taken her along. But one thing was in her favor; whoever had escaped, no one seemed interested in looking for them in the sublevels of the great castle. As far as she could tell, the guards were searching the ground level and above, which was all very logical—who would escape to a torture chamber? That logic served her well.

She reached the chamber quickly; she was still panting as she pushed against one of the great ironwood doors. But the door would not budge; it had been locked. Feverishly she took the bailiff's key ring and fumbled as she tried each key, one after the other, until the lock finally gave with a groan. She was in. It was not quite dark inside the chamber, which looked the same as it had the first time she had seen it. The tables and racks brooded silently, their leather and brass fittings shining evilly in the dim light.

The only sounds she could hear were the snores of the prisoners and an occasional soft groan as one of them stirred in his sleep. She hurried to her father's cell and again fumbled with keys, but none of them would even go into the rusty lock, let alone turn; the bailiff did not carry keys to such unimportant doors as that one.

Her mind worked frantically until she remembered the watchman who had slept at his post. She looked out past the angle of the wall. There was no one at the desk. The watchman must also have joined in pursuit of the mysterious escaped prisoner. She ran across the room toward the deserted post, hoping against hope that there would be another key ring there—but there was not. The watchman had taken it with him. What was she going to do? She was too frail to batter the lock open by main strength.

A sound made her turn; someone was coming. Her eyes searched for a hiding palace and she spotted a shadowy corner, hidden from the uncertain torchlight by one of the massive pillars which supported the ceiling. She scuttled into the cranny just as a door opened and two men entered.

"That's strange," she heard one of them say. "I locked that door when I left." Bessina cursed herself; she had not thought to try locking the door from the inside.

"I don't see why they'd have come here, but you'd better have a look around." The other voice was low and guttural, and she had heard it before; it belonged to one of the torturers.

"Who'd escape just to come to this pit?"

"Only the gods know that. Search every corner."

Bessina shrank as far into her niche as she could force herself, pressing her head against the cool stone of the wall. There was something hard and cold beside her; she felt the back of her hand brush against the smooth, chilly surface. Curious, she felt it again. It was a stack of lead weights, smaller ones stacked on top of larger—she had learned their purpose two days earlier. They were used for pressing. A plank was strapped across the victim's chest and the weights were placed upon it, first lighter ones, then heavier ones; as more and more weight was added, breathing became difficult, bones cracked, and respiration halted. She removed her hand.

She had other things to worry about. She could not see the watchman as he started his search, but the sound of his voice told her he had begun on the far side of the chamber. He did not seem to enjoy his task. She heard him call out sarcastically, "Do you want me to look in the water butt?"

"You don't need to be funny. You'll be getting a very strange sensation if you don't search and it turns out she was here all the time."

Bessina tried to make herself even smaller and less conspicuous. Had Gymon been found or were they still seeking the other prisoner, the Princess? She began to sweat; the drops stood out on her forehead and trickled down her cheeks. The watchman was making a slow circuit; she could hear his footsteps as he stopped at each of the cells which faced into the chamber. Some of the prisoners stirred and one of them must have asked a question because she heard the watchman say, "Shut up and go back to sleep. You'll have little enough as it is."

He entered her field of vision and she turned her head to peek at him out of the corner of one eye. Even though he was on the far side of the great chamber, would he see her white face shining in her dark corner? No. His attention was directed at closer things and he passed on, kept searching, and circled the chamber until he came toward her along the near wall. "You can't be wanting this to go on," he said to the other. "They're not here."

The other man must have grown disgusted. "Suit yourself. I don't care." She heard the great door slam.

"I'd not have made you look," the watchman shouted at the departing footsteps, waking more prisoners. Then he broke off his search and walked toward his table, muttering as he went. Bessina shuddered. He would pass within a few fingers' lengths of her. What would happen

if he saw her? Her fingers traveled to the pieces of lead
once more and she picked one up. It was all the weight
she could lift with one arm; she had to use both hands to
hold it over her head. And he must have heard the tiny
sound, because his footsteps suddenly quickened.

When he came into range, she brought the weight down
with all her strength but he was too quick; he dodged and
the momentum of her blow almost toppled her. The weight
slipped from her fingers and went rolling across the floor
with a loud cobbling sound, while more prisoners awoke
and some cried out.

"Now who be you?" His eyes widened, and he lunged
for her. She tried to draw the bailiff's dagger, but she was
too slow; he grasped her wrist and twisted it behind her
back until the weapon clattered to the floor. "You be a
regular spitfire, don't you? You be his lordship the bailiff's
wench."

"Let me go," she cried. "Let me go. Let me go."

More prisoners awoke and their cries filled the chamber, but the watchman paid them no heed. He pawed at
her; he was trying to hold her and hike up her clothing
all at the same time. "We'll see you back to wherever you
run off from, but we'll have a little fun first."

Bessina burned with shame; it seemed as if nothing
she could do would stop this from being her night of
humiliation. It was all too much to bear. With an insane
shriek, she drove her body against his. She tried with all
her might to knock him down or jar him hard enough to
make him let go. She leaped and screamed and kicked
while the prisoners took up the cry, and the place filled
with the din. It was bedlam; it sounded like a corner of
Hades.

His eyes bulged with surprise, his mouth twisted in
anger, and then he backed her against the door to one of
the cells and pounded her head against the grating until
she was sick and giddy. But she struggled harder than
ever, with all the strength of her madness. They whirled
and struggled and fought; but through the red haze of her
rage came the realization that she was never going to
escape his grasp. He was much stronger than she. He

would defeat her as surely as the mantis defeated the lacewing.

Then a great pair of arms emerged from the grating behind him; bony fingers locked about the watchman's neck, until he finally released her with a throttled shriek, to batter at the hands of the man who was strangling him. Bessina fell to the floor, gasping. She had been saved by some unseen prisoner who had his own score to settle with the watchman, but the watchman was drawing his sword; he would cut himself free and come for her again. In desperation, she grasped the sword-bearing hand and hung on for dear life.

It took at eternity. Any moment, it seemed, he would shake her off and then he would kill her and her unseen savior. But it did not happen. His struggles became weaker and weaker until the weapon dropped. She did not even wait until his feeble motions ceased; she tore his key ring from his belt and ran away, toward her father's cell, ignoring the cries from the man who had saved her. "Please, little sister, please set me free."

Count Clauvis was at the door of his cell and he went pale at the sight of her. "Bessina. By the gods, how can it be?"

"I'm too ashamed to tell you. Father, please, accept me once again and let us be away from this foul place." She opened the lock and they embraced in the doorway to the cell. But it could not be a long embrace. There was no time.

Every prisoner was screaming for his own release. The place rocked with the din; the sound alone was as frightening as anything she had seen there. While her father went to a wooden bin full of the prisoners' clothing, she saw the body of the watchman and ran to the cell behind it. But she was afraid to unlock her benefactor's door, to release the gods knew what sort of man.

Her father donned some ill-fitting clothing, then took the keys from her. He quickly found the proper one for the lock, turned it, and flung the lock to the floor. A tall, nearly naked man appeared, but neither the Count nor

Bessina said anything to him; they thrust the key ring into his hands and ran toward the chamber's double doors.

"How will we escape?" Count Clauvis asked, panting. "I know I cannot run far, and this place is filled with knights and guards and soldiery."

"We'll trust to stealth and ask the gods for aid." She took him by the hand, then started along the dark corridor. The din from the torture chamber was nearly deafening, even with the doors locked, and she could hear the crash of approaching soldiery. The two of them ducked down a black side corridor as a body of armed men plunged past with their swords drawn. Shortly after, they both heard the unmistakable sounds of fighting, accompanied by the screams of the wounded and dying.

"I pity them," Bessina said.

"No more than I," Count Clauvis replied. "But still, a quick death is a victory in there and they make cover for our own escape." Bessina thought his attitude harsh, but she said nothing; it had only been by the grace of the gods that they themselves had escaped, and she was too pleased at his freedom to begin an argument. Perhaps the night's humiliations had not been fruitless.

The passage to the castle's ground level was a nightmare filled with wrong turns and hiding from the soldiers. Only the tumult that saturated the castle made it possible at all. At times it seemed as if they would surely be recaptured. But while night still cloaked the sky, they found themselves creeping through an unguarded exit into the castle's great outer bailey. The gatehouse or the wall still lay between them and freedom, but they had already made it farther than she had ever thought possible.

And there was an anthill of activity in the courtyard as well as in the halls; a large wagon moved past them, pulled by a team of a dozen oxen. Mounted cavalrymen surrounded it. Neither of them could guess at what it carried—perhaps a valuable shipment of some kind. But whatever it was, disorder surrounded them. The air was full of shouting, and the men who guarded the wagon seemed to have been hastily gathered, judging from their many different states of uniform. Some of them were hardly even dressed.

But the sight gave Bessina and Count Clauvis hope. As the disorganized cortege moved toward the gatehouse, they slipped along in the shadows and reached the gate when it opened. It seemed that every eye in the courtyard would be on the strange procession, but no one challenged them. They were taking a great risk, as they both knew. If even one of the cavalrymen paid them any heed, they would surely be ridden down and killed. But Count Clauvis did not seem to care after his terrible imprisonment, and Bessina was filled by a strange kind of thrill, an almost mystical sense that they would not be stopped when they had come so far. They waited beside the towering gate. The procession moved near, and the leader shouted orders to the gatekeepers.

The two heavy panels swung apart on massive iron hinges. Bessina could also hear the rumble of the drawbridge being lowered, along with a command for the outer gate to be opened. The horsemen and the wagon moved into the gatehouse. Just as the portcullis began to descend after the last horseman had passed beneath it, she and her father darted through, practically beneath the horses' hooves. Bessina made a silent prayer as she ran, but there was only the clopping of the horses and the creaking and groaning of the heavy wagon a few cubits from them.

The double doors of the outer gate were open before them; the two halves swung apart on their great hinges and the horsemen flooded through. Bessina and Count Clauvis did not hurry; if they had not attracted attention already, it made no sense to do so now. Then, as the horsemen passed onto the drawbridge, they increased their pace and the wagon moved ahead, leaving the two fugitives behind and in the open. They heard a shout from the wall above them, then another shout, but the cavalrymen paid no heed; the procession made its way along the causeway toward the great harbor of Buerdaunt.

They ran. They were not sure they were being pursued, but they ran as fast as they were able, down the causeway's embankment, across the common which separated the castle's walls from the nearest buildings, and down the nearest street. The Count's breathing came like thunder, and Bessina's ankle filled her with pain; neither of them would be able to run much farther, even though they could still not tell whether they were being followed.

They plunged down an alley as black as a troll's heart and too narrow for horses to follow, then slowed to a walk because Count Clauvis could go no farther. At last they slumped down and collapsed in the blackness of the alley, amid the stink and the noise of scurrying vermin. Count Clauvis wheezed as if his breast would burst. The night's events at last came crashing down on Bessina—the horror, the terror, the fear and exertion, and the relief of being able to rest at last. She collapsed into a crumpled heap and wept as if her heart would break. She wept bitterly and continued to weep, even as exhaustion overtook her.

Chapter Twenty-two:
Ursid

AELIA STOOD BESIDE the fallen chess table and watched as Ursid's cohort strode toward the chamber door, opened it a crack, and spoke soft words to the men outside. Suddenly Ursid moved at the corner of her vision; before she could stop him, he had reached down, snatched a longsword from the scabbard which had been lying next to his chair, and threw his free arm about Berengeria's throat. "We have them here," he cried. "Come in with weapons drawn."

Surprise and rage fired Aelia's veins. She leaped toward Ursid but he halted her. "One false aggressive move by anyone, and I will slit her veins as if she were a shoat, to be bled out for pudding. You, you Knight of Pallas, cast away your heavy mace. You'll win no battles here."

Sir Phebos did as he was ordered. "I'll have no maiden come to harm. Put down your weapon, sir."

But Ursid did not do that. Berengeria struggled and shrieked insults at the young warrior, but her hard imprisonment had weakened and drained her. Ursid easily forced her to her knees. She cried out with pain and humiliation, but he only turned his eyes toward the guardsmen who had rushed into the room. "Send a messenger unto the King, to tell him that the prisoner is held securely. And the rest of you, apply the bonds to all of them."

One man dashed out with the message while the others prepared to bind the three captives. For her part, Aelia was livid as rough hands trussed her; she snarled at Ursid and spat at him as if she were a cat protecting its young. "You foul and loathsome traitor. How I wish my eyes were gouged away so I'd not have to look upon you. Honor hides her face; she cannot look at men who turn upon their benefactors thus. You traitorous, treacherous dog."

"A traitorous dog, you say? Indeed I am." Ursid gave Berengeria up to the hands of the guardsmen, turned toward Aelia, and glared back at her. "Yes, I betrayed my country and my King for love of that false woman." He gestured toward Berengeria, who sobbed bitterly as the men bound her arms behind her. "Without my aid she never would have left this high keep's walls last spring, nor would you ever have survived your journey home. For her sake have I spilled my blood and risked my life. Indeed, my life was all but lost. I'm hacked with scars which pull my skin and give my countenance a look of grisly horror."

He advanced toward Berengeria, who turned her eyes from him. "You'd never kiss this face now, would you, dear? The weals which track across my flesh were got while fighting for your honor, but you'd not offend yourself by touching one of them. When I arrived in Carea, the land I'd chosen over my own native state, I quickly learned how deeply you loved me. You threw me over for another man and even when you could not marry him, you still would not accept my suits. So then I knew that I was but your fool; I was the animal you turned to your own ends by promises."

He paused for breath, his face red behind its webwork of scars. "And there I stood, betrayed and countryless, alone within a land that laughed at me."

Aelia interrupted. "And yet 'twas Palamon who saved your life. You've not been so ill-used as you make out."

He glared at her. "Your Palamon betrayed me most of all. He promised me the hand of Berengeria if ever he should fail to marry her. And did he marry her? Of course not; 'twould have been a blasphemy for him to marry his own sister. So the path lay open and I pressed my suit, my honorable suit—and then your Prince, that Palamon, curled back upon his word the way a viper curls about a root. I'd looked upon him as a conqueror, a man of strength and honor and a saint in earthly garb, but then he turned and used me as his fool the same as all the others. I'd have been less wretched had I died before I had a chance to learn of human perfidy."

Berengeria bit her lip and Aelia knew what she was thinking. She had listened while Palamon had made that promise; it had seemed meaningless at the time.

"And when the mystic warriors conjured forth by Alyubol attacked me in my rooms, I still fought gallantly. But to no end, for I was taken and they brought me back to my Buerdaunt defeated, in disgrace, and made ridiculous. And what befell me then? My uncle, Lothar, had no reason to be kind to me. He could have sent me to the meanest death which ingenuity could e'er devise; instead he took me to his heart. When he forgave me, telling me that I was not the first young man to fall into a trap laid down by devilish womankind, I all but wept. And then he gave me back my post while he advised me to avail myself of wiser counsel in the future. That I shall. I have no further use for you or your deceit, for I have been retrieved out of the trap which I had fallen in on your behalf." He had to pause for breath, but he glared at the two women. "Enough. Now take them all to face the King."

Aelia understood what had happened to him. He had indeed been ill-used in Carea, though neither Palamon nor Berengeria had wanted it what way. Was the Princess to blame, after all, for the fact that she did not love him? He had never once taken her feelings into account or even acknowledged that such things mattered.

But Lothar the Pale had understood Ursid. The King of Buerdaunt was no fool; he had seen the young man's remorse and frustration and had turned them to great advantage. After all, of what use would Ursid have been as a mutilated corpse? So Lothar had forgiven him, had played on his bitterness and his despair, and had turned him into a loyal subject and a valuable ally. Even as the three prisoners were hustled out of the chamber to be taken to the King, Aelia had to respect the astuteness of Lothar's decision.

But Ursid was still being unfair. "Young man," she said to him. "You have forgotten that one thing which brought us into your tight clutches. Our Princess endangered her own life and freedom that she might help you escape imprisonment which she thought you were subject to. 'Twas her desire to rescue you which led us to your rooms. The simple fact that she was not inclined to be your bride is not a reason for condemning her."

He looked back at the older woman, his eyes haughty and full of contempt. "I have no further need for your advice, false doxy. Muzzle your deceit."

At that moment, the messenger ran back along the winding corridor with the news that the King wished to see them in his audience chamber rather than in his personal quarters. Ursid nodded and the group turned along the appropriate hallway, walking rapidly.

"I hope you feel great pride at what you do," Aelia said as a last swipe at him. "You send three innocents to likely death."

"I have no further need to parry thrusts from a deceiver such as you."

"Perhaps. But can you name for me the cruel disease which twists a man and brings his budding life to end all prematurely, turning him into a soulless mass of hatred?"

Judging by his reaction, Aelia was not sure Ursid even understood her question. He stared at her with a blank look, then gazed ahead. But she had not expected him to understand until she had explained the answer. "You have it, sir—a vengeful memory."

He did not respond and they entered Pomfract Castle's

great audience chamber. It was a large, eight-sided room with a high ceiling and walls of stark, quarried quartzite. It was normally full of courtiers, attendants, and petitioners, but it now stood empty because of the awkward hour; the only ones there were the servants who were hurriedly lighting lamps, a few messengers, and the man who sat atop the towering dais—Lothar the Pale.

Aelia had seen the inside of the chamber before, although not willingly. She had also seen Lothar the Pale previously. He had not changed. The dais was high and he sat with his feet far above the heads of everyone, the lantern light gleaming off his stringy, white, shoulder-length hair. She had always suspected him of having such a high seat to compensate for his lack of physical stature; he was a very small man, shorter than she was. Even so, he was an intimidating figure as he sat silently on his throne, his large, pink-centered eyes measuring them, one after the other. One index finger flicked at the hem of his embroidered purple robe, and he did not allow himself the luxury of an expression. He was, as always, Lothar the Pale.

There was hardly a sound in the chamber. Everyone, captured and captors alike, had been silenced by that cool gaze. All looked up at him, from Aelia to the King's chamber boy, who sat at the foot of the throne, blond, tanned, almost girlish looking, with one bare arm resting against the King's perfectly formed calf. The chamber boy met her eyes brazenly, glanced up at his master, then back at the other prisoners.

Lothar the Pale's eyes fastened on Ursid. "Our nephew, we can see you have done well; you have recovered what was lost to us. Come up to us and tell how this was done."

Ursid mounted the dais to bow before the King, who crooked a finger and pointed to one ear. The young warrior stepped to his side and bent to whisper. Ursid was not interrupted; no one, not even the prisoners, was willing to brave the King's stare. The only motion came from the chamber boy, who turned to listen to the hushed conversation.

When the account was finished, Lothar said a few words

in return and evidently ordered Ursid to remain beside him. The young warrior saluted, straightened, and stepped back a pace. Ursid looked very proud; there was no doubt Lothar the Pale had captivated him. Then the monarch's eyes fastened upon the prisoners. "We meet again. What have you three to say?"

"We have the right to flee to our own land, or to attempt escape and flight at least," Aelia said. He made no reply to her words, so she went on. "Your Grace, detention of the Princess can no longer serve your policy. You must have learned by now that there's another heir. Would it not serve you better to relent, to send her back unto her father's side and gain Carea's thanks and friendship too?"

The King replied matter-of-factly. "We know this story and we see that you are twisting it, as often is your wont. Buerdaunt once held the friendship of your land and it was little use to us. Your kings were glad to be our friends and allies in our weakness of those years. Buerdaunt grew up in status and your envious Berevald no longer showed a friendly face to us—that is, until his daughter came to be our guest. Now she is ours once more and he would be our friend again. We like that well; she shall remain with us.

"The two of you have made a fitting pair, my Lady Aelia. Your Princess we have found to be as shallow as one would expect of any representative of your own devious sex. She seeks to hide this trait by being haughty, stubborn, overproud. And you have filled the role of guardian through deceit and cunning treachery. The gods put womankind upon the earth to test mankind, who are their true creations. You have done this very well, and now it seems old Pomfract Castle has become too weak to hold you and your wholesale subterfuge. This problem shall be solved."

He paused in his remarks and gazed at an attendant. "Now where is our Lord Gymon? Does he come? I've questions for him."

The page spread his hands. "My Liege, he has been sent for more than once."

"Then go to him yourself. I know the hour is late but still I want him here."

The attendant bowed and left. As the footsteps echoed from the chamber, Lothar the Pale turned his gaze to Sir Phebos. "We know your armor, fellow, and it shows that you have membership within the ranks of Pallas' Knights. Buerdaunt does not desire strife with such a worthy company. Just how you came to be in league with all this lot, we do not know; still, you are free to go if you so wish. We will not hold you here."

"I thank you, sir." Sir Phebos bowed his head but he did not smile. "I have no yearning to escape the wage brought down by my participation; thus, I shall accompany my loyal friends."

Lothar the Pale appeared vexed. "We make the offer one more time; you may withdraw and so escape the sentence we pronounce. If you refuse this time, we have no choice but to include you in the punishment."

"So be it."

The King frowned. "There may be hidden factors behind that choice which complicate our course and policy. I would the bailiff came at once, because I find his mind is quick and sharp on such affairs." His voice became a brooding murmur.

Ursid looked troubled. Lothar the Pale noticed that and looked up at him. "Ah, good nephew, we believe you are distressed. If you have words to say concerning all these matters, we would hear them."

"Your Grace, my King, I know I have no right to offer you this counsel. Still, I would be glad to take her—that is, the Princess—into my custody and guard her well."

Lothar gazed at the young noble with an expression so blank it seemed as if his eyes had turned into lead. After a moment, he became more friendly and patted the younger man on the wrist. "I shall not place that burden in your arms. Already you have suffered far too much at the accounting of this base and shallow woman." He turned back toward the prisoners. "No, indeed. Now hear me, all of you, for this is what I say shall be your fate. Though Pomfract Castle is a citadel which has not fallen through the centuries, it seems that it becomes a porous sieve when touched by you. Therefore, you shall be placed aboard a ship and sent back to the holdings of our ally, the great wizard known to all as Alyubol. There you, fair Princess, shall take up your residence within a place you'll surely not escape. The others he may do with as he wishes; you shall be well treated till the time our thoughts about this matter may be changed."

There was a shriek. Berengeria had stood through the audience in stony silence, but as the sentence was pronounced she cried out and buried her head against Aelia's bosom. "I'll starve myself to death," she cried. "A better fate than to be prisoned by that miscreant."

Lothar the Pale ignored her and turned back to Ursid. "And for your role, Ursid, to show that we have not lost faith in you, you shall be captain of the escort we shall order to accompany them. You shall reside at Alyubol's retreat for long enough a time to see to it our wishes are borne out."

"I thank you, Sire." Ursid looked somewhat cheered.

Then the hearing was interrupted. The messenger who had been sent to the bailiff's quarters returned, throwing a door open with a bang. "Your Grace," he cried. "I bring you news which teeters on the brink of the impossible. I fear to tell you what I have to say."

The King looked at him narrowly, then signaled him to speak. The page swallowed, then obeyed. "The bailiff has been murdered. Now he lies all cold and naked in a chamber in the highest tower. And a female guest, a stranger, so they say, has done the deed, and then fomented insurrection in the donjons. All the midwatch guard still battles with the prisoners."

"By the gods!" The King's voice rang through the chamber like thunder and brought gasps of surprise and consternation everywhere. Lothar the Pale looked at Aelia, his brow dark as a thunderhead's belly. "You fiend from darkest Hell, was this your doing? This act confirms me in my policies, and what is more I'll have you under way before the night has passed." His eyes flashed about the chamber, so terrifying that messengers threw themselves toward the foot of the dais without even being summoned. "I want a vessel readied now, immediately. It shall set sail before the morning stars have faded from the skies. Ursid, assemble all the men you want, and whomsoever you may choose shall be provided. Ready some conveyance; take this trio from my sight. If they remain here at the day's first light, I swear they shall be slain."

Each person in the chamber quailed before the King's rage. It was not his manner to decide anything in anger; his policies hatched in the cool light of reason. But now he labored in the heat of a passion which catapulted men and women into frenzied activity, as if they were being struck by lightning bolts. For their parts, the prisoners were bound tightly, then bundled outside. A blacksmith was roused from his sleep to heat his forge and put them into heavy irons, as if they had been so many criminals. An ancient wagon was dragged forth and horses were found and harnessed to it, all in an atmosphere of haste and confusion. The guards roughly threw the prisoners into the back, and they started on the first leg of their journey to the unknown retreat of Alyubol.

Chapter Twenty-three:
The *Spada Korrigaine*

STINKING, LEERING USMU caused Palamon's head to bob as he carried the Prince like a baby along the corridors beneath the Library of the Polonians. Palamon had been held for days before the door to his chamber had flown open and revealed two beings, Navron and the flesh servant, Usmu. They had leaped in and seized him the way a kidnapper picks up a child.

Usmu's great tongue lolled over the half-crescents of his teeth as he carried Palamon along; Navron had to hurry to keep up. Palamon looked at Navron. He hated the thought of speaking to Alyubol's evil minion, but he needed to know many things. "The man who once inhabited these halls, the mystic sage Reovalis, what did you do with him?"

Navron looked up at him smugly. "He left."

"Where did he go?"

"That has no importance," Navron said.

"This noble monster; tell me how it is he serves your master? He was conjured up by old Reovalis."

Navron laughed evilly. Palamon did not like the sound

of it. "Reovalis' talents were limited. Never did he fully understand all of the qualities of his own beast. A flesh servant requires some excitement." He looked up at Usmu's great, smiling jaws. "He likes to play games. That is so, is it not, mighty Usmu?"

The flesh servant's wolfish face formed a smile and a hideous, low rumble of a laugh came from the great throat. It was a horrible sound, dark and evil and full of cruel intent. Palamon thought about the time in the Library of the Polonians, far above these tunnels, when Usmu had played a game. It had been a game which had nearly cost Palamon his life. "So Alyubol plays games with him and thereby steals his loyalty. What sort of games?"

Navron grinned at him unpleasantly. "You'd better just hope that you never find out."

It was a grim answer; everything about the situation was grim. Then they entered the quarters Reovalis had once occupied, strode through them, and into the next chamber. Palamon remembered that place, also; it was the cave which held the Glass of the Polonians, a mysterious pool of blue vapors which had given Reovalis much of his mystic power. And Alyubol was waiting for him.

Alyubol stood with two of his vassals on the far side of the pool as Palamon was carried in; the mad wizard's pinched features looked ghastly in the cave's blue light. And there was another prisoner also; Flin had been strapped to a pair of rings set into the wall, and his head was hanging as if he were asleep. Palamon's heart missed a beat at the sight of the young swashbuckler. What had Alyubol done to him? What had he wanted from him?

Alyubol wrung his hands with glee and leered evilly as he greeted the Prince. "And now you are here. That is good." His eyes flicked to the hulking flesh servant. "Tie him up to the wall. We'll begin."

Palamon found himself shoved against the chamber's cold wall while the henchmen seized his arms and used leather thongs to strap his wrists to rings like the ones which held Flin. Alyubol had added that feature; Palamon could not remember such rings being in place when he had been there before. He looked up at one of them; it shone with the gleam of new brass. A hole had been bored into the limestone of the cavern wall with great difficulty, the molten metal had been forced in to form the anchor, and the ring had been set. Alyubol had evidently planned Palamon's capture for a long time. Or perhaps such preparation had been the reason for Palamon's long stay in a locked room. It was not important; either way, Palamon knew he would not enjoy what was about to happen. He had lost all optimism. Usmu finished binding the Prince's wrists, then turned wordlessly and departed while Palamon gazed warily at the mad wizard. "I have no secrets you may hope to steal, therefore you torture me to no good end."

"Now what makes you think there is torture in store for you, Prince?" Alyubol sneered up into his face, mocking him.

"Your hospitality has always lacked a certain friendly note," Palamon said. "The last time I reposed with you, it lacked so much that we were forced to bid farewell, my Lady Aelia, Berengeria, Ursid, and I myself. Perhaps I shall be forced to leave again."

Alyubol's face contorted into an expression of rage. He snarled, leaped at Palamon, and slapped him sharply. "It may be you fled from me once, but you had vital help; the Sword of the Fairies was waiting to hear your command and Reovalis, too, had provided a means of escape. You've no such advantages now, for your sword is locked safely away; I have plans for it. As for your sister, 'twas not a long time she was out of my grasp, and she'd have remained, had I not needed funds to deliver myself and my chattels to this mountain fastness." He placed an ugly accent on the word "fastness." It was a taunt, Palamon knew, a reference to the Fastness of Pallas, stronghold of the knightly order which had cast Palamon out.

The wizard's scowl went away as he spoke, and he began to revel in his advantage. "So the Princess is mewed up in Lothar's stout keep in Buerdaunt. She is gone. But that fact does not matter; I've lines in the water which make my revenge on your father seem trivial indeed. Your own sword has been fetched from the pyrothere's carcass

where it was stuck fast; now it lies once again in its case."
He gestured toward the wall behind him. The ornately
scrolled box which had once held the *Spada Korrigaine*
lay closed on the floor, its latch fastened.

Palamon stared at it. The sword could come at his call.
It was a mystical weapon and he did not begin to understand all its powers, but he knew it would fly through the
air to his grasp if he called it, which meant he could still
cling to hope. He was surprised that Alyubol had allowed
the weapon to be placed within the sound of his voice.

But Alyubol looked at him and grinned slyly. "By the
way, if you're thinking of calling your weapon, please do.
I've a bond on it now which prevents that particular tack.
Go ahead."

"I do not think this is the time to call."

"You're correct."

"The Smiths of Muse, who forged my ancient blade,
would doubtless spin within their clammy graves to know
your magic had surpassed their skill."

Alyubol snickered at him and looked superior. "You're
so uninformed," the wizard gloated. "You do not know
the origins of the great weapon you've carried for months;
why, you're not fit to bear it. The sword shall be mine."

Flin had revived and had begun to watch the exchange;
Palamon could see the young warrior out of the corner
of his eye, though the mad wizard was paying no attention
to him. "I can't see why," Flin interrupted. "You've hardly
got the look of a man who'd need a sword."

Palamon grimaced; Flin plainly had a talent for nettling
people he disliked. As for Alyubol, the mad wizard whirled
toward the young warrior, and rage gleamed in his eyes.
"As for you, my young vagabond, know that your suffering's been slight. I have been very patient; it's plain
you know nothing and therefore are not worth much effort
from me. You will die in due time. Fret me not, or I swear
by the name of the Lord of the Universe, He Who Is Not
To Be Named, you shan't live to draw twenty more
breaths."

"Indeed, young Flin, endanger not your life. You have
no part in this." Though he knew Flin was headstrong,

Palamon prayed the young warrior would heed his word.
Palamon did not want to see Flin risk his life by needlessly
taunting the wizard. Besides, Alyubol had said something
which bothered Palamon. What had he meant by He Who
Is Not To Be Named? The Twelve Divinities all had names;
what strange force did Alyubol worship?

But Alyubol did not mention that again. He only smiled
at Flin and nodded. "Indeed, lad. Believe he speaks true."
Then he turned back to the Prince. "My Palamon, you're
a brave man, and quite sensible, too—so be sensible now.
All your bravery will do you no good." He backed away,
leering. "Your young friend has no concept; he knows not
the stakes of the game. If you have the impression your
blade was devised upon Muse, you could not be more
wrong, for your twelve gods themselves worked the steel,
beat it out, and presented the product to Parthelon. They
blessed the blade with such properties you only guess at,
and now it is mine. But you have to renounce it, reject
it, and cast it away. I'll no longer play games with you.
Yield to my logic; comply, and I'll grant you a life which
is free of the torments you'll otherwise suffer."

"And if I should refuse the deed you ask?" Palamon
knew what course he had to take. Whatever Alyubol's
reasons for demanding the *Spada Korrigaine*, the weapon
would make the mad wizard stronger; therefore, Palamon
could not surrender it.

"Oh, you'll not refuse me. Perhaps you may dally a
bit, but I'll win in the end. Once your hold is relinquished,
the blade shall conform to my will. It's connection with
you has impeded my wishes a bit, but we're practical
men. You will soon see the wisdom in being my ally, and
then my great plan will proceed."

"If, as you say, the blade's a holy sword, it never shall
surrender to your will, no matter what I come to say or
do."

Alyubol laughed. "You do not have my schooling and
art. All your holiness is but a state of the mind. Just a tilt
of the axis shall free all the mystical strengths which are
dormant within that stout blade. You must speak as I tell
you: 'I, Palamon, son of old Berevald, now surrender my

claim and renounce any kinship of thoughts and ideals twixt myself and the blade which is known by the name of *Spada Korrigaine*."

The statement repelled Palamon, quite apart from the words themselves. He knew in his soul as well as he knew his own name that he would never be able to comply; he could not do it, even though he did not yet know the full implications of the act. "I cannot speak the lines you have laid down," he said. His wrists were strapped to the bronze rings by stout thongs. He knew what his position was, what he was letting himself in for with such words. But he was responsible for the welfare of a nation. He could not weaken.

Alyubol's face twisted evilly. "Think again, for you err. You'll say all of the things which I ask before long. It is all quite inevitable. I will ask you again, so comply. Save my time and yourself."

"Inflict what pain you wish; I shall not speak. My blood may flow like any other man's; we both may stand and watch. Do what you will."

Alyubol cackled and rubbed his hands together as if he were about to play the winning trump in a game of cards. "I do not have the need to spill out any blood, Pallas' Knight. You forget that you stand in the presence of one of the prodigies of our fair world—the Glass of the learned Polonians. I know your stoic disposition. To tear out your eyes would not bring your submission. But I still have the means. I can show to you sights which will torture you more than the rack or the wheel. So you must speak the words I have asked."

"I shall not speak."

Alyubol stalked to the far side of the chamber with evil intent written all across his dried, pinched-up features. Between them lay the boiling pool of mystic blue vapors which was called the Glass of the Polonians—but Palamon kept his eyes away from that. He knew its powers were strange and awesome and he knew he did not dare gaze into the blueness to tempt those powers. Alyubol released a sinister chuckle. "I see you avoid the blue gift which is spread out before you. And yet you must look to the

Glass—for it's there you will learn of the world." He gestured and Navron grasped the hair on the back of Palamon's head, grunting as he forced the Prince's gaze down toward the pool. Navron had to use both hands and all his strength to overcome his victim's bulging neck muscles, but he did succeed. Palamon's head bent lower, his eyes swept across the rolling clouds of the pool, and he was captured as surely as a gnat encased in amber. He was trapped. He was a prisoner of the blue vapors and could only await what the evil wizard was about to subject him to.

Alyubol's voice rose and cracked; he laughed and cackled and whooped. "Gaze into the Glass—it is good. It will show you sights which will break your proud spirit."

The pool held Palamon's gaze as though he had been paralyzed, but still he found the strength to speak. "My mind is still my own. That cannot change."

Alyubol laughed even more. "Look and see. Go within the great rooms of the Fastness of Pallas once more, to observe all the acts which took place just a cubit or two from the cot where you slept. Your superiors chastised you well for the trespass with which you were charged. Now look closely and see what hypocrisy is."

Alyubol gestured. The vapors of the pool seemed to rise up and surround Palamon, caress him, and permeate him; it was a weird and somehow wonderful sensation, one he had felt once before. The blueness shifted, became many colors, and solidified into an image, into a reality. He was within the Fastness of Pallas. He even recognized the room; he had only been allowed into it a few times, but he knew it was in the quarters occupied by the Grand Master of the Knights of Pallas, Sir Photinus, who was old and holy and had relinquished all earthly pleasures to become the leader of the order. Sir Photinus was there. He and his chambers appeared with unearthly realism, looking more lifelike than they had when Palamon had seen them for himself.

But it was strange and puzzling; there were a dozen people in the chamber, both men and women. Women were never allowed into the Fastness of Pallas, but there were several here, talking to one another and drinking wine. The sight was disturbing and disquieting. Palamon did not like to see Knights of Pallas on free terms with so many young and attractive females.

But the sight became even more disturbing. The Knights in the chamber were all men of status within the order and their familiarities with the women increased. Hands were placed about waists, kisses were exchanged, and there was laughter and a great raising of eyebrows. Articles of clothing fell to the floor, there was fondling, and some of the couples embraced.

It became a drunken orgy. Knights and their women coupled before the others in the chamber, to inebriated laughter and applause. It was sickening. Sweat erupted from Palamon's forehead, trickled down his face, and stung his eyes. Then he understood Alyubol's strategy; what better way was there to torture an idealist than to show him such sights? Alyubol plainly knew Palamon would never respond to physical pain—so the wizard was employing torture of an emotional nature. Palamon would not yield to such a gambit; still, the image was hard to bear.

"Now see what you've missed," came the voice of the wizard. "It is time to renounce all your claim on the sword. Join with me. We shall triumph together."

Palamon could not speak. How was Alyubol making him see such things? Why did the setting of the vision appear so horribly real? That was what made the torture ghastly—the reality of the scene.

"You refuse me? Then you will see more." Alyubol's words merged into a cacophony of wheedling and threats. "Give it up, give it up, give it up, give it up." The words echoed and re-echoed inside Palamon's head. "You'll see more, you'll see more, you'll see more."

At that instant, the scene before Palamon vanished. The Grand Master's quarters disappeared, the Knights and the women went away, and the laughter and other sounds faded, along with the odors of wine and sweat. Palamon sagged with relief.

But the scene was replaced by another one, which had

been etched into his memory like an inscription on a monument. He stood in the square before the Temple of Pallas in the city of Oron, near the Fastness, and there was a great gathering of Knights present; they looked splendid in their armor as they straddled their great horses and held their gleaming weapons. And he could see himself, too, standing before that body of Knights, listening with downcast eyes while the Grand Master read to him of his sin.

He, Palamon, a Knight in good standing, had disgraced his order by lying with and impregnating the maid Arlaine. Sir Photinus cast the parchment away and strode toward Palamon. He grasped Palamon's helmet, ripped it from his brows and cast it into the dust, all the while reviling him. It was a scene even more painful than the last because it had actually happened and it had happened exactly as Palamon was seeing it now; each humiliation paraded before him exactly as it had occurred. In fact, it was even more vivid than the actual event had been; it happened all about him and to him and in his head, all at once.

He had withstood the degradation in stony silence. He had made no sound as he had been stripped of all his laurels, as the townspeople had rushed to the troughs to hurl mud at him, as they had spat upon him, and as he had been strapped to the back of a refuse wagon and dragged from the city to be left along the road. Palamon closed his eyes, but it made no difference; the vision would not go away. He heard a groan. It came from his own throat.

He had to speak. He had to call his marvelous sword, had to escape. His lungs bulged as he tried to scream for the weapon, and his tongue and lips writhed to form the words, but nothing happened. He felt as if a great hand had clamped his mouth, and he was being smothered by bestial fingers. The wizard had placed a spell on Palamon or the chamber and Palamon could not call the sword's name any more than fly. He was helpless; he could only writhe against his bonds and suffer all the visions the wizard wanted to place before him.

The wizard laughed insanely, told him to renounce the

sword, and threatened him with worse; but still Palamon could not give up the weapon. Why not? A tiny voice of doubt pondered that question and he could not answer; but he could not find the words, he could not do it. He heard himself shriek at the top of his lungs, call to the holy Maiden herself, and implore his patron, Pallas. That made Alyubol laugh even harder, then cackle that Pallas was lowest of all.

A new scene attacked Palamon and swept him to a completely different setting. All about him loomed snow-covered mountain peaks, with the pure white snow matching the alabaster gleam of a heavenly city. Alyubol was actually showing him the abode of the gods. Palamon marveled to look on the divine sanctuary. He stood inside a gleaming hall, laughing, surrounded by young men, satyrs, and other beasts. And again Pallas appeared, exactly as she had when Palamon had seen her in his vision. It had been the most cherished moment of his life, one that he had shared only with Aelia and his immediate family, and even then only in part. How could it be a trick? He was actually seeing the real Pallas; there could be no doubt of it.

She laughed and her laughter sounded on his ears like little bells, just the way he remembered it. And then she began to disrobe. She removed every stitch of her clothing before the youths in the hall, the hairy satyrs who leered and giggled at her, and the beasts which brayed and grunted and milled about. Palamon tried to close his eyes, tried to look away from the scene, to see something else, but it did no good. The vision would not go away, could not be denied; it hovered in front of him, no matter how he thrashed back and forth with his head. He looked upon Pallas revealed—the pure white arms and the divine smoothness of the belly and the thighs. He stared as if hypnotized, filled with unbridled shame. He cursed himself for seeing and for believing. His mind became a cauldron.

He felt the floor of the chamber go from beneath him as his knees buckled. He struggled to regain his footing amid a nightmare of his own writhing anguish and the voice of Alyubol.

Then Pallas, divine Pallas, the daughter of purity and the mother of man's divine soul, knelt before one of the satyrs, caressed the creature's hairy hips, and embraced him. All the young men and animals, all the gathering of unspeakable sexuality, closed in about her, touched her, fondled her, and degraded her in unspeakable ways while she smiled and laughed and submitted.

It was the worst of all. It was a blasphemy, a crime. Palamon heard himself cry out once, then again and again in a great void. He felt the hot tears scald his cheeks while Alyubol witnessed it all and laughed. His mind rebelled. He could not think; he could only leap against his bonds like a fish on the end of a spear and thrash his head against the cold stone until he could no longer hear Alyubol's words. But he could not make the horrible scene go away. This was torture indeed; his mind would not long withstand such visions.

Something inside him ballooned to a huge size and burst in a surge of insane strength; he felt one of his arms lurch free. Somewhere at the edge of his consciousness, he realized the stone of the cavern wall had given way against his struggles. There was the weight of a brass ring heavy and loose in his hand. He reached and hurled it at the white shadow which danced and cackled away in the distance.

The whiteness collapsed, the vision went away, and Palamon's eyes began to clear. He could hardly comprehend his surroundings, but at least he could see them. The vision and all the bad sights had gone away. Navron and the others were rushing toward him, and Alyubol was lying on the floor of the chamber with the brass ring lying beside him. Flin was still bound; he struggled and shouted to Palamon to get up. And on the far side of the chamber lay the wooden case which held the *Spada Korrigaine*. The wood was smoking; it had been charred into blackness. Even as Palamon glanced at it, the box burst into flame.

"The sword." Flin's shout was urgent. "Get your sword. The box is burning. You can reach it now."

Palamon scrambled to his feet and lurched toward the box. Though Navron and the others tried to tackle him, he flung them away like small things. The box crumbled as he ran toward it and the mystic blade lay before him, red-hot; but the handle was cool to his touch. The two men who had tried to stop him now huddled about Alyubol, trying to drag the wizard to his feet.

Alyubol began to regain his senses and to look about. There was no time to lose; Palamon leaped to Flin's side and slashed at the rings which held the youthful hands. The gleaming blade sang through air, struck brass, hissed a great sound, and sundered metal. The blade would cut anything. The prisoner was free.

They had to turn to their captors. Alyubol clambered to his feet and looked about drunkenly; then his eyes filled with fire and he glared at Palamon. He lifted his arm. If the wizard's magic was still intact, it was hopeless for them to face him. Palamon and Flin dashed toward the chamber's entrance. Even as they reached it, a bolt of lightning leaped from the wizard's extended finger and seared the air as it sought Palamon.

The bolt struck the Prince in the small of the back, but the armor he had been given by Pallas protected him; he was unharmed, even though the force of the thunderclap knocked him through the doorway.

There was no time to think; all actions had to come from his fighter's instinct. Many tunnels lay between them and the outside world. Even as Flin helped him to his feet, Palamon could hear the wizard and his henchmen, their footsteps scuffling behind them. Palamon smote the stones above the entrance with his blade. There was the scream of exploding stone as the metal cleaved into the solid rock; the rock fell, and the access was closed. Palamon swung again and the blockage became complete. They were free.

But they had to be cautious even as they fled; there was no telling how long the cave-in would hold Alyubol, considering what magical ways he possessed to remove it—and Usmu still lurked somewhere ahead of them. They had to be cautious, but they also had to hurry. They rushed up the corridors with Palamon in the lead, then dashed toward the Library of the Polonians and the pathway which led to the river bank.

They rounded a corner and ducked into the tunnel which led to the great temple, only to come to a sliding halt. In the distant darkness at the other end of the tunnel, Palamon could see two pinpoints of light in a great, hulking shadow; Usmu was waiting for them there. They would have to find another way out.

Even as they hesitated, the shadow started toward them, approaching with a quickness that frightened. Palamon reacted instantly. He was still shaky from his experience, but he was able to function as a warrior. He used his sword twice more to cause cave-ins like the one which had blocked off Alyubol, then the two fugitives fled a different way.

There was still another way out—through the dining area and up the great brass staircase which led to a garden at the top of the cliff. Palamon led Flin that way, stopping a couple more times to cave in tunnels; Alyubol had more henchmen somewhere in the labyrinth and Palamon did not wish to be surprised. They reached the dining hall and hurtled through it, through the great kitchen, through the pantry, and up the brass stairs which rang with their steps. Would the garden still be there or would they be trapped again?

The garden was there, though the green of spring had given way to the brown of autumn. They ran across the garden, past the livestock pens, vaulted the stone wall together, and lay gasping on the hard ground outside. Flin pulled Palamon to his feet and they ran on, into the wilderness of cliffs, rocky crags, and ravines which surrounded the Library of the Polonians. Would they ever reach a place where they could not be found?

Chapter Twenty-four:
Reovalis

THEY FLED THE garden and hid in a crevasse which split the limestone cliff. It was not the best hiding place, but it was all they were able to find under the circumstances. Palamon blinked and looked at Flin. "It seems we have escaped, at least for now."

Flin looked back at him uneasily. "It's still hard to believe the way you tore that ring out of the wall. If someone had told me about it, I wouldn't have believed him."

Palamon smiled at the younger man. It was the first time he could remember seeing Flin awed by anything. "The strength derived from fright's considerable," he said.

Flin whistled. "They must have been hard, hard visions. You went quite mad, you know."

"Indeed, it's not a thing I can deny. The whole experience was interesting, although I have no wish to see such stimulating sights again." Palamon stopped speaking. They really needed to seek a better refuge than the narrow fissure which overlooked the garden. He looked about; then he saw movement below them, back along the rocky way they had come. He clutched his *Spada Korrigaine* and stood.

Someone had walked past the entrance to the ravine where they were hiding. Palamon lifted his blade and stalked forward, while Flin picked up a rock and followed him. At least, if it came to blows, the ravine would be more easily defended than some open place. He and Flin crept to the entrance of the fissure and looked out. A bent, white-haired old man stood looking to and fro a few cubits away. Palamon recognized him; it was Reovalis, the ancient sage who had once occupied the abandoned caverns which now housed Alyubol.

Before either Palamon or Flin could speak, the old man saw them. "By all the gods," he whispered. "Tall Palamon. I never would have thought you'd come back here."

"It wasn't my idea," Palamon said. "What's occurred? Why do we find you here among these cliffs with Alyubol a tenant in your halls?"

"The story's long and difficult to tell." The white-haired, white-bearded old man glanced nervously about as he spoke, looking mainly toward the garden they had fled. "Are you pursued?"

"We do not know."

"I sensed a presence here, although I did not know it would be you. The garden is unoccupied as long as it is daytime. Alyubol does not concern himself with it, and Usmu would prefer to work at night. Therefore I go there in the afternoon to gather sustenance. I've lived this way since Alyubol subverted Usmu's heart and occupied the hallways down below."

Palamon asked the old sage how that disastrous event had taken place, and Reovalis answered almost reluctantly. "I think your Princess let him know of this. Do you remember when you came here last she asked of me to let her look at him, foul Alyubol, by using the Polonians' far Glass? Her unschooled scrying warned him of this place and put him on the trail to capture it . . . at least that is as much as I can guess."

"But how did you escape?"

"I saw the wizard coming in the Glass. Before he landed,

I transported goods up to a cave which I shall take you to. And then I placed my Usmu in the Library to turn back the attack and found, to my surprise, he joined with them. But even so, his mental powers are so weak he can't recall my hiding place. I've seen him lead them searching through the rocks, and watched them throw their hands into the air in anger and disgust at strange, conflicting guidance he would give."

"The dark side of his nature fancies them," Palamon observed. "They have subverted him, corrupted him, made him an evil servant. So it's well his mental faculties are low or he would do such harm we'd not survive. But now I need to know another thing. What is the interest Alyubol has shown in my strong blade, the *Spada Korrigaine*, which you presented to me months ago?"

"The *Spada Korrigaine*. Ah, yes indeed. He would want that if he has learned as much as I now know about its powers and its history."

"It seems he does," Palamon said grimly.

"I see that you still cling to it," Reovalis said. "That's good. It did not interest me to any great extent until I saw its mystic powers, saw it fly to you and mold into your grasp, as you remember. So then I studied it, both in the Glass and also in my books. The things I learned of it are most momentous; would that I had known them then, that I might have told you of them ere you went away."

Then Reovalis told Palamon the full story of the mighty blade; it was a strange tale. First of all, Palamon could hardly have been more wrong in thinking it had been manufactured on the island of Muse. Alyubol had told the truth for once. The sword had been forged by the gods themselves and presented to Parthelon the Great as the weapon with which he would build his Great Empire. He had been called "the Good King" by the common people, and the gods had favored him with a prodigious weapon.

Each of the Twelve Deities had given the sword a separate gift. It knew where it was at all times, as well as who was wielding it. It had the powers of thought and movement when triggered by the proper phrases, and could carve through any object with ease.

But there was something more. The last gift had been the greatest; the *Spada Korrigaine* possessed the power to grant life itself. The gods had presented the sword to Parthelon, a good, courageous, and pious man, to give him extended life and dominion over the peoples of the Thlassa Mey, to enable him to rule them and keep them forever on the true path.

Parthelon had fulfilled the first part of the bargain. He had gathered great armies, had conquered all the lands about the Thlassa Mey, had granted them enlightened and benevolent rule, and in the process he had grown old and wise. When the time to die had come to him, he had elected to send the sword away, to hide it deep in the vaults below the Library of the powerful Polonians, so that it would never be used again. The reason he gave was simple, as well as impeccably correct. He had declined to use the sword's gift and had ended his life with an enigmatic statement: "If I should rule too long, I would become the very thing the deities oppose."

Then Parthelon had died and had been carried down to his secret tomb below Sparth's Head Castle, while the sword had lain hidden from mankind. All mention of it was stricken from records, except for the folk ballads which could not be erased and the archives of the Library of the Polonians, which that powerful sect would not allow to be altered.

The story moved Palamon. How many men confronted by death would have had the courage to face it, rather than accept prolonged life from the gods themselves? "But tell me," he asked. "How great is my sword's power to prolong the life of him who would accept that gift? Would it give life to anyone, or was that gift reserved for Parthelon alone?"

Reovalis mused for a moment. "It is not written in so many words," he finally answered. "My guess is that, while it was given to old Parthelon alone, a decade or a score of years could flow to any man. It's capable of giving life back to the newly dead, enabling them to live the normal span of years that would have been allotted them, or it can see that span extended on for several decades."

Palamon's jaw dropped. "Then that is why foul Alyubol desires the mystic blade—to give him added life. By holy Pallas, think of all the evil deeds that he could do with twenty extra years." The truth put a heavy weight on Palamon's shoulders.

"Far more than you or I can guess, for I have learned another fact. Foul Alyubol is riddled by disease. He shall not live beyond the year; his only hope is to secure your sword and its great gift."

There was morbid hope in that statement, though it also drove home to Palamon the fact that Alyubol's pursuit of the *Spada Korrigaine* would be relentless in the meantime. "Though it is sin to yearn for someone's death, the world would be a safer place without him."

"That is true, for he has deeds afoot which threaten to unhinge the very roots of our existence as we know it." With that, Reovalis stopped, faced Palamon, and told him a tale which chilled the tall Prince to the center of his bones. Even though Alyubol had been a canker on the world, the things he had done thus far were nothing compared to the great evil he would unleash if he had the chance.

In his insane studies, Alyubol had learned of an entire pantheon of evil gods which sought control of the world. They had contested with the Twelve Divinities aeons before men had even appeared on the scene. The Twelve had won that cosmic war and had sealed the defeated deities away in an unknown place, to make the world safe for the coming of men.

But the evil ones still existed, beings so blasphemous that even their names could not be mentioned, not even by the cults who worshiped them secretly. And Alyubol led such a cult and worshiped the dreadful powers, the huge, amorphous masses of indescribable evil. He knew they lurked in their forbidden city; he knew they only waited for the right person to set them free in the world, to let them in from their own dimension to work their havoc upon men. They would destroy the divine balance of the Twelve Deities and haul the world off to their own part of the universe for their indescribable ends. Alyubol considered himself the one chosen to open that door, and even though the Twelve would certainly win the cosmic struggle eventually, it would mean the end of the race of men, if it took place.

But the wizard needed time; five years had to pass before the stars would be right for him to usher in the dark deities; if he did not succeed, a generation would have to expire before the experiment could even be attempted again. And Alyubol did not have five years to wait, not unless he could seize the added life offered by the *Spada Korrigaine*.

The explanation turned Palamon's brow as cold as sleet in winter. So that was the game the wizard was playing. He would subvert the *Spada Korrigaine* and turn it to his own ends to gain time to unleash indescribable evil on an unsuspecting world. It was unbelievable, impossible. But from what he knew of Alyubol, Palamon realized that nothing could be safely judged beyond the wizard's reach. Possession of the sword was the key to Alyubol's schemes and Palamon's renunciation of the weapon was the key to that possession. Palamon could never allow that to happen. He would see the sword and himself destroyed before he would allow the wizard to make the attempt again.

At that point Reovalis was interrupted. They had arrived before the mouth of a cave, and rain began to fall; a deluge erupted from clouds which had piled up over their heads with disconcerting suddeness.

"That's Alyubol," Reovalis said as he led them into the cave. "He's made it rain on different days to force me to return to him to be destroyed."

"I can believe that," Palamon said. "I have seen him do such things before. What's worse, it means he's well and has begun to seek us out. I hope he does not find us in this place for it would mean our deaths and yours as well." Still, Palamon could only note glumly to himself that his own death would be a small matter beside the greater evil the wizard was plotting.

"You need not be afraid. He shall not find you while you are with me or in this cave. I found this place full many years ago." As Reovalis spoke, he bent and used a flint to light a lantern. The flickering light revealed a narrow cavern of great depth, and they could see that the floor was worn by the endless treading of feet. He rose and led them further in, speaking over his shoulder. "Far in the rear, beneath a pile of stones, I found a little chest containing gems. Each one was special, placed there, I suppose, by the Polonians themselves. I'll show you one."

He opened his robe and showed them a large, dirty-yellow gemstone which appeared to be of slight value. "This one has saved my life," he said. "It hides me from the scrying eyes of those who wish to seek me out. While you remain with me, you'll not be seen by anyone you do not wish to see you."

Palamon looked at the stone and whistled.

"I have some more," the ancient sage offered. "If we are to defeat this Alyubol, we each must carry one."

Flin looked doubtful. "I don't have much faith in magic," he said. "That pool of blue vapors in the cave, what if he uses that?"

Palamon smiled at him. "I thought you had no faith."

"I've seen that at work."

"Tush, tush, young man," Reovalis said. "Believe I've verified that statement, for my own life depended on it. The Polonians' great Glass is far more to be feared than human eyes if Alyubol has gained the use of it. But still these gems are proof against the Glass itself. I tested them."

As they spoke, Reovalis led them toward the rear of the cavern. He had plainly had time to plan against Alyubol's invasion, because the rear of the place was stacked high with goods. It had been well that the Glass of the Polonians had given him that warning, even though its properties would now be used against all of them. Even so, Palamon could see that the experience of being driven from his refuge had been hard on the old man; he seemed much humbler, more approachable, and less imperious than he had been before.

"I need your true opinion," Palamon said to the ancient sage. "Should it pass that Alyubol recaptures me and once again attempts to place his hands upon this blade, will it be possible for him to gain success in turning it to suit his purposes?"

Reovalis thought for a moment. "His skill is great," he finally said. "It might be possible, with great experimentation and hard work, for him to turn the sword without your help. Should he succeed, he'd gain rewards to justify the time and effort spent."

Palamon nodded and a frown worked its way across his features. He was silent for a long time, as if he was deciding something, then he spoke once more. "He must be stopped, then."

"I agree," Flin said. "But how do we go about stopping him?"

"We've proved the *Spada Korrigaine* can cleave through stone. If we can fill both entrances with rock, perhaps he might be trapped within his lair."

"He has that monster, not to mention his henchmen," Flin said. "No one likes digging but they'd do it if they had to."

"We might be able to dislodge more rock than they could dig. At least we have to try; we cannot set him loose upon the world."

"Your plan is difficult," Reovalis said. "While we might easily seal off the hall which leads back from the temple to the caves, the exit to the garden will be hard. The one is narrow while the other leads through open chambers and expansive rooms. It will take long; we must do that one first."

The sage rummaged through the potions and materials he had transported to the cave, but he could find nothing which the magic of Alyubol would not overcome. At last the sky began to grow lighter; the heavy storm clouds which had been hanging over the area began to thin and fade away. The lightning still struck occasionally but no longer seemed a threat.

Had Alyubol and his henchmen managed to dig free of the blockages Palamon had caused? There was no way to know, but the fugitives could not allow the wizard any more time. They ate some dried fruits by way of a meal, then started to make their way back toward the garden.

But something deterred them. As they crept along the cliff face, they could look down at the broad Stilchis which rolled toward the sea, and Palamon saw a ship. It was a many-oared war galley; the banks of oars rose and fell, rose and fell as the vessel made steady progress against the stout current. Its flags and pendants showed that it was from Buerdaunt.

"This changes things," Palamon said, stopping to watch the vessel.

"Maybe we should just hurry," Flin suggested.

"No, we must get closer." Palamon turned to Reovalis, who also watched the vessel labor past. "Is there a better place from which to look?"

"Perhaps." The old man led them along the face of the cliff until they were below the colonnaded porch of the Library of the Polonians itself. And all the while, the Buerdic galley drew closer. There were several figures standing along the rail and one of them was taking constant depth soundings with a lead line. There was no doubting the ship's destination. More warriors began to spew from the hold onto the deck, a whole company of them, and armored knights besides. What was the ship's purpose? Was there hope that Lothar the Pale and Alyubol had had a falling out? Palamon doubted that. All that was sure was one simple fact—their attack on the mad wizard would have to wait on this new development.

Chapter Twenty-five:
Flight From Buerdaunt

BESSINA AND COUNT Clauvis had escaped from Pomfract Castle. But the night dragged on, an endless nightmare of running and hiding. An occasional patrol passed and filled them with fright; at the slightest sound, they hid in alleys, beneath bridges, in doorways, and in piles of refuse.

But their flight assumed a shape as the night wore on; they had to escape from Buerdaunt. It was time for Bessina to follow her father now, for he was familiar with the city and she was not. They darted along narrow streets like living shadows, Count Clauvis in the shapeless robe stolen from an executioner, Bessina in the clothing she had removed from the dead bailiff.

Bessina had been to Buerdaunt only a couple of times. She did not know the streets, but she could tell they were going toward one of the older, poorer parts of the city. She stumbled over loose cobblestones in the dark; sharp odors assaulted her nostrils, and an occasional dog barked or growled at them as they slipped past. She hoped her father knew what he was about.

At last they came before a rattletrap of a shop amid a block of equally flimsy buildings. It was a pawnbroker's shop; a signboard hung over the street and the three balls were visible even in the darkness. To her surprise, Count Clauvis pounded on the door. The rapping echoed through the building and along the street till she expected a patrol to come along at any moment. "What place is this?" she asked. "Why do you knock here so?"

"The man who operates this little shop has many contacts. Crecche had dealings with him." Count Clauvis rapped again until the windows rattled.

The mention of Crecche's name made Bessina cringe; after all, she and her father had both suffered because of that worthy's dealings. What nameless commerce had he had with the man her father was seeking now, she wondered, and what had her father known of it? She was disappointed. Her father must have known something about the chamberlain's crimes; at least, he seemed familiar with this area and some of its people.

Count Clauvis paused in his rapping and looked up. They heard movement from the room over the shop; someone was fumbling about. Then a light sprang into being through the window, shadows danced for a moment, and the light disappeared. But they did not have to wait long; the light reappeared in the lower story of the building, someone worked at the door bolt, and the door swung open on protesting hinges.

The man who peered out at them was short and heavy-set, with a face the color of an overripe peach. He was a drinking man; his eyes were bloodshot and veins stood out darkly under the skin of his cheeks. His gaze went from Bessina to Count Clauvis, then back again. "Who be you?"

"You've seen me once or twice. My name is Clauvis." The Count pushed past the fellow, entered the shop, and motioned for Bessina to follow him. The shopkeeper looked perplexed, but said nothing. He only shut the door and turned to face his midnight customers. "I've done ye a service even opening the door, but if yer money be not good, all ye'll get above that is bruises." He whistled and

there came a low growling from the back of the shop,
almost like the rumbling of a mill wheel. There was breathing and a clacking noise. A great dog moved into the
lantern's light, the end of its nose as far from the floor as
Bessina's navel.

Count Clauvis snorted. "I know that dog. He'd never
hurt a mouse. My man, whom you addressed as Crecche,
has been here sundry times. As for myself, I am in need
of horses. We have dealt with one another; each trans-
action made you richer. Now you must get horses for us
both, so we may quit this cursed city."

"Yes, yes, I know you." A spark of recognition burned
in the man's florid face. "But I don't know what I can
find at this time of night."

Clauvis wrapped his arm about the fellow's shoulder
in an aggressive manner; Bessina could tell that he was
determined to have his way and perhaps was close to
violence, in spite of the shopkeeper's dog. "I know your
qualities and that you have your contacts; you've procured all manner of goods for those who have the asking
price. I promise I shall make it worth your while, but I
will not accept a negative response."

"I can try. Two horses?"

"Two horses," Count Clauvis said as he eyed some of
the goods hanging along the walls. "And this sword." He
took up a sword which hung with the other items, an old
weapon which had a badly nicked blade but was better
than nothing. "And clothing, sir. We'll want a change of
garments ere we go."

"Indeed, indeed." The shopkeeper took them into
another room, a wardrobe. There was nothing decent there.
Every article was old and worn and some were moth-
eaten; still, they could provide a change of clothes, which
was the main objective at the moment. The fugitives picked
out clothing, Bessina stepped into the dark to change, and
they were soon ready for travel. Count Clauvis even purchased a skin of wine and a loaf of bread from the shopkeeper's pantry.

The three of them slipped into the alleyway, wearing
dark clothing and worn traveling capes. The proprietor

seemed to specialize in that type of clothing. It made
sense; providing a change of garments for fugitives could
provide him a thriving business.

After they had stepped into the cold autumn shadows
of the alley, he locked the door and spoke to them. "I'll
be awhile getting the horses; after all, it's a hard thing to
do this late with no notice beforehand. You wait here and
I'll find nags for ye and come back. Both of ye wait right
on this very spot."

He lifted a knuckle to his forehead, then hurried away,
his rotund shape moving through the darkness with surprising speed. They could only stand in the shadows and
study the incomprehensible dark depths of the alleyway.
The city was as dead as a vault; nothing stirred, there
was not a sound. But as they waited, the silence formed
into the scurrying of rats, heavy snoring beyond an invisible window, and the breathing of the dog on the far side
of the shop's back door.

Bessina worried. She did not know the shopkeeper.
What if he had gone to the authorities? Did he guess how
his two customers would be sought, once Gymon's murder was found? She looked up at her father, who was only
a blacker blackness against the shadow. "I hope this fellow's to be trusted. If he wishes to betray us both, he'd
never have a better chance than now."

Count Clauvis' voice came heavy and deep out of the
darkness. "He'll not betray us. Trust me, I will get us out
of here and to a place of refuge. We'll be safe."

Bessina did not reply.

A long time passed. The sky above them became a
washed-out blue before the shopkeeper returned; but when
he did come, he led two horses that were saddled and
ready to ride. They were far from the best; they were
swaybacked, rangy, and looked as if neither of them had
had many full meals. Still, they were better than nothing.
Count Clauvis relieved Bessina of her purse and paid the
man, though he complained about the price.

Then they mounted and made for the nearest city gate.
That was the next crucial phase of their flight. The guardsmen who manned the gates could never be pigeonholed.

Some were fanatics who searched every person and item passing before them. Others seemed to have no greater concern than passing out the term of their watch as quickly and conveniently as possible.

But to Bessina's relief, her father bluffed his way past the guards very well. There were questions about destination and reason for traveling at such an early hour, but Count Clauvis carried it off convincingly in his gruff manner. One of the guards looked a bit suspicious, but he said nothing, and they rode on.

Only as they passed out of Buerdaunt did Bessina begin to notice the morning's chill or take pleasure in the awakening of the new day. The city wall fell away behind them, and the tension fell away with it, like a heavy coat which she could only now shrug off. She was free. She and her father were free to ride unhindered across the autumn countryside.

They followed the road away from the gate and went in whatever direction it should lead. But as the city fell toward the horizon behind them and the sense of freedom became complete, Bessina thought about her ring. It rested on her right hand, but she had forgotten it in the excitement and horror of the night's events. Now she lifted her hand and gazed at it; it shone softly in the light of the climbing sun, and she recalled all that Peristeras had told her.

The ring was strange. Plain, unadorned, it seemed to cling to her finger, to plead with her, lecture her, and hypnotize her. It was true that her father had been in Buerdaunt and that Peristeras had erred in telling her he was dead. It was true that her quest had cost her greatly in terms of her own dignity. But she still had to finish that quest. If it had been Peristeras' word alone, she would have given up the journey, she was sure of that; she repeated the fact to herself even as she rode along. But she looked down at the ring and she knew that she would never feel like a complete human being until she had looked upon Sparth's Head Castle. She did not need a soothsayer to tell her that; she knew it in her soul.

So she turned her horse toward the north, toward the

Greenlands and the promontory where Sparth's Head looked out over the Thlassa Mey. Count Clauvis was surprised by her sudden change of direction; he looked after her, then he dug his heels into the side of his horse and cantered after her. "Where do you think you're going?"

"Father, I must go to Sparth's Head Castle. I have told you why and we've discussed this point. And I should think that you would be too glad to travel there and leave these lands where we are fugitives."

"That's foolish, girl." His tone had a patronizing quality to it. "There's nothing in that place. The walls are falling down; no man lives there. And we are strangers in the Greenlands; there, no man will know us and we'll have no friends."

"We've none in Lothar's realm." She looked at him. "Cannot you see? They've branded you a traitor in this land and if we're found, you shall be taken to the donjons once again. We must away from here and I must touch the walls of that high keep which stands on Sparth's Head."

"No. You're very wrong." He caught her horse's reins and halted her. "We'll go to Maix, which lies a dozen leagues southward from Tolq. I have a cousin there who likes me well and has been Count of Maix for many years. He shall protect us from the royal wrath until I've time enough to clear my name and come again into the King's good grace."

But it was he who was wrong, not she, and she knew it. "Cannot you see?" she demanded. "You are a count no more. Your fief is taken and your house and goods are all turned over to some vassal of the King. He does not want to pardon you. You have no friends in Maix or Galliardy or Jolier or any province which lies within the reach of Lothar's fingers." She looked at him and saw unhappily how her words battered him. She placed her hand on his own rough fingers. "Oh Father, can't you see? Perhaps someplace beyond the King's long reach you have a friend but it will be within some northern land, not near Buerdaunt."

"The Count of Maix will not desert me, though I may be fallen now from grace."

"He will not have a choice."

They sat on their horses and gazed at one another while Count Clauvis' eyes grew dark. "Then we shall go up to Lacourd. I still may have friends there."

She brightened. "A better choice. And on the way to that fair city, we can journey up the coast to Sparth's Head."

"You are still my daughter, child. You shall not tell me where I'll travel, where I'll not, and where I shall detour to satisfy your little girlish whim. It cannot mean so much to see a ruin."

Bessina looked from his face down to the ring which embraced her finger, then back into his face. They had disagreed many times over the years and he had been her master. He had forced her to give up Flin, to let her lover be impressed onto some ship, and now he was forcing her to go to a senseless place simply because Sparth's Head had not been his idea. But she would be reunited with Flin as surely as the sun rose in the morning and set at night and she was going to go to Sparth's Head Castle. "I told you of the man who spoke to me, an elderly soothsayer whom I knew as Peristeras. When he spoke, he told me that this journey was my destiny. And then he spoke of all the Fates, the Moirae, and he said it was their choice. If it's my fate to go there, then I shall."

Count Clauvis released her with a snicker. That made her blush deeply; she would rather he had slapped her across the mouth. "Your destiny's to go to some old ruin, to watch the seagulls fly about the battlements, and watch the sheep a'grazing on the hills while rooks and magpies hold their councils where old Parthelon once had his golden court. If that's your destiny, then I must say it is a noble one. But you've no need to do it suddenly; you'll come with me, and we shall be established where I say. When there is opportunity, perhaps we'll make a journey to your ruin."

"I have to go there now. It is my fate."

He laughed and shook his head. "As you told me the story, your soothsayer also swore that I no longer lived. He's not too accurate, this saint of yours."

The words dripped with sarcasm and they made Bessina blush all over again. It was true, of course: Peristeras had been wrong when he had told her of her father's demise. But she also had the ring. She could never describe the feeling the ring imparted to her; she knew he would never understand. But she had to go to Sparth's Head Castle for the ring's sake, if for no other reason; it was pulling her there.

She knew he was watching her keenly; he would try to say something, comfort her, persuade her. She also knew that it would have nothing to do with the real situation. He was not wearing the ring. He could not understand her now, just as he had never understood her before. He began to speak but she did not listen; she knew his words would be cheap, trite, meaningless little things, borne of his own mediocrity and destined to be forgotten, even if she did listen. Her mouth tightened with her anger, and she kicked her heels into her mount's flanks and tore away from him at a gallop. Why did they always have to argue? She did not know the answer but she knew the only thing she could do was ride away, ride north. Let him find his own way.

She could hear the thudding of his horse's hooves as he pursued her. And he was gaining; he had selected the better of the two mounts and she realized she would not be able to outrun him on the nag she was riding. He overhauled her quickly, grasped her reins again, and hauled her to a stop. "You little fool," he snarled. "You never ever listen."

"If I am such a fool, then tell me how it was that I had guile enough to free you from the cell you had been placed into. You didn't rescue me, sir. I saved you." She knew her words were stinging him, slashing into his pride, even as she shouted more. "You did not have the skill to win your freedom. Where were your friends then? You had none."

His face became red. He drew his arm back and struck her on the cheek; the slap brought tears that came more from humiliation than from the pain. "If it were not for all your maiden's pride and vanity, I'd not have been in

gaol. You flaunted all your charms before the court and
in their jealousy they ruined me."

That hurt. It was a stupid statement, a desperate, stupid statement from a man who was saying anything just
to avoid being caught without a reply. But in all its stu-
pidity, it pricked at the truth. Gymon had told her that he
had destroyed Count Clauvis in order to possess his
daughter. Bessina blinked back her tears of pain, shame,
and guilt. She could not let him win the argument or she
would be plowed into the soil of her own mind by him as
surely as the winter's dead grass was plowed under in the
spring. "'Twas Crecche's treachery which brought you
down," she cried. "If you and he had paid the proper tax,
the King would not have marched upon our fief." The
blow landed effectively; she could tell that by looking at
him. But then over his shoulder, along the lower slopes
of the Priscus River Valley, she saw something which
made her forget the argument. There was a great body of
riders, of Buerdic cavalrymen, moving along the slope.
"By all the gods' good graces, they are coming."

"Who's coming?" He looked over his shoulder and saw
the riders. "It's Pale Lothar's cavalry. I wonder if they
still are seeking us, or if some other quarry interests them."

"They're seeking us," she said.

"How can you know that?"

Her voice nearly failed her. How could she tell her
father the awful truth, the pivotal truth she had not yet
revealed to him? "The reason I was free to steal the keys
which opened up your cell last night is this—I gained my
freedom with a dagger's blade. I was a prisoner in my
own right and killed the bailiff, gaining my escape." Even
as she spoke, she could see the company of riders change
direction. She and her father had been seen.

"The gods," Count Clauvis said. "It is not so. Old
Gymon?"

"Yes. He had designs upon my chastity." It was as
much explanation as was needed; they were suddenly
father and daughter once again as they set spurs to their
horses, to ride up the hillside. They breathed a sigh of

relief when the pursuing horsemen disappeared below the crest of the hill.

The forest sprang up at the valley rim, eerie, naked, and leaf-stripped, like dead weeds at the edge of a path. But though the leaves had fallen, the forest was still a good hiding place. They guided their horses toward the trees and plunged headlong between the stout boles, kicking up dead leaves, mud, and sticks. The forest was thick. Clumps of brush sprang up like gray walls, hiding everything. They could not see whether they were still being pursued; they could only ride on and hope the horsemen had lost track of them.

They remained in the forest for the better part of the day. Fatigue rotted their bones but they did not dare stop. It was awful; the only bright side of the nerve-racking hide-and-seek was that at least they were heading in the general direction of Sparth's Head.

They reached the northern edge of the forest late in the afternoon; they were both nodding in their saddles and they did not even stop to discuss the wisdom of riding back into the open. It had been more than a day since they had slept, and neither had any thought except to keep going. They plodded across dead meadow grass which had been green a month before.

But they had made a disastrous mistake. They had only gone a league when something made Count Clauvis turn in his saddle. His face went pale. They had never eluded the cavalry; all those riders and more were hotly chasing them. The scores of sleek horses had broken out of the trees and were less than a league away; the earth shook with the distant pursuit.

The fugitives spurred their horses, but they had little chance of escaping. There were more trees ahead of them, another large patch of forest, but it was atop the next ridge of hills, a distant black line on the horizon. But they tried. Their horses were poor ones, ridden all day, but the pursuers were nearly a league back. If they could reach the trees, there was always the chance of finding a hiding place, a patch of brush or a rill where they might escape pursuit.

They rode as fast as their two nags would carry them; Count Clauvis broke ahead of Bessina, but then he slackened his pace to allow her to keep up. The cavalrymen were gaining; each time she glanced over her shoulder, they had moved measurably closer. But the trees were measurably closer, also. Then the Count's horse gave out. They had come so close! The trees were only a hundred cubits away, but his horse slowed and collapsed into a heap of lather and awkward angles. Count Clauvis managed to leap free, rolled through the grass and then clambered to his feet.

There was only one thing to do. "Come, Father," Bessina shouted. "Ride with me upon this horse." It was a hopeless gesture. Even when it had borne only her, the horse's only redeeming quality had been that it was too slow even to run itself to death. But Count Clauvis clambered up in back of her with wheezes and grunts and they started off once more.

Then they were astonished to see mounted, armored knights appear from the trees in front of them. The new warriors were as different from the company of cavalrymen as the mastiff from the greyhound. Each knight was encased by heavy plate armor and so was each broad courser. Each carried a lance and on each lance waved a scarlet banner, made more scarlet by the rays of the waning sun. The horses' caparisons were scarlet, as well.

There appeared to be four to five score of them, a formidable force, considering that each knight was accompanied by squires and attendants bearing extra weapons. And they had spotted the fugitives. They formed into a battle line which cantered toward Bessina and Clauvis as ominously as a cat approaching a bird's nest.

Bessina reined in her mount; there was no sense riding any farther. Any hope of escape was gone. They could tell nothing about the company of knights, other than the fact that they were plainly mercenaries. But whoever the stoutly armored men were, the fugitives' freedom could last only moments longer.

Chapter Twenty-six:
The Red Company

STUNNED, BESSINA AND Count Clauvis watched as the two companies of horsemen approached; weapons glinted in the dying sun as helmeted heads faced one another. From their place in the middle, the two fugitives could only watch and listen as their prospective captors decided who would possess their bodies.

The cavalry commander rode forward and addressed the knights. "Who are you armored men who cross the borders of Buerdaunt? And do you offer shelter to these two, these murderers? I hope that's not the case."

One of the knights threw up his helmet visor, rode forward, and replied. "We don't know them and we don't care what business you have with them. But we'll take them or not as we decide, for we're of the Red Company and we go where we please. And that's an answer to both your questions."

"Our King's our strength. Yield up the prisoners. Say we may take them with us to our keep and we shall let you leave these lands untouched."

The leader of the Red Company burst into derisive

laughter which was echoed all up and down the line of his fellows. "Yield them up, and you'll let us leave? Why, my lads, that's extortion. They'll let us leave their lands untouched." He turned back to the cavalry officer and shouted, "Tell your men to see their blades are loose in their scabbards, my young friend, because we're the Red Company. Cities tremble at our coming and it's we who decide who's to be touched and who's not to be touched. Have at them, lads; show this king of theirs we're not frightened of plowboys on horseback."

He slammed his visor shut, leveled his lance, and charged into the midst of the cavalrymen, followed by his fellows. Bessina was thrown from her horse by the fury of the charge. It knocked the wind from her, but neither she nor her father was hurt. As for the horse, it galloped away in panic while the two companies of warriors battled to and fro along the hillside.

The light cavalry had been an innovation of Lothar the Pale himself; it was something only Buerdaunt possessed and was famous all across the Thlassa Mey. Units were stationed across the land; they pursued fugitives, posted official messages, and put down riots in the provinces. They curbed thievery; they served every useful purpose. The men wore the lightest armor, carried light weapons, and their fine palfreys were provided by the crown. The ranks of the cavalry often included young noblemen as well as promising career soldiers and bureaucrats. They were not like knights of the heavy horse, who had to be nobles with enough income to afford their own armor, horses, and attendants.

So it was that the nobles of Buerdaunt were freed from all the tasks taken care of by the cavalry. But cavalrymen were not knights, they lacked the fearsome weapons and the heavy armor; they were a less powerful force.

There were many cavalrymen while the number of the Red Company was only some four or five score lances; even so, the cavalrymen had a hard time of it.

The battle was terrible, brutal. Knights on broad coursers charged into the light cavalrymen like iron-clad comets, knocking their opponents this way and that, running men and horses through with their steel-tipped lances. It was no tournament, after all. The lances were not capped on the ends; they terminated in deadly points and they had a man, a horse, and over a hundredweight of armor behind them. They pierced flesh and leather like bodkins piercing pears.

The cavalrymen answered with equally brutal tactics. If a number of them could surround a knight, one would seize his reins while the rest hacked the victim to pieces. Bessina and Count Clauvis cowered in the dead grass, afraid to run as men wielded bloody swords, horses stamped and screamed, knights thundered by with lances couched, and bloody bodies fell here and there, littering the hillside.

But all the while, the battle went against the cavalrymen. There were too few of them to withstand massed charges by their heavily armored opponents; their horses began to panic at the smell of spilled blood and the screams of other wounded horses. The knights of the Red Company gradually swept the cavalry down the hill toward the forest. And as the tide of the battle swept away from them, Bessina and Count Clauvis were left lying amid scattered bodies and fallen horses. They could hear the shouting and the clashing of weapons as the battle faded into the distance, so they leaped up as one and dashed in the opposite direction.

But it was a useless attempt. They had made only a few cubits when a cluster of attendants gave chase and ran them down, pulling them to the turf before they could reach the shelter of the trees. The captors dragged the two roughly to their feet, then made them walk to the spot where others watched the battle. The cavalry had been badly mauled and had retreated pell-mell through the trees. The mounted knights had not bothered to follow; they galloped back up the slope, trumpets blaring and banners dancing.

Their leader halted his horse before the captives, dismounted, and handed his great helmet to a young man who appeared at his side to take it. The leader was a pleasant-looking fellow, a bit older than Count Clauvis, with dark, sweat-soaked hair that had much gray mixed in. He studied the two of them without speaking.

For her part, Bessina was horrified by the carnage and the purposeless spilling of blood. "You mean you fought a battle for the sake of taking us? You seem a foolish man; by my troth, you've left full many bodies on the field for captives who have neither gold nor hope of raising ransom."

He smiled at her; the smile looked strangely familiar. "Young lady, the gods will decide the price to be placed on your heads. People who are pursued by as many of the King's men as you were must be of worth to someone. Besides, if you look, there are a great many more of their bodies lying on that hillside than there are of ours. They'll remember us, you see." He quaffed wine from a flagon which was offered to him, then continued. "Always fight, that's what I say. They'll remember us and the next time we meet they'll say to one another 'Let's not tackle them ourselves this time. We'll just pass the word they were here.' And so a few blows exchanged now can save us many later on." He smiled again. "Besides, it was enjoyable. Would you like some wine?" He offered the flagon to her but she declined.

He shrugged and handed the flagon to one of his fellows. "And now we come to cases. Who are you two and why have you come all this way to fall into the hands of the Red Company? Speak up now, it'll do neither of you any good to dissemble."

Count Clauvis hesitated and Bessina was also silent. She knew of the Red Company. They were a band of mercenary knights, soldiers of fortune who had roamed the Greenlands for years, exacting tribute from villages, mauling local militias, even capturing castles and whole towns. The Red Company—her Flin had been a member of the Red Company. "My Lord, perhaps the Fates have made us meet, for it is likely that you know one dear to me. His name is Flin and he was taken from my side some weeks ago."

The man looked at her. "By the gods' eyes, I know him as sure as my name's Leuval and I lead this company.

He's my son, as fine and strapping a lad as a man could wish." He looked down at her. "And you, perhaps, are some maiden he's left in his wake. Don't feel bad on that account; you've company enough. But I can tell you he's met his match at last, the daughter of some count, and she's tricked him and sold him into slavery." He paused; his smile went away, and his expression hardened. "And that's why we've come here, you see; the Red Company will ravage Buerdaunt and Galliardy and all the other provinces of this realm until my boy's restored to me."

A menagerie of emotions attacked Bessina. She had met Flin's father at last—that explained the familiarity of the smile and the carriage—and the man already hated her. What would she do? She was not one of the strumpets Flin had known earlier; she was the woman he loved. Fear, shame, and pride fought within her for possession of her tongue, but one fact towered over the rest—Flin had not returned, not to her, not to the Red Company. "My Lord, I see you hate me. That is just, for I am she, Bessina, daughter of the Count of Galliardy. But hear me out. I did give him to the guards but it was done to save his life, to save him from a fate far worse. And when 'twas done I learned the tale. They shot his haughty steed from under him and hauled him to the ground—and every bruise and bleeding wound they laid on him is duplicated in my soul, for I adored him and still do. I fain would give my eyes to have him here and safe once more."

Leuval seemed moved by her words. Compassion warred with anger in his face. "Then I have found you," he said simply. "You're lovely enough; I should have known the instant you spoke of him." He seemed to teeter on the brink of a great decision; his face was very grave. "I'm not sure what to do with you. Why did you betray my son?"

Bessina looked at her father. He was watching her; his face had become red and his expression was belligerent. "Tell him," he said.

She could not face either of them. It had begun at the Douzainium; she had been captured, harassed, and threatened. Now she had to stand before a gathering of hard-armored men and describe the second most painful moment of her life. She looked at the dead grass, at the articulated plate which covered Leuval's feet. It was hard, and she did not know what to say. "Because of what I saw," she finally stammered.

"What could that have to do with it?" The voice which came from among the knights was hardly sympathetic.

"My father took me to a donjon cell and there I saw a poor, decaying man who once had been a noble. He'd been kept in that same cell for seventeen long years to grieve and rot. And even as I watched, he passed away from all afflictions he had borne from moldering in that awful, foetid place. My father..." She looked at Count Clauvis; his eyes were hard as iron. "My father told me that would be Flin's fate for touching me." Tears began to lace her words. "Unless I would agree to see him captured and impressed aboard some merchant ship, to ply the seas and never see me more." The tears came faster; she could hardly speak. "And so I did it. I gave up my love and sold him to an unknown destiny."

She could not go on. She was only a maiden, three years shy of a score, and her experiences over the last weeks had been enough to bow any neck. There was no one to turn to; her father was glaring at her, knights were frowning at her, Leuval himself gazed at her as if she were some species of insect. Where was her mother now? More than anything else, she wished she could be with her mother, but the Countess had disappeared from her life many a year ago. She felt herself wilting the way a flower wilts when a bonfire is built too close to it. She crumpled to the ground, because there was nothing for her to cling to, and she sobbed hopelessly. "Of all this broad world's creatures, I'm most wretched."

She lay on the dead grass sobbing as she heard Leuval's voice. "And you're her father. Is she telling the truth? Did you cause her to betray my Flin?"

Whatever faults Count Clauvis had, cowardice was plainly not among them. He glared back at the leader of the Red Company. "I did it and I'm not ashamed of it. If my portion for that act is death, then let the deed be done.

I'll gladly die before I see my daughter in the arms of any common man."

He pointed toward Bessina. "She had to learn her lesson—that a woman must be dutiful, must bear the burden nature gives to her, and, most of all, must learn obedience to a man who is her husband or her father." His voice thundered through the darkening air and made the dead leaves rattle. "Her mother learned those lessons at too great a cost, and therefore my Bessina shall be taught while still she's young and has not yet been wed."

He glared into the angry eyes which surrounded him. "That had to be established. When she weds and whom is chosen and whatever things she does through all her years of maidenhood must be at my decision. I'm her father. As to why your son was sent away, I'd see her dead and parceled out to beasts, or with a beast as husband, ere I'd see her give herself in love to some mere rogue. So do your worst. But when I'm dead and gone and you have had your carnal way with her or given her to some base man you choose, remember me, you men who have fair daughters of your own, remember that the mighty gods look down upon your acts and I shall be avenged."

Bessina had stopped weeping. She looked up at the bearded faces above her and at Leuval's face most of all, for she could see that he was very angry. But he did not shout as her father had shouted. He looked into Count Clauvis' red face and said in a quiet voice, "You're courageous. You've spoken your heart before your captors and I can say that if I needed a man to fight, I'd choose you as easily as any. And if I needed a man to guard my beasts from wolves, I'd choose you for the task—but your daughter isn't a beast. You don't select proper blood lines for her as if she were a mare or a ewe. It's plain to me you set her to the deception of my son, so this is my decision: we'll take both of you with us. You'll stay with us until he's found. If he's well, then you'll be released unharmed. If he has lashes across his back, you'll receive twice that number. If he's lost a finger, you'll lose your hand. And if he's crippled in any way so he can't ride and can't wield a sword or lance, then you will die."

He bent to take Bessina's hand and helped her to her feet. "And as for this maiden, she'll also go with us. When we find Flin, the two of them can choose what they want to do. If Flin still wants her for his bride, then it will come to pass." He looked at her gravely. "And if he decides otherwise, then I can see from the tears that wash her cheeks it will be punishment enough."

He faced his cohorts. "She'll ride with us. As for this Count, I want his hands bound. Put him on a horse and if he tries to escape, he's made his choice." Then he turned back to Bessina. "Now, where might my son be?"

She looked up at him. "Sparth's Head."

"What would he be doing there? There's nothing but a ridge of hills and a deserted castle."

"My destiny awaits me at Sparth's Head," she replied. "And Flin's my destiny. So it must be that he is there or I, perhaps, may find a way to reach him." She then told him the story of her escape from the Douzianium, her meeting with Peristeras, and how the mystic soothsayer had told her she was ordained to bring Parthelon's ring to Sparth's Head Castle. Then, as an afterthought, she removed the ring and showed it to him.

He took it from her and examined it, turning it over in his hand to read the inscription. Another knight of the Red Company looked at the ring over Leuval's shoulder and soon it was being passed through the company. There were few comments—only a nodding of the head here or a pursing of the lips there. Although the ring was solid gold, its value was nothing new to men who had seen rings many times its worth; it was the antiquity of the piece which drew the respectful silence, as well as something about the very plainess of it that was mystical. At last it completed its circuit and Leuval handed it back to Bessina.

"Is there any man among you who doesn't wish to go to Sparth's Head?" He asked the question, then repeated it. There were no negative answers, only some murmuring. He turned back to Bessina. "Then we'll take you to this Sparth's Head and see if there is a mystery, as you say there is."

Bessina bowed her head. "I thank you for your help but there is one more thing which I must ask."

"You may ask it, though it may not be given."

Bessina hesitated. "Release my father from his bonds. He is a man of courage and he shall not flee." She spoke in a small voice because she was afraid of the reaction she might draw down on herself.

But Leuval did not become angry; he looked at Count Clauvis. "If we cut your bonds, do you forswear flight?"

"I shall not be released by young girls' pleas. Leave all your bonds in place and choke on them."

Leuval turned to Bessina. "It seems he's made his choice."

"I cannot go until his hands are free."

Leuval began to chuckle, then his chuckle turned into laughter. "What sort of match is this? They turn every word and every gesture into a contest, yet they say they're a father and a daughter, bound by blood and fate. By the gods, even a tiny kindness becomes a contest of wills between these two." He waved a hand at one of the attendants. "Release him, then, and if he should flee, good riddance to him; we'll tend to him in all good time. Lovely maid, it would seem to me that my Flin has chosen a pretty family to marry into, for all your noble blood."

Leuval's orders were followed and then a horse was brought for Bessina. Once the dead and the wounded had been tended to, all mounted up and the Red Company made toward Sparth's Head, which rose out of the sea up the coast from Verdast.

It was a finer escort than Bessina would have believed possible a day earlier. They covered many leagues each day, their big horses eating up endless stretches of grassland with even strides. They did not bother to bind Count Clauvis when they made camp at night. And insulted by that aspersion on his character, as well as reluctant to leave Bessina, he declined to flee.

Early on the third day they approached Sparth's Head itself; there stood the great, deserted castle, still magnificent, with sheep grazing among the fallen stones of its lower outworks and rooks wheeling and calling among the towers.

In its day, the castle had been the most powerful on the banks of the Thlassa Mey. A high wall had been built a hundred cubits below the castle itself, its gatehouses and towers evenly spaced along it. But that wall had fallen into disrepair. They rode through one of the gaps in single file, then started up the last stretch of hillside toward the great pile itself.

But there was no riding into Sparth's Head Castle; the towering curtain walls stood unbreached by time or enemies, and, while the great gate hung open, the drawbridge was long since rotted away. The rear of the castle had been built at the edge of the high cliff; the battlements looked out over the sea itself, five hundred cubits below. Around the rest, a moat had been built; it was dry, but the stone sides were so steep that any attempt to cross it on horseback would have been suicidal. They had no choice but to dismount.

For all his naysaying, Count Clauvis demanded to accompany Bessina; he would not release her from his sight. So it was decided that Bessina, Count Clauvis, and Leuval would enter. The rest of the knights would wait at the gate for fear of losing their horses and equipment to bandits or surprise.

The three of them dismounted, clambered down the bank of the dry moat, and climbed up the other side. It was as if they were climbing into another era as they walked beneath the massive gatehouse and into the eerie silence of what centuries earlier had been the seat of an empire.

Chapter Twenty-seven:
Palamon and Aelia

WHEN THE NIGHT had been darkest, Aelia had heard crewmen shouting on the deck as the galley's single broad sail had been furled. The ship's motion had changed and the rowers had stepped up their efforts; she had made a mental note of that. At first the sounds had disturbed her. Were they preparing for battle? Had Carea's fleet already appeared? But time had gone by and there had been no further noises or changes of direction, so she had relinquished that hope.

The slaves labored like oxen at their benches. She could hear the steady beat of the hortator's drum sounding through the ship's timbers and, because her berth was near the rowers, she could hear the occasional crack of the whip. Then the realization came to her that they were traveling upriver. She did not know which river it might be; Ursid had kept her belowdecks and separated from her Princess ever since they had left Buerdaunt—and perhaps it did not matter anyway. They were traveling the last leg toward Alyubol's new stronghold; that was all that mattered.

She lay back and fell once more into a desperate, hopeless sleep. She rolled and twisted; she could not find a comfortable position and could not quiet the dread which held her. Then everything changed; a deep calm swept over her, she drifted into deep slumber, and she dreamed the same strange dream she had dreamed before. Once again she lay in the unknown dream-chamber with dark tapestries covering the walls. Once more the dream-priestess chanted over her and the chant was the same as before. The same voices issued from the dream-priestess' mouth. "The question must be asked. Consent shall then be given." But there was a new phrase added to those two: "The deed shall soon be done."

Aelia could again sense a presence on the other side of the arras at her feet. Someone watched the strange ceremony, a woman of regal bearing. The dream had advanced again, then. Even in her sleep, Aelia could remember that she had not been able to determine the spectator's sex before. But there was no doubt now. It was a woman, a young woman, and she looked familiar; Aelia could almost identify her. The curve of the face, the cut of the hair, all were maddeningly familiar. The spectator watched the scene intently, as if preparing to show herself, but she never did; the chanting went on endlessly. Then the scene faded into another, different dream. But when Aelia awoke, she remembered it, even though she had forgotten the dream that had followed.

She slept until a guard came to take her to the main deck and she did not receive his morning's greeting with joy; she knew it meant they had reached their destination. Still, she felt rested and refreshed, which was a far cry from the way she had felt the two mornings before.

When she reached the deck, she was amazed by what she saw. She had been right; they had traveled upriver, and the galley was landing at a place she recognized, the Library of the Polonians. So that was why Alyubol had not been at the Dark Capes—he had ousted Reovalis and had taken this refuge. She felt concern for the ancient sage. The wizard was not known for kindness toward his victims.

Berengeria was also there, her hands bound before her the same as Aelia's. Even so, Aelia held forth her own tied hands, grasped the maiden's wrists, and they looked into one another's eyes for a moment. Then Ursid came on deck, splendid in heavy armor that gleamed like jewelry. "The lesser prisoners will go ashore this instant," he ordered. "I will wait with the Princess until the wizard has replied and has accepted the provisions of the pact."

The order was plain enough. But as Aelia was taken away and put into company with Phebos once more, she knew the young knight had ulterior motives; he wanted more time beside the Princess, more time to plead or threaten her and to make her accept his wooing. It was almost pitiful; after all, Lothar the Pale had made that decision for him.

Sir Phebos was already being escorted down the gangplank. He carried himself with dignity but it was plain that he was greatly discomfited because his armor had been taken from him and he was wearing nothing more than a prisoner's loincloth. From what Aelia knew of Alyubol, it was likely that Sir Phebos was only beginning to suffer for his gallantry.

There was no time for them to do more than exchange morning pleasantries. Gags were shoved into their mouths—the guard who performed that task apologetically explained that it was Ursid's order—and they were hustled down the plank, through the two cubits of water at the bottom of it, and onto the shore. They plodded toward the Library of the Polonians, heads bowed.

They started up the path but they had not gone far when three men dropped onto the trail behind them. The escorts were astounded but no more than Aelia was, because she recognized all three of the rescuers—young Flin, Reovalis, and Palamon. Her face went slack with her surprise, but she did not let that paralyze her; she dropped to the ground and threw her shoulder against the legs of the guardsman nearest her. He lost his balance with a cry, fell, and was easy prey for Flin's club.

And Palamon! The sight of the Prince aroused a hurricane of emotions within her. She was tearful with relief to find that he had survived to strive beside her once more. However he had gotten to that place, he was fighting furiously for her and Sir Phebos. He laid right and left with the *Spada Korrigaine* as only Palamon could do with a two-handed sword, scattering the soldiers the way a big dog would scatter a flock of chickens. The great blade felled two of them before they could flee, while a third vaulted down the face of the cliff to avoid combat, falling and rolling a dozen cubits to the sandy ground below.

Reovalis was too old for fighting, but he removed Aelia's gag and cut her bonds with a small knife, while Flin battled another guard. Sir Phebos, after a moment's surprise, used his feet to sweep the last guard's legs from beneath him, then kicked him over the edge of the trail after his fellow. The Knight of Pallas had recognized Palamon; Aelia had seen it in his eyes. They had widened in astonishment, but then he had joined the battle, and the expression had vanished almost instantly.

Flin finished his opponent, Reovalis cut Sir Phebos' bonds, and there was an instant's greeting between old friends. The expressions which washed over Palamon's face were as intriguing as those of his former squire; he stood motionless before Sir Phebos, his jaw working silently. Then he turned to help Aelia up.

That was all the time there was for greetings. "We must make haste. Our dear Princess has not yet left the vessel's deck." Palamon leaped down the trail, racing breathlessly, but it was no use. Though the scuffle had lasted only instants, even that had been too long; the crewmen had cut the lines holding the galley alongside the beach and the Stilchis' current was sweeping her away. Berengeria had been hauled below.

Palamon raced like a madman toward the river's edge, followed by the others. But his quest was hopeless, for Buerdic archers had scrambled to the vessel's rail, and the arrows began arching from their bows. He was forced back; even his *Spada Korrigaine* was useless against such weapons.

Palamon pursued the galley as far as he dared, but he

had to retreat in the face of the singing shafts, one of which struck his chain mail and glanced away harmlessly. His face and his voice were full of anguish. "My sister, I have failed you." He grimaced with bitter frustration, then stooped, picked up a stone, and hurled it after the departing vessel. The force of the throw carried him to his knees, but the stone still fell far short.

It was Flin who grasped the Prince by the shoulder and hauled him back, away from the withering flights of arrows. "Bravo," he said. "It was a marvelous throw, but rocks can't sink warships, so let's go away."

Palamon stood and smiled darkly as he turned toward the cliffs. "Indeed." Aelia had seen that smile before; she had watched his jaw drop at the first sight of Sir Phebos—his face had looked as if musty old memories would carry him away then. But now that Berengeria's loss was added to that shock, all that registered was his mask of a smile.

Then his expression softened as he gazed at them, and he threw his arms about Sir Phebos' shoulders. "Ah, Phebos. It is good to see you once again, although the circumstances could be better. We're in trouble, as you see." Then he turned to face Aelia. "And Lady Aelia." His look of joy surprised her as he grasped her wrists and loosed the severed cords from them. "I had thought I might not see you ever, but I should have known the truth. Your skills protect you better than iron mail."

Aelia was surprised and gratified by the compliment. For her part, she was happy to see him again, happier than she would have expected, even under such circumstances as these. "My knight, my Prince. It was a hard time, but we both have overcome the forces laid against us." She would have said more, but she could not find words as she looked up at the man who stood before her, perspiring and clasping her hands.

Then Reovalis ended the moment. "But now we all must flee. Success has gone a'glimmering; your good Princess has sailed away, and Alyubol could bring his mystic wrath about our ears at any moment."

Aelia watched Palamon's face fall as he looked one last time across the river's waves at the galley. The forest of long oars was moving again. The pilot was once more jockeying for position to put people ashore. "You're right. Once they suspect how few we are, they'll land a force and we shall be pursued."

"Then let's go back to the cave," Flin said. "And lay the best plans we can."

Palamon heaved a great sigh and turned from the river. He reached for Aelia's hand but she had knelt to remove one sandal, for a rock had settled into the bottom of it and she could hardly walk. "You go ahead, for I won't be an instant," she said. Then, as she was straightening, she saw something lying in the dirt where Palamon had thrown the rock at the galley. It had slipped from the loose metallic sleeve of his hauberk and now it lay before her, half unfolded. Oddly enough, she could see her name at the top of what looked like a page torn from a ship's log. That puzzled her. It was her name with a question mark, scribbled hastily: Aelia? Without thinking much about it, she picked it up, slipped it beneath her belt, and hurried after the others. But as they walked up the trail, she pulled the paper from her belt and began to read it. After all, it was her name that was at the top of it.

What she found written there surprised her. It was Palamon's handwriting, a sonnet written in the same form as the prayers he offered up to holy Pallas. But Pallas was not the object this time; Aelia herself was. Her mouth fell open as she read the fourteen lines over twice. She nearly stumbled; she was mystified.

Even though her name was scrawled at the top of the paper, she could tell Palamon had never planned to show it to her. She felt uncomfortable reading his words, but she could not put them from her, because the letter was too sharp a glimpse into the workings of the Prince's soul for her to resist reading it. Perhaps the Fates had intervened.

It's no emotion I can understand.
I thought I felt it once; 'twas but to find
That I was seeking sin. It is unkind.
But should I doubt the gift of your fair hand?

Gray Pallas tells me that a golden band
Unites our fates. Perhaps. And yet my mind
Cannot begin to duplicate the kind
Of passion which our Princess dear once fanned.
And still, and still, your image lingers in
My thoughts. I cannot rest till you are free,
Till you are safe and sound. I'll not begin
To name the fears your absence breeds in me.
My brain's become a stone; no thought's within.
The heavens keep you—what will be, will be.

It was flattering. Palamon was writing of love—that
was obvious—yet he never mentioned the emotion by
name. The implications and risks plainly unnerved him
so much he would not use the word, even in a paper he
had never planned to show to anyone.

It surprised her that he thought enough of her to write
the poem, even though he would doubtless never have
showed it to her on his own. And one thing stunned her—
he was plainly contemplating marriage. Such a thing was
impossible, because she was, after all, a priestess. But he
mentioned Pallas; had he not told her once that he had
seen Pallas in a vision? Had the holy Maiden actually
promised him that he was to marry Aelia, a priestess of
Hestia? He had never indicated that to her—but then he
never would have.

It was all very strange, a match arranged by a deity.
That was a marriage made in heaven with a vengeance.
But Aelia's own patron had not been heard from, and it
seemed unlikely a priestess could slip away and marry
the Prince of Carea without divine Hestia, the second of
the three holy virgins, knowing of it. It was impossible,
laughable.

Marriage. It was ridiculous, of course, but even the
concept, new and unfamiliar as it was, fascinated her. It
was threatening, frightening, interesting. What could it be
like, marriage to Palamon, with its binding of souls and
its physical love? They had traveled many leagues together,
and he had filled her thoughts at times, yet the vision of
marriage was beyond her.

What would she say if he asked her for her hand? The hurdles were obvious, and above all of them stood the ultimate conflict—she was a priestess pledged to Hestia. She turned her eyes upward for an instant and mouthed the question: "Oh Hestia fair, what must I make of this?"

She had to escape her own thoughts. She put the paper away; she would ponder other things awhile. And there were plenty of other problems for her to consider. She caught up with the group and listened to their plans. They would watch the cliffs through the day, wait for Ursid to send Berengeria ashore, then attack the escort and free her. There was little hope in the plan, but no less than in any other.

So they watched the shore through the remainder of the day. The galley moored again, and a stream of messengers traveled between the warship and the Library of the Polonians. But no move was made to send the Princess ashore. When night fell, the quintet watched long after the last light had faded, watched the sentries parade back and forth along the rail. They conferred once more, and Flin proposed a novel plan. They might be able to slip one or two of their number into the warship and release Berengeria before she could be sent ashore.

But they never had the chance. Their conference was interrupted by a parade of torches that emerged from the colonnaded porch of the Library, an endless stream of white-robed warriors who marched down the path toward the beach. It was an army. Archers passed, then men bearing battle-axes, swordsmen, and men with war clubs. Palamon and Aelia both knew the army for what it was— the warriors were illusions, all but a few. But Alyubol was a master of that device; he would have his henchmen mixed with the illusion, just enough that one could not face them without some doubt whether his opponent was real or not. And that doubt would make the illusion deadly; a particle of belief would make each axe real, each arrow swift and true.

So they could only watch. Palamon's expression was invisible in the darkness as the procession from the Library of the Polonians met a score of torch-bearing knights from the galley. Berengeria was surely with them. But there were too many to attack; even with the *Spada Korrigaine* in Palamon's hands, it would have been madness for them to oppose such a force. Berengeria was lost, at least for the moment.

They all watched until the last of the torches had disappeared into the temple. Then Palamon stood with a sigh and said it was time for all of them to return to their lair. He said nothing more; he simply began walking. His face was an indistinct blur in the darkness.

It was hard for them to feel their way along the rocky ledges; everything had been dissolved by darkness and they did not dare make any light. But when they reached Reovalis' refuge, Palamon turned toward Aelia and Sir Phebos. "I must regret that our reunion's ruined because we still have lost our dear Princess. But still I thank you, Phebos, that you've come."

Sir Phebos also smiled. "When Lady Aelia spoke your name, I knew that I would ne'er forgive myself if I did not accompany her. She is a wondrous woman, so I say, as competent as anyone I know."

"Indeed she is." There was a strange inflection in Palamon's voice and he glanced uncertainly at Aelia; she would have noticed the movement of his eyes, even if she had not read his letter. But she did not remark on it; the conversation turned to other things as Flin and Reovalis joined in. The main topic centered on Berengeria's predicament and how to gain her release, but that was a hard question to answer. There were five of them there, most experienced strategists, but not one could produce a decent plan to remove Carea's Princess from the tunnels beneath the Library. Even so, Palamon vowed more than once that he would not leave until that objective had been achieved.

Reovalis grew weary after a time and excused himself. He went into the cave, stretched out one of the many blankets he had stored there, and faded off to sleep. Flin did the same. Both of them lay snoring a few cubits from where the other three still sat at the mouth of the cave, discussing bygone days and immediate problems. At last

Sir Phebos became weary and he also retired, leaving Palamon and Aelia alone. But Palamon plainly did not feel like sleeping and neither did Aelia. "We cannot move until we have a scheme," she said, for perhaps the dozenth time.

"On that we are agreed. And we must have one by tomorrow. We cannot allow the grip of Alyubol the time to tighten. Yet my mind is like a jaded horse; it does not function."

Aelia said nothing. There was nothing for her to say. She was no more able to produce a scheme that would work than he was.

Palamon spoke once more, quietly, thoughtfully. "One thing I ne'er will do. I'll not allow the *Spada Korrigaine* to come again into the hands of that outrageous man. The stakes are far too high. Before that's done, I'll fling it off the highest cliff into the deepest pit and then I'll follow it."

It was an unusual burst of emotion from Palamon. Aelia looked at him. "I thank you that you trust enough in me to tell me what your heart says. We will hope the time may never come when you will have to act upon that pledge." She touched him on the arm.

Palamon looked at her hand, then he seemed to notice something was missing. He felt the metallic sleeve of his hauberk and looked distressed.

"What are you looking for?" she asked.

"A trifle."

She hesitated. "When I bent to fix my sandal, I perceived a letter lying in the sand where you had passed. It had my name inscribed upon it and I paused to read it. I apologize."

He stared at her, then shrugged and smiled. "It's nothing. Please forget the words you've read, for they were meaningless." Then he hesitated and she could tell strong forces were warring within him. "No, that's not true." He struggled to force more words out. "I was concerned and I am very glad to see you once again."

"You mew your thoughts up, Palamon. It was a revelation as I read them."

"I doubt you read profundity in that; I should have burned it." He smiled again, ruefully this time. "Muddled bits of thoughts and tired verse were all it offered you."

"Those bits of thought were honest, noble, and kind. I thank you that you thought that much of me."

"Young Flin has told me that I think too much and that I have no concept of the mind of womankind. Perhaps it's true." He hesitated. When he spoke again, the words flowed over like a warm river, suddenly released. "I told you of my vision months ago when I saw holy Pallas on the verge of that high cliff which rises from the sea not far from our own capital. But I did not tell all. The Maiden said that it would be my fate to find a bride, that she was someone I already knew. She told me that this woman's mind was quick and that her character was strong. And I knew then she spoke of you alone." With the last phrase, his voice failed once more; he looked away from her, out toward the river which lay hidden by cliffs and darkness.

"I'm pleased to hear your patron thinks that well of me." It was hardly a witty response, since Aelia had read Palamon's words about marriage in the letter. But how could she make any better? It did not matter what she thought of Palamon; she was a priestess of Hestia. Marriage was a distant shore across a rushing torrent.

"Flin has told me that it's all so easy," Palamon said. "He revels in the intricacies of his wooing and he laughs at those of us who do not know the proper words. He tells me that I think too much and yet I cannot think of what is right to say. But Pallas tells me you're to be my bride." A note of desperation had entered the Prince's voice, the sound of a man who had ventured too far and could not turn back.

Aelia interrupted him. "My Palamon, you need not flog yourself. I think the world of you, but still I am a priestess of the goddess Hestia. I cannot wed. I must admit that I have been attracted to you since the first time we locked eyes. But how am I to change the rôle which claims me?"

It was barely a refusal to the proposal Palamon had not made yet, but it made Aelia feel like a murderess. Palamon was silent for a long time. She could not tell whether he was disappointed or relieved that she could not marry him. "That's very true," he said at last. "And yet you are the bride my deity has chosen for me. You have told me that you cannot change you rôle, but how can we deny the wishes of the holy Maiden?"

A thought rose from the back of Aelia's mind and presented itself to her. It was a momentous thought, a chilling thought, a revelation. She was not yet ready for it. She was unsure; questions still had to be answered. "Good Palamon, please tell me one small thing. You say that we should wed. Am I correct?"

He nodded weakly. The gesture was ludicrous when made by him; the obvious uncertainty behind it was touching. "I think that you should be my wife."

In spite of the fact that Aelia had known what he would say before she had even asked her question, she felt a strange thrill upon hearing the words from his lips. And she felt that thrill, that idea, that memory threatening to overwhelm her, to cloud all logic from her brain. "Yours is an honorable thought. But still I wonder—do you think it for my sake, or do you merely follow the belief your Pallas wishes that we two should wed? The state of love which should exist between a man and bride—do you feel love for me? Or are you simply following the course you think your patron's chosen for you?"

It was the first time the word "love" had even been spoken during the conversation. But Palamon did not appear as if the word were new to his thoughts. Rather, he spoke of it in a tone which made Aelia believe the word had opened a gate into his soul. Doubts and questions began to pour forth. "I wish that I could tell you that I knew." His voice nearly left him. "I'm sorry."

He paused, then tried again. "You ask of love. I know not what it is. I thought I did but now I've no idea; I shall not lie to you on that account. You know that once I loved fair Berengeria—at least I thought I did. The thoughts I have of you are different and yet they still are powerful. What's love? Can you tell me? I do not know the name of every thought which pulses in my brain, and yet I can say that I have a great respect for you, that you are in my mind, and that I've missed your counsel all the time you have been gone." He took her by the shoulders. "Perhaps no love springs up between us two; perhaps the thoughts I have of marriage are because of Pallas' will. But yet if we should marry, I would be as proud to live with you and see your face each morning..." He made a helpless gesture. "I would not hesitate to give my royal title up for such a fate." He released her and turned away hopelessly, with the air of a man who had forced himself into a desperate gamble only to find he had blundered on the verge of winning the prize. "I've told you nothing. Please forgive me."

But he had said a great deal, more than he seemed to realize. It was almost funny to see a rawboned tower of a man fumbling for words and turning away to hide his face from her like a small child. He knew nothing of women; he was a helpless innocent. Still, it was funny in a way that made her catch her breath.

And misgivings were all being blotted out by the great thought; his proposal had answered one question, a question which had puzzled her for weeks. It explained everything. "Perhaps I ought to tell you of my dreams."

He looked at her. "Dreams?"

"Since we were torn apart that night at sea, I've had some dreams—not every night but still with regularity that gives me pause."

He said nothing. His expression masked the thoughts behind it, but she went on quickly and did not look at him again. "They're very vivid. I am in a room, a cloister or a temple, I'm not sure. A sibyl stands above me and she sings an endless chant. She has three voices; each one is as clear as if it came from out a separate mouth."

"What does she say?"

"I shall repeat the words." Aelia found herself faltering. It had been only moments since she had begun to understand the visions' meaning and her voice wavered as she repeated the three phrases to him. "At first she said 'The question must be asked.' And next she spoke the phrase 'Consent must then be given.' 'The deed shall then be done' was what came next." She stopped and looked up at him.

"But tell me this," he said. "Were they good dreams or bad?"

"Good dreams, for I slept well upon the nights they came and hardly slept at all on other nights."

"And woke up rested?"

"Yes."

He drew a long breath, then smiled uncertainly. "'Consent must then be given.' That is what she said?"

"Indeed."

"Then all my fears were empty, and the gods had opened up the path into your heart before I ever took a step." He began to laugh quietly. She also laughed as the tension eased; soon they were leaning against one another, laughing in the darkness.

Then Aelia stopped. "What shall become of me when this is known within the temples of our Carea?"

Palamon put his arm about her shoulder, surprising both of them with the gesture. "I am a Prince. Your safety is assured e'en though a scandal shakes the palace stones. If Hestia's clerics are as reasonable as it is said they are devout, this tale of visions and of vivid dreams will sway them to accept that 'twas in truth a pious act."

"I hope that shall be so."

"Besides," he said, "the chance is very poor that we will even live another day. If Alyubol can have his way with us, then we'll both die unwed, before we can return to Carea to post the bans."

"Indeed, whatever strategy we use, our lives shall be at risk tomorrow." She was quiet for a moment. "I have a small suggestion."

"Yes?"

Her mouth formed a line, her lower lip was pressed thoughtfully between her teeth. "It's true, you know. Tomorrow well could be the last day of our lives. E'en if we fled..."

"We shall not flee. That's sure." There was an unwonted harshness in Palamon's tone.

"Bear with me now," she said, vexed by the interruption. "For even if we did, we'd still be at the mercy of Ursid and all his knights and archers."

"And your suggestion?"

"Since that's the case, let's have it done tonight."

Palamon looked stunned. Still, it was quite logical. "We need a priest," he said.

Aelia laughed. "Sir Phebos is a priest, and so are all you Knights of Pallas and myself as well, for I am still a priestess. I would say the one thing that we have in great abundance, even in our present straits, is clergy."

"It's a sudden step."

"How is it? You have pondered it for weeks." She grasped his wrist. "Tomorrow morning we may both be dead or separated once again, or we'll have lost the fortitude to take the risks involved. Let's have it now."

He nodded. "Indeed. Indeed, you're right. I'll wake Sir Phebos." They embraced and gazed into one another's eyes for a moment. Then Palamon went to fetch his former squire. They did not wake the other two sleepers. Palamon did not want to do that; he was obviously embarrassed. But they explained the situation to the Knight of Pallas at some length, he nodded his understanding, and they walked out into the starlight.

The ceremony was a short one. They declared their desire to marry, Sir Phebos invoked the blessing of Pallas and enjoined them to be true to one another in body and spirit, to make their marriage a reflection of their stout faith. Then it was done. On the rock ledges of the Cauldron of the Stilchis, Prince Palamon and Lady Aelia were joined in matrimony; Sir Phebos dabbed both their foreheads with borrowed oil and they kissed for the first time.

Chapter Twenty-eight:
Usmu's Game

THE MORNING FROST clung to the rocks, and there was an icy crust around the puddles left by the rain Alyubol had sent the day before. A chill breeze swayed the tassels of the dead weeds which clung to the hollows and cracks about the mouth of Reovalis' cave, but far back in the depths of the cavern, beneath the blanket which covered Palamon and Aelia, it was warm. After the two of them had spoken their vows, Sir Phebos had helped Palamon clear a space where the newlyweds could have some privacy, had hung a blanket by way of a partition, and had departed. A bed of blankets had provided a comfortable nest through the hours of darkness.

Now Palamon lay awake. He had slept well, though he had not slept long, and he knew it was morning because he could hear bodies moving about at the cave's entrance. But it was still dark in the improvised bridal chamber, too dark to see his hand in front of his face.

He could hear Aelia's breathing and he could feel the warmth of her body as she slept. That was a strange feeling; in fact, it was a morning of strange feelings. In

306

his thirty-and-ninth year, after a life of celibacy, Palamon had taken a wife and had known physical love for the first time. It had been a strange experience, a marvelous experience, and now he was awake, contemplating that night of rising emotions and sensations.

He listened to Aelia's breathing and he drank in her warmth. Cautiously he reached out and touched her hair. The night had come so suddenly he had not been prepared for it, but he had to smile at that thought. Had he had time to prepare, he likely would have lacked the resolve to go through with it.

It had been a night of learning for him. He had had moments when he had pictured the female form, when he had dreamed of the touch of a woman. But in the warmth and darkness of his wedding night, he had found Aelia's body to be a hundred times more subtle and marvelous than any figment of his half-suppressed thoughts. He had known her well before; together they had gone through some of the most harrowing tests the Fates could offer, but he had not known her until last night, not the way he knew her now. He smiled at himself again. They had shared secrets men and women had been sharing for many thousand years, yet it seemed that what they had experienced together could never have been experienced by anyone else.

They had been able to shut out the disappointments of the day before, at least to a degree. They had conspired in the act, determined that it should take place before they, whom the gods had paired, could be cut down by Alyubol's magic or separated once more by Ursid's machinations. It had been a night of learning, a night of warmth and breathing, of lips touching lips, of exploring, of softness. And the wonder was that, if they could survive the day, there would be other such nights in store for them.

Aelia was his wife. It was morning and shortly they would have to go out and risk their lives together. It would not be the first time they had done that. He reached out his hand and touched her in the darkness, felt a shoulder, then her throat, and then her chin. He leaned forward and kissed her. Her lips were soft and warm.

She yawned, stretched, then spoke. "Are you awake already? Is it morn?" Though her voice was low and soft in the darkness, it was louder than he had expected it to be.

"It's morning and I've lain awake awhile."

She nestled against him. "I must be very sinful for a priestess," she said.

He evaded that statement with a question. "Was your sleep a sound one?"

Her voice came out of the darkness with a quaint edge on it. "My sleep was calm and deep, and in its midst there lay another dream, a repetition of the ones I mentioned."

"Was it a good dream?"

"It was interesting. And vivid, as they all have been." Her voice was very thoughtful. "I still was in the chamber I described to you; the sibyl chanted as she did before, except the words were slightly changed: 'The question has been asked. Consent was given, and the deed has now been done.'" She paused and he heard her swallow. "And then I saw the goddess."

"Goddess?" Palamon's curiosity cut through the darkness.

She nodded. He could not see the gesture but he could feel her hair move against his arm, her cheek against his bare chest. "Indeed, the patron of the hearth and home, of marriage, and of the love of man for wife. High Hestia was the figure who was watching me behind the arras. Then she stepped..." Aelia paused and swallowed once again. "'Twas *through* the cloth she stepped, her face and form as beautiful as dawn or sunset e'er have thought of being."

"Did she smile?"

"Her look was enigmatic. 'Satisfied' might be the word best used. She looked on me as if to say, 'It's done. How does it feel to be a wife, to know the joys that I, a goddess, cannot ever know? Is it enough, this small reward I give to you for being what you are?' Then she spoke to me."

"What did she say?"

Aelia hesitated an instant. When she did speak, it was

with words that came too fast. "I am not sure. Her words were strange; I can't recall them all."

There was something evasive in her answer, something unsatisfying. Palamon wanted to ask for more, to jolt her memory. After all, how could she not remember the words of a goddess, even in a dream-vision?

But they were interrupted. A voice sounded from the other side of the blanket that had been hung across the cave. "I have to speak to the newlyweds." The voice belonged to Flin.

Palamon assured himself that he and Aelia were snugly concealed, then he answered. "Feel free to enter."

The blanket moved to one side and there stood Flin, holding a lantern. He wore an infectious smile—not the leer that Palamon might have expected but the radiant expression of one who gladly shared the joy of another. "When I went to sleep you were the Prince and the priestess and when I woke up you were married. How do these things happen?"

Palamon smiled dryly. "I do not know myself, to tell the truth. The world is strange."

"It is indeed. May I ask my Lady a question."

Aelia nodded.

"This man, this new husband of yours, did he ask you last night?"

"He did."

Flin knelt and clasped Palamon's wrist. "I'm proud of you, you know. And happy for you, too. If marriage agrees with you, I might try it myself sometime."

For all Flin's good intentions, Palamon was uncomfortable. "I thank you. Did you come to tell us something?"

"Yes, I did. We've cooked a breakfast, that's all. It can wait, so come out when you want to." His voice lowered to a whisper. "They elected me to tell you that. I don't know why." Then he resumed speaking in more natural tones. "I'll leave the lantern here because it's easy to trip on this rough floor." He turned toward Aelia once more. "Lady, I know I'm intruding but I have to say something. He's a very good fellow, this Palamon, even though he does think too much. And he's very fond of you. I think he's fonder of you than he knows himself." Then he was gone. Palamon watched him depart, looking at the swaying blanket where he had passed and not knowing quite what to think.

"An interesting fellow," Aelia observed. "And it seems he loves to smile. But does he ever stop?"

Palamon laughed. "He smiles because he's Flin. He takes no heed of threats that lie on some horizon far away. I've only seen him daunted once or twice and then 'twas for a moment and no more. He sees no reason not to come and speak with us upon the morning of our wedding night, not any more than that defeat should come to him when all the day's events are through. Life's all the same to him. At times like this, when narrow straits lie to be passed before the day may end, I think it stimulates him." Palamon paused. "He enjoys a pleasant life."

"Yes. So it seems." Aelia looked up at Palamon. "And now it's time for us to face the day, so kiss me, love. Our pleasure time must end and we must see what Fate's prepared for us."

It was true. They had to rise and rescue Berengeria. Palamon kissed Aelia: they embraced one last time in the warmth of their little chamber. Then they rose, and Palamon put on his hauberk while Aelia also dressed. He did not look at her in the lantern light; it seemed as if there was a kind of sacrilege in that. Her body was her own, not to be rudely devoured by his ravenous eyes.

Besides, it was time to think of Berengeria. He had put her from his mind for the night and had taken his pleasure and his love while his sister lay in Alyubol's caverns. Now it was time to face the day and either see to her release or join her in her fate.

But then they were interrupted. A great voice boomed from the sky, as if the very heavens had begun shouting. But it was not the heavens; it was the disembodied voice of Alyubol, as Palamon and Aelia had heard it before. "Come out of your hiding place if you would be entertained. In just a few moments, a carnival shall run its course in the garden above my abode. Come alone, Palamon, for you'll not need your friends."

Palamon and Aelia ran to the front of the cave, where the booming tones brought consternation and discussion. "You cannot go alone," Aelia said. "It's surely death."

"Indeed," Reovalis cried. "For treachery has ever been his way."

Flin agreed. "Besides, I want to see what the old viper has planned."

At last Palamon agreed. "Then very well. I shall not go alone. We'll take the crystals which have guarded us against his scrying eyes and hide up in the rocks and crags. And one more thing—whate'er may come to me, it shall not guide your actions. That's to say, if I should fall and you have opportunity for your escape, then you must fly to safety."

They rose as one, took up their weapons and the crystals which prevented Alyubol from seeing them through his magic, and crept out of the cave. They kept a diligent lookout; there was always the chance the wizard would have his minions searching for them since he knew they would be moving about. But they did not see a sign of such activity. They found a good location which looked down upon Reovalis' old garden from beneath an overhanging ledge. There they would be invisible from below, though they would have a view of whatever happened.

There was no one in the garden but they did not have long to wait. The first to emerge was Ursid, who had doffed his great helmet, but was still wearing his armor. Then came the knights who had accompanied him, and in their midst was Berengeria, looking terribly gaunt and alone.

Aelia turned to Palamon and whispered, "It ever was his way to lie behind and let the others take whatever risks of ambush or attack there were."

Palamon nodded but said nothing. Berengeria looked tired and hopeless, and he gnawed the knuckle of his index finger as he leaned against a rock and watched her. Then huge, wolfish Usmu appeared, followed by all six of Alyubol's minions, and finally the wizard himself. He had his white robes gathered tightly about him to protect his disease-racked body from the morning air.

Alyubol stopped and glanced about the garden; but to Palamon's surprise, there was still no evidence that anyone might be searching for the fugitives. Instead, the wizard addressed his remarks to empty air, not even bothering to use the magical voice which had boomed out earlier. "When Reovalis fled from this stronghold on seeing my ship, I must say that he did the right thing. For my magic was stronger than his; he could not have withstood all the forces which I could have brought down upon him. Therefore he departed and left me his servant to see to his interests and drive me away. What a pitiful gesture."

Palamon glanced at Reovalis, who was watching the harangue without expression. The Prince felt a pang of sympathy for the sage as Alyubol continued. "He could not even trouble me there, for his Usmu defected to me. You may ask of me, 'How, mighty wizard, did you come to gain the allegiance of that fearful beast?'" He smiled a grand smile. "'Twas with ease. Old Reovalis' ways are too dull. A flesh servant loves good recreation and needs to relax, yet Reovalis worked him too constantly. I have allowed him to play a small game now and then, when all his chores are complete, and therefore he has followed me. Now you may like to observe him as he plays, for I know you are up in the rocks and can see what I do."

Alyubol waited as his words echoed away, to die in the chilly air. There was no reply, but that did not seem to trouble him. He walked to his minions and spoke quietly to them for a moment. Two went to the pens where the sheep, chickens, and goats were kept. Then Alyubol approached Usmu and stood before the hulking flesh servant, dwarfed by the monstrous form.

The two white-robed servants returned from the pens leading a sheep, a young ewe. They took her to the center of the garden, dropped the lead rope, and left her absently nibbling a tuft of dead grass. Then the wizard spoke again and his voice was loud enough to be heard by the spectators hiding up in the rocks. "Would you like recreation now, creature?" Usmu's head bobbed a clumsy affirmative and his lips peeled back to reveal gleaming teeth. Revolting laughter floated up from the garden. Alyubol made a sweeping, stagy gesture. "You see, the poor beast wants to play. Well then, play all you wish; show my friends how I let you amuse yourself."

The hulking apparition leaped to the center of the garden and crouched over the ewe, laughing another blood-curdling laugh. He leaned back, bared his teeth once more, and then extended a talon toward the victim. The ewe was frightened and tried to trot away, but Usmu's hand lashed out, and a claw sliced wool and skin like a razor. The blood spurted forth, staining the white fleece.

The ewe panicked. She stumbled to the ground in her hurry to escape, then scrambled to her feet and dashed toward the safety of the pens, bleating in terror. But Usmu was far too quick for her; he made a leap and landed in her path. His clawed hand flicked forth again, and one of the ewe's ears fell to the bloodstained ground.

Palamon looked away from the awful sight. "I'll not imagine how a man could be so warped as to allow such things to be. How can he stage an exhibition such as this?"

The other three had also turned away. The sheep was bleating in a frenzy of pain and fright; that combined with Usmu's laughter to breed sounds which could never be described. Each of the fugitives shuddered.

"It's my mistake," Reovalis said. "I never should have left my Usmu where foul Alyubol could get his hands on him. A fleshen servant is a creature which is summoned from a tartarus—a hell. He is a sort of demon and his way, in fact, is evil. But his mind is so unworldly and so empty of all thoughts there's little threat in him, if his slight evil's kept in check. I never would have thought he'd do such things."

"Yes. Alyubol's perverted him," Aelia said.

"That's it. Unfortunately he has shown he has a mighty talent for such things." Reovalis hung his head, obviously shaken.

The ewe's bleating turned into unspeakable screams of terror and pain, then all sound except Usmu's laughter died away. They all turned to look back down at the garden and saw that the ewe was dead, bathed in blood from dozens of fine wounds. The flesh servant was laughing hysterically, gnashing his great teeth, clenching and unclenching his clawed hands, putting little rips into the flesh of his own breast in his ecstasy.

Aelia grimaced. "The fiend."

"A pair of fiends," Sir Phebos observed.

"There's just one fiend," Reovalis said. "A cat cannot be blamed for killing mice. Tormenting them in their last moments. It is how the feline spirit works." It was an interesting observation, given the circumstances. "This Alyubol's the fiend, the only one, for his perversion of a stupid beast. That's all my Usmu was before they met." His tone was bitter.

Alyubol spurned the dead ewe, then looked up at the rocky crags. "Was it amusing?" he cried. "Was it pleasant to see how he played?" His voice was strident. "You, Palamon, you are the one who's to blame for all this, with your stubbornness and your refusals. But now you'll come down here to me, to my will, or there shall be more games before we are done."

"That's terrible," Aelia said. But Palamon said nothing.

"A moment or two shall I wait, but no more," Alyubol cried. "Then the games will begin once again, so surrender your coveted sword." He walked about, circling the inner confines of the garden while he waited impatiently for Palamon's surrender.

For his part, Palamon watched in grave silence. There were lives riding upon his decision, he knew. But there were more lives to forfeit if he surrendered and if Alyubol should manage to unlock the secrets of the *Spada Korrigaine*. How could he let Alyubol pervert the world and usher in the beings he planned to usher in? Palamon could flee and cast the sword into the river or bury it or hide it in some other way, but that would not keep the wizard from finding it. The best thing for him to do at the moment was to remain where he was and keep a stout grip on the wondrous blade.

All was silent below them. Even Usmu's laughter had died away, and he stood stupidly in the center of the garden. Animals stirred in the pens, and a chill breeze whispered through the rocks, but that was all until Alyubol shouted once more. "I'll not wait for you longer; you've made your decision."

He gestured toward a pair of his henchmen and they strode toward Berengeria. Palamon heard Aelia gasp and he caught his own breath as he watched them drag the Princess screaming toward the center of the garden. Would gods save men from other men? Would holy Pallas protect him from going mad at what was about to happen?

"You've sentenced your sister to torture beyond your worst dreams," Alyubol howled. "So have joy in your pride, in your stubbornness, for what now will occur." He whirled in his steps, grasped the cringing woman's gown, and heaved at it with surprising strength, tearing it in one sudden jerk so that she was exposed to the waist. "I will give you the best view I can as the blood starts to flow. Count each drop, for 'twas you drew it forth."

Berengeria crossed her arms in front of her in a poignant attempt to fend off the cold eyes of Ursid's knights. She was already shivering against the chill and her fear, but she shouted a gallant answer to the wizard's tortures. "Oh, Palamon, you must flee from this place. My death, however painful it may be, is much to be desired before a life of torment in this horrid wizard's halls. Oh flee, my Palamon, and Aelia too, seek refuge..."

Her words were cut short, transformed into a shriek of pain. Alyubol had made a gesture to Usmu and the monster now stood over her; with a single dagger-keen claw he had drawn a furrow from the nape of her neck down the length of her back, to where the remnants of her robe were held together at her waist. The blood followed after his talon the way the inked line follows the quill, dark against her pale flesh.

Palamon closed his eyes. His heart threatened to explode and the tears seared his clenched eyelids. "By holy Pallas, I have not the heart to watch this horrid deed."

"Then flee away from here, as your Princess has said." Aelia's whisper was harsh. "She sacrifices her own life

for you and for the world. You must forbear." Yet for all
her stout words, there was a tremor in her voice; her soul
was plainly bleeding.

When Palamon opened his eyes, it was to see Usmu
drawing another crimson line, giggling as his talon traveled the length of Berengeria's bare arm; the pain must
have been immense. She had borne the two agonizing
wounds with great courage, but her suffering became too
much for anyone to withstand. She rose and tried to flee
from the next slash, but Usmu leaped after her; it was
what he had been waiting for. Her terror plainly excited
him even more than her blood; his laughter rose up out
of the garden again, mocking the very gods themselves.

Palamon clenched his eyes once more, but it did not
help; he could see more of the horror in his mind than he
could with his eyes open. A low groan rose up from the
depths of his being and became a cry of anguish. He stood,
even as Aelia clutched at his elbow. "Enough," he cried.
"I shall surrender all to you, if only she is harmed no
more."

Joy and triumph sounded in Alyubol's voice as he
answered. "You must swear you shall not cast away the
great sword. And if you should leap down to your death
from your ledge, then the game will begin all anew."

"I have it in my hands," Palamon shouted back. "I
shall come down."

Even as Palamon spoke, Alyubol ordered the flesh
servant away from the hysterical Berengeria. Ursid ran
to her, threw a robe about her shivering shoulders, and
led her away, toward the interior of the Library of the
Polonians. Alyubol and the others stood waiting for the
Prince, smiling broad smiles.

Chapter Twenty-nine:
The Glass of the Polonians

PALAMON WAS DEFEATED and he knew it. Alyubol had won because the sight of Usmu's keen claws slowly shredding Berengeria was impossible to bear, more impossible than the thought of what the wizard would do once he got his hands on the *Spada Korrigaine*.

Palamon stood and made his way down the rocks toward the garden. To his surprise, he found he was not alone; Aelia had followed him. He turned to stop her. "My bride, you should not go. The choice and all its punishments are mine."

"You shall not go alone," she responded. "Our lives are joined; thus, I shall go with you."

He sighed and touched her on the cheek. Then they walked together. Sir Phebos and Flin also followed, as did Reovalis. The five of them streamed down the cliff side and into the waiting clutches of the wizard.

Alyubol was plainly delighted by such a bag. "Move quickly and hold up your hands. One false move and your Princess will die."

He did not even try to take the *Spada Korrigaine* from

317

Palamon. The Prince knew that was because such a precaution was unnecessary. After all, Palamon did not dare use the weapon. Berengeria and Usmu had gone ahead of them, into the labyrinths which lay below the Library of the Polonians. It would be impossible to reach her alive if he began wielding the blade.

As they reached the brass staircase to descend to the lower levels, he saw Ursid. The young knight had changed greatly since they had met five months earlier. The face was no longer rounded and without personality; instead it had become dark and intense. The man was plainly consumed by hatred. Even the sight of Palamon brought low by Alyubol had not lessened the passion which gripped the knight's features. Palamon had not meant for things to happen in the way they had happened, but Ursid still glared at him, lurid scars gleaming like lightning bolts against a stormy sky.

They passed to the lower chambers where Usmu waited with Berengeria, his fangs shining in the torchlight. Reovalis frowned at him. "My Usmu, how could you have lent yourself to such misdeeds as these? I am ashamed of you. You have done badly."

Surprisingly enough, the flesh servant looked uncomfortable. His bestial smile faded and he glanced at the floor. Then, at the sound of Alyubol descending the steps behind the prisoners, the flesh servant ushered blanket-robed Berengeria out of the chamber and on ahead of the procession.

Palamon knew where they were headed; they were going back to the Glass of the Polonians. It was a great source of mystical energy, and Alyubol apparently wanted to use it in gaining his prize. The walk along the familiar course took a long time; still, it did not take long enough. At its end, after all, lay humiliation, final surrender, and probably death.

The company filed into the chamber. Usmu and Berengeria had already arrived, as had some of Alyubol's henchmen. Ursid and his Buerdic knights followed the prisoners, along with the wizard, whose face was alight. Oddly enough, Alyubol did not approach Palamon directly.

He was unusually relaxed, a man who knew he had all objectives well in hand and could afford to take his time and enjoy himself.

He walked to Reovalis, and the two of them eyed one another like two chess masters, sizing one another up, appraising skills and weaknesses. Alyubol's smile was infuriating. He was plainly enjoying his victory. "I defeated you handily, sage," he said at last. "But then, how could it have been otherwise?"

Reovalis said nothing. He looked angry, but he held his peace. In truth, it would have been foolish to speak. As for Alyubol, he seemed pleased with the point he had made. He turned and walked toward Palamon. "And now we have traveled full circle; we're here once again." He smiled up at Palamon, but there was a volcano of suppressed violence in his eyes. "You shall give up your weapon to me; you shall do all I say; you'll renounce it, renounce your religion, whatever I choose. And if you do not, then your sister will bleed once again." He gestured across the room toward where Berengeria stood, trembling in Usmu's grasp.

Alyubol was right, of course. Palamon cold not see Berengeria hurt again, even if it meant victory for the wizard. The siblings stood several cubits apart, separated by the blue turbulence of the Glass of the Polonians. It was probably as close as they would ever stand; they were not likely to leave the blue chamber alive, either of them, no matter what Palamon did. He allowed his gaze to stray to the Glass of the Polonians itself. The rolling blueness of the Glass was distilled magic, the essence of the mystical arts. He had been told it was deadly to the touch. How deep into the bowels of the earth did the well extend? A fathom? A league? How much ethereal substance was there?

Reovalis broke into the conversation. "Beware, O Alyubol. You must recall the *Spada Korrigaine* has had two owners. One is Palamon, the other Parthelon, the ancient Emperor. The stamp of both of them is on the blade and that bodes ill for any who would tamper with its magic. Though you may harass good Palamon and make him speak against that bond, he shall not be your ally in his heart and you will be no closer than before to the possession of the mystic sword."

Alyubol took an angry step toward the ancient sage, the light of madness and genius in his eyes. "And you think I'll give up its promise because of that fact? You old fool, I have made preparations; I know what I'm at. Had our brave, foolish Palamon done the intelligent thing and renounced the great blade..." The wizard shrugged. "He'd have saved me much labor. But still, it's the same in the end. I shall tear out his heart while he lives; I shall burn it in front of him. That done, his stamp will be gone. And then, if I have to search all of the world's tombs and graves, I will root out the body of Parthelon, tear out his heart, and repeat all my actions and chants. Both the seals will be loosed, and then I can do all the sorcery which it may take for this blade to be drawn to my service. I am little surprised at your attitude. There is no doubt you possess but a second-rate mind. The corrections I contemplate only a genius could do, which is why I can do them and you cannot even begin."

He pulled his dagger from its sheath and faced Palamon. "And now it is time. I will demonstrate all I have said."

But Palamon leaped away from him. The Prince knew better than to defend himself with his weapon; Alyubol would already have taken some precaution against that. There was only one chance, one possibility of keeping the wizard from his goal, though the act would doubtless mean many deaths, deaths which were going to take place anyway. Palamon vaulted into the Glass of the Polonians itself, into the turbulence of the magic well. He had to die; he and his weapon had to perish together in the dreaded ether of pure magic. As oblivion swept over him, he thought a silent prayer for Aelia, for Berengeria, and for the friends he had left in Alyubol's clutches. They would pay for his leap.

He plunged down and down, toward the center of the world, for all he knew toward the center of eternity. Yet he retained his senses. He was in a whirling blue void, surrounded by visions from an archaic past, by monsters

which bared fangs at him as he hurtled past them, and by
his own memories and the memories of others. He was
in a universal emptiness, a divine ether, and he only knew
that he was falling, traveling at great speed. Was Pallas
there? Was Hestia there, or Actaea? Were any of the
divinities there, or all of them? Visions blurred and tumbled, and he swept onward, hardly conscious.

He found himself standing on solid stone in an unfamiliar chamber. The pool was still there; it bathed everything in an eerie blue glow. But on the far side of the pool
stood a huge sarcophagus. Beyond that, a narrow flight
of steps led up the high wall to a door.

Palamon leaped toward the stone staircase. The deadly
reputation of the Glass was false; if he had made the
transit through the ether to this strange place, others could
follow. He was dizzy. His feet hardly obeyed his commands, but he knew he had to get out of the chamber.
He was not fast enough, however. There was a great
crackling sound and hulking Usmu appeared behind him,
leaped after him, and caught him at the base of the steps.

Palamon swung his blade at the flesh servant but again
he was not quick enough. Usmu struck with his own great
weapon, his huge battle-axe, and the *Spada Korrigaine*
was knocked from Palamon's grasp. Usmu, brandishing
his battle-axe, herded Palamon back toward the pool.

"You must wait here," he said. "I will make you wait
here."

There were more noises from the pool, and Palamon
looked to see Aelia and Berengeria appear. They rushed
toward him, but the flesh servant glared at them. "You
must all be still or I will kill you. That is what my Master
told me to do." Then he sidestepped and picked up
Palamon's fallen blade. "My Master told me not to let
you have this."

The weapon hissed and crackled as the flesh servant
took it up, and the air about them was full of the smell
of burning flesh—but Usmu only laughed. He did not
seem to mind the smoke and stink rising from his own
charring hands. "I don't know why my Master wants your
sword, but he's very angry at you. He's not sure he can

come through the magic colors; but, if he's not here soon,
I'll kill you and return."

Palamon looked at Berengeria, then at Aelia. "The two
of you are here? How did you come?"

"We leaped in after you," Berengeria said, putting her
arms around him.

"Yes, both of us," Aelia said. As she spoke, she also
embraced Palamon and the three of them stood together
beneath the threatening gaze of the flesh servant. "The
chamber was confusion at your act and both our minds
took up the selfsame thought at once. The Glass was
preferable to what would be our future in the hands of
Alyubol."

"You could have both been killed," Palamon said.

"We both assumed that fact, the same as you,"
Berengeria said simply.

Palamon looked from her face to Aelia's and the older
woman nodded. He reached out and caressed Aelia's cheek
and would have done the same for Berengeria, except
that it did not seem proper. Then there was another crackling from the pool and he turned his head to see Ursid
and other knights standing beside the boiling blue vapors.

"Do we still live?" one knight asked.

"Of course we live," Ursid replied. "The Prince of
Carea would not have risked his life."

"You've seen the horrid acts of Alyubol," Palamon
cried. "You've seen his tortures and his other crimes.
Now will you stand with us and be our allies?"

"I'll never stand with you again," Ursid replied.

"But Alyubol desires to ruin the world," Aelia said.

"You three have lied to me, while he has not," Ursid
snarled, his voice dripping with hatred. "And as for torture, those few shallow scars of Berengeria's will heal and
be dissolved. Do they exceed the ones I bear for love of
her who thrust my hand away?" He did not wait for an
answer. "I have not come to be a friend to those who
have deceived me. I have come to post a solid guard and
wait for Alyubol. He may be mad, but if he can destroy
you three and your Carea, then he is a friend to me. For

now, he studies in his books and scrolls to find where we've arrived, thus is delayed. But he will be here soon."

Aelia glowered. "More likely, he must seek a way to pass his monstrous evil through the Glass without destruction. He's unnatural and you're a fool to stand beside him."

Ursid did not reply. He would plainly never recover from the wounds his heart had sustained; there was no sense in arguing with him. There were more snappings and flashings until the rest of Ursid's knights had arrived. He posted them evenly about, some by the prisoners, some here and there, a pair of them at the base of the stone steps.

There was no more conversation. Palamon stood beside the two women and gazed about the chamber at the stone steps and at the great sarcophagus. He wondered where they had arrived. Then there was one last burst of light and Alyubol appeared, his face contorted with anger and triumph. He stepped to Palamon's side, reached out, and struck him. "You thought you'd escaped. You're a fool; you have actually helped. Now do you know the name of this chamber to which you have guided me?"

Palamon did not reply; he knew Alyubol would tell him soon enough. And such was the case.

"You have answered a question of mine," the wizard said. "In the past, when I gazed far down into the depths of the Glass, I would note what looked like a reflection. It was. It was this surface here." He pointed toward the roiling vapors behind him. "I'd have found all these secrets in time, but the threat of some violence sufficed to unlock the old lips of Reovalis; thus, I came quickly."

Was Reovalis still living after Alyubol's threat of violence? Palamon knew he might never find out as the wizard went on triumphantly. "We've come to the place that I needed to find, where the Glass has its outlet upon the far side of the great Thlassa Mey. We are now in the tomb of old Parthelon."

Palamon groaned. His escape had been short-lived and fruitless; what was worse, he had guided Alyubol to the one place he least wanted him to find, the tomb of the

Great Emperor. Parthelon's body was the next require-
ment for Alyubol's usurpation of the mighty *Spada
Korrigaine*.

As for Alyubol, he turned to Usmu and bade him release
the weapon. Then, with mystical gestures, he caused the
sword to rise from the flesh servant's scorched hands. Up
it went, hissing and crackling in protest, with little bands
of blue flame playing along the blade. Alyubol levitated
it until it was pinned against the stone over their heads.
Then a maniacal gleam glazed his eye and he leaped toward
the top of the sarcophagus, fairly hopping as he strained
against the stone lid. He screamed for Usmu to help him;
the flesh servant pushed the lid off the great vault. It
crashed to the floor, shattering and raising a cloud of dust.

But Alyubol paid no attention. He had already directed
Usmu to the gilt inner cover, which was also removed
and cast to the floor. Then the huge claws of the flesh
servant pierced the lead lining. Alyubol gave a scream of
delight, reached in, and used all his strength to haul out
a human form wrapped in shrouding.

The sacrilege did not seem to bother him in the slightest; he cackled with excitement, laid the form on the
sarcophagus, and plunged his dagger into it. "Thus do I
treat him who meekly surrendered to death. With my
dagger I rip at him; when I have cut out his heart, I will
burn it to ashes. And Palamon, you who have helped me,
shall quickly meet death in a similar fashion." His hand
rose and fell as he slashed through long-dead tissue and
hacked through bone. He whooped with glee and his
laughter filled the chamber.

Chapter Thirty:
Sparth's Head Castle

BESSINA PASSED INTO the broad, empty courtyard of Sparth's Head Castle a few paces ahead of Count Clauvis and Leuval, then she had to pause. A strange dizziness overtook her, and the air filled with a pungent fragrance, an aroma that was pleasantly sweet and musty. She heard a multitude of voices which sounded muted and mournful. Nonplussed, she looked back at the two men who were still following her, breathless from the climb out of the dry moat.

Then she looked down at the ring. It sat on her finger as before, its beaten gold surface glinting in the sun's rays. It felt strange. It had become warm; the heat flowed into her finger the way warmth spreads into the belly from a goblet of wine too quickly consumed.

But even more strangely, she felt as if her finger could actually taste the ring, as if the digit had become a tongue and the ring had become a warm, sweet mass dissolved across it, like the hot wine sauces on her childhood desserts. It was tangy and irresistible. The sensation spread along her finger, across her hand, and up her arm. Her body melted into rapture at the taste of the ring. Her extremities tingled, her breath came in little gasps, and her vision became faded and blurred.

She could hear the voices more clearly now—the keening and grieving of noble ladies sorrowing over some great loss. And in the midst of the sad music, she could actually see them moving slowly across the courtyard with their men, the colors of their gowns vividly vibrant. But to her surprise, she could see the stones of the wall through their bodies; it was as if they were shadows made of color, rather than darkness. She was transfixed by curiosity. She had to follow them.

A multitude filled the castle's inner ward. There were knights, guardsmen, and horses; the courtyard was filled with people and animals. But she was most attracted by the ladies who walked and mourned in their colorful costumes of another age. She had to walk after them.

She sensed loss profoundly. Some great man had died. Although she had no idea who he could be, she knew his death had affected her life and the lives of all the people at the great gathering. She realized, in fact, that she was going to the great man's funeral. The people moved toward the castle's chapel and poured through the doors, trudging to the tolling of phantom bells. She knew her place was within and she walked quickly through the door.

No one paid her any heed, except the two men who had followed her. They hurried after her, trying to say something to her, but she could not understand them above the other sounds. Besides, they were not part of the throng she had joined. But to her surprise, she found the funeral service over. The gilded pall was being lifted from its place before the altar and borne to the rear of the chapel; stout knights carried it into a curtained alcove, while guards prevented the noble ladies from following it. The mourners had already departed, in fact.

It did not matter. Her place was not with them anymore; her place was at the side of the casket itself, a fact she knew as surely as she knew her own name. She tried to push past one of the guards and found she had actually walked through him, as if he were nothing more than a spirit. She caught up with the priests and the pallbearers and followed, to stone steps which descended out of the torchlight.

The mournful procession plodded down into the bowels of the mountain beneath the castle—priests, pallbearers, torch-bearing guards, and Bessina. Behind them, trying to keep up, feeling their way, stumbling, and almost falling, followed the two men. They were ludicrous compared to the rest of the dignified and mournful company. But Bessina became so weary she hardly noticed them; the journey into the mountain's depths was terribly taxing. The pallbearers became exhausted and a pair of them actually had to yield their places to a pair of the guards.

At last they came to the bottom of the steps, walked along a short tunnel, and reached a plain wooden door. The high priest placed his hand on the casket for a moment, then turned and unlocked the door with a great key. He pushed the portal open, and soft blue light bathed them all. He hesitated for a moment, then walked through; the others followed after.

But Bessina hesitated. There was something bad beyond the door as surely as there was a body within the casket; her fear warred with her desire to follow. She glanced at the two men behind her, then rushed through the portal, only to stop in confusion. The casket had disappeared. The priests, the pallbearers, and the guards were gone, and she found herself on a stone landing, looking down at a treacherous flight of stone steps which led to the floor.

She gazed at the ring. It no longer filled her with the pleasant sensation of wine and sugar; all the warmth it had injected into her was flooding back into it. She had become cold—in fact she was shivering. The ring was suddenly too hot to wear; she yanked it from her finger so violently it hurt and she dropped it in her haste. It fell to the stone landing and rolled between her feet.

When she dropped the ring, all the strange sensations faded from her, the way a person's breath fades on a wintery day. She was weary, so weary she could hardly stand, and she saw a cluster of people moving below her.

A pool of what appeared to be surging blue liquid produced the light which filled the room. It fell on armored knights, two women, and some kind of horrid apparition, the appearance of which made her shudder.

There was someone else. He was old and wore a white robe and he stood atop a great stone sarcophagus, plunging his dagger into the body he had snatched from it. That made her feel sad because she knew it was the body of the great man whose pall she had followed into the cavern. Still, she was so fascinated by the scene that she nearly lost her balance and toppled from the landing. She just caught herself in time.

Then she heard a voice from below. "By all the gods, intruders have arrived, and two of them have faces that I know. Count Clauvis—what has brought you here from our deep donjons of Buerdaunt? Why is your daughter here to help you watch these grim proceedings?"

She recognized the knight who had spoken. It was Ursid, Lothar the Pale's nephew, whom she had met two summers earlier. But he had not looked then the way he looked now. His face had become lean and dark, and he was transfixed with gruesome scars. As he shouted up at them, her father's hand clapped onto her shoulder. "Now see the harm you've done," he said. "You've led us to some secret ceremony, and we'll have to flee once more and be pursued. Now come away, for we must flee again."

"Stop." The command sounded through the room like thunder and it caused Bessina and the two men to halt in their tracks. They turned and saw the madman peering up at them, laughing with inscrutable glee. "My bag is now full, for the last of old Berevald's line stands before us. She has come to my grasp uninvited. You, Palamon, you Berengeria, look on your niece. Now the Fates show approval of all of the things I have done, as they cast this last glittering bauble down into my hands."

He stood and giggled, his face covered by the dust from the corpse's wrappings. Even at the distance between them, his look made Bessina shudder. He was ugly; his features were pinched, and his entire countenance was contorted by the grip of madness. His sneer twisted his lips in a way that was painful to behold as he used the back of one hand to wipe the dust from his face.

Then he spoke again. "All the strings of old Berevald's progeny dangle in air, for they're slashed by the blade of my vengeance. What's left are you three: Berengeria, pretty Bessina, and Palamon, too. And you all shall be dead by the time that the sun sets. And then my revenge will have run to the end of its course. With the life that I gain from the sword, I can turn to new things." He returned to the body and his grisly play.

But Count Clauvis was beside himself with rage. He no longer attempted to flee; rather, he stood at the edge of the landing and screamed down at the crazy old man. "You charlatan. I know not who you are, but you should be strung up before the gates of Castle Gnoffe and left there till you rot. How dare you cast aspersions on this child of lawful marriage, got from my own loins? My own is what she is; my own she'll stay, and your foul lies can never alter that. Why, I have flogged much better men than you for even hinting at such cuckolding or that my wife was not a virtuous bride, or that this lovely girl is not my own." On the verge of apoplexy, he scoured the narrow perch with his eyes, seeking something to throw at the man who had insulted him.

The old man grew as enraged as Count Clauvis. The laughter fell from his lips and he glared up at the intruders, his eyes beaming hatred. "The man who makes threats at me lives to regret his rash words—but no longer than that. You shall die with the rest, dog. When I have completed the work I do here, you shall writhe in the grip of the punishment I shall prescribe. But first, I shall tell all the story of what was your shame, for though you may say otherwise, you were a cuckold indeed and this sweet, pretty child is the bastard that lechery produced."

He wheeled to shout his sordid tale to the chamber. "To the great hall at Galliardy, seventeen winters ago, came a traveler. Singing and jest were the products that he had to offer the nobles therein; and his voice was so sweet and his manner so gentle and soft that the Countess was taken with him from the moment they met." He snick-

ered and turned back toward Count Clauvis. "For your
way as a lover was poor—you were rough and unkind.
Now you see, not a secret of yours has escaped my wide
glance.

"But the love that grew between the Countess and
paramour was too sweet to be seen by her husband. He
swore that the vengeance he took would make laughter
a prize never known by the one or the other, his victims
of rage. So he tore the young troubadour out of the wife's
loving arms and imprisoned him deep in his donjons. He
castrated him and preserved him all caged in a cell for
the rest of his days. Yes, and as for the Countess, she
never felt laughter again, for salt tears and reproaches
became the hard lot of her days. And the offspring of their
short romance is the maiden you see." He pointed at an
astounded Bessina. "It was punishment I could approve
of, I'll add, for he died covered up with his shame and
his grief, did this young Berethar."

Bessina was crushed. She could feel the stares of the
people below her, yet no one was more shocked than she.
She was not her father's daughter! She was the product
of some other man; she was illegitimate. Her cheeks burned
with the shame. She was the bastardized product of a
great house in a foreign land, the poor, half-blooded cousin
of royalty she had never met.

But that was not the worst. Her hand went to her lips
and her knees turned to sand as the thought descended
upon her. She had met her real father. She had met him
at the end of his terrible imprisonment, at the worst of
his shame and suffering as he paid the price for his forbidden love with the Countess. She wept, and the sounds
of her grief echoed through the chamber. Her real father
was the man she had pitied in the prison beneath Castle
Gnoffe, the man Count Clauvis had forced her to look
upon. She had watched her own father die in that foetid
cell.

Count Clauvis had been scrabbling about for an object
to throw at the laughing madman below. As Bessina sagged,
he reached down and picked up the ring she had dropped.
It had become steaming hot; it even gave off its own faint

light, which blended with the radiance that filled the chamber. It was so hot Bessina would not have dared picked it up, but Count Clauvis ignored the pain. The cords of his neck stood out like bowstrings, his face turned the color of raw meat, and he shrieked at the top of his lungs as he drew back his arm. "The day will surely come when you regret what you have done to me." Then he hurled the ring with a horrible cry. He had become an animal blinded by his own rage.

He made his throw from the edge of the landing and the force of his effort carried him forward, out into the void. He teetered an instant, tried to cycle his arms and regain his balance, but leaned ever farther into emptiness. His feet slid from the stone before Bessina's horrified gaze and he plunged toward the floor.

She never looked down. Her eyes fixed themselves into space, glassy and unseeing; she did not need to look, did not need to listen to the ugly thud of flesh and bone smashing against stone. He never made another sound. That was good; perhaps he had died without pain. Her head swam; Count Clauvis had been her father, yet he had destroyed her father. She had argued with him, had fought, and now he had gone to his death. She had not even had the chance to bid him farewell, to be the daughter that he wanted one last time. She had lost two fathers in the time it takes to recite the alphabet. Her legs gave way and she fell backward, away from the edge, but she was unconscious even before her head struck the stone wall behind her.

Alyubol ducked the Count's wild throw, but the ring curved away from him and toward the shrouded corpse of Parthelon.

Something curious happened when it struck. It did not bound away on impact; it stuck to the cloth and its great heat brought a wisp of smoke from the burning fabric. Alyubol turned back toward the body, but stopped in surprise. The long-dead flesh beneath the ring began to swell and bulge upward. Then there was a slight popping sound and the ring was absorbed into the body's swollen tissues through the burned shroud.

Alyubol's laughter ceased. Clouds of smoke billowed from the hole where the ring had entered the corpse. Then a beam of blue light shot from the opening. The entire body began to glow and tremble. The cavern started to vibrate as another sound crackled above—the *Spada Korrigaine*, which Alyubol's magic had pinned against the roof, was also glowing. It became a bright, brittle blue, then plummeted downward, searing its way, curving in its descent until it landed atop the body.

The body moved. It grew and trembled; blood seeped from the wounds made by the wizard's dagger. The long-dead form sat up, then stood. Hands which had been stilled for generations rose, moved, and unwound the wrappings from the face. The eyes came into view—they glowed pale blue and brilliant, like little stars.

Alyubol looked up as if hypnotized. The madness had left him; stark terror brewed in its place. His dagger dropped from nerveless fingers and he backed away, toppling from the sarcophagus and landing with a thud and a cry. He tried to crawl away, but was captured by the sight of the apparition. He could only sit as motionless as a stone.

The ancient lips moved, and the tongue which had not felt breath for generations shaped words, as the croaking voice of long-dead Parthelon filled the chamber. "The three great seats of my past power are joined and thus I have been summoned from my rest to lend fulfillment to the prophecy inscribed within the ring. I sense the presence of an evil one who desecrates my tomb. He tampers with great powers and will find what happens when his art outstrips his soul."

The croaking ceased and the resurrected Parthelon raised the brilliant blue line which had been the *Spada Korrigaine*. A beam of light shot from the tip of the great weapon and transfixed the wizard, lifting him into the air while he struggled feebly, his limbs moving like the legs of a dying spider. Tongues of fire licked him. He screamed. Then he was enveloped by flames. The light was almost unbearable as he burned and his ashes dropped to the chamber's floor.

Once more the croaking voice of the ancient ruler filled the chamber. "The moment has arrived when I must return into the place from which I came; but though I pass, the three great gifts remain: the sword, the ring, and lastly the great pool. The evil man has perished from this world; now let his apparition go with him." The brilliance increased, and all present were forced to place their hands over their eyes. A faint humming sound grew into a roar that soon died away, giving way to silence. All became dark, except for the original soft light cast by the Glass of the Polonians.

But when Palamon looked toward the sarcophagus, he could see what had happened; there were two large piles of ash, one atop the monument, one at its base. The pile of ash at the base was as black as despair; it was all that was left of Alyubol. The other was pure white, and on it lay the sword and the ring. Usmu had also disappeared; his great axe was left lying on the cavern floor. Palamon blinked in astonishment.

"By the gods, that was a bright light. What happened?"

Palamon turned to look at the new voice. To his surprise, he saw Flin standing beside the pool, along with Reovalis and Phebos. It was certainly a time for prodigies. "I must say I am glad to see you three," Palamon exclaimed. "But how came you to join us in this place?"

Flin did not give either of his companions time to answer; his enthusiasm made him tell the story himself. "This old gentleman, this practitioner, had tricks he never showed us." He gestured toward Reovalis. "He drew mystic signs and shapes in the air and the guards were so dazzled by them that we escaped to join you. But the light—what was the light?"

"I do not know, exactly," Palamon said. "But it's destroyed an evil which the world may do without."

"And Usmu, where is he?" Reovalis asked.

"He also disappeared."

Flin beamed. "Then it's all come out well, as I knew it had to. The gods had to make it all right in the end. . . . Father!" He had been looking about the chamber and his eyes had fastened upon the middle-aged man who was slowly descending the steps. "I don't know how you got here but you're a welcome sight."

"My son, you've been away a long time." The older man also beamed as the younger rushed up the stone steps and embraced him in joyful reunion.

Then Flin lifted his eyes and saw the maiden who was only now struggling into consciousness at the top of the steps. Astonishment seized his face, followed by a look of ecstasy. "And she's here," he cried. "My Bessina, my precious love, the bride of my dreams."

He left his father and made his way up to her, to kneel beside her and support her shoulders tenderly, allowing her sagging head to fall against his breast. Accompanied by Aelia and Berengeria, Palamon also made his way up to her, still shaking his head at the fact that she was the missing heir. But Flin did not suspect such a thing yet; he only rejoiced at seeing her.

Bessina was plainly speechless. She had lost her father and the man she had called her father. But with Flin to reconcile her, Palamon could not doubt that she would survive. Already the sight of the young rogue had done much to relieve her shocked spirit: she wrapped her arms about him, buried her face against his chest, and wept. It was obvious that their love would be strong enough to heal all parts of her which needed healing.

Flin grinned up at Palamon. "So now you see the way it is. Among the women of our world, she's a star among candles. The gods could never have been cruel enough to tear us apart forever. Can you deny she's all I told you of?"

Palamon had to smile. "She's that and more besides." It was all a revelation to him. Given the Oracle's prophecy, he had never dreamed Berethar had produced a child. But the wording had been the least bit obscure—Berethar "had no child to feed or call his own." And so it had been; Bessina had been reared by another.

He was interrupted by a voice from below. "Indeed, that may be true. But still and all, from what I can deduce you have become my prisoners." The voice belonged to Ursid, who walked to the foot of the steps, drew his sword, and gathered his knights about him. "You might well flee, but I am confident my knights and I will gather you all up and bring you to our donjons in the end. So it is best you yield yourselves to me and to my men without delay."

Palamon, Aelia, and Berengeria all stared down at the knight's features, but Flin's father threw back his head and laughed. "You may have captured us, but the bulk of the Red Company, over a hundred lances, is waiting at the gatehouse. And I, Leuval, command them. If you can find a way to slip us past them, you'll deserve great credit."

"And there is more than that." Reovalis had been examining the remains of Parthelon and Alyubol and now he addressed the Buerdic knights. "The *Spada Korrigaine* retains its powers. And though my Usmu has been sent away, I soon shall summon him once more, relieved of evil thoughts. So it is that you shall have to deal with awesome forces in this very chamber."

Ursid's face fell as he considered the might arrayed against him. Then his features contorted into a bitter smile, and he looked up at Palamon again. "So it seems that you have won again. Shall I be chained and bound, or is it best that I should simply fall upon my sword?"

Palamon shook his head. "You shan't be bound or chained. The time which we have spent together seeking common goals and all the suffering which has come to you have purchased your freedom. Leuval, might you give to all these knights a pass which will allow them exit past your force?"

Leuval began to answer but Ursid interrupted him with a shout. "No. I shall not take your charity. Far better I should let out my own blood then grovel for the kindness of a man I hate."

"Then slash away," Aelia said, her features pale with anger. "This is the second time that Palamon has given you the gift of life itself, and all his motives are as honorable as yours are selfish. He has not seen fit to make you hostage, as your pallid King two times has done to Berengeria. So if you wish to sacrifice your life to your own hatred of a righteous man, then do it now in this deep, hidden place as far as possible from heaven's eyes. The gods should not be forced to look upon the face of one who will not seek to live and bear the disappointments dealt to him by fate." She paused, her breast heaving with the exertion of her speech.

Her words cut Ursid deeply. A scowl seized his features. Then he began to lead his knights in single file toward the door which led from the chamber. He accepted a pass from Leuval without comment. But after his knights had pushed past the crowd on the landing, he paused at the door. "No, Palamon, do not think you have seen the last of me. The time will come when I shall have revenge, for all you three have treated me with scorn." Then he turned and was gone."

For those who remained, there was much to do. Count Clauvis had to be carried back to the surface, there to be decently interred. The ashes of Parthelon had to be respectfully placed in the sarcophagus which had held him through the generations. But they left Alyubol's ashes where they lay. It was best that the mad wizard be allowed to rest in the place where he had come so close to triumph and had suffered his great catastrophe.

As for Reovalis, he announced that he would not leave with them. He would summon up his flesh servant, go back the way he had come along the vortex of the Glass of the Polonians, and vie with Alyubol's minions for his old refuge. Even as they left the chamber, Palamon gazed through the closing door to see the flesh servant standing once more before his true Master. Usmu seemed a trifle less hulking, his broad back a trifle bowed. Perhaps, even with his minuscule brain, he had come to learn something.

The sun was setting by the time they had at last completed all their tasks and ridden from Sparth's Head Castle. And as they descended toward the plains, Palamon paused to twist in his saddle one last time, to pass his gaze over the towers and battlements of the ancient fortification, black against the setting sun. Sparth's Head. It was an obsolete term, a combination of words which had not been used in common speech since the times of Parthelon's Great Empire.

He understood the words. Sparth had been the word used to denote a battle-axe, as well as the name given to the sharp ridge of hills upon which the great castle had been built. And it was an appropriate name; from the east, the ridge really did look like the cutting edge of an axe head.

"And by the Axe's Blade is found the truth." The last line of the prophecy had been fulfilled. Palamon smiled at himself grimly. It was obvious enough now. But obvious did not mean visible. And even if he had understood, would it have made a difference? No one could ever know the answer to that question.

His smile faded. He turned in his saddle, spurred his horse, and cantered after the others.

ABOUT THE AUTHOR

DENNIS MCCARTY was born on June 17, 1950, in Grand Junction, a small town in western Colorado. His family traveled a great deal because of his father's work. By the time he had graduated from high school, Dennis had attended eight different public schools, most of them before he was twelve.

He graduated in English from the University of Utah and served four years in the United States Coast Guard. Over the years, his hobbies have included fishing, hunting, photography, and automobile racing.

His greatest love has always been reading and writing fiction, however. He made his first attempt at a novel of science fiction when he was seven. He began writing seriously at the age of twenty; *Flight to Thlassa Mey* was his first published novel.

Dennis and his wife, Kathy, were married in 1972. They have two daughters and reside in Naples, Utah.